William H. Ainsworth

Cardinal Pole

The days of Philip and Mary - an historical romance

William H. Ainsworth

Cardinal Pole
The days of Philip and Mary - an historical romance

ISBN/EAN: 9783337273781

Printed in Europe, USA, Canada, Australia, Japan

Cover: Foto ©Andreas Hilbeck / pixelio.de

More available books at **www.hansebooks.com**

OR,

THE DAYS OF PHILIP AND MARY

An Historical Romance.

BY

WILLIAM   HARRISON   AINSWORTH,

AUTHOR OF

"CONSTABLE   OF   THE   TOWER,"

"LORD MAYOR OF LONDON,"

"THE TOWER OF LONDON,"

"WINDSOR CASTLE,"

ETC.

NEW   EDITION.

LONDON:

CHAPMAN AND HALL, 193 PICCADILLY

CARDINAL POLE.

BOOK I.

PHILIP OF SPAIN.

CHAPTER I.

HOW A MARRIAGE WAS AGREED UPON BETWEEN MARY QUEEN OF ENGLAND, AND DON PHILIP, PRINCE OF SPAIN.

NO sooner was Mary, eldest daughter of Henry VIII., securely seated on the throne left vacant by the premature death of her brother, Edward VI., than the Emperor Charles V., already related to her through his aunt, Katherine of Aragon, determined to bring about a marriage between the Queen of England and his son Philip. By the accomplishment of this project, which had been conceived by the Emperor during Edward's last illness, the preponderance obtained in Europe by the House of Austria would be largely increased, and Charles's dream of universal dominion might eventually be realised.

Philip, who was then a widower—his wife, Doña Maria, Princess of Portugal, having died in 1545, in giving birth to a son, the unfortunate Don Carlos—readily acquiesced in his father's scheme, as he fully recognised the vast importance of the match, and Mary alone had to be consulted. But little apprehension could be entertained of her refusal. All the advantages were on the Prince's side.

Eleven years younger than the Queen, who was then thirty-eight, Philip was not merely in the very flower of manhood, but extremely handsome, and, as heir to a mighty monarchy, unquestionably the greatest match in Europe. No princess, however exalted, on whom he deigned to smile, would refuse him her hand.

But there were difficulties in the way of the projected alliance, only to be overcome by prudential management. For many reasons the match was certain to be obnoxious to the English nation, which would not unnaturally be apprehensive of being brought under a foreign yoke. Neither was the Queen altogether her own mistress. Governed by her council—especially by the Lord Chancellor, Gardiner—she could not act in contradiction to their decisions; and some of her ministers would infallibly be hostile to the alliance. However, the Emperor did not despair of silencing the objectors. Neither treasure nor pains should be spared to effect his darling scheme.

The moment, however, for entering upon public negotiations of the marriage had not yet arrived. The realm was still agitated by Northumberland's abortive attempt to seize the crown for his daughter-in-law, the unfortunate Lady Jane Grey; religious dissensions prevailed, rendering the meditated re-establishment of the old worship extremely hazardous; while the violent opposition certain to be experienced from the whole Protestant party, might intimidate the Queen and deter her from following her own inclinations.

Proceeding with the caution required by the circumstances, the Emperor enjoined his ambassador at the English court, Simon Renard, a man of great subtlety, in whom he had entire confidence, to sound the Queen warily as to the marriage, but not to propose it to her formally until assured of her assent. Acting upon these instructions, Renard soon discovered that Mary's affections were fixed on her young kinsman, Courtenay, Earl of Devonshire, who had been long held captive in the Tower during the reign of Edward, and whom she herself had liberated on her accession. The wily ambassador instantly set to work to undo this knot, and by his machinations succeeded in convincing the Queen that the indiscreet and fickle young Earl was wholly undeserving of her regard, as he had become enthralled by the superior fascinations of her sister Elizabeth. Courtenay was therefore quickly discarded.

But another obstacle arose, which Renard had not foreseen. Ashamed of the weakness she had just exhibited, the Queen began seriously to think of uniting herself with Cardinal Pole, at that time attainted with treason by an act passed in the reign of Henry VIII., and banished from the realm. Regarding the Cardinal, she said, with feelings akin to veneration, and owing him reparation for the many and grievous injuries he had endured from her father, she would make him amends by bestowing upon him her hand. As he was only a cardinal deacon, a dispensation for his marriage with her could be easily procured from the Pope. She would implore his Holiness to grant her request, and to send Pole as legantine ambassador to England, when the nuptials might be solemnised. The union was sure to meet with the approval of the Holy See, which would perceive in it an earnest of the complete return of the realm to obedience to the Church. Renard did not attempt to dissuade the Queen from her design, feeling his efforts would then only be thrown away, and might serve to confirm her in her purpose, but contented himself with acquainting the Emperor with her Majesty's design, suggesting that Pole should be detained until after the marriage which they sought to bring about should have taken place.

The hint was not lost upon Charles. At the hazard of incurring the displeasure of the Sovereign Pontiff, Julius III., he determined to prevent the Cardinal from passing into England.

No man of his time possessed higher and nobler qualities than the illustrious Reginald Pole. Sanctity of manners, erudition, wisdom, eloquence, combined to render him one of the most shining lights of the age. Devout without bigotry, tolerant, strictly conscientious, and pure-minded, he was utterly free from debasing passions. Guile and hypocrisy formed no part of his character. Self-denying, abstinent, and laborious, he was ever generous and charitable. Descended from the royal house of York, his mother being Margaret, Countess of Salisbury daughter of the Duke of Clarence, brother to Edward IV., Pole attached no undue

I—2

importance to this adventitious circumstance, but maintained an almost apostolic meekness of deportment. At the advanced period of life he had attained at the period of our history, his looks were in the highest degree venerable and impressive, offering a complete index to his character. A master of the Latin language, which he spoke and wrote with facility and classical elegance, he had delighted in earlier years in the Greek poets and philosophers, but of late had confined his studies wholly to theology. At one time he had enjoyed the favour of Henry VIII., who was fully alive to his great merits, but he incurred the displeasure of the tyrant by the bold opinions he delivered as to the injustice of Katherine of Aragon's divorce and the King's marriage with Anne Boleyn. This opposition to his will was never forgiven by the implacable monarch, and unable to get Pole, who had taken refuge in Italy, into his power, he deprived him of his benefice and possessions, declared him guilty of high treason, laid a price on his head, and sought to procure his assassination. At last, unable to accomplish his fell purpose, Henry wreaked his vengeance on the Cardinal's mother, the venerable Countess of Salisbury— the last of the whole blood of the royal line of Plantagenet —on his brother Henry Pole, Lord Montague, Sir Edward Nevil, Sir Nicholas Carew, and other of his friends, all of whom were attainted of high treason, and brought to the block. The slaughter of the aged and unoffending Countess, who was only put to death because she was Pole's mother, is perhaps the deepest stain on Henry's character. These wholesale murders deeply afflicted Pole, and cast a gloom over the rest of his days; but he did not cry out for vengeance upon the perpetrator of the foul crimes, knowing that Heaven would requite him in due season. That the snares spread by the tyrant had failed to catch him—that the daggers aimed at his breast had been turned aside— convinced him he had work to do for which he was miraculously preserved. So he resigned himself to the heavy calamity that had befallen him, but though there was no show of grief on his countenance, the deep-seated wound in his heart never healed. Raised to the Purple by Paul III., on the death of that Pontiff, in 1549 (five years before the date of our history), the eminent and virtuous

Cardinal appeared the most fitting person in the conclave to assume the tiara, and, in spite of the intrigues against him, he was elected to the Pontifical throne ; but when the news was brought him at a late hour, he modestly bade the messengers wait till the morrow, and his answer being construed into a refusal, another election took place, when the choice fell upon Cardinal del Monte, who took the title of Julius III.

This occurrence caused a little disappointment to Pole. He retired to the Benedictine convent of Maguzano, on the margin of the Lago di Garda, where he was visited by Commendone, a secret envoy from the Pope to England, and made acquainted by this discreet messenger with the Queen's gracious intentions towards him. But with characteristic humility he declined them, alleging that, apart from any other considerations, his age and infirmities forbade him to think of marriage. Her majesty, however, he added, might count upon his zealous assistance in the great work she had before her, and the rest of his life should be devoted to her service.

Appointed legate from the Holy See to the Queen of England, the Emperor, and Henri II., King of France, with full powers and credentials, Pole set forth on his mission, but by the Emperor's order he was stayed at Dillinghen on the Danube. After some delay, he was suffered to proceed as far as Brussels, where he received a letter from Mary, telling him that matters were not yet ripe for his advent, and that his appearance in England might lead to a religious war. The Emperor also peremptorily enjoined him to remain where he was, but assigned no reason for the mandate.

Anxious to obtain some explanation, Pole besought an interview with Charles, which, at last, was reluctantly accorded. When the Bishop of Arras brought him word that his Imperial Majesty would receive him, alleging some excuse for the delay, Pole replied, " Truly, I find it more easy to obtain access to Heaven in behalf of the Emperor, than to have access to the Emperor himself, for whom I daily pray." The Cardinal gained nothing by the interview, and could not even learn the cause of his detention. Charles feigned anger, and taxing Pole with unnecessary impatience, reiterated his orders to him not to leave Brussels.

Having secured Pole, who he fancied might interfere with his plans if suffered to go into England, the Emperor wrote to the Queen, expressing his entire approval of her rejection of Courtenay, and hypocritically regretting that the Cardinal's extraordinary indifference to worldly honours rendered him insensible to the great dignity she designed for him, concluded by offering her his son.

The proposal was well timed, Mary being in the mood to receive it. She did not waste much time in consideration, but sent for Renard, who was fully prepared for the summons, and saw at once by the Queen's looks that his point was gained. She entered upon the business in a very straightforward manner, told him that, having always regarded the Emperor as a father, since his Majesty had graciously deigned to choose a husband for her, she should not feel at liberty to reject the proposal, even if it were not altogether agreeable to her. So far, however from that being the case, no one could please her better than the Prince of Spain. She, therefore, charged his excellency to acquaint the Emperor that she was ready in all things to obey him, and thanked him for his goodness. Thereupon, she dismissed Renard, who hastened to communicate the joyful intelligence to his imperial master.

But though the Queen had been thus won, much yet remained to be accomplished, and all Renard's skill was required to bring the affair on which he was engaged to a triumphant issue.

Informed of the proposal of marriage which their royal mistress had received from the Prince of Spain, the council, with the exception of the old Duke of Norfolk, the Earl of Arundel, and Lord Paget, arrayed themselves against it; and Gardiner, who had supported Courtenay, earnestly remonstrated with Mary, showing her that the alliance would be distasteful to the country generally, would alienate many of her well-disposed subjects, and infallibly involve her in a war with France. Finding it, however, vain to reason with her, or oppose her will — for she was as firm of purpose as her royal sire—the Chancellor desisted, and being really solicitous for the welfare and safety of the realm, proceeded to frame such a marriage-treaty as should ensure the government from all danger of Spanish interference, and maintain inviolate the rights and liberties of the people.

So much obloquy having been heaped upon the memory of this great prelate and statesman, it is right that his conduct in this important transaction, and the care taken by him to guard the country from foreign intervention, should be clearly understood. That Bishop Gardiner was subsequently led into acts of unjustifiable severity towards the adherents of the new doctrines, and became one of the chief instruments in the terrible persecution of the Protestant martyrs, cannot be denied. But it should be borne in mind, that he himself had suffered much for his religious opinions, and the harshness and injustice with which he had been treated in the late reign, chiefly at the instigation of his enemy, Cranmer, the sequestration of his revenues, and long imprisonment in the Tower, had not tended to soften his heart. Neither side when in power showed much pity for its opponents. But whatever judgment may be formed of Gardiner's acts towards the Protestant party, and his desire to extirpate heresy and schism by fire and blood, it must be conceded that he was one of the ablest statesmen of the day, and that Mary was singularly fortunate in choosing him for her chancellor and prime minister. He speedily replenished an exhausted treasury, repealed obnoxious taxes, and conducted the administration of the kingdom with so much zeal and ability, that, making himself both feared and respected, he obtained the greatest influence at home and abroad. The best proof of his capacities is to be found in the confusion that reigned after his death, and the impossibility on the moment of finding an adequate successor. Even Cardinal Pole, who was by no means favourably disposed towards him, declared that, as a minister, his loss was irreparable.

All-powerful as he was in the government, and high as he stood in the Queen's favour, Gardiner was not free from jealousy and distrust, and Pole's appointment as legate from the Holy See to England filled him with uneasiness lest he should be superseded on the Cardinal's arrival. Like the Emperor, he did not give that lowly-minded man entire credit for disinterestedness and disdain of worldly honours. Persuading his royal mistress that the legate's presence in the kingdom at a juncture when nothing was settled, would be fraught with infinite peril to herself and to the Church, Gardiner induced her to write to Pole to delay his coming to a more convenient season; and her letter furnished the Emperor with a plausible pretext for continuing to detain Pole at Brussels.

Obviously it was Charles's interest to win over Gardiner, who, if so minded, might unquestionably mar the marriage-project, even though it had gone thus far, and Renard was, therefore, instructed to spare no pains, and to hesitate at no promises calculated to propitiate the Chancellor. By the wily arts of the imperial ambassador, a certain under-standing was arrived at with Gardiner, who thenceforward withdrew his opposition, and warmly promoted the match; satisfied he could do so without sacrificing the interests of the country. The concurrence of others was procured by promises of pensions and gifts, and Charles V. remitted the vast sum of four hundred thousand crowns of the sun to his ambassador for this purpose.

Matters, therefore, being in good train, an extraordinary embassy, consisting of the Counts D'Egmont and Lalain, the Lord of Courrières, and the Sieur de Nigry, were despatched by the Emperor to the English Court, to demand formally the Queen's hand in marriage. In anticipation of their arrival, a treaty was prepared by Gardiner, its terms having been already discussed with Renard.

The chief stipulations of this treaty were, that the government of the realm should remain, as heretofore, absolutely and entirely with the Queen, so that, although Philip would have the name of King, he would have no regal authority whatever, and no power to dispose of lands, offices, revenues, and benefices. Spaniards were to be strictly excluded from the government, and from all court offices. The Queen could not be taken out of her kingdom save at her own desire. A jointure of sixty thousand pounds a year, secured on lands in Spain and the Netherlands, was to be settled on her Majesty by Philip. If there should be no issue, and Philip should survive his consort, he engaged to make no claim to the succession. The crown was to descend as provided by the laws of the country. A perpetual league was agreed upon between England and Spain, and the league already subsisting between the former country and France was not to be disturbed.

These conditions, insisted upon by Gardiner, and submitted to by the imperial ambassador, were, it must be owned, sufficiently advantageous to England. Count D'Egmont and his companions returned with the treaty to the Emperor, who was well enough content with it, being determined to obtain the throne of England for his son at any price.

So far all had gone tolerably smoothly, but a storm was brewing, and soon afterwards burst forth, threatening to dash to pieces this well-planned fabric.

Amongst the powers dissatisfied with the projected match, the most adverse to it was France. Henri II., the reigning monarch of that country, and the Emperor's inveterate foe, had already secured the youthful Queen of Scotland, Mary Stuart, for his eldest son; but the union between Philip and the Queen of England would be more than a counterpoise to his own anticipated aggrandisement. At all hazards, Henri was determined to thwart the alliance.

He therefore secretly instructed his ambassador at the English court, Antoine de Noailles, whose genius for intrigue eminently qualified him for the task, to stir up a revolt among the discontented nobles, the object of which should be to depose Mary, and place the Princess Elizabeth on the throne. De Noailles was authorised to assure all such as entered into the plan, that France and Scotland would lend them aid. By this adroit intriguer's machinations, aided by those of the Venetian ambassador, an extensive conspiracy was soon formed to oppose Philip's landing, to marry Courtenay to the Princess Elizabeth, and proclaim them King and Queen of England. Already indisposed to the match, the people were easily set violently against it. Every imputation that could be cast upon Philip and on the Spanish nation, was employed by the conspirators to excite the popular animosity. An army of imperialists, it was asserted, was about to invade the English shores and enslave the people. The terrible

Inquisition would be introduced into the country, and atrocities worse than those committed by Torquemada, the first inquisitor-general, who burnt eight thousand, eight hundred heretics and Jews, would be perpetrated. By such representations as these, aided by the undisguised hostility of the Protestant party, the nation became greatly disturbed, and an insurrection seemed imminent.

The Duke of Suffolk, father of Lady Jane Grey, with his brothers, the Lords John and Thomas Grey, entered into the plot. Courtenay, dazzled by the prospect of a crown and the hope of wedding Elizabeth, engaged to put himself at the head of the rebels, but, as the hour approached, he shrunk from the perilous enterprise, and confessed the design to Gardiner. Thus betrayed, the conspirators were obliged to precipitate their plans, which were not intended to have been put into execution till the arrival of Philip. A rising was attempted at Exeter by Sir Peter Carew, but met with little support, and was quickly suppressed by the Earl of Bedford. Several of the conspirators were apprehended, and Carew fled to France. The Duke of Suffolk and his brothers were equally unfortunate, and after a futile attempt to make a stand in Leicestershire, were arrested and lodged in the Tower.

A far more successful attempt was made by Sir Thomas Wyat in Kent. Speedily rallying a large force round his standard, he marched towards London, and defeated the veteran Duke of Norfolk, who was sent to oppose him. The rebellion had now assumed a formidable aspect. Wyat was in Southwark, at the head of fifteen thousand men, menacing the metropolis, in which he expected to find an immense number of supporters.

Undismayed by the danger, the Queen repaired to Guildhall, addressed the Lord Mayor and citizens in language so stirring and energetic, that they promised to defend her to the last; and when Wyat, designing to take the city by assault, was prevented by the Tower batteries from crossing London Bridge, but subsequently effected a passage higher up the river, and so approached the capital from the west, his partisans became alarmed at the vigorous preparations made for their reception, and began to desert him. An engagement took place at Charing Cross, which resulted in the defeat of the insurgents, and though Wyat gallantly fought his way with a few followers to Ludgate, none rose to join him, and he was compelled to retreat to Temple Bar, where he surrendered to Sir Maurice Berkeley, by whom he was taken to the Tower.

By this rebellion, in which she had no share, the ill-fated Lady Jane Grey was sacrificed with her husband. Even Elizabeth was placed in great jeopardy. Both she and Courtenay were sent to the Tower, the dungeons of which were crowded with those implicated in the conspiracy. The Emperor counselled severe measures, representing to the Queen, through his ambassador, that she would never be safe while those who could be put forward by the disaffected as claimants of the crown were permitted to live. But Mary, though thus urged by Charles, and by the imperial faction in the council, was reluctant to put her sister to death, and Gardiner encouraged her feelings of clemency, as well towards Elizabeth as Courtenay. Neither of them, therefore, though their complicity in the plot was indubitable, were brought to trial, but Elizabeth, after a brief confinement, was sent under a strong guard, and in charge of Sir Henry Bedingfield, to Woodstock, and Courtenay was taken to Fotheringay Castle. The Duke of Suffolk, with his brothers, paid the penalty of their treasonable acts with their lives, dying unpitied. But Wyat's fate excited much commiseration, his daring and gallantry having won him the sympathy even of his opponents. Many rebels of lesser note were hanged in different parts of the country, but multitudes received pardon on expressing contrition for their offence.

In this manner was the insurrection crushed. Its contriver, De Noailles, remained unmolested, though Renard denounced him to the council, declaring that he had forfeited his privilege as an ambassador by fomenting rebellion. But the Queen did not desire war with France, which would have certainly followed the plotting minister's arrest. Emboldened by this apparent immunity from personal risk, and utterly regardless of the calamities he might bring on others, De Noailles continued his secret intrigues as actively as ever, encouraging faction, and hoping to the last to defeat the alliance.

The rebellion, however, was serviceable to Mary. It confirmed her authority, and enabled her to perform many acts which she had not hitherto ventured upon. Above all, it elicited undoubted manifestations of loyalty from the great body of the people, and though the dislike to the Spanish match could not be extinguished, the Queen's emphatic declaration that regard for her husband should never interfere with her duties to her subjects, was held a sufficient guarantee for the security of the country.

The negotiations in regard to the marriage, so rudely interrupted by the outbreak, were now renewed, and Count D'Egmont and the other ambassadors returned to the English court, with the treaty duly ratified and signed by the Emperor. Introduced by the Lord High Admiral and the Earl of Pembroke to the royal oratory, they there found her Majesty surrounded by the lords of the council. After an address from the Queen, delivered with a dignity and feeling that powerfully moved the auditors, she exchanged the ratification of the treaty with the Count D'Egmont, who now acted as Philip's proxy. No better representative of the proud Prince of Spain could have been chosen than D'Egmont, himself one of the first lords of the Low Countries, and as distinguished for graces of person as he was for military genius and prowess in the field.

Kneeling at the altar beside the Queen, D'Egmont espoused her on the part of the Prince; and at the close of the ceremonial, which was performed by Gardiner, the Count placed on her Majesty's finger a diamond ring of great value, sent to her by the Emperor.

His mission completed, Count D'Egmont repaired to Spain to confer with Philip, who was then at Valladolid.

Gardiner's next step was to have an act confirming the marriage-treaty passed by both Houses of Parliament, and this was accomplished without delay. Lords and Commons were equally satisfied with the provisions of the treaty, and unanimously agreed to it, assuring the Queen that the Prince of Spain would be heartily welcomed on his arrival by all her dutiful subjects.

All being now arranged, the Earl of Bedford, lord privy-seal, and Lord Fitzwaters, with other noblemen and gentlemen, were sent to Spain to conduct Philip to England.

Landing at Corunna, the ambassadors proceeded to Santiago, then the capital of Galicia, where they waited for the Prince, who was journeying towards them, with a large train of attendants, by easy stages from Valladolid. During their stay at Santiago, the ambassadors were sumptuously entertained by the Marquis de Sara, and by others of the Spanish nobility.

On Philip's arrival at Santiago, high mass having been performed in the ancient cathedral, containing the shrine of St. James of Compostella—the patron saint of Spain—the Prince, in the presence of a large assemblage of grandees, dignitaries of the Church, and other important officials, received the treaty of marriage from the Earl of Bedford, ratified it, and solemnly vowed to abide by its conditions.

After a day or two devoted to feasting and pastime, Philip set out for Corunna, and on the 13th July, 1554, all being ready for his departure, he embarked for England in the "Santissima Trinidada," the finest vessel in the Spanish navy. He was escorted by a hundred and fifty ships, well provided with men and ordnance, and had with him many of the chief nobility of Spain.

During all this time, De Noailles continued his intrigues, vainly endeavouring to excite a fresh revolt, and to his agency may be traced an imposture, which created an extraordinary sensation in London, and might—if it had not been speedily detected—have led to dangerous popular tumults.

A man and his wife, occupying an old tenement in the heart of the city, forming part of a despoiled religious establishment, declared that from a stone wall adjoining their habitation an unearthly voice was heard to issue, proclaiming many strange and terrible things. Ere long, as may be supposed, a curious crowd collected within the court, and the assemblage was gratified by hearing the spirit denounce the approaching marriage of the Queen, which it declared would be full of bale and mischief to the realm. Some of the bystanders called out, "God save Queen Mary!" whereupon the spirit was silent. When they mentioned the Prince of Spain, a deep groan was the response; but when Elizabeth was named, the voice loudly replied, "So be it!" Furthermore, on the question being propounded, "What is the mass?" it discreetly answered, "Idolatry;" with many other utterances to the same purpose.

A report of this wondrous circumstance quickly spread throughout the city, and on the following day, upwards of seventeen thousand persons assembled in the neighbourhood of the structure whence the mysterious voice proceeded. Such as were able to get near the wall heard many treasonable speeches against the Queen, and fresh denunciations of her marriage, which they repeated to those further off, so that the sayings of the spirit were circulated amongst the immense crowd. Much excitement being caused and tumults apprehended, the persons belonging to the house were arrested, and strict search being made, a girl, named Elizabeth Crofts, was discovered, artfully hidden in a hole contrived in the thickness of the wall, whence she had managed to speak through a crevice, with the help of a small trumpet. The impostor was very leniently dealt with, being only made to do public penance for the offence at Saint Paul's.

Another incident occurred about the same time, which, though ridiculous in itself, is worthy of note, as showing that aversion to the Spanish match pervaded all classes, and was even shared by the young. Some three hundred boys, armed with clubs and staves, assembled in Finsbury Fields, and got up a mock fight, which they styled "The Queen against Wyat." Though intended as a sport, the conflict was carried on with so much good will, that several were wounded on either side, and the boy who represented Philip of Spain, being taken prisoner by the opposite party, was hanged to a tree, and only cut down just in time to save his life.

Calculating on the unconquerable antipathy to the match manifested in so many ways, De Noailles pursued his schemes, persuaded that, when Philip set foot on the English shores, the people by whom he was so much detested would rise against him, and massacre him and his attendants.

Meanwhile, Lord Clinton, the Lord High Admiral, who himself had no special liking for the Spaniards, or for the Spanish match, though he was full of loyalty towards the Queen, was cruising about the Channel, with eight-and-twenty of the tallest ships in the English navy, to protect the Prince, in case any attempt should be made by the French to attack him on his way, it being reported that four Gascon regiments had been ordered to Rouen, to attempt a descent upon the Isle of Wight and Portsmouth. Lord Clinton was accompanied by the Count de la Chapelle, the Vice-Admiral of the Low Countries, with some fifteen ships, which, however, the rough Englishman did not rate very highly, but called them in derision "mussel-shells."

As the time drew nigh when the Prince's arrival might be expected, Mary exhibited an impatience foreign to her character, but by no means unnatural under the circumstances. Sumptuous presents had been provided for her intended husband by her order, and preparations on a magnificent scale were made for the marriage ceremonial, which it was arranged should take place at Winchester. All the principal nobility were bidden to the solemnity, and the chief officers of the royal household, and, indeed, all connected with the court, had parts assigned them in the grand reception to be given to the Prince, and in the celebration of the nuptials.

Many, therefore, shared in the Queen's anxiety for Philip's safe and speedy arrival. Up to this time the breezes had been propitious, but contrary winds might arise, and delay the royal bridegroom on his voyage. Some, indeed, prayed that the vessel that bore him might founder, and would have exulted in such a catastrophe, and deemed it a special interference of Providence.

Their prayers were unheard. Tidings were brought by the Marquis de las Naves, the Prince's avant-courier, who landed at Plymouth, to the effect that his royal master might be daily looked for, and this welcome intelligence was immediately communicated to the Queen, and served to allay her anxiety.

Escorted by a strong guard, and attended by a sumptuous retinue, she forthwith proceeded to Guildford, where the Marquis de las Naves was presented to her by Renard, and gave her most satisfactory accounts of the Prince. Next day she continued her journey, and, on reaching Winchester, the loyal inhabitants of that fine old city welcomed her with very demonstration of joy. Well pleased by her reception she took up her abode at the Bishop's palace, which had been prepared for her by Gardiner.

At the same time, De Noailles, accompanied by some trusty agents, whom he required for a dark scheme he had hatched, journeyed secretly to Southampton, where the Prince meant to disembark.

CHAPTER II.

EARLY on the morning of the 19th of July, 1554, the long-looked-for Spanish fleet, conveying the royal bridegroom to our shores, was descried from the loftiest hill of the Isle of Wight, and presented a most magnificent spectacle as it neared that lovely island.

Consisting, as we have intimated, of a hundred and fifty sail—a third of the number being vessels of large size—the fleet formed a wide half-moon, in the midst of which rode the stately ship bearing Philip and the principal nobles of his suite. The "Santissima Trinidada" rose like a towered castle from the water. From the lofty crenellated turret at the stern floated a broad banner, embroidered in gold, with the arms of Castile and Aragon; its masts, and the turret at the forecastle, corresponding with that at the stern, were gaudily painted; and the sides elaborately carved and covered with devices, were so richly burnished, that the waves shone with their glow. Armed with the heaviest guns then in use, this splendid vessel had on board, besides her crews and the Prince's suite, three hundred fully equipped arquebusiers.

Other ships there were scarcely inferior to the "Santissima Trinidada" in size and splendour, displaying banners and streamers, and richly painted and decorated according to the Spanish fashion, and all well provided with men and ordnance.

Never before had such a superb fleet ploughed those waters; and when, at a later hour in the day, the Lord

2

High Admiral caught sight of it, he was sore angered, and internally vowed to lower the Spaniard's pride.

A soft westerly breeze filling the sails, impelled the ships gently on their way, though the surface of the sea was but little agitated. Having risen with the dawn, Philip was now on deck with the Duke of Alva, enjoying the ravishing beauty of the morning, and gazing at the land he was approaching. He could not help being struck by the bold outline and precipitous cliffs of the island in his immediate vicinity, and noted with wonder the tall sharp-pointed rocks, detached from these cliffs, that sprang like pinnacles from the sea.

Passing the Needles, the fleet entered the Solent Sea. On a far-projecting causeway on the left was Hurst Castle, a fortress erected by Henry VIII., and on the right loomed Yarmouth, with its castle. Salutes were fired from both forts. The scenery of the coast now possessed great beauty. On the mainland, noble woods, forming part of the New Forest, at that time of great extent, and full of deer, grew down to the very margin of the lake-like sea; occasional creeks and openings exhibiting sylvan scenes of extraordinary loveliness, and affording glimpses of ancient towns or sequestered habitations. On the other hand, the verdant slopes and groves of the island formed a delicious picture wholly different from that presented by the bold cliffs on its southern coast. Here all was softness and beauty, and to eyes accustomed to the arid and sunburnt shores of Spain, such verdure had an inexpressible charm.

For some time Philip remained wrapped in contemplation of the enchanting scenery of the island, unable to withdraw his eyes from it. At last he exclaimed, "And this is England! the land I have so longed to behold. How deliciously green is yonder island, and what a contrast it offers to our own coasts! And yon noble woods on the left, which they say are those of the New Forest, where William Rufus hunted and was slain! What magnificent timber! We have nothing like those oaks."

"It may be hot, your Highness," replied Alva; "but I prefer our olives and vines and chestnut-groves to those woods, and our bare brown mountains to those green slopes. If the sun scorches our herbage and burns our soil to brickdust, it makes abundant compensation. We have oil and wine and a thousand luxuries that these English lack, to say nothing of our fiery men and dark-eyed women."

" Your excellency is a true Spaniard," replied the Prince ; " but you forget that as soon as I set foot on these shores I shall become an Englishman."

" Heaven forfend ! " exclaimed Alva ; then checking himself, he added, " I crave your Highness's pardon. Inasmuch as the country will belong to you, you may be right to call yourself an Englishman."

" But I shall be King of England only in name," said Philip. " As you know, I am debarred by the marriage-treaty from any share in the government, neither can I appoint you, nor any of my nobles, to a post."

" Out on the treaty ! " cried Alva. " Your Highness, I trust, will little regard its terms. Once wedded to the Queen of England, the country will be under your control. This the Emperor well knew, or he would have spurned the conditions proposed to him by the wily Gardiner. Bind you as they may, the council cannot hold you fast, and ere long you will have supreme sway. In two years' time England will be as much a province of Spain as the Netherlands is now. Then you will reap abundantly the harvest you are sowing. Moreover, by that time the crown of Spain and the imperial diadem may grace your brow."

" Why do you think so, Alva ? " demanded Philip, quickly. "My father suffers much from gout ; but gout, physicians tell me, keeps off all other ailments, and those afflicted with it live long in consequence. When he last wrote to me, the Emperor reported himself in good case."

" Saints keep him so ! " cried the Duke. " Yet, as I have just said, ere two years are over, your Highness will surely be King of Spain and Emperor of Germany."

" What means this prediction ? " inquired Philip looking inquiringly at him.

" It means that the Emperor your father, tired with the cares of government, designs to surrender his kingdoms to you."

" Has he said aught of his intent to you, Alva ?—or is it mere surmise on your part ? " demanded the Prince, unable to disguise the interest he took in the question.

2—2

" Your Highness will excuse me if I decline to state how I obtained the information," rejoined the Duke ; " but I will stake my life on its correctness."

Philip said nothing more, but remained for some time with his hand upon his lips, absorbed in thought. The flush that overspread his cheeks showed he was much excited. Alva kept his keen eye fixed upon him, and seemed to read what was passing in his breast. After a while, Philip broke the silence.

" It may be as you say," he remarked ; " yet I do not think my father will part lightly with his crown. In a moment of weariness he may talk of abdicating in my favour—but when the fit is over, the design will pass away with it. How would he spend his days if not employed by state affairs ? "

" In retirement and holy meditation—in preparation for eternity. Such is his Majesty's intent."

" If it be so it is a praiseworthy resolution ; and it is to be hoped that Heaven may keep him in it. However, all is uncertain—the firmest man may change his mind."

" Your Highness says right. Therefore, it will be well to secure a crown in case of accident. Neither do I despair of your doing so. The English nation, they say, hate us Spaniards. What matter ? They cannot hate us worse than we hate them. They fear our yoke. Yet us give them reason for their fears by ruling them so severely that they shall not dare to move hand or foot, save at our pleasure. With such a people nothing but hard and sanguinary measures will do. Their late King, Henry VIII., knew that well, and his subjects obeyed him, crouching at his feet like beaten hounds. But to impose our yoke upon them, we must go beyond the despot Henry. We must pour forth the blood of the English nobles like water, seize upon their possessions, and assume their titles. Do this, extirpate heresy, establish the Inquisition, and your Highness need fear no rebellion."

Alva's eyes blazed as he gave this counsel, and his countenance assumed an expression so terrible that even Philip regarded him with awe.

" The time is not yet come for acting thus," observed the

Prince. "I must first try to ingratiate myself with the people, and win over the council and the nobles by gifts and promises. If those fail, I may have recourse to other means."

"There, to my mind, your Highness is wrong," rejoined Alva. "Begin as you mean to go on. You cannot make yourself beloved by this perfidious nation, but you may easily make yourself dreaded. Hesitate not to shed blood—the best blood. Strike boldly, and at the highest. If you have any misgivings, let me do the work for you, and it shall be done effectually. I shall not object to be grand justiciary of the realm."

And again his features wore the terrible look we have just noticed.

"It is too soon to talk of this," said Philip. "We will speak of it hereafter."

"It may then be too late," rejoined Alva, in a sombre tone. "Once again, I counsel your Highness not to delay. As soon as you are fairly wedded, throw off the mask."

"And be driven disgracefully from the kingdom," cried Philip. "No; I shall adopt a safer course. A time may come—and that at no distant date—when I may profit by your counsels, and ask your aid."

And he turned to watch the numerous white-sailed little barques steering towards him from Portsmouth.

CHAPTER III.

CHARLES V. has been described as more of a
Fleming than a Spaniard, and his son Philip as
more of a Spaniard than a Fleming. But the
Prince bore a strong resemblance to his sire,
though he was not so tall as the Emperor, and more slightly
and elegantly formed than that martial monarch. Apparently, Philip must have looked like a Scotsman, since he
was compared by a Highlander, John Elder, "the Redshank," who saw him on his entrance into London, to
"John Hume, my Lord of Jedward's kinsman." The Redshank seems to have been greatly struck by the royal
Spaniard's personal appearance and deportment, for he says,
"his pace is princely, and gait so straight and upright as he
loses no inch of height;" adding, "he is so well-proportioned of body, arm, and leg, as nature cannot work a more
perfect pattern."

But we have Philip actually brought before us as he lived
and moved at the period in question in the portraits of
Titian and Sir Antonio More. There we see his slight and
singularly elegant figure, and admire his striking costume.
There we may peruse his remarkable lineaments, every trait
of which has been preserved by the great painters with
extraordinary fidelity. Philip's face was a perfect oval, and
all the features good, except the mouth, the lower lip of

which was too full, and projected beyond the upper—a defect inherited by the Prince from his father, who was considerably under-jawed. Philip's complexion was fair, of almost feminine delicacy and clearness, his eyes large and blue, and shaded by thick brows meeting over the nose. His hair, worn short, according to the Spanish mode, was of a golden yellow—a circumstance which, no doubt, caused the Redshank to liken him to "my Lord of Jedward's kinsman;"—and his pointed beard of the same hue. His forehead was lofty, and white as marble, and his nose long, straight, and perfectly proportioned. In regard to his attire, he was extremely particular, affecting dark colours, as they best suited him; and he had the good taste to dispense with embroidery and ornament. On the present occasion he had in no wise departed from his rule. Black velvet haut-de-chausses, black taffetas hose, velvet buskins, doublet of black satin, all fitting to perfection, constituted his habiliments. Over all, he wore a short black damask mantle furred with sable. His neck was encircled by the collar of the Golden Fleece, and on his head sat a black velvet cap, having a small chain of gold as its sole ornament.

This costume, chosen with great judgment, was admirably calculated to display the graces of his person, and set off the extreme fairness of his complexion. Moreover, the Prince's demeanour was marked by extraordinary loftiness, and an ineffable air of the highest breeding pervaded his every look and gesture.

Philip was only nineteen when he was first married. Doña Maria of Portugal, the Princess to whom he was then united, died in giving birth to a son, the half-crazed and savage-natured Don Carlos, whose fate is involved in mystery, though it is supposed he was poisoned by his father's orders. It will be seen, as we proceed, how Philip treated his second consort; but we may mention that to neither of those who succeeded her—he was twice again married—did he manifest much affection. To his third wife, the young and beautiful Elizabeth de Valois, eldest daughter of Henri II. and Catherine de Medicis, he was unaccountably indifferent, repaying her tenderness and devotion by constant neglect and infidelities. At all times, he seems to have preferred any other female society to that of the one entitled to his regard. His fourth wife, Anne of Austria, was but little better treated than her predecessors. Philip long survived her, and would have married again if he could have found among the royal families of Europe an alliance sufficiently tempting. The sole being he entirely loved was the Infanta Isabella, his daughter by his third wife. She served him as his secretary, during his retirement in the Escurial in his latter days, and when dying, he commended her to his son and successor in these terms: "Philip, I charge you to have always the greatest care of the Infanta, your sister. She has been the light of my eyes."

At the period under consideration, the darker qualities inherent in Philip's nature had not become developed. He grew more impassive, sterner, and severer, as he gained power, and advanced in years. He was a profound dissembler, and his designs were inscrutable. None knew when they had forfeited his favour. He caressed those he meant to destroy; whence it was said that there was no difference between the King's smile and the knife. His self-restraint offered a striking contrast to the fiery impetuosity of his father. His policy was subtle, perfidious, Machiavellian. He had not Charles's sagacity, nor Charles's towering ambition, but he had more craft and hypocrisy than the Emperor, equal love of power, and equal capacity for rule. His industry was astonishing, and when his mighty monarchy devolved upon him, comprehending Spain, Flanders, Burgundy, the Two Sicilies, the Indies, and the New World, he passed many hours of each day, and often of each night, in reading petitions, annotating upon memorials, writing dispatches, and other toils of the cabinet. No sovereign ever wrote so much as Philip. Everything was submitted to his inspection. In hatred implacable, in severity unrelenting, fickle in friendship—if, indeed, he could form a friendship—he was equally inconstant in love matters, so that no syren could long hold him in her thrall. His affairs of gallantry, like all the rest of his proceedings, were shrouded in mystery. To none did he give his full confidence, and not even his confessor was allowed to peer into the inmost recesses of his breast. More inflexible than his father, if he had once formed a resolution, whether for good or ill, it was unalterable. But he was slow in coming to a decision. In religion he was bigoted, and firmly believed he was serving the cause of the Romish Church by the rigour he displayed towards heretics. He declared he would rather put to death a hundred thousand people than the new doctrines should take root in his dominions. Throughout his reign the terrible tribunal of the Inquisition was constantly in action. Such was the detestation felt for him in the Low Countries and in England, that he was called the "Demon of the South;" while his Spanish subjects spoke of him, under their breath, as the "Father of Dissimulations." Despite, however, his perfidy, his bigotry, and his severity, he was a great monarch, and raised the power of Spain to its highest point. After him its splendour began to decline.

In his latter years, Philip led the life of a religious recluse, shutting himself up almost entirely in the Escurial, and performing devotional exercises, vigils, fastings, and penances, with as much zeal as a brother of some severe order. Yet, notwithstanding this austere life, he continued to the last to conduct the affairs of state from his closet. His end was a grand and solemn scene, of which full details have been left us.

After receiving extreme unction, Philip said to his son, "I have sent for you that you may know what death is." He then caused his coffin, which had already been prepared, to be brought into the chamber where he lay, and the crown to be placed on a death's head on a table beside him. Then taking from a coffer a priceless jewel, he said to the Infanta, "Isabella Eugenia Clara, my daughter, this jewel was given me by the Queen, your mother. It is my parting gift to you." He next gave a paper to his son, saying, "You will see, from this, how you ought to govern your kingdom." A blood-stained scourge was then brought him, and taking it in his hand, he said, "This blood is mine, yet it is not mine own, but that of my father, who used the discipline. I mention this, that the relic may be the more valued." After another paroxysm, he again received extreme unction, and feeling his end approach, he asked for a crucifix, which the Emperor held in his hands when he breathed his last, and which he also desired to hold when dying. In another hour he became speechless, and so continued to the end, his dying gaze being fixed on a taper of Our Lady of Montserrat, burning on the high altar of the church, which was visible through the open door.

We have stood in the little chamber in the church of the Escurial in which Philip died, and have looked from it at the altar whereon burnt the sacred flame that attracted his last regards.

Philip's suit, as we have already intimated, comprised several nobles of the highest importance, who had been ordered to attend upon him by the Emperor. Besides the Duke of Alva, there was the scarcely less important Duke de Medina Celi, Don Ruy Gomez de Silva, Prince of Eboli, the Admiral of Castile, who was in command of the fleet, the Marquis de Pescara, the Marquis del Valle, the Marquis D'Aguillara, the Conde de Feria, the Conde Olivares, the Conde de Saldana, the Count D'Egmont, and several others equally distinguished. Each of these haughty hidalgos had a train of attendants with him.

With the Prince, also, was the Alcalde of Galicia, the Bishop of Cuença, Father Alfonso de Castro, and several other priests.

Moreover, he had a great painter in his train, Sir Antonio More, who had been previously sent into England to take the Queen's portrait (which may still be seen in the gallery at Madrid), and had now the honour of accompanying the Prince on his voyage.

Two other important personages had preceded Philip to England—namely, the Marquis de las Naves, previously referred to, and Don Juan Figueroa, Regent of the Council of Aragon, a nobleman much in the Emperor's confidence, and to whom an important part had been assigned in the approaching ceremonial.

Shortly after his discourse with the Duke of Alva which we have reported, Philip withdrew to his state cabin to perform his orisons, and listen to a discourse from the Bishop of Cuença. On his reappearance, he found most of his nobles assembled on deck, making, as they were all superbly attired, a very gallant show. Only three or four of their number removed their plumed and jewelled caps on the Prince's approach. The rest being grandees of Spain, and entitled to remain covered in the presence of royalty, asserted their privilege. Foremost in the group were the Duke of Alva, the Duke of Medina Celi, Ruy Gomez de Silva, and the valiant Marquis de Pescara—one of the great captains of the age. All these had the cross of Santiago on their mantles. Some of the assemblage were Knights of Calatrava, others Knights of St. Lazarus, or of St. John of Jerusalem, and all wore their orders. Numbering about fifteen, they presented a remarkable array of noble-looking figures, all more or less characterised by pride of look and haughtiness of deportment. It would have been easy to discern at a glance that they belonged to the most vainglorious people then existing—a people, however, as valiant as they were vain-glorious.

As we cannot describe these haughty personages in detail, we shall select one or two from the group. The most striking among them was undoubtedly the Duke of Alva, whose remarkable sternness of look arrested attention, and acted like a spell on the beholder. There was a fatal expression in Alva's regards that seemed to forbode the atrocities he subsequently committed in the Low Countries. His gaze was fierce and menacing, and the expression of his countenance truculent and bloodthirsty. His complexion was swarthy, and his short-clipped hair and pointed beard were jet-black. His figure was lofty, well proportioned, and strongly built, and his manner excessively arrogant and imperious. His attire was of deep-red velvet and damask. His mantle was embroidered with the Cross of Santiago. and round his neck he wore the collar of the Golden Fleece.

Full as noble-looking as Alva, and far less arrogant, was the Count D'Egmont, whose tall and symmetrical figure was arrayed in a doublet of crimson damask. His hose were of black taffetas, and his boots of bronzed chamois. His black silk mantle was passmented with gold, and his velvet hat was adorned with a tall panache of black and white feathers. Like Alva, he wore the order of the Golden Fleece.

Next to D'Egmont stood Sir Antonio More, for whom the Count had a great friendship. The renowned painter was a man of very goodly appearance, and richly dressed, though not with the magnificence that characterised the hidalgos around him. A doublet of black satin, paned with yellow, with hose to match, constituted his attire ; his hair and beard being trimmed in the Spanish fashion.

Such was the assemblage which met the Prince, as he came forth for the second time that morning. Returning their salutations with the dignity and solemnity of manner habitual to him, he seated himself on a throne-like chair, covered with purple velvet, which had been set for him on the raised deck.

By this time the fleet had passed the Solent Sea, and was off Cowes. The extreme beauty of the Isle of Wight, as seen from this point, might have excited Philip's admiration, had not his attention been drawn to the English and Flemish fleets, which could now be seen advancing to meet him. On came the two armaments, proudly and defiantly, as if about to give him battle, or oppose his progress. When they got within a mile of the Prince, the English ships were ordered to heave to, and soon became stationary ; but the Flemish squadron continued to advance until it met the Spaniards, when it wore round and came on with them.

As yet no salute had been fired by the Lord High Admiral.

" I do not understand such matters," said the Duke of Alva, approaching the Prince ; " but it seems to me that the English Admiral gives your Highness but a cold reception."

Philip made no reply, but, after a moment, observed, " Those are fine ships."

" They are so," replied Alva ; " but their commander should be taught to show due respect to his sovereign."

Just then an incident occurred which caused the utmost astonishment, not unmixed with indignation, throughout the Spanish fleet. A shot was fired by the Lord High Admiral across the bows of the Spanish ship nearest him. Philip was made instantly aware of the occurrence, and for a moment exhibited unwonted emotion. His pale cheek flushed, and he sprang from his seat, seeming about to give an angry order, but he presently became calmer. Not so the grandees around him. They were furious ; and the Duke of Alva counselled the Prince immediately to fire upon the insolent offender.

"I am as eager to resent the affront as the Duke," said Count D'Egmont; "but first let an explanation be demanded."

"Make the inquiry with our cannon," said Alva, fiercely; adding, with a scornful look at D'Egmont, "timid counsels smack of treason."

Regarding the Duke with a glance as disdainful as his own, D'Egmont said, "My loyalty to the Emperor has been often approved. His Highness will be better served by prudence than by rashness. There must be some mistake."

"There can be no mistake, and no explanation ought to be accepted," cried Alva, yet more fiercely. "The affront is a stain upon the honour of our country, and can only be avenged by the destruction of that insolent fleet. Count D'Egmont is not a Spaniard, and therefore does not feel it."

"I should regard the matter differently, if I could believe that insult was intended," rejoined D'Egmont. "But I cannot think so."

"Here comes the explanation," said Philip, as the Admiral of Castile approached. "How now, my lord?" he added to him. "What means this interruption? For what reason was that shot fired?"

"Because our topsails were not lowered in deference to the English navy in these narrow seas," replied the Admiral. "It is the custom to exact this homage to the flag, and Lord Clinton will not abate a jot of his demands. I am come to ascertain your Highness's pleasure."

"Pour a broadside into the insolent fellow," said Alva. "That is the only answer to return consistent with your Highness's dignity."

"It is not for me to offer counsel," said D'Egmont; "but it is better, methinks, to submit to this affront, which, after all, may not be intended as such, than to hazard the loss of a prize that is so nearly gained."

Philip looked thoughtful for a moment, and then said, in an authoritative tone, "Let the topsails be lowered—in this ship—and throughout the fleet. Since the demand is warranted, we ought to comply with it."

The Admiral instantly gave the requisite orders to the officers near him, and ere another minute the topsails were lowered, amid the murmurs of the Spanish grandees, whose glowing cheeks and flashing eyes proclaimed their wrath.

"I did not think this affront would have been endured," cried Alva.

"Nor I," cried the Marquis de Pescara, and some others.

"Be patient, my lords—be patient," observed Philip, significantly. "Our turn will come anon."

In another minute all the vessels in the Spanish fleet had followed the example of the "Santissima Trinidada."

This was no sooner done than a loud salute was fired from all the guns in the English navy.

Before the smoke had rolled away, the Spanish fleet replied by a deafening roar of artillery. Lusty cheers were then given by the sailors thronging the ropes and cross-bars of the English ships, and amid the beating of drums and the shriller music of the fife, a large boat was lowered from the Lord High Admiral's ship, in which Lord Clinton, attended by several officers of distinction, was rowed towards the "Santissima Trinidada."

On coming on board, the Lord High Admiral was ceremoniously received by Count D'Egmont, who acted as the Prince's major-domo, and, after a brief interchange of compliments, on the Admiral's request to be presented to his Highness, he was ushered through two lines of bronze-visaged and splendidly-equipped harquebuzeros to the bulk-head, where Philip was seated, with his nobles drawn up on either side. By all the latter, Clinton was regarded haughtily and menacingly, but, apparently heedless of their displeasure, he made a profound reverence to the Prince, who received him with a graciousness that offered a marked contrast to the defiant looks of his entourage.

"In the Queen's name, I bid your Highness welcome to her dominions," said the Admiral; "and I trust I shall be excused if I have appeared uncourteous in the discharge of my duty, which is to maintain her Majesty's sovereignty in these seas."

"No need of apologies, my lord," replied Philip. "The fault was ours, not yours. We ought to have recollected that we are now in English waters. How fares her Majesty?"

"Right well," said the Admiral, "and only anxious for your Highness's safe arrival."

"Is she at Southampton?" pursued Philip.

"No, my lord," rejoined the Admiral. "Her Grace came these two days past to Winchester, where she will await your Highness's coming. I had tidings of her so late as yester-morn, brought by my nephew, who is now with me."

"Is this your nephew, my lord?" inquired Philip, glancing at a tall, well-proportioned young man, standing behind the Admiral.

The blooming complexion, clear blue eyes, brown waving locks, and features of this very handsome young man, proclaimed his Saxon origin.

"Ay, my lord, this is my nephew, Osbert Clinton," replied the Admiral, eyeing the youth with a pride which the good looks and gallant bearing of the latter might perhaps justify. "He is fresh from her Majesty's presence, as I have just declared to your Highness. Stand forward, Osbert, and tell the Prince all thou knowest."

On this, the young man advanced, and bowing gracefully to Philip, gave him particulars of the Queen's journey from London, of her stay at Guildford, of her meeting with the Marquis de las Naves, and of her arrival at Winchester—to all of which the Prince listened with apparent interest.

"What office do you fill at court, young Sir, for I conclude you have some post there?" demanded Philip, when young Clinton had done.

"I am merely one of her Majesty's gentlemen," replied Osbert.

"I would willingly have made a seaman of him," interposed the Admiral, "and but that he dislikes the service, he might now be in command of one of yon gallant ships. Sorry am I to say that he prefers a court life."

"He is in the right," said Philip. "Unless I am mistaken, he has qualities which will be better displayed in that field than in the one your lordship would have chosen for him—qualities which, if properly employed, must lead to his distinction."

"Your Highness judges me far too favourably," said Osbert, bowing profoundly.

"Not a whit," rejoined Philip; "and to prove my confidence in you, I will attach you—if you list—to my own person."

"My nephew cannot quit the Queen's service without her Majesty's consent," said the Admiral, in a tone which, though deferential, showed his dislike of the proposition.

"That is always implied," said Philip. "But supposing her Majesty agreeable, what says the young man to the arrangement?"

"I am entirely at your Highness's commands," replied Osbert, overwhelmed with gratitude.

"And ready to become a Spaniard, and forswear your country, if need be, I make no doubt," observed the Admiral, gruffly.

"I shall violate no duty to the Queen by serving her consort," said his nephew; "and England and Spain will be so closely linked together by this most propitious union, that they will become as one land, wherein there will be no divided service or interests."

"That time is not yet arrived, and never will arrive," muttered the Admiral.

"You are doubtless anxious to return to your ship, my lord," said Philip. "I will no longer detain you."

"I thank your Highness," replied the Admiral. "We will make all haste we can, but there is little wind, and I fear it will be somewhat late ere we can reach Southampton."

"It matters not," said Philip. "I shall not disembark till to-morrow."

"Your Highness will exercise a wise discretion in the delay, as a better reception can be given you," returned the Admiral. "I humbly take my leave. Come, nephew."

"It is my pleasure that your nephew should remain with me, my lord," said Philip.

"But I am about to despatch him in a swift galley to her Majesty," remonstrated the Admiral.

"You must find a fresh messenger, my lord," said Philip. "I have other business for him. However, I would place no constraint upon the young man. He can depart with your lordship if he is so minded."

"Nay, I desire nothing so much as to remain with your Highness," cried Osbert, eagerly.

"The Prince was right in saying he was born a courtier," muttered the Admiral. "I can do nothing with him."

Making another obeisance, he then quitted the Prince's presence, and, being formally conducted by D'Egmont to the head of the vessel's stairs, re-entered the boat, and was rowed back to his ship, in no very good humour.

On reaching it, he immediately issued orders to his fleet to make all way to Southampton, and the noble vessels were soon bending in that direction. The Spanish and Flemish fleets followed in the same track. But so slight was the breeze, that some time elapsed before they passed Calshot Castle and entered Southampton Water.

As the Admiral had predicted, evening was at hand ere the fleets had cleared the broad and beautiful estuary, at the northern end of which stood the ancient and then highly picturesque town of Southampton. The grey walls circling the town, the spires of the churches, and the castle on the hill, were glowing in the last rays of the setting sun.

Crowds could be seen gathered upon the quays, and upon every point of observation. A loud salvo was fired from the castle batteries, and from the ordnance placed on the walls and on the gates. Except the "Santissima Trinidada," the Lord High Admiral's ship, and that commanded by the Vice-Admiral of the Netherlands, all the other vessels now cast anchor. The three large vessels got as near the port as they could, and then came likewise to an anchor, the ship containing the Prince occupying the foremost position. These movements excited great interest amongst the spectators, whose shouts were loud and continuous.

Intimation having been given to the authorities of the town that the Prince's disembarkation would not take place till next day, his Highness needing repose after his long voyage, no one went on board the royal ship. The ceremonial of the reception, and all public rejoicings and festivities connected with it, were postponed to the morrow; but it was not until it grew dusk, and they had in some measure satiated their curiosity by gazing at the superb vessel which had brought the illustrious stranger to their port, that the crowd on the quays began to disperse and return to their own dwellings.

3

It was at this hour that Philip called Osbert Clinton to his state cabin, and, dismissing his attendants, said to the young man, as soon as they were gone,—

"I intend to go ashore, incognito, to-night, and pass an hour in Southampton. I would judge with my own eyes of the people I shall have to govern. You shall go with me— I think I can trust myself with you."

"I will guard your Highness with my life," said Osbert, resolutely. "But I cannot conceal from you that it is a hazardous step you are about to take."

"Hazardous or not, I am resolved upon it," said Philip. "I like a nocturnal adventure, and the opportunity for one now offers, under circumstances that heighten its zest. My nobles would infallibly oppose my design, and therefore must know nothing of it. One person alone can be trusted, the Count D'Egmont, and he will lend me aid. I must about it at once, for it grows late."

"Your Highness will be in time, for this will be a night of revel and rejoicing in the town," said Osbert. "Pray Heaven no ill may come of the adventure!"

D'Egmont was then summoned, and on his appearance the Prince disclosed his plan to him. The Count strongly opposed it, representing its danger, as Osbert had done, but in the end he was obliged to yield.

"For an hour you and I will change parts," pursued Philip to D'Egmont. "You shall be the Prince, and I the Count. The Count will remain here, and the Prince will go ashore with this young Englishman as if sent on some special errand. None will be the wiser—not even Alva or Ruy Gomez. Go, order a boat to be got ready instantly. Make some change in your attire. Put on the long dark mantle I have seen you wear at night, and a black cap without a plume. Speak to the attendants as you pass, and tell them you are going ashore."

"It shall be done," replied the Count, departing.

While he was gone, Philip retired into an inner chamber and made some change in his own apparel. Just as he had completed his preparations, D'Egmont returned, habited as the Prince had directed. Philip took the Count's mantle, and wrapping himself in it, said, so as to be heard by the attendants, "See the Count D'Egmont and the English caballero to the boat, and let watch be kept for their return. Till then I would not be disturbed."

Having uttered these words, he muffled up his features and went forth, followed by Osbert. The ushers took him for the person he represented, and attended him to the stairs.

In this manner the Prince and his companion got into the boat without stoppage of any kind, and were rowed to a landing-place at the quay near the South-gate of the town.

CHAPTER IV.

SOUTHAMPTON IN 1554.

GIRDED round by high embattled walls, flanked with numerous towers, all in good repair, and well ordnanced, old Southampton had a proud and defiant look, especially when viewed from the water. Within the walls, situated on an elevated point on the north-west, stood the castle, now totally destroyed, the donjon of which, erected at the time of the Conquest, if not before, commanded with its guns all the approaches to the harbour, as well as the country to the north. This strongly fortified town possessed no less than eight gates, besides posterns. It was defended on the north and east by a moat of extraordinary width and depth, crossed by drawbridges connected with the gates, and on the south and west by the sea, which washed the foot of its walls ; and it contained many large and important mansions, amongst which may be noted the antique palace of Canute, besides several fine churches, hospitals, religious establishments, conduits, and great storehouses, together with a long and goodly street, described by old Leland, in his Itinerary, "as one of the fairest streets that is in any town of all England."

From the summit of the castle magnificent views were obtained of the lovely Isle of Wight in the distance ; of the vast woody region known as the New Forest ; of the broad estuary spread out like a lake before it, almost always thronged with craft, and sometimes, as now, filled with larger vessels ; of the ruthlessly-despoiled but still beauteous abbey of Netley, embosomed in its groves ; of the course of the Itchen, on the one side, and of the Test on the other ; or, looking inland towards the north of a marshy tract, caused by the overflowing waters of the Itchen ; of more marshes on the low ground further on, then more forest scenery, with here and then a village and an ancient castellated mansion, until the prospect was terminated by Saint Catherine's and Saint Giles's hills near Winchester.

Situated at the point of a piece of high land lying between the confluence of the two rivers just mentioned, namely, the Itchen and the Test, old Southampton was completely insulated by the deep ditch connecting these streams on the north, and continued along the east side of the walls. Without the walls, on the east, lay an extensive suburb, occupying the site of a still older town, which had been sacked and in a great part burnt by French and Genoese pirates in the time of Edward III.—a disaster that caused the second town to be as strongly fortified as we have described it.

And now let us examine the gates, the noblest of which, the Bar-gate, happily still exists. Built at different epochs, the two semicircular towers composing the north frontage being added to the central arch, which dates back at least as far as the Conquest, this stately structure, which formed the sole entrance to the town from the north, surpassed all the other gates in size and grandeur. Even now, crowded as it is with habitations, and standing in the midst of a busy throughfare, it is very imposing. Its massive towers, reverent with age, and carrying back the mind of the beholder to a remote period, are strongly machiolated, and retain much of their pristine character, but the once beautiful pointed archway between them has been disfigured by enlargement. Anciently, there was a double moat on the north of this gate, crossed by a stone bridge and a drawbridge. On the parapets of the first of these bridges the lordly sitting lions now guarding the archway were set.

We may complete our description of the Bar-gate by mentioning that it contains the Guildhall of the town, or Domus Civica, as old Leland terms it. Underneath, below the level of the moat, there was formerly a dungeon.

It may be questioned whether the good folk of Southampton are half so proud of their noble gate as of two extraordinary paintings hanging on the right and left of the central arch, which represent the renowed Sir Bevis, the legendary hero of the town, and the giant Ascapart, who, according to tradition, being conquered by the doughty Danish knight, became his squire. We do not quarrel with these paintings, or with their position, but why should not pictorial representations be likewise given of the peerless Princess Josyan, of whom Sir Bevis was enamoured, and of his marvellous charger, Arundel? The pictures, we venture to suggest, might serve to screen the grievous disfigurements on the south side of the Bar-gate.

The Water-gate and the South-gate, both of which faced the harbour, though inferior in size and grandeur of appearance to the Bar-gate, were very strongly built, machiolated, provided with double portcullises, and flanked by towers. The other five gates were nearly similar in character; the most important being the East and West-gates.

High, and of great solidity, the walls were further strengthened on the south and west sides by huge buttresses, as may still be seen in the picturesque remains left in these parts of the modern town. The parapets were embrasured, and had bastions at the angle of the walls. Towers were also built for the protection of the flood-gates required to admit the sea to the trenches.

All the fortifications, as we have said, were in good condition, having been repaired and strengthened by Henry VIII., who was a frequent visitor to the town, and, still more recently, in the reign of Edward VI. The batteries were furnished with fresh artillery by the former monarch, and a large piece of ordnance, graven with his name and title of "Fidei Defensor," is still preserved.

Separated from the town by the broad deep moat which was traversed in this quarter by a couple of large drawbridges, the quay extended along the shore to some distance on the east, and was laid out in wharves, and provided with cranes and other machines for landing or embarking cargoes. The harbour was marked out by huge piles driven into the banks, like those which may be seen in the shallow lagunes of Venice. Ordinarily the quay was a very busy scene, but its busiest and blithest time was on the arrival of the Flanders galleys, which came twice or thrice a year, laden with rich freights. Then all the wealthy merchants of South-hampton, with their clerks and serving-men, and even with their wives and daughters, repaired to the platform eager to inspect the goods and rare articles brought by the fleet.

Inhabited by a body of merchants who traded largely with Venice and the East, and almost rivalled the merchants of London in wealth, Southampton gave abundant evidence in its buildings of power and prosperity. In English-street, now known as the High-street, dwelt the chief merchants of the place, and though their habitations were not marble palaces, like those of the Venetians with whom they traded, nor stately structures, like those of the Flemings, who brought rich cargoes to their port, they were substantial timber houses, with high roofs, picturesque gables, and bay-windows. Not only did these houses possess large entrance-halls, and spacious chambers panelled with black oak, hung with costly arras, and otherwise luxuriously furnished, according to the taste of their wealthy owners, but they boasted, in many cases, large, dry, well-arched vaults, stored with casks of good Bordeaux, Xerez, Malaga, Alicant, Malvoisie, and Gascoigne wines. Some of these famous old cellars yet exist. Let us hope they are as well stocked as of yore.

Most of the houses in English-street were remarkable for the elaborate carvings adorning their woodwork, while the handsome porches were embellished with shields and escutcheons charged with armorial bearings. In all cases the upper stories projected beyond the lower, so as to over-hang the footways. It is satisfactory to add that the Southampton merchants of that day were noted for the liberality of their dealings, as well as for their princely hospitality to strangers.

About midway in English-street stood Holyrood Church, an antique pile, of which we shall have occasion to speak anon; and contiguous to the South-gate, which then formed one of the outlets to the harbour, was the Domus Dei, or God's House, an ancient hospital, in the chapel of which, now used as a place of worship by French Protestants, were buried the three lords, Cambridge, Scrope, and Grey, beheaded for conspiring against Henry V., as that warlike prince was about to embark for France to win the glorious battle of Agincourt. And while on this theme, let us not forget that it was likewise from Southampton that the victors of Cressy sailed.

Such was Southampton in the middle of the sixteenth century. It was during the reign of Henry VIII. that its power and importance as a seaport culminated. At the period of which we treat it had begun to decline, though the vast wealth previously acquired by its merchants helped for a while to sustain it. But its trade continued sensibly to diminish in Elizabeth's time, while its rival, Portsmouth, grew in consequence. However, a great future was in store for Southampton. The present century has witnessed its revival and restoration to far more than its mediæval prosperity. With its secure harbour and noble docks, wherein ride the superb steamers that connect it with the East and West Indies, and indeed with the whole world, few ports in the kingdom can now vie with that of fair Southampton.

CHAPTER V.

THE platform on which the Prince of Spain and
young Clinton stood, after leaving the boat, was
entirely deserted, the vast concourse, recently
assembled there, having returned, as already stated,
to the town. Here and there a sentinel, in steel cap and
breastplate, and armed with a halberd, strode to and fro
along the solitary quay. One of these sentinels challenged
the Prince and his companion on their landing, but a word
from Osbert caused the man to retire.

As Philip first set foot on English ground a thrill of exultation ran through his breast, but he allowed no outward
manifestation of the feeling to escape him; but after a
momentary halt, signified his desire to Osbert to enter the
town.

The night was dark, but clear and perfectly calm. Behind, on the smooth sea, which reflected the stars shining
brilliantly above, and the lights of the large lanterns hanging at the poops of the vessels, lay the "Santissima Trinidada," with her scarcely less colossal companions beside her,
looming like leviathans in the darkness. Here all seemed
buried in repose, for no sound arose from the mighty ships,
or from the squadron in their rear. But in front there was
a strong light proceeding from a blazing barrel of pitch set
on the top of the Water-gate, the flames of which, rising to

a great height, illumined the battlements and keep of the
castle, as well as the steeples of the churches and the roofs
of the loftier buildings, casting a ruddy glare on the moat
beneath, and making the adjacent walls and towers look
perfectly black. Moreover, a loud hum, with other sounds
arising from the interior of the town, showed that its inhabitants were still astir.

Traversing a drawbridge, near which another sentinel was
stationed, Osbert and his royal companion speedily reached
the Water-gate. Three or four halberdiers were standing
beneath the archway, and advanced to question them, but
satisfied with young Clinton's explanation, one of them struck
his pole against the massive door, whereupon a wicket was
opened, and the pair entered the town.

They were now at the foot of English-street, with the
principal features of which the reader is familiar. Active
preparations of various kinds were here being made for the
anticipated ceremonial of the morrow. Men were employed
in decorating scaffolds erected near the gate, and other arti-
ficers were occupied in adorning the fronts of the houses.
Though the hour was late, owing to the bustle of preparation,
and the numerous strangers within the town, few of the inhabitants of this quarter had retired to rest. Festivities
seemed to be going on in most of the houses. Lights
streamed from the open casements, while joyous shouts,
laughter, and strains of music resounded from within.

All was strange to Philip—the quaint and picturesque
architecture of the habitations, the manners, and to some
extent the very dresses of the people. But though he was
amused by the novelty of the scene, the rudeness, noisy talk,
boisterous merriment, and quarrels of the common folk, were
by no means to his taste. Naturally, his own arrival in the
harbour and expected disembarkation on the morrow formed
the universal topics of discourse, and he heard remarks upon
himself and his nation, such as he had not hitherto conceived
that any one would venture to utter. Little did the heedless
talkers imagine that the haughty-looking stranger, with his
face closely muffled in his mantle, who passed them in the
street, or lingered for a moment beneath a porch to watch
their proceedings, was the Prince of Spain. Well was it,
indeed, for Philip that he was not recognised, since there

were some discontented folk abroad that night who might not have held his royal person sacred.

Philip took no notice of his opprobrious discourse to his conductor, who would fain have shut his ears to it; but he said within himself, "I begin to understand these people. They are insolent, audacious, and rebellious. Alva was right. They must be ruled with an iron hand."

As he walked along, the Prince glanced through the open windows into the dining-chambers of some of the larger houses, and seeing the tables covered with flasks and flagons, and surrounded by guests, whose condition proclaimed that they had been drinking deeply, he inquired of Osbert whether his countrymen usually committed such excesses?

"They are somewhat prone to conviviality, I must admit," replied the young man. "But joy at your Highness's safe arrival has doubtless made them carouse longer than their wont to-night. Besides, there are many strangers in the town, and the hospitality of the Southampton merchants knows no limit."

Whether this explanation was entirely satisfactory to the Prince may be doubted, but he made no further remark.

By this time, Philip and his conductor had arrived within a short distance of Holyrood Church. An arch had here been thrown across the street, which some young women were decorating with flowers and ribbons; while a knot of apprentices, in jerkins of grey or russet serge and flat caps, were superintending their operations, and holding torches for them.

All at once a great shouting was heard in the upper part of the street, whereupon the maidens suspended their task, and called out gleefully to the youths that Sir Bevis and Ascapart were coming. At this intimation the apprentices drew back, and with some others of the townsfolk who were assembled there, ranged themselves on either side of the arch.

Presently the clamour increased, showing that the knight of Southampton and his gigantic squire must be close at hand, and in order to get out of the way of the crowd, the Prince and his companion withdrew into a porch, whence they could see what was going on without molestation.

Scarcely had they thus ensconced themseves, when a

tumultuous throng burst through the arch. These were followed by a troop of Moors—for such they seemed, from their white garments, turbans adorned with the crescent, and blackened features. The foremost of these Paynims bore torches, but three of them, who marched in the rear, had golden fetters on their wrists, and crowns on their heads. After these captive monarchs rode their conqueror, bestriding his mighty war-horse, Arundel. Sir Bevis, who was of gigantic proportions, was equipped in an enormous steel corslet, with greaves to match, and had on his head a white-plumed helm, the visor of which being raised, disclosed a broad, bluff, bearded visage. Arundel was of extraordinary size and strength, as he had need to be with such a rider, and had a tufted chamfron on his head, with housings of red velvet.

On the right and left of Sir Bevis strode two personages, whose frames were as gigantic as his own. One of these, clad in a tunic of chain armour, which fully developed his prodigious amplitude of chest, wore a conical helmet surmounted by a crown, and having a great nasal in front, which gave peculiar effect to his burly features. This was the Anglo-Danish King, Canute. His majesty bore on his hip a tremendous sword, the scabbard of which was inscribed with mystic characters, and carried in his hand a spear that would have suited Goliath. His shield was oval in form, with a spiked boss in the centre.

Loftier by half a head than the royal Dane was the giant Ascapart, who marched on the other side of the valorous knight of Southampton. Ascapart's leathern doublet was studded with knobs of brass; a gorget of the same metal encircled a throat thick as that of a bull; his brawny legs were swathed with bands of various colours; and on his shoulders, which were even broader than those of Canute or of his master Sir Bevis, he carried a ponderous club, which it would have puzzled an ordinary man to lift. At his back hung a dragon's head, no doubt that of the terrific monster slain by Sir Bevis. Despite his attire and formidable club, there was nothing savage in Ascapart's aspect. On the contrary, his large face had a very good-humoured expression; and the same may be asserted both of Sir Bevis and Canute. It was evident from the strong family likeness distinguishing them that the three giants must be brothers.

As if to contrast with their extraordinary stature, these Anakim were followed by a dwarf, whose appearance was hailed with universal merriment by the spectators. A doublet and cloak of silk and velvet of the brightest hues, with a cap surmounted by a parti-coloured plume of ostrich feathers, formed the attire of this remarkable mannikin. A rapier, appropriate to his size, was girt to his thigh, and a dagger, tiny as a bodkin, hung from his girdle. He rode a piebald horse, and behind him on a pillion sat a plump little dame, representing the Princess Josyan, whose transcendant beauty had bewitched Sir Bevis, and softened the adamantine heart of the ferocious Ascapart. It can scarcely be affirmed that the Princess's charms were calculated to produce such effects on men in general, but there was doubtless a sorcery about her, which operated more potently on certain subjects than on others. To ordinary eyes she appeared a fat little woman, neither very young nor very tempting, with a merry black eye and a comical expression of countenance. Princess Josyan's gown was of green velvet, and her embroidered cap had long lappets covering the ears. In her hand she carried a fan made of peacock's feathers.

In Sir Bevis and his companions Osbert Clinton at once recognised (as perhaps some of our readers may have done) three well-known gigantic warders of the Tower, yclept Og, Gog, and Magog, who, on account of their prodigious stature, were constantly employed in state pageants and ceremonials, while in the consequential-looking pigmy riding behind them he did not fail to detect the Queen's favourite dwarf, Xit, who of late, having received the honour of knighthood from her Majesty, had assumed the title of Sir Narcissus le Grand. The plump little occupant of the pillion, Osbert felt sure must be Lady le Grand, formerly Jane the Fool, whom the Queen had been graciously pleased to bestow in marriage upon Xit. While young Clinton was detailing these circumstances to the Prince, an incident occurred that brought a smile to Philip's grave countenance.

As Og, the representative of Sir Bevis, was passing through the arch, which his plumed helmet well-nigh touched, he perceived a very comely damsel looking down from a ladder on which she was standing, and laughing at him. Without more ado, he raised himself in his stirrups, and putting his arm round her neck, gave her a sounding salute. Indignant at this proceeding, the damsel requited him with a buffet on the cheek, but in so doing she lost her balance, and would have fallen if the giant had not caught her, and placed her behind him on the broad back of Arundel, which done, he secured his prize by passing his belt round her waist.

Great was the amusement of the bystanders at this occurrence, and several of them clapped their hands and called out, "The Princess Josyan!—the Princess Josyan!" One young gallant, however, did not share the general mirth, but, shouting to Sir Bevis to set the damsel down, made an effort to release her. But he was thwarted in his purpose by Magog, or rather, we should say, by the terrible Ascapart, who, seizing him by the jerkin, notwithstanding his struggles, handed him to Sir Bevis, and by the latter he was instantly transferred to the highest step of the ladder which the damsel had just quitted. Satisfied with what he had done, Sir Bevis rode on, carrying away with him his fair captive, amid the plaudits and laughter of the spectators. Highly incensed at the treatment he had experienced, the youth was preparing to descend, when he perceived Xit beneath him, and stung to fury by the derisive laughter and gestures of the dwarf, who was mightily entertained by what had taken place, he pulled off his thick flat cap, and threw it with such force, and so true an aim, that hitting Xit on the head, it nearly knocked him off his horse.

Greatly ruffled by the indignity thus offered him, Xit, as soon as he recovered his equilibrium, drew his sword, and shrieking out to the apprentice that he should pay for his insolence with his life, bade him come down instantly. But the youth did not care to comply, but joined in the laughter of the spectators, all of whom were prodigiously entertained by the enraged dwarf's cries and gesticulations. At last, Xit, who was preparing to scale the ladder and attack his foe, yielded to the solicitations of Lady le Grand, and rode on, delivering this parting menace: "We shall meet again, thou craven flat-cap, when I shall not fail to avenge the insult offered me."

He then quickened his pace, for the laughter and jests of

the bystanders displeased him, and speedily overtook the cavalcade.   On coming up with it, he found that the damsel, who was universally saluted as the Princess Josyan, still maintained her position behind Sir Bevis, and, indeed, seemed perfectly reconciled to it, as she was now chatting in a very amicable manner with her captor.   Perhaps her vanity was a little excited by the effect she evidently produced upon the lookers-on.   This may account for the proffer she voluntarily made to Sir Bevis, to enact the Princess Josyan on the morrow — a proffer which the courteous knight readily accepted, provided the matter could be accommodated with Lady le Grand, who had a prior claim to the part.

Great was the tribulation of the luckless apprentice who had thus lost his sweetheart.   From his elevated position he watched her progress down the street, and could perceive that she manifested no disposition to dismount.   But he soon lost sight of her, since, before reaching the bottom of English-street, Sir Bevis and his *cortége* turned off on the right in the direction of the West-gate.

CHAPTER VI.

WHAT PASSED BETWEEN MASTER RODOMONT BITTERN AND THE PRINCE.

AS soon as the street was clear, Osbert inquired whether his Highness would proceed as far as the Bar-gate, but Philip having now seen enough, declined, and they began to retrace their steps. The tipplers in the houses were still at their cups. Some of them, it is true, had staggered to the windows on hearing Sir Bevis and his *cortége* pass, but by this time they had got back to the bottle. However, a party of half-inebriate guests issued from a large house so suddenly, that the Prince and Osbert had no time to get out of their way, but were instantly surrounded.

"Ah! who have we here?" cried one of these roysterers, struck by Philip's haughty air. "By the life of the Emperor Charles V., a Spanish grandee! Perchance, one of the Prince's suite."

"You are right, Sir," interposed Osbert; "this noble cavalier is but newly-arrived at Southampton with his Highness the Prince of Spain, and, having come ashore on business, is now returning to his ship."

"How does the noble cavalier style himself?" demanded the other.

"Call me Don Philip—that will suffice," said the Prince, haughtily.

"Bezo las manos, Señor Don Felipe," rejoined the other, taking off his cap. "Your lordship is right welcome to

Southampton. Suffer me to introduce myself to you as Master Rodomont Bittern, a caballero y hombre de honor, who will be proud to do your lordship a service. These are my friends, Nick Simnel and Jack Holiday—both caballeros like myself, and courageous and haughty as bulls. Be known to Don Philip, señores. If your lordship will permit us, we will escort you to the quay."

"Ay, and go on board with his lordship, an he likes our company," cried Simnel. "We are in the humour for an adventure."

"I am ready for aught, save the couch," said Jack Holiday. "Don Philip will find us jolly cocks, that I promise him."

"Why should not Don Philip, if he be not pressed, enter worthy Master Tyrrell's house, and crush a flask of Bourdeaux?" said another of the party. "He shall be welcome, I will answer for it."

"Ah, that he shall, good Master Huttoft," cried the host, who was standing in his doorway, and heard what was passing. "He shall have the best my cellar can produce. I pray you, noble Sir, come in."

"Enter by all means," said Rodomont to the Prince. "Master Tyrrell is well worth knowing. He is the richest merchant we have—richer than the Italian merchants Nicolini and Guidotti, who dwell near St. John's. Master Tyrrell is a descendant of the famous brothers Gervase and Protasius, who founded the hospital of God's House. His daughter, Constance, is surnamed the Pearl of Southampton. A ravishing creature, I vow. You will lose your heart the instant you behold her. Your Andalusian beauties are nothing to her."

"What do you know of Andalusian beauties, Sir?" said Philip.

"By the mass! a good deal," rejoined Rodomont, significantly; "as your lordship will guess, when I tell you I have been at Seville. That is how I knew you for a grandee. I could not be deceived. Enter, I pray you, and make Master Tyrrell's acquaintance. You will find his daughter as I have described her—the fairest creature you ever clapped eyes on. Not, however, that you will see her to-night, for she is at her devotions. She is as pious as Saint Elizabeth. Had I the

4

choice, I would take Constance Tyrrell in preference to our Queen, whom the Prince, your master, has come hither to marry—ha ! ha ! "

And the laughter in which he indulged was echoed by his companions.

"Heaven grant that the Prince may not have raised his expectations too high on the score of his consort's beauty, or he is like enough to be disappointed," pursued Rodomont. " Hath your lordship ever beheld her Majesty ? "

"How could I, Sir ? " replied Philip, "since I have never set foot in England before this hour. But I have seen her portrait by Sir Antonio More."

"Sir Antonio is a court painter, and has doubtless flattered her," said Rodomont. "By my beard ! she is as thin as a whipping-post, and as sour as verjuice."

This sally was followed by a shout of laughter from the party.

" Let me impress upon you the necessity of a little caution, Master Bittern," said Osbert. "You seem to forget that Don Philip is attached to his Highness's person."

"But he is not going to marry the Queen, therefore the question of her good or ill looks can have no interest to him," laughed Rodomont. " After all, tastes differ, and the Prince may think her Majesty charming, though I do not."

"Are you allowed to talk thus freely of great personages in England, Sir ? " demanded Philip, sternly.

" For the present we are, Señor Don Felipe, but there's no saying what we may come to, now the Prince, your master, is about to take us in hand, and teach us manners. Ere long, we shall have a padlock placed upon our mouths, I make no doubt. They say we are to have the Inquisition, and an Auto-da-fé once a month to purge us of heresy, and bring back the stray lambs to the fold. What with the Prince, your master, and Cardinal Pole, who is shortly expected, we are likely to have a pleasant time of it. Familiars of the Holy Office will become too familiar with us, and after a few months passed in secret cells, with red-hot pincers and the rack for recreation, we shall be burnt alive in the market-places, shrouded from head to foot in a san benito, as I have myself seen done in your delightful city of Seville."

" You are trying to frighten us by these horrid descriptions of red-hot pincers and the rack, Rodomont." said Simnel. "But it won't do. Such things will never come to pass in England."

"Be not too sure of that, Nick," rejoined Bittern. "You yourself may march at the head of a procession of penitents to Smithfield before the year is out."

"May be I shall," rejoined Simnel; "but if I am burned at the stake, you will bear me company. However, I refuse to believe that the Prince of Spain has any such fell designs as you calumniously attribute to him. Don Philip will give us an assurance to the contrary. Doubtless he is in his Highness's confidence. I pray your lordship to contradict him. Give him the lie direct."

"Set your mind at ease, Sir," rejoined Philip. "The Prince is a good Catholic, but that you need not be told. But even his abhorrence of heresy will not induce him to interfere with the religious affairs of this realm, which belong, of right, to the Queen and the Church. You need not fear the establishment of the Inquisition."

As the words were uttered, a passer-by, who had lingered to hear what was going forward, exclaimed, " 'Tis he!" and then, hurrying on his way, speedily disappeared.

The exclamation troubled Philip, and he felt the necessity of instant departure.

"I am sorry I cannot longer continue this discourse, gentlemen," he said, "neither can I accept Master Tyrrell's hospitality. I bid you all good-night."

And bowing to the party with a dignity that strongly impressed them, and prevented them from attempting to accompany him, he walked away with Osbert.

"My mind misgives me," said Rodomont, looking after him. "Did I not feel sure the Prince must be on board the 'Santissima Trinidada,' I should think this haughty hidalgo was he. What an air he has!"

"A princely air, indeed!" exclaimed Simnel.

"Who was it cried ' 'Tis he?'" demanded Bittern.

"Nay, I know not," returned Jack Holiday. "Whoever the fellow might be, he went away quickly."

"From the glimpse I caught of him, he looked like the French Ambassador," observed Huttoft. "His Excellency is in Southampton. I saw him this morning."

4—2

"The French Ambassador!" exclaimed Rodomont. "Nay, then, my suspicions are well founded. Gentlemen, we have been conversing with the Prince of Spain."

Expressions of incredulity arose from the whole party.

"If it be the Prince of Spain, I would not give much for your ears, Rodomont," said Simnel, laughing. "Bethink you how disrespectfully you spoke of the Queen."

"I but affirmed the truth in saying she was not a beauty," rejoined Bittern.

"Ay, but the truth must not be spoken when her Majesty's looks are in question," observed Simnel. "You are in for it, friend Rodomont."

"Bah! I am not afraid," cried Bittern, "The Prince will be of my opinion when he beholds his royal consort. Mark what I say. There is not a gallant in the Two Castiles fonder of a pretty woman than Don Philip—a pretty woman, d'ye heed? How then will he reconcile himself to one so much the reverse of beautiful as the Queen? But we must watch over his Highness's safety. The French Ambassador is the Prince's worst enemy, and capable of doing him a mischief. Good-night, worthy Master Tyrrell. We will have another merry bout to-morrow. Come along, gentlemen—but caution!—caution! —The Prince must not perceive that he is followed."

With this, they all marched down the street.

CHAPTER VII.

INSTEAD of proceeding to the Water-gate, near which a noisy throng was still assembled, Philip and his conductor turned off on the left, with the intention of making their exit from the town by the South-gate.

Passing through a Gothic archway, they entered a narrow sombre street, or alley, with old monastic looking buildings on either side. In this street stood, and still stands, the *Domus Dei*, or God's House, a hospital founded in the reign of Henry III. by two brothers, Gervase and Protasius, merchants of Southampton, and dedicated by them to Saint Julian, the patron of travellers. Connected with this hospital, ancient even at the period of our history, was a beautiful little chapel, where, as we have already mentioned, the three conspiring lords were buried after their decapitation.

Vespers were being celebrated within the sacred pile as Philip and his conductor passed it; perceiving which, the Prince determined to go in and perform his devotions. Accordingly, they entered the little edifice.

Dimly lighted by the tapers burning at the altar, its massive round pillars, semicircular arches, small windows, and deeply-recessed doorway could only be imperfectly seen. Within the chancel, the arch of which was of great beauty, three black marble flags told where the traitororous nobles were laid. Here, also side by side, were recumbent statues of the founders of the fane, sculptured in alabaster.

Except the officiating priest and his assistants, there were only two female devotees in the chapel, both of whom were kneeling before the altar.

Philip took a place near them. For some minutes he was so absorbed in his devotions that he did not notice the person beside him, further than remarking that she was young; but as he raised his eyes, he caught sight of a face that at once riveted his attention. Never had he beheld features so exquisitely beautiful, or so sweet in expression. No nun could have a holier or purer look. A tender melancholy pervaded this angelic countenance, adding an inexpressible charm to it. The face was seen by the Prince in profile, but the attitude served to display the classic regularity of the lineaments, the noble brow, white as murble, the delicately-chiselled nose, the short upper lip, and rounded chin. The complexion of the lovely devotee was of dazzling fairness, which lent additional effect to her resplendent black eyes, her finely-pencilled brows and dusky and luxuriant tresses. Her figure was slender, and its perfect symmetry was defined by her black taffetas dress. From her girdle hung a silver rosary. A small ruff encircled her swan-like throat, and a velvet hood fastened to a coverchief lay at the back of her head.

Totally unconscious of the effect produced by her charms, she pursued her devotions, and it was only towards the close of the service, that she became aware of the Prince's propinquity, and of the ardent gaze he fixed upon her. The discovery gave her evident annoyance. Whispering to her attendant, she arose hastily, with the design of quitting the chapel. She could not avoid Osbert, who was leaning against a pillar directly in her way. Young Clinton had been as much struck by her beauty as the Prince, and with looks betokening the extent of his admiration, he bowed to her respectfully as she passed. Coldly returning the salute, and drawing the hood over her head, she went forth, followed by her attendant.

Philip did not move till the fair devotee had quitted the chapel. He then arose, and with undisturbed gravity of deportment left the building. As he issued into the street, which we have stated was dark and narrow, the two females could nowhere be discerned. Yet, feeling confident they must have proceeded towards the main street, he speeded in that direction. Osbert went with him, but was not sorry to find, on reaching the archway opening into English Street, that nothing was to be seen of them.

"Whither can she have gone?" cried Philip, in a tone of fierce disappointment; and then, without waiting for an answer, he added, "But perhaps you know her."

Osbert replied in the negative.

"I did not believe the world contained such a paragon," cried Philip. "But to lose her would be intolerable. Stay! the priest can tell us who she is. Let us go back and question him."

"Such a step would excite the holy man's suspicions, and infallibly seal his lips," replied Osbert, "To-morrow I will obtain information for your Highness."

"But I must be satisfied to-night," cried Philip. "I cannot rest till I feel sure I shall behold her again."

"She appears to have made a great impression upon your Highness," observed Osbert, in a tone that slightly evinced his dissatisfaction.

"More than I like to confess," rejoined the Prince. "I am not accustomed to be thwarted. I must find out who she is, and that without delay."

"I see not how your desire can be gratified," said Osbert. "We have lost all traces of her for the moment."

"You seem reluctant to do my bidding, Sir," said Philip. "Are you smitten with her yourself? Take heed! I will endure no rival."

"Far be it from me to dream of rivalry with your Highness," rejoined Osbert. "I am ready to execute any orders you may deign to give me, but I cannot blind myself to the risk of continuing this quest."

"You are too young to talk of risk, Sir," said Philip. "Difficulties and dangers only add zest to an affair of this kind."

"That would be quite true, were I alone concerned in it," rejoined Osbert. "But it is risk to your Highness, and not to myself that I dread. You would not care to have it known that you have privily visited Southampton to-night.

Yet it may become so, without due caution. Even now, methinks, we are watched. Cast your eyes across the street, and beneath the gate of yonder convent of Grey Friars you will perceive the party of tipsy revellers from whom we have but just escaped. Unless I am mistaken, they are playing the spy upon us."

"By Heaven you are right!" cried Philip, looking in the direction indicated, and remarking the group beneath the convent gate. "If we go on, we shall have those fellows at our heels, or they will join us, which will be worse."

"Not a doubt of it," replied Osbert. "And to speak truth, I am not without uneasiness on another score. That sudden exclamation of a passer-by would seem to indicate that you were recognised—perhaps by an enemy. If I may be so bold, I would counsel your instant return to the ship."

"And leave this adventure unfinished!" exclaimed Philip. "It goes against my inclination. 'Tis not the custom with us Spaniards to halt on the threshold of a love affair. But I yield to the prudence of your suggestion."

"Heaven be thanked!" mentally ejaculated Osbert. "He shall never behold her again, if I can help it."

On this, they once more tracked the dark and narrow street. In another moment they were near the little chapel, and Osbert would have hurried on, but the Prince paused to consider the locality. Possibly the damsel might be still thereabouts, or she might have entered the hospital which adjoined the chapel, and indeed was connected with it. A lateral passage led to a small quadrangular court, and down this passage Philip went, hoping to make some discovery. Nor was he this time destined to disappointment. On gaining the court, he found that the fair object of his search was advancing towards him with her attendant. She had evidently just left the hospital, as the door was being closed at the moment by an ancient porter, carrying a lamp.

"At last I have found you, Madam!" exclaimed the Prince, springing towards her. "I have looked for you everywhere in vain. But I thought fortune would not present such a treasure to my view, only to rob me of it instantly."

"Let me pass, I entreat you, Sir," cried the terrified maiden.

"Not till I have told you of the passion which your charms have inspired in my breast," pursued Philip, detaining her. "You must—you shall hear me."

"Not another word," cried the damsel, haughtily; "I command you to let me go. You will repent this rudeness. Know you whom you thus insult?"

"Pray Heaven she do not tell him who she is!" said Osbert, internally.

"I know you for the fairest creature I have ever beheld," said Philip, "and if I offend you by my speech, blame me not for it, but rather blame your own charms, which compel me to give utterance to my feelings. Did I but know your name, I would at once release you."

"Then learn to your confusion, forward Sir," interposed the old attendant, "that my young lady is Mistress Constance, daughter of Master Tyrrell, the rich merchant of English Street, whom you must know by repute."

"What! the Pearl of Southampton!" exclaimed the Prince. "By my faith, the title is well bestowed. She does not belie her reputation."

"Ay, the Pearl of Southampton," cried the old woman. "And a pearl she is, above all price, I can tell you, and not to be meddled with by profane gallants like you, when she is engaged on works of charity."

"What goodly work has your fair mistress been employed in?" inquired Philip.

"In ministering to the sick within this hospital," replied the old woman. "But she is always occupied in good works, and hath no time for idle vanities. You would do well to follow her example. When the Prince of Spain arrived in the harbour this evening, and all the town flocked to the quay to welcome him, what did my pious darling do but hie to yon little chapel to return thanks to Heaven for giving him a safe voyage."

"Indeed!" exclaimed Philip. "The Prince ought to be much beholden to her. I thank you in his name, Madam," he added to Constance.

"You are a Spaniard, then, Sir?" said Constance, for the first time raising her eyes towards him.

"One of his Highness's suite," replied Philip. "I am sure it will delight the Prince that one so fair should take an

interest in him.   I trust you will again remember him in
your prayers."

"I have prayed for him," said Constance—"prayed that
having arrived here in safety, he may escape all danger
from the disaffected—prayed that his marriage with our
Queen may be fraught with happiness to both of them, and
conduce to the welfare of the realm, and the benefit of
religion."

"I rejoice to hear such sentiments fall from your lips.   I
have heard few like them since I landed.   You wish well to
the Prince of Spain?"

"I wish well to him because he is to be the Queen's husband, and she has no more loyal subject than myself.   I
could not wish him better than to be the chosen spouse of
so excellent a Princess."

"He might be better pleased, Madam, if her Majesty
resembled you," observed Philip.

"The Prince cannot be of your opinion, Sir," returned
Constance, "for I hear he is singularly devout.   He will
require no other graces in her Majesty save those of her
mind and heart."

"You have been rightly informed as to the Prince's zeal
in religious matters, Madam," said Philip.   "He is as
strict as you appear to be ; but he is by no means indifferent to beauty, and I am certain he could not behold
you unmoved."

"You do him wrong, Sir," said Constance.   "The Queen
must now exclusively occupy his heart.   A thought of any
other would be sinful, and a pious prince would never
indulge such a thought."

"A very pertinent remark.   I trust he may profit by it,"
muttered Osbert.

"The sin being involuntary, would lie lightly on his conscience," observed Philip.   "But I must prevail on the
Prince to mention your name to the Queen.   She ought to
be made acquainted with your merits, and might, possibly,
find some place for you near her royal person."

"I pray you, Sir, do not.   I have no desire to emerge from
my present obscurity.   But for my father, I should embrace
the life of a cloister.   That is my real vocation."

"It must not be, Madam!" exclaimed Osbert, unable to

restrain himself. "You would do a wrong to society to deprive it of its chief ornament."

"You see, Madam, that this gentleman is as much opposed to the step as I myself should be," observed Philip. "You must not quit a world you are so well calculated to adorn. No, no ; you must be one of her Majesty's attendants—you must grace a court."

"I grace a court !" exclaimed Constance. "I am not fit for it. But you are mocking me, Sir."

"By Saint Iago I am not !" cried Philip. "I was never more serious in my life. I will prove to you I am in earnest ——"

"Nay, I desire no such proof, Sir," interrupted Constance, alarmed by his impassioned tone. "I must go. Do not detain me. I have stayed too long already discoursing with a stranger."

"It will be your own fault if I continue a stranger to you, sweet Constance," said Philip. "Rather than you should doubt my sincerity, I will declare myself."

"Hold !" exclaimed Osbert. "Pardon me," he added to the Prince ; "I feel it my duty to interpose."

"It would avail me nothing to know your name and quality, Sir," said Constance. "Henceforth we must be entire strangers to each other."

"Not so !—not so ! sweet Constance !" cried the Prince. "Will you not suffer me to attend you to your home ?"

"I am too well known to need an escort," she rejoined. "Nay, I am peremptory," she added, seeing the Prince meant to accompany her. "You will not, I am sure, disoblige me. Come, Dorcas. Fare you well, Sir."

"Adieu, sweet Constance !" exclaimed the Prince ; adding, as she disappeared with her attendant, "notwithstanding your interdiction, we *shall* meet again."

CHAPTER VIII.

OF THE MURTHEROUS ATTACK MADE UPON THE PRINCE IN THE COURT OF THE HOSPITAL.

"CONSIDERING that I have been little more than an hour in England, I have employed my time not unprofitably," remarked the Prince, gaily.

"If your Highness was in search of an adventure, you have certainly been lucky in meeting with one," observed Osbert. "But I presume you are now content, and disposed to go on board."

"Presently," replied Philip. "But I must pause for a moment to think over the interview—to recall her words, and the music of her voice. She has cast a spell upon me."

"So it would seem," muttered Osbert. "Hah! she is here again!" he exclaimed, as Constance and her attendant suddenly re-entered the court.

"Returned so soon!" exclaimed Philip, springing joyfully towards the damsel. Then remarking her agitation, he added, "But what has happened? Have you come to claim our escort?"

"I am come to warn you," she replied, trembling. "Your life is in danger."

"The danger is welcome, since it procures me the happiness of seeing you again," said the Prince.

"Oh! trifle not thus," she rejoined. "'Tis no imaginary peril. Listen to me, I beseech you. There are some evil-minded men in the street, whose design, I am certain, is to set upon you as you come forth. They have weapons in their hands, and their talk left me no doubt as to their sanguinary purpose."

"But why should they lie in wait for me?" rejoined Philip, carelessly. "However, be that as it may, I am infinitely obliged to them for proving to me that you are really interested in my safety."

"How could I fail to be, when I learnt from some words that fell from these miscreants, what I might have conjectured before, that you are no less exalted a personage than the Prince of Spain?"

"In what way did the villains obtain the information?" cried Philip. "It must be mere guess-work on their part. But make yourself easy, sweet Constance. They will not dare to assault me; or, if they do, I shall know how to defend myself. Besides, I am not alone. This gentleman, Master Osbert Clinton, I make no doubt, is a tolerable swordsman, and will help me to give a good account of the rogues."

"Your Highness may depend on me," said Osbert. "But you must not place yourself in this jeopardy. The street is dark and lonely, and favourable to a murtherous attempt of this kind. Already, more than one foul deed has been perpetrated within it."

"The wretches are lying in ambush ready to attack you unawares," said Constance. "I saw them extinguish the only lamp in the street, and then retire behind a buttress in the wall."

"By Holy Mary! my young mistress speaks the truth," said old Dorcas, her teeth chattering with fright. "I counted the villains. There are six of them."

"Then they will be three to two," rejoined the Prince, lightly. "We can manage that odds, eh, Master Clinton?"

"Your Highness must not thus expose yourself," said Constance. "It will be impossible to escape them. I pray you to be ruled by me, and enter the hospital till a guard be procured."

"I am well content to do so, if you will tarry with me," answered Philip. "But who will bring the guard?"

"Be that task mine," cried Osbert. "As soon as your Highness is in safety, I will fly to procure assistance."

"Nay, you must not go, Sir," said Constance. "The peril will be as great to you as to the Prince himself. You will only throw away your life in the attempt. I will summon the watch. I shall run no risk."

"She will, at least, pity me if I fall—I will go!" mentally ejaculated Osbert.

"I will procure your Highness instant admittance to the hospital," said Constance, "and then ——"

"Nay, you must bear me company, or I will not enter," interrupted Philip.

Osbert waited till they had nearly reached the door of the hospital, and then, drawing his sword, rushed down the passage leading to the street.

"Ah! rash young man!" exclaimed Constance, in accents of pity which might have gratified Osbert if he could have heard them. "He is rushing to certain destruction."

Scarcely were the words uttered, when the clashing of steel was heard without, accompanied by other sounds, proving that a desperate conflict was going on.

"I must leave you, Constance, and fly to his assistance," cried the Prince, plucking his rapier from its sheath.

"No," she rejoined, holding him. "Your life is too precious to be thus sacrificed—too precious to the Queen."

"I will strike down these assassins in her name," rejoined Philip. "I am proof against their blades. The son of Charles V. is not destined to perish thus obscurely."

"'Twere far better you sought an asylum here; but, if go you will, may Heaven and all good saints guard you!"

And as she relinquished her hold of him, and sought to enter the hospital, she found the door was fastened.

Perceiving this, old Dorcas knocked against it, calling out lustily, "Within! I say, within!" But there being no answer to the summons, she added despairingly, "Deaf old Absalom, the porter, must have gone to bed. What will become of us?"

Meanwhile, the Prince had quickly divested himself of his cloak, and, wrapping part of it round his left arm, leaving the other half hanging down, he flew to the passage, rapier in hand. On reaching it, he found it occupied by Osbert and his assailants. The young man was defending himself like a lion against his opponents, one of whom he had already disabled, but he was compelled to retreat; his position being such, that for the moment the Prince could render him no assistance. But the foremost of the assassin band caught sight of Philip, and shouting out to his comrades,—

"There stands the accursed Spanish Prince who would enslave us! We have him now—we have him!" Whereupon, incited by the words, they attacked Osbert so furiously that they drove him down the passage.

"Ah! why do I find your Highness here?" cried young Clinton, despairingly, as the Prince joined him, and helped him to keep off his assailants.

"You hear what he says, comrades," cried the leader of the band, a formidable-looking ruffian in a buff jerkin and steel cap, who looked like a disbanded soldier. "I was not mistaken, you see. 'Tis the Prince in person. 'Tis the bloodthirsty tyrant who would rob us of our liberties, and place us under a foreign yoke; who would force us by fagot and fire and other severities, conceived in hell, to return to the Romish idolatries we have abjured. But he has been delivered into our hands ere the wicked devices of his heart can be accomplished. It is Heaven's will that he should die, and in putting him to death we shall earn the gratitude of our country."

"Besides the hundred rose-nobles each that we are to have for the deed," cried one of his comrades.

"I would do the deed for nothing," shouted another of the band, "for it will redound to our credit. So have at him!"

"Harkye, young Sir," cried the leader of the band, addressing Osbert. "We do not desire your life—nay, we would willingly spare you. Our sole object is to crush this spawn of hell. Retire, and leave him to our justice."

"Think you I will stand tamely by and see you execute your ruthless purpose?" cried young Clinton. "No; I will defend the Prince to my last gasp."

"Your blood be upon your own head, then," rejoined the ruffian. "Upon them, comrades! Strike, and spare not."

"Thou, at least, will never be executioner," cried the Prince.

And as the ruffian made a desperate lunge at him, he

dexterously caught his sword in the hanging part of his cloak, and returning with a full thrust, transfixed his antagonist with his rapier.

"This comes of Spanish practices," groaned the wretch, as he fell to the ground. "Had he fought like an Englishman, without the cloak, I had killed him. Revenge me, comrades," he added, with his last breath.

"I have done thee too much honour in killing thee, vile caitiff," cried Philip, spurning the body with his foot.

The death of the leader caused a momentary pause in the assault. But determined to make sure of their prey, three of the ruffians now attacked the Prince, leaving the fourth engaged with Osbert. But for his activity and address it might now have fared ill with Philip. His cloak saved him from many a deadly thrust aimed at his breast, and distracted his assailants. Strange to say, he was entirely untouched, though all three of his opponents had felt the point of his weapon. He tried to separate them, but without success. They were too wary to be caught by the stratagem.

In this way, he was driven back towards the door of the hospital, before which stood Constance and old Dorcas, unable to gain admittance, and filling the court with cries for help. Presently at this juncture, and as if to afford him a means of retreat, the door of the hospital was thrown open by old Absalom, the porter, who held a lamp in his hand, and was shaking with terror. While stepping nimbly backwards in the hope of passing through the doorway, Philip encountered some obstacle, and fell, thus lying at the mercy of his opponents.

In another moment all had been over with him, if Constance had not heroically thrown herself before him, and the ruffians, having some touch of manhood in their breasts, forbore to strike. With terrible oaths, however, they ordered her to stand aside, but, with unshaken resolution, she maintained her place, and they were preparing to execute their fell purpose in spite of her, when a loud clatter in the passage leading to the street warned them that succour was at hand, and made them pause. The next moment Rodomont Bittern and his friends, shouting and flourishing their swords, and accompanied by two or three torch-bearers, rushed into the court.

"A Rodomont to the rescue!" roared Bittern. "Where is Don Philip? Heaven be praised, we are not too late!" he exclaimed, perceiving the Prince, who by this time had regained his feet. "Down with your swords, villains!" he added to the ruffians. "Down with them instantly, or we will hack you to minced-meat."

"Know you whom you aid?" cried one of the men, regarding him fiercely. "It is the Prince of Spain—the arch-foe of England. But for this foolish damsel we had already destroyed him!"

"Soh! you unblushingly confess your villany?" rejoined Rodomont. "A precious rascal, truly!"

"Ay, and I should have exulted in the deed, if I had accomplished it," retorted the man. "A day will come when you will regret this interference. Think not to detain me."

"Stay him! kill him! suffer him not to escape!" shouted Rodomont to his companions.

But, in spite of the many weapons directed against him, the man fought his way desperately towards the passage, and was close upon it, when a cut on the head staggered him, and he was captured and disarmed. He was followed by his two comrades, both of whom were more successful than himself, and effected a retreat. The ruffian who had been engaged with Osbert likewise escaped, having broken away amid the confusion caused by the arrival of Rodomont and his party. Some pursuit was made after the miscreants, but it was ineffectual.

No sooner was Philip freed from his assailants, than he turned to express his gratitude to Constance.

"I owe my life to you," he said; "nay, more, you have risked your own life to preserve mine. How can I requite you?"

"By forgetting that you have ever beheld me," she replied.

"That were impossible," he rejoined. "Ask something that I can perform."

"I desire nothing," she returned; "and, indeed, I do not merit your gratitude. It is the hand of Heaven that has guarded your Highness, not mine—guarded you for the Queen, to whom your safety is dearer than her own life, and

5

who might not have survived your loss. I must now retire for a short space, to compose myself ere I return home. Once more, I implore you to forget me. Farewell for ever!"

And without another word, and in spite of Philip's appealing looks, she entered the hospital with Dorcas.

"It would be well if I could forget her," thought Philip, as Constance disappeared; "but that is beyond my power. I could not tear her from my heart without a pang greater than I could endure. Yet it would be a crime to trouble the peace of one so pure and holy-minded. No matter! I should be wretched without her. Come what will, we must meet again."

CHAPTER IX.

DERRICK CARVER.

FROM these thoughts he was recalled to what was going on by Rodomont, who called out, "Here is one of the murtherous villains who attacked your Highness. Will it please you to question him?"

Philip turned at the words, and by the light of the torches which were held towards him, was enabled to examine the captive. The man, whose hands were tied behind his back by a belt, was of middle height, and rather powerful frame, and seemed to be decently attired; but his garments were sullied with blood, which flowed from several bodily wounds, as well as from a deep gash across the temple. His head was uncovered, and his matted black locks were dabbled in gore. His features, which were strongly marked, and remarkably stern in expression, were of a ghastly hue; but notwithstanding the smarting of his wounds and evident faintness from loss of blood, his looks were resolute and his black eyes blazed fiercely. He did not quail in the least before the searching and terrible glance fixed upon him by the Prince.

"Do any of you know this man?" demanded Philip, after regarding him stedfastly for a short space.

"By the body of Saint Alphonso, which reposes at Zamora! I should blush to avow myself acquainted with the felon hound," rejoined Rodomont. "But luckily I have never seen him before; and everyone else appears to be in the same predicament. How art thou called, fellow?

5—2

Speak out, or the thumb-screw shall force the truth from thee."

"Torture would not make me speak," replied the man, firmly. "But I have no desire to conceal my name. It will profit you little to know it. I am called Derrick Carver, and I am of Brightelmstone, in Sussex."

"Derrick, thou art most appropriately named Carver," rejoined Rodomont; "but instead of carving his Highness, as was thine atrocious design, thou shalt thyself be carved by the knife of the executioner."

"By whom wert thou instigated to this attempt?" demanded Philip. "Some greater hand than thine own is manifest in the design."

"A far greater hand," rejoined Derrick Carver. "The hand of Heaven is manifest in it."

"Deceive not thyself, insensate villain," rejoined Rodomont. "'Tis the Prince of Darkness who hath inspired the black design. He has deserted thee, as he deserts all his servants."

"I am no bond slave of Satan, but a faithful servant of the Most High," said Carver. "It was Heaven's wish that I should fail; but though my sword has been turned aside, there are others left that shall find the tyrant out."

"There is clearly some conspiracy on foot," said Osbert, who by this time had joined the Prince. "I have my own suspicions at its author, which I will presently communicate to your Highness. But that these are hired assassins is certain. By their own showing, they were to have a hundred rose-nobles each for the deed."

"Said I not right that Beelzebub was at the bottom of it?" cried Rodomont. "A hundred rose-nobles! Is that the sum for which thou hast bartered thy soul, thou damnable Derrick? Wert thou to be paid in *French* coin— ha! Carver?"

"Your suspicions tend the same way as mine own, I perceive, Sir," observed Osbert.

"Mine tend towards the French Ambassador, M. de Noailles," rejoined Rodomont. "I speak it openly. I'll be sworn this attempt is his excellency's contrivance."

"Like enough," said Philip. "But the truth must be wrung from that villain's lips."

" Nothing can be extorted from me, seeing I have nothing to confess," rejoined Derrick Carver, boldly. " I cannot answer for the motives that actuated those engaged with me, but my own were righteous in intent. I meant to free the Protestant Church from its deadliest enemy, and my country from subjection to Spain. I have failed ; but, I say again, others will not fail, for there are many to take my place. The blood of the saints will not be shed in vain, but will cry out incessantly for vengeance."

" Peace, blasphemer !" exclaimed Rodomont, "or we will have thy tongue plucked forth."

" Hear me out, and then deal with me as you list," said Derrick Carver. " I am no hired assassin. Scarce half an hour ago I was lamenting the perilous condition of the Church and the realm, when I heard that the enemy of both was in Southampton, almost unattended. Those who told me this designed to slay him, and I unhesitatingly joined them, without fee or promise of reward, being moved thereto, as I deemed, by a divine impulse. That is all I have to say."

" Let him be kept in some place of security till he can be further interrogated," said the Prince. " And let the clothes of the villain who fell by my hand be searched to see whether there are any papers about him that may lead to the discovery of his employer."

" It shall be done," replied Rodomont. " As to this Derrick Carver, he shall be clapped in the dungeon below the Bar-gate, the strongest prison in Southampton, and if we have to put him to the question, ordinary and extraordinary, we will have the truth from him. But your Highness may take my word for it, 'tis a *French* design."

" I thank you for your zeal, good Master Bittern," said Philip, "and in consideration of the services you have rendered me, I am content to overlook the freedom of speech in which you indulged a little while since. But I must enjoin you to be more careful in future."

" I shall not fail," replied Rodomont, bowing respectfully. " My excuse is, that I knew not whom I was addressing. Your Highness may ever count on my loyalty and devotion," he added, placing his hand upon his heart.

At this juncture the priest, who had officiated in the little chapel of the Domus Dei during Philip's visit to it, entered the court with his assistants, and after inclining himself reverently before the Prince, proceeded to congratulate him on his miraculous preservation.

Replying in suitable terms, Philip declared he was so fully convinced of Heaven's interposition in his behalf, that he desired at once to offer up thanks for his providential deliverance, and prayed the holy father to accompany him to the chapel for that purpose.

The priest readily assented, and led the way to the sacred edifice, into which, after a brief delay, Philip, with Osbert and the rest of the assemblage, including even Derrick Carver, were admitted.

Again the tapers were lighted at the altar, and again the Prince knelt down before it; but this time there was no fair devotee beside him to distract his thoughts, and his prayers were full of fervour and gratitude.

It was a strange and solemn scene, and impressed even Rodomont and his companions, whom recent events had served to sober.

The demeanour of Derrick Carver was stern and unmoved; but when the priest uttered a heartfelt prayer for the Prince's deliverance, he could not repress a groan. As Osbert looked round at this moment, he fancied he could discern, within the deep recess of the doorway, the figure of Constance Tyrrell. If it were so, however, she had vanished before the others quitted the chapel.

His devotions over, Philip arose, and in taking leave of the priest, promised the holy man an offering to Saint Julian, the patron saint of the chapel. He then bowed to the others, and declining further attendance, passed forth with Osbert, and proceeding to the quay, entered the boat which was waiting for him, and returned to the "Santissima Trinidada,"

At the same time Derrick Carver was conveyed by Rodomont and the others to the Bar-gate, and locked up in one of the gloomiest cells of its subterranean dungeon,

CHAPTER X.

NO suspicion whatever had been entertained of the Prince's absence from the ship. He was supposed to be alone in the state-cabin, where, as we know, the Count D'Egmont had been left as his representative, and, after the strict orders given to that effect, the Count remained entirely undisturbed. As time wore on, and midnight drew near, D'Egmont began to feel uneasy, and it was a relief to him when, shortly afterwards, the Prince appeared with Osbert.

"I fear you must be fatigued with waiting for me, Count," said Philip, as soon as the usher had retired. "I have stayed longer on shore than I intended."

"I trust your Highness has been amused," observed D'Egmont, assisting the Prince to take off his mantle. "Heavens! what do I see?" he exclaimed. "The cloak is cut in pieces."

"Not unlikely," replied Philip, laughing. "It has warded off more than one deadly thrust. Your cloak has done me good service, Count. Without it, Queen Mary might have wanted a husband, and the Emperor an heir to his dominions."

"Your Highness has acted rashly and unwisely in thus exposing yourself," cried D'Egmont. "Recollect how much hangs upon your life. The destinies of the world would be changed if aught befel you. The saints have guarded you at this moment of peril, and will continue to guard you, but it is tempting Heaven to jeopardise your safety unnecessarily."

"You assume that I have acted rashly, D'Egmont," rejoined Philip, "but I did not provoke the conflict. Set upon by assassins, I was compelled to defend my life. Thanks to your cloak and to my own right hand, I have come off without a scratch."

"I do not presume to ask for particulars," said the Count. "But I trust you have not been recognised. If so, your secret visit to the town will be known to all within it tomorrow, and will assuredly be reported to the Queen."

"I have thought of that," rejoined the Prince. "Precautions must be taken lest any idle tale be told her Majesty. No tidings of the occurrence can reach her tonight, and at daybreak you shall convey a letter to her, wherein I will inform her that I landed privily with the design of hastening to Winchester to throw myself at her feet, when my purpose was prevented by this untoward circumstance. Osbert Clinton shall accompany you. Having been with me at the time of the attack, he will be able to answer any questions the Queen may put to him relative to it."

"Your Highness will be pleased to give me my lesson previously," remarked Osbert. "I presume I must say nothing of Constance Tyrrell?"

"Nothing but what will recommend her to the Queen," rejoined Philip. "Her Majesty will be pleased to learn that the damsel preserved my life by stepping between me and the weapons of the assassins."

"And did she so?" inquired D'Egmont.

"Ay, in good sooth," returned Philip; "and it was worth the risk I ran to be so protected. Constance Tyrrell is the fairest creature my eyes ever lighted on. Her charms have completely enthralled me."

"Then let me counsel your Highness to shake off the fascination as speedily as possible," said D'Egmont, gravely. "It was an unlucky chance that threw the temptress in your way at this juncture."

"Lucky or not, I shall not relinquish her," rejoined Philip. "Were you to preach to me as energetically as Father de Castro, you would produce no effect, so you may spare your breath. And now to prepare the letter to the Queen."

So saying, he withdrew into an inner chamber, from which he presently emerged with the letter, sealed with a broad seal, and tied with a silken thread.

"This for her Majesty's own hands," he observed, with a smile, while delivering it to D'Egmont. "Be it your business to obtain an audience before any messenger from Southampton can reach her. All will then go well. As you serve me discreetly," he added, significantly to Osbert, "so shall you prosper."

With this he dismissed them, and summoning his groom of the chamber, prepared to retire to rest.

In obedience to the Prince's commands, Count D'Egmont, accompanied by Osbert and a small train of attendants, went ashore at an early hour in the morning, and as soon as horses could be procured, started for Winchester.

A glorious day dawned upon Southampton. A morning gun, fired from the batteries of the castle, awoke the slumbering town into sudden animation, while another gun from the English admiral's ship had a similar effect upon the crews of the combined fleets studding the smooth waters. Men could be seen on the decks, or amidst the rigging, actively employed in decorating the vessels with banners and streamers. Hundreds of boats came ashore to obtain fresh meat, bread, fruit, vegetables, and milk; and the quays, which were speedily thronged, became a perfect Babel. Horses and mules, bearing heavy panniers, laden with provisions, crossed the drawbridges, and were soon sent back for fresh stores, the supply being far from equal to the demand.

In the town all was bustle and excitement. The church bells began to peal joyously, and the streets were soon thronged with townsfolk, clad in holiday attire. But there was considerable misgiving amongst those who were aware of the occurrence of the previous night. At an early hour the mayor and aldermen repaired to the Guildhall, which, as we have previously mentioned, occupied the interior of the Bar-gate, and here they found the Earl of Arundel, Lord Steward of the Queen's Household, the Marquis of Winchester, Lord High Treasurer, and other noblemen, who had met to investigate the attempt upon the Prince's life, and to consider the measures necessary to be adopted to ensure his Highness's safety on his disembarkation.

Nothing, it appeared on inquiry, had been found upon Derrick Carver; but on the body of the man slain by Philip, a letter, written in the French language, was discovered, which, though very cautiously worded, bore evident reference to the dark transaction. The plan, no doubt, had been precipitated by the recognition of the Prince during his secret visit to the town. Diligent, but hitherto fruitless, search had been made for the four other ruffians engaged in the attack. These daring miscreants being yet at large, it was possible some further attempt might be made, and no precaution, said the Earl of Arundel, who presided over the meeting, must be neglected to ensure the Prince's safety. The guard must be doubled, and persons of assured loyalty must be placed near his person, while the slightest attempt at outbreak or commotion must be instantly repressed.

"It would have been a lasting disgrace to the country," continued the Earl, "if the Prince whom our Queen has chosen as her spouse, and whom we are all bound to love, honour, and defend, had been basely assassinated on setting foot on our shores, and we may be thankful that we have been spared that foul reproach—thankful, also, that the design was not conceived by an Englishman. But for the present, for reasons which will be apparent to you all, a veil must be thrown over the mysterious occurrence. Out of these walls none of you will speak of it. The preservation of public tranquility necessitates this caution. Some rumours of the attempt may be bruited abroad, but it will be best to discredit them. Doubtless the Prince desires to keep his nocturnal visit to the town secret. Nothing, therefore, must be publicly said of it. This you will carefully observe. Bear in mind, also, that you will have many Spaniards in your town to-day. They are a fiery nation, easily roused to anger, and if this unlucky affair be talked about, they may resent it, and quarrels and bloodshed will ensue. It is the Queen's desire that all who come with her destined consort be cordially welcomed. As loyal subjects, I am sure you will carry out her wishes."

The mayor and the town authorities having promised compliance with his lordship's instructions, the meeting broke up.

Before leaving the Bar-gate, however, the Earl of Arundel desired to see the prisoner. Accordingly, he was conducted by the mayor to the subterranean dungeon, where, in a dark and noisome cell, the floor of which was humid with the drippings from the stone walls, they found the miserable wretch stretched upon a few trusses of straw. His wounds had been bound up, but little beyond had been done for his comfort. Pained by the light of the lamp flashed upon him by the officer in attendance on the visitors, he tried to turn aside his head, but ineffectually.

"Raise him, that I may look at him," said the Earl of Arundel to the officer.

The execution of the order gave the poor wretch so much pain that he could not repress a groan. But though he was suffering excruciating agony, his courage did not desert him, and his answers to the interrogations put to him showed unfaltering resolution. Threats of torture could wring nothing from him, and he sternly refused to betray his accomplices.

"I gave no orders to have his wounds dressed," said the mayor. "By whom hath he been tended, Piers?"

"By Master Malwood, the chirurgeon," replied the officer.

"I thank him not for his care," said the prisoner. "Had he let me be, I had ere this escaped man's malice."

"He speaks the truth, an please your worship," observed Piers. "Master Malwood declared, that if left to himself, the poor wretch would die before the morning."

"But who sent for Master Malwood, answer me that, Sirrah?" demanded the mayor.

"Nay, I am not to blame, your worship," rejoined Piers, humbly. "The chirurgeon was sent by Mistress Constance Tyrrell, at her proper charge."

"This is the second ill turn she hath done me," said Derrick Carver. "But for her, the idolatrous tyrant had not escaped me, and now she preserves me for a lingering death."

"Thou art like the wild beast, who would tear the hand

put forth to succour him," cried the mayor, in disgust. "Will it please your good lordship to qnestion him further?"

"Not now," returned the Earl of Arundel. "Who is this Mistress Constance Tyrrell of whom he has just spoken?"

"The daughter of one of our wealthiest merchants," replied the mayor. "A very pious damsel, and ever engaged in acts of charity."

"Is she a heretic?" demanded the Earl.

"Not so, my lord; she is a most zealous Catholic, and it is most like she will enter a nunnery," replied the mayor.

"Accursed be she, then!" cried Derrick Carver. "Had I known this, I would have resisted the chirurgeon."

"Let us hence, my good lord," cried the mayor. "If he continues these blasphemies, we shall have the walls fall upon us and crush us."

"Before your worship goes, I would fain know whether I may admit Mistress Constance Tyrrell to the prisoner," said Piers. "She hath asked to see him, but I would not grant the request till I had your worship's sanction."

"Let her not come near me," cried Derrick Carver. "Her presence will trouble me."

"For that very reason she shall have admittance to thee," rejoined the mayor. "She hath helped to cure thy body— may she now help to save thy soul!"

"I need not her aid," rejoined Derrick Carver. "She hath more need of my teaching than I have of hers."

"If I thought thou wouldst taint her with thy heresies, I would keep her from thee," said the mayor. "But I have no such fear. Admit her when she will, Piers."

And he quitted the cell with the Earl.

CHAPTER XI.

BEFORE noon the preparations for the Prince's reception were complete. All the houses in High-street had been hung with carpets and costly stuffs, and otherwise decorated. From the Water-gate to the porch of Holyrood Church, where high mass was to be performed for the Prince, the street was kept clear by archers and arquebusiers fully equipped, and drawn up on either side, their steel caps and breastplates glittering in the brilliant sunshine.

By-and-by a grand cavalcade of richly-apparelled nobles, well mounted, and followed by long trains of esquires and pages wearing their liveries, rode towards the quay. Notice-able amongst these were the Earls of Shrewsbury, Derby, and Sussex, but the personage who attracted most attention was the Duke of Norfolk.

This venerable peer, whose long confinement in the Tower, commencing at the latter part of the reign of Henry VIII., and extending throughout that of his son, Edward VI., had neither broken his spirit nor impaired his bodily vigour, rode a high-spirited charger, which he managed with all the address and grace of a youthful cavalier. Norfolk's attire was of almost regal magnificence, being of purple velvet, edged with miniver, and richly embroidered, and his charger was trapped in cloth of gold, of red and yellow sheen. Behind him rode eighteen pages, each mounted on a handsome courser, and each clad in cloth of gold.

After the Duke of Norfolk and his attendants had ridden by, six mounted trumpeters, with the royal badge on their scarlet surcoats, came on, and made the welkin ring with the din of their silver clarions. After the trumpeters walked a troop of lacqueys, sumptuously attired in silk and velvet. Then came other nobles and gentlemen of the train, all superbly mounted, and vying with each other in the splendour of their apparel, and the number of their pages and esquires.

Next came a band of minstrels playing upon tambours and rebecs. Then more lacqueys in the royal liveries, and after them Sir Edward Hastings, Master of the Horse, who was followed by two grooms leading a Spanish jennet, caparisoned in cloth of silver, the bridal, poitral, and saddle being studded with silver roses. This beautiful animal had been sent by the Queen for her intended consort.

Next came Sir Robert Rochester, Comptroller, and after him rode the Marquis of Winchester and the Earl of Arundel. Each of these noblemen was magnificently attired, and followed by a long train of attendants. Then came a mounted guard, preceding the town authorities, who marched two abreast, this part of the procession being closed by the mayor on horseback.

Passing through the Water-gate, on the summit of which the royal standard now floated, the whole of the splendid cavalcade crossed the drawbridge, and proceeded to that part of the quay where it was intended the disembarkation should take place. A vast concourse had here assembled, but a wide space near the water was kept clear by the guard, and within this the procession drew up.

It was now high tide, and close to the strand lay the Queen's barge, gorgeously decorated, and having a broad banner embroidered with the arms of England on the stern.

The Earl of Arundel with the Duke of Norfolk, the Marquis of Winchester, and the principal nobles, having dismounted, entered this barque, and were immediately rowed by two banks of oarsmen to the Prince's ship. In front of the royal barge stood six trumpeters. Four other gilded barges followed. The course of these gorgeous barques was watched with momently-increasing interest by the thousands of spectators on the quays, on the town walls, and on other points of observation.

With her decks crowded with arquebusiers in their full accoutrements, and banners floating from her turrets, the "Santissima Trinidada" made a most gallant show, exciting the wonder and admiration of all who gazed upon her. Her companions on the right and left were likewise splendidly decorated, and, indeed, every vessel within sight fluttered with banners and streamers.

As the royal barge approached the Prince's ship, loud fanfares were sounded by the trumpeters, and immediately several officials in rich habiliments, and bearing white wands, appeared at the head of the stairs. On gaining the deck, the Earl of Arundel and the other nobles were conducted with the utmost ceremony to Philip, whom they found surrounded by the Dukes of Alva and Medina Celi, Don Ruy Gomez, and the rest of the grandees composing the Prince's suite.

On this occasion Philip had laid aside his customary black habiliments, and wore a doublet and hose of crimson silk, with a robe of cloth of gold. His boots were decked with golden strings, and bordered with pearls. All the grandees forming his *entourage* were dressed with extraordinary magnificence, and made a most splendid display.

Philip received the English nobles with the greatest courtesy, and being informed that the Earl of Arundel was the bearer to him, from her Majesty, of the insignia of the most noble Order of the Garter, he immediately bowed his head, and while the collar was passed over his neck by the Earl, the Duke of Norfolk buckled on the garter. When this ceremony had been performed, and an interchange of formal salutations had taken place between the English nobles and the Spanish grandees, the Prince was conducted to the royal barge, the English nobles entering it with him. The Spanish grandees, with various officials, gentlemen, and pages, in attendance upon the Prince, went ashore in the other boats.

On the part of the quay reserved for the disembarkation, a rich Turkey carpet had been laid, and upon this stood four henchmen in parti-coloured attire of crimson velvet and yellow silk, sustaining an embroidered canopy of red damask, fringed with golden thread. The pages, esquires, and other officials having first landed, the royal barge was brought close to the strand, and a railed plank, covered with striped cloth, being laid upon it, offered an easy passage to the Prince, whose deportment as he slowly traversed it, was singularly haughty and majestic.

On the instant that Philip stepped ashore a royal salute was fired from the castle batteries, the roar being prolonged by every gun in the English fleet. At the same time vociferous acclamations arose from the spectators.

"Heaven save your Highness!—welcome to England!" exclaimed a voice from amidst a group near the canopy.

The voice sounded familiar to Philip, and glancing in the direction of the speaker, he recognised Rodomont Bittern, who, with his friends, had managed to obtain a position with the mayor and the town authorities. Rodomont's exclamation, uttered in a loud voice, and with unmistakable heartiness, found many an echo. Pleased by the cordiality of the welcome, Philip bowed graciously around, and in so doing addressed a slight smile of recognition to Rodomont.

A brief pause now ensued, but as soon as the grandees had landed, and ranged themselves behind him, Philip drew his sword, holding it aloft till he got beneath the canopy, when he again stood still, and returned the blade to the scabbard. This action surprised all the lookers-on, and gave rise to many comments.

"By Saint Jude! a strange proceeding!" observed Jack Holiday to his companions. "Are we to understand that the Prince intends to rule England with the sword?"

"By the mass! it looks like it," rejoined Simnel.

"Tut! you are wrong in your surmise," cried Rodomont. "His Highness draws the sword in the defence of our country. That I take to be the meaning of the act."

Attended by the aldermen, the mayor now advanced towards the Prince, and reverentially presented him with the keys of the town, laid upon a velvet cushion.

Philip did not take the keys, but graciously bidding the mayor arise, said in clear and distinct accents, "I thank you, Sir, and I thank all those with you for this welcome. You know what has brought me here. I come not in search of men or treasure, having sufficient of both in the country I have left. As the chosen husband of your wise and virtuous Queen, I come to dwell among you, not as a foreigner, but as a native Englishman. To you, my good lords," he added to the English nobles, who were ranged on either side of the canopy, "I am much beholden for the assurances of loyalty and devotion which you have already proffered me, and I here publicly declare that you, and all her Majesty's faithful subjects, shall ever find me anxious to promote the welfare of the kingdom, to observe its laws, conform to its customs, and defend it against all enemies."

Then, turning to the Spanish grandees, who were standing behind him, he said, "My lords, you all, I am well assured, share the gratification I experience at the very friendly reception that has been given me. Hitherto, you have been strangers to the people of England, but this must be so no longer. Spaniards and Englishmen must henceforth be brethren, bound together by ties of strictest amity. It shall be my aim to encourage and maintain a good understanding between the two nations, and, seconded by you, and by these noble English lords, I cannot fail in my design."

"We are ready to obey your Highness in all things," said the Duke of Alva, with a haughty inclination of his head, while the other grandees made similar professions.

"He may talk till he is tired," muttered the Lord Admiral. "There will be no cordial understanding between us."

This opinion was shared by several others. Indeed, the English nobles were deterred by the arrogance of the Spanish grandees from making advances towards them.

"It is my wish to observe all good old English customs," pursued the Prince. "If I unintentionally neglect any of them, I hope to be made aware of the omission. I would fain drink a health to all present."

"A cup of wine for his Highness!" cried the Earl of Arundel.

"Nay, my good lord, let me have a flagon of English ale," said the Prince. "I should prefer your national beverage."

6

"As your Highness pleases," rejoined Arundel, bowing. "A flagon of ale on the instant."

The Prince's choice caused considerable merriment, and warmed many a heart towards him.

"A cup of ale!" exclaimed Simnel. "This is carrying complaisance to the highest point."

"His Highness is resolved to become an Englishman, that I can plainly perceive," observed Rodomont, "and takes what he conceives to be the shortest way to his object. Heaven bless him! he is a most gracious Prince."

At this juncture, a silver flagon, filled with ale, was brought on a salver, and presented by the Earl of Arundel to the Prince, who, taking the cup, bowed graciously around.

"His Highness drinks to you all, good Sirs!" cried the Earl of Arundel, in a loud voice.

"To all, of whatever degree!" said the Prince, raising the goblet to his lips.

Most opportunely, at the moment, another discharge was fired from the castle guns, followed by a loud flourish of trumpets and drums. From the shouts that were also raised, it was evident that the Prince was rising rapidly in popular favour.

"How does your Highness like the beverage?" inquired the Earl of Arundel, as he took back the goblet.

"It will improve upon acquaintance, I make no doubt," replied Philip. "At present, I find it somewhat too potent."

"A strong head is needed to stand it," observed the Lord Admiral, with an ill-disguised sneer.

After this, Philip remained for some little time beneath the canopy, conversing with the English nobles, and evidently striving to propitiate them, and he appeared to be successful in his efforts. He showed himself extremely easy of access, and amongst other persons presented to him was Rodomont Bittern.

"This is not the first time we have met, Sir," observed Philip, to the surprise of most who heard him.

"Since your Highness deigns to recollect the circumstance, be assured I shall never forget it," replied Rodomont.

"Nay, you have rendered me a great service," said the

Prince, "and it shall not pass unrequited. Is Master Tyrrell here?"

"Ay, your Highness," replied Rodomont. "He is yonder, with the town-council."

"Let him come forward. I would speak with him," said Philip.

Accordingly, the worthy merchant, much to his dismay, was brought before the Prince. He was so confused that he would have neglected the necessary obeisance, if he had not been prompted by Rodomont, who, indeed, half forced him to incline his person.

"I am glad to see you again, good Master Tyrrell," said Philip, smiling, "and have to thank you for your hospitable intentions towards me last night."

"Your Highness will forgive me. I knew not whom I was addressing," stammered Tyrrell. "It is true that I subsequently learnt from my daughter ——"

"That she had rendered me a most signal service, which I trust adequately to requite," interrupted the Prince. "No more of that now, Sir. But rest assured that her Majesty will not be less grateful than myself to fair Mistress Constance."

"I am not quite so sure of that," thought Rodomont.

With further assurances of his consideration, the Prince then dismissed Master Tyrrell, who retired with Rodomont, both being charmed with his Highness's affability.

Though the foregoing conversation was not altogether intelligible to the Spanish grandees, it caused them great surprise, and even disquietude.

"As I live, his Highness seems to know these people," observed Alva to the Duke of Medina Celi. "Where can he have met them?"

"I am as much in the dark as yourself," replied the other. "But, in my opinion, he must have gone ashore secretly last night."

"By my faith! you are right," rejoined Alva, bending his heavy brows. "Some idle affair of gallantry, I'll be sworn. He is ever engaged in such adventures. I must inquire into the matter, and take him to task for his imprudence."

The English nobles, who were somewhat better acquainted than the Spaniards with the Prince's proceedings, laughed amongst themselves at what was passing.

Influenced by their royal master's deportment, the Spanish grandees showed a disposition to relax from their stiffness and hauteur, and ere long engaged in friendly discourse with the English nobles, though their manner still continued grave and formal.

Meantime, another boat had come ashore, bringing the Bishop of Cuença, and Father Alfonso de Castro, the Prince's confessor. On landing, these ecclesiastics immediately knelt down and recited a prayer, and as he arose, the bishop pronounced a solemn benediction on the assemblage.

Several other boats followed, filled with Spanish arquebusiers, who, being very fine-looking men and splendidly accoutred, excited much curiosity as they ranged themselves on the platform. The object of this guard was made speedily apparent by the arrival of some thirty large coffers, each enveloped in a cover bearing the Prince's escutcheon. These coffers, supposed to contain gold in bullion, were subsequently conveyed to the castle under the guard of the arquebusiers. Many speculations were indulged in as to how this treasure was to be employed—the general impression being, that it would be used in bribing certain of the council and of the nobility.

As soon as the treasure was landed, the Prince mounted his jennet, the Master of the Horse holding the stirrup, and the *cortége* returned to the town. Richly-caparisoned chargers were brought for the Spanish grandees who rode behind the Prince, while the English nobles preceded him.

CHAPTER XII.

AMID the thunder of cannon, the ringing of bells,
the beating of drums, the braying of trumpets, the
clash of cymbals, the waving of scarves and ker-
chiefs, accompanied by joyous acclamations,
Philip entered Southampton by the Water-gate.

Bending lowly in return for the clamorous welcome given
him by the occupants of the gallery adjoining the gate, the
Prince continued to bow gracefully right and left as he rode
slowly up the street. Philip was never seen to greater advantage than on horse-back, and his stately figure now commanded universal admiration. As he went on, he descried
many a comely damsel at the windows, but she he most
desired to behold was not visible.

Passing through the triumphal arch reared across the
streets, which, now that it was completed, had a charming
effect, he dismounted at the Gothic porch of Holyrood
Church, near which the English nobles were ranged to receive him.

Internally, the church presented an imposing appearance,
being richly decorated for the occasion. The aisles were
densely crowded, but the broad nave was kept clear, and
along it a crimson cloth was stretched. The pillars were
also covered with embroidered cloths, and ornamented with
paintings. Superb vessels of gold and silver, chalices, reli-

quaries and pixes, decked the altar, above which stood an image of the Virgin, then but newly set up. Large tapers burnt on either side. Priests and deacons in their stoles, with white-robed choristers and incense-bearers, filled the chantry.

As Philip, preceded by the Bishop of Cuença and Father de Castro, and followed by a splendid train of English and Spanish nobles, marched along the nave, the priests advanced to meet him, while the air was filled with fragrance. At the same time the roof resounded with jubilant symphonies. A large velvet cushion had been placed on the right of the altar for the Prince, and on this he knelt down, while the English and Spanish nobles grouped themselves on either side. Mass was then solemnised, the Bishop of Cuença and Father de Castro officiating with the English priests.

On issuing from the church, Philip was greeted with loud acclamations from the crowd, which he graciously acknowledged. Mounting his jennet, and attended by a gallant train, consisting of the English and Spanish nobles, he proceeded along High Street towards the Bar-gate, where he was told by the Earl of Arundel that a pageant awaited him.

The same manifestations of popular satisfaction that had hitherto attended him continued during this part of his course, and no untoward incident occurred to mar the general harmony.

On approaching the Bar-gate, Philip perceived beneath its archway the gigantic Sir Bevis of Southampton, armed as he had appeared on the previous night, and seated on his mighty charger Arundel. Royal Canute was stationed on the right of the puissant champion, and savage Ascapart on the left. Behind were the Moorish kings.

Thus placed, the gigantic figures had a very picturesque effect, and harmonised well with the ancient structure. A trumpet being sounded, a fancifully-attired dwarf issued from a postern in one of the flanking towers, and strutted towards the Prince.

"Who art thou, and what is thy business?" demanded Philip, as the dwarf made him a very ceremonious obeisance.

"My name may perchance have reached your Highness's

ears," replied the mannikin, proudly. "I am called Sir Narcissus le Grand, and am one—perchance not the least distinguished—of her Majesty's attendants."

"I am aware that her Majesty has a dwarf to divert her," replied the Prince, laughing. "But I fancied the diminutive valet's name differed from thine."

"There is no other dwarf but myself in her Majesty's household," returned the mannikin. "Before I received the honour of knighthood, I was called Xit, and I am still occasionally so designated by those who are on familiar terms with me."

"That name has brevity to recommend it, and therefore suits thee better than the other," observed the Prince.

"Nay, an your Highness thinks so, I am ready to resume the appellation. Xit is a name of which I have no reason to be ashamed, seeing I have ever borne it with honour. Perchance your Highness designs some distinction for me. The Cross of Santiago, or the Toison d'Or, would not be ill bestowed."

"By Saint Anthony! a modest proposition!" exclaimed Philip. "I marvel thou dost not ask to be made a grandee of the first class."

"That is indeed my ambitiom," replied Xit. "I shall then be privileged to remain covered in your Highness's presence, like the proud lords I see yonder. But, though dazzled by the thought, I must not forget the business in hand, which is to acquaint your Highness that the Knight of Southampton, the redoubted Sir Bevis, with his slave Ascapart, and the regal Canute, all of whom you behold under yon archway, welcome you to England, and shout with me 'God save Prince Philip!'"

"God save Prince Philip!" vociferated the three giants in concert.

"Thanks for the welcome," replied Philip. "Your pageant is good, but it lacks its chief character. Where is the Princess Josyan?—she should be with Sir Bevis."

"Highness," said Xit, somewhat embarrassed, "there are two princesses, and since they cannot agree as to which shall take precedence, it was deemed best that neither should appear. They are within the Bar-gate. If you desire it, they can be summoned."

"Bring forth the youngest and fairest of them," rejoined Philip.

Xit bowed, and hastened to execute the Prince's command.

In another instant he reappeared, leading by the hand a comely young damsel, attired in a kirtle of green velvet, and having a glittering caul on her head, in whom Philip was at no loss to recognise the captive made by Sir Bevis on the previous night. A bright blush suffused her cheeks, serving to heighten the effect of her charms, but otherwise she did not seem much abashed, but tripped gaily with her little conductor towards the Prince.

"Highness," said Xit, as he presented her, "in this damsel, ordinarily known as Lilias Ringwood, you behold the Princess Josyan."

Scarcely were the words uttered, than a lattice, immediately above the central arch of the Bar-gate, was thrown open, and an angry female face appeared.

"'Tis false!" screamed Lady le Grand, for she it was— "'tis false, I say! I am the real Princess Josyan, and no one shall usurp the part. I am shut up here under lock and key, or I would soon strip that vile hussy of her attire, which belongs of right to me. Doff it at once, minion."

"Retire on the instant, I command you, Madam," screamed Xit, shaking his hand furiously at her.

"I shall obey no orders of thine, thou contemptible little monster," rejoined Lady le Grand, in a shrill voice. "Let me out, or it shall be worse for thee. How dare you put another woman in my place? Lilias Ringwood shall not enact the part assigned to me."

"Marry, but she shall," rejoined Xit. "His Highness desired that the youngest and fairest of the two claimants should be brought forth. Thou art neither so young nor so lovely as Lilias, and art consequently superseded. Retire, I say."

Before Lady le Grand could make any further rejoinder, Philip interposed.

"But what says Sir Bevis himself?" he demanded. "Since he is chiefly concerned in the matter, the choice of a princess ought to rest with him. Methinks he cannot hesitate."

"Assuredly not, your Highness," rejoined the gigantic

warrior, inclining his head. "I am right glad of the exchange."

"Then take fair Lilias to him," said Philip. "Remember the fate of the strong man of Israel," he added to Sir Bevis, "and be not subdued like him. Otherwise, thou mayst have reason to repent thy choice."

"No Delilah shall enslave me, your Highness," rejoined the giant, as the damsel was placed behind • him by Ascapart.

"That remains to be seen," laughed Lilias, as she settled herself on the pillion.

Mortified by the success of her young rival, Lady le Grand retreated from the window, amid the jeers and laughter of the beholders, all of whom were mightily entertained by the incident.

No sooner was this important point settled, than Sir Bevis rode forth from the archway with the fair Lilias behind him, her countenance radiant with triumph. Bending in knightly fashion to the Prince, the gigantic warrior bade his companions attend him, and struck into a street on the right. Calling for his piebald steed, Xit followed the procession, without troubling himself further about Lady le Grand.

CHAPTER XIII.

THE ABBESS OF SAINT MARY.

PHILIP next proceeded to the castle, in the principal court of which he found his arquebusiers drawn up. Long before this, the treasure had been locked up in one of the strongest chambers of the donjon. Not being familiar with a Norman castle, the Prince examined the ancient fortress with much interest, and, ascending to the summit of the keep, enjoyed the magnificent view commanded from it.

His inspection of the castle completed, Philip was conducted to a public place in the centre of the town, which derived its name of Saint Michael's Place, from a venerable and beautiful church standing in the midst of it. Facing the east end of this reverend pile was the habitation designed for his temporary abode.

In Saint Michael's Place, as elsewhere, a large crowd had congregated, who cheered the Prince lustily on his appearance, and did not seem inclined to disperse even when he had dismounted and entered his lodgings.

The quaint architecture of the habitation, the bay-windows filled with painted glass, the low-raftered roofs, the walls panelled with oak darkened by age, the numerous small apartments, the stiff cumbrous furniture—all so different from the vast gilded saloons and open courts suited to another clime, with which he was familiar—were far from displeasing to Philip, and when the Earl of Arundel apologised for the scant accommodation of the place, the Prince courteously assured him that the house was very much to his taste. "What sufficed for your great monarch, Henry VIII.," he said, "may well suffice for me."

Pleading fatigue, he then retired to a private chamber, and was not disturbed until the return of the Count D'Egmont and Osbert Clinton from Winchester, when they were immediately admitted to his presence.

D'Egmont brought a letter from the Queen, which he delivered to the Prince, but, without manifesting any impatience to ascertain its contents, Philip laid it on the table beside which he was seated, and proceeded to question the Count as to his visit.

"Pass by all other matters," he said, "and come to the point. What did her Majesty think of my nocturnal adventure ? Was she satisfied with the explanation offered her ? "

"Not entirely, I fear, your Highness," replied D'Egmont, "though she said little to warrant such a conclusion."

"You were careful not to alarm her ? " said Philip, turning to Osbert.

"She pressed me very shrewdly," replied the young man, "but I trust I succeeded in allaying her suspicions, which were evidently aroused by the description I was obliged to give of your fair deliverer, Constance Tyrrell. Her Majesty inherits something of the disposition of her august sire, and is inclined to jealousy."

"That does not augur well for my future comfort. Jealousy in a wife is intolerable," replied Philip. "Let us see what is said in her letter," he added, opening it. "There is nothing here but congratulations on my safe arrival, and deep concern at the attack upon my person. Not a word as to my intended visit to Winchester. Apparently, her Majesty does not attach much credence to that part of the story."

"She is not easily imposed upon," observed D'Egmont. "It must be admitted that your Highness has given her just cause for suspicion. She will not believe that eagerness to behold her induced you to quit the ship privily at night. Her penetration pointed to a different motive, and all she heard seemed to confirm her doubts. At one moment she had resolved to come over to Southampton, but fortunately she relinquished that design. Mischief might else have been made by the opponents to the marriage."

"Pshaw! I have no fears on that score," said Philip. "But I am glad she did not come. She might have interfered with my plans."

At this moment an usher entered, stating that Mistress Constance Tyrrell was without, and besought an audience of the Prince.

"By Saint Iago! this is better than I expected," cried Philip, overjoyed. "Is she alone?"

"No, your Highness," replied the usher. "The lady abbess of St. Mary, Winchester, is with her."

"I would the lady abbess were in her nunnery, or anywhere but here!" exclaimed Philip, in a tone of pique. "Admit them."

On this the usher withdrew, and the next moment Constance entered the room, accompanied by a religious dame of very stately deportment. The abbess of Saint Mary was attired in a long black gown, the ample folds of which swept the ground. The sleeves of her robe were loose, and over her shoulders was spread a sable mantle, with a hood attached to it. A barbe of plaited linen covered the lower part of her face, and, with the close-drawn hood, effectually concealed her features. On the entrance of the two ladies, D'Egmont and Osbert retired.

Stepping quickly towards Constance, Philip took her hand, preventing her from making the lowly obeisance she contemplated. After greeting her very courteously, he turned to the abbess, and saluting her respectfully, said,—

"Holy mother, to what am I indebted for this visit? Can I serve you in aught?"

"For myself I seek nothing, Prince," replied the abbess, in a voice that vibrated through Philip's breast, occasioning him an uneasy feeling. "I am a messenger from the Queen to this young maiden. Her Majesty, having been informed that, under Heaven, the chief instrument of your preservation from a great peril was Mistress Constance Tyrrell, who heroically shielded you from the weapons of assassins, has sent me to bring the damsel to Winchester. This is my mission, which I was enjoined to execute without delay; but I have consented to defer my departure for a short space, as Mistress Constance hath a request to prefer to your Highness."

"I thank you for your consideration, holy mother," replied Philip. "The fair Constance can ask nothing of me that I will not readily grant."

"Make no rash promises, Prince," remarked the abbess. "First hear her request."

"I pray you speak, then, fair mistress," said Philip, in an encouraging tone to Constance. "You need not apprehend a refusal."

"The boon is greater than I ought to ask," said Constance, trembling. "Yet I must summon courage to make it. In a word, then, your Highness, I would solicit pardon for the miserable wretch who dared to raise his sacrilegious hand against your royal person."

"Pardon for that miscreant!" exclaimed the abbess. "Impossible!"

"For myself I would willingly grant your request," replied Philip, in a troubled tone, "but I have not the power. The Queen alone can pardon this offender against her laws. You must appeal to her."

"But your Highness will second me," observed Constance. "A word from you, and it will be done."

"Be not too sure of that," said the abbess, sternly. "The Queen is compassionate, but just. To pardon a wretch like this would be fraught with evil consequences. It may not be."

The force and decision with which these words were pronounced struck the Prince, and he looked hard at the abbess. But her features were wholly undistinguishable.

"The lady abbess is right," he said, after a pause. "I fear the appeal to the Queen will be in vain. Yet say to her that, if possible, I would have the man spared."

"The man is a heretic, as I understand," remarked the abbess. "If he will abjure his errors, and discover his accomplices, mercy may, perchance, be shown him—not otherwise."

"I fear, then, he must die," replied Constance. "He is obstinate in his opinions."

"Then he deserves to perish," rejoined the abbess, "and you are wrong in seeking to save him."

"My hope is to make him profitable to the Catholic Church," said Constance. "If he be put to death now, he will be deemed a martyr by those of his own faith. In time I may bring about his recantation."

"'Twere a good act, if you could accomplish it, fair Constance," observed Philip; "but I fear you deal with impracticable material. But how comes it you take so much interest in this Derrick Carver, for such, if I recollect aright, is the caitiff's name?"

"I know not whence my compassion for him springs," she replied. "But I have visited him in his cell, and fancy I can discern something of good in him."

"Be not deceived, damsel," said the abbess. "There can be no good in one capable of the crime which this man hath attempted. But if you are in earnest as to his conversion, I promise you you shall have an opportunity of attempting the work. I have interest enough with the Queen for that."

"I am glad to hear you say so, holy mother," observed the Prince. "And I shall rejoice if the fair Constance succeeds in her attempt. But be this as it may, I do not feel relieved from the weight of obligation I am under to her. When you present her to the Queen, say I shall be well pleased if her Majesty can place her among her gentlewomen."

"I will do more," rejoined the abbess. "I will use all the influence I possess with her Majesty to see the damsel well bestowed in marriage."

"Not if I can prevent it," thought Philip.

A suspicion in regard to the abbess, which the Prince had begun to entertain, being confirmed, he begged a word with her in private, and on her ready assent, led her into the deep recess of a bay-window.

Entirely changing his manner towards her, he then said, "I know not how to account for it, holy mother, but while talking to you I could almost imagine myself engaged in converse with her Majesty."

"A strange supposition," observed the abbess, in a blander tone than before.

"It is the highest compliment I could pay you," pursued Philip. "That you should resemble so admirable a sovereign is the best proof of your merit."

"I am much flattered by your Highness's good opinion," returned the abbess, still more blandly; "but how can you tell that I am like the Queen, since you have never beheld her Majesty?"

"I can perfectly judge by the many descriptions given me of her," said the Prince. "In disposition I am sure you are exactly like her. Remove your hood, I pray you, that I may see whether the resemblance extends to feature."

"I cannot comply with your Highness's request, as I have a vow which prohibits me from disclosing my countenance to any of your sex," she replied; "but I will own that I am like the Queen."

"I was quite sure of it," said Philip. "Permit me for a moment to address you as her Majesty."

"'Tis a strange whim," replied the abbess, complacently, "and I ought not to consent to it. But your Highness is singularly persuasive. I am not without curiosity to know what you would say to the Queen."

"What I have to say may sound like the language of passion, and may not suit your ears," rejoined Philip.

"But, as the Queen, I may listen to it," she rejoined, with something of tenderness in her tones.

"Then I would throw myself at your feet, as I do now," cried Philip, kneeling as he spoke. "I would press your hand to my lips, and assure you of my unalterable love and fidelity. I would tell you how I have burned with impatience to behold you—how I have counted the hours of my long voyage, and have rejoiced as each day brought me nearer to you. In the strongest terms I could employ I would express my sense of the honour you have conferred upon me in choosing me for your husband, and I would endeavour to convince you that it will be the chief business of my life to increase your felicity and to extend your power. Not a cloud shall overshadow your future existence if I can drive it away—but all shall be serenity and sunshine. This is what I would say to the Queen," he added, rising.

"Your language is so impassioned, Prince," she returned, "that I am almost as much moved as her Majesty could be by your words. For the moment, I will suppose myself the Queen ——"

"It is so understood," interrupted Philip.

"I fear you feign this passion, Prince," she continued. "To love one unknown, unseen, with the ardour you profess, is impossible, and yet I ought not to say so, for though I have never beheld you till now, your image has long occupied my breast. I hope you may not be disappointed in me. It shall be my anxious study to win your affection by entire devotion and submission to your will, and I trust, with Heaven's grace, to succeed."

"Doubt it not," replied the Prince, fervently. "You are sole mistress of my heart, and will ever maintain paramount sway over it."

"I am foolish to ask it," she said, "yet I would fain have your assurance that it is not my crown that has enticed you hither?"

"Rest easy on that score," rejoined the Prince. "You yourself are the magnet that has attracted me. You would have been as much prized without your kingdom as with it."

"I cannot believe you; yet the assurance is so sweet, that I will yield to the delusion," she rejoined. "But I must listen to these honeyed words no longer. Once more I must become the abbess."

"To others, but not to me," rejoined Philip.

On this, they left the recess, and returned to where Constance was standing.

"What shall be done for this damsel?" said Philip. "It pains me that I cannot grant her request."

"Her request is most unreasonable. Still, she has a great claim upon you," replied the abbess. "I make no promise, but order the prisoner to be brought here for examination, and I will consider what can be done."

Thanking her with a smile, Philip instantly summoned Osbert Clinton, and bade him bring Derrick Carver before him with all possible dispatch. He likewise ordered the immediate attendance of the Bishop of Cuença and Father de Castro.

With a profound obeisance, Osbert departed on his mission.

While this was passing, the abbess proceeded to the table,

on which writing materials were placed, and wrote a few words on a sheet of paper, which she folded up, and, delivering it to the Prince, observed, in a significant tone, "You may need this anon. Not a word," she added, with a gesture of caution.

After glancing at the paper, Philip placed it within his doublet.

CHAPTER XIV

FATHER ALFONSO DE CASTRO.

SHORTLY afterwards, the usher announced the Bishop of Cuença and Father Alfonso de Castro. No fitting opportunity having hitherto occurred of describing these two personages, we will now say a few words respecting them. The Bishop of Cuença was a perfect courtier, polished in manner, witty, sarcastic, and a *bon vivant*. His features were handsome, and his looks intelligent, but wily. His attire was as elegant as his position as an ecclesiastic permitted. His person was tall, well formed, his complexion olive, his eyes dark and intelligent.

A far more striking personage than the bishop was Father Alfonso de Castro. He possessed one of those austere countenances in which the old Spanish painters delighted. In age he was about sixty, and his long life seemed to have been spent in practices of penance and devotion. A few scattered locks, marked by the tonsure, clothed his reverend head. His figure, once tall and erect, was now bent, and his gait feeble and slow. His complexion was sickly, and his eyes deep sunken, but still full of lustre.

Father de Castro was a profound theologian, and had written much against heresy, menacing the professors of the new doctrines with such severe punishments, that he had not unjustly acquired the title of "*Hæresio-mastrix acerrimus.*"

A grave salutation passed between the Bishop of Cuença and the abbess, but, when the Prince presented his confessor to her, she said,—

"I am already acquainted with Father de Castro through his writings. I have perused his learned commentary on the Twelve Minor Prophets, and his homilies on the Psalms. I have also read his three books on the Just Punishment of Heresy, and I entirely agree with him. But the work that has afforded me the deepest gratification is his masterly treatise on the Validity of the Marriage between Henry VIII. and Katherine of Aragon. That treatise has been the Queen their daughter's constant companion, and has solaced her during many an hour of affliction."

"I grieve to hear that so excellent a Princess has endured so much," replied Father de Castro; "but it was the consciousness that truth and justice were on her side, and not my poor production, that sustained her during her trials. Yet I must rejoice that I have been able to pour balm into her soul. However, her sorrows are now over, and she will reap the reward of her long suffering and patience. Heaven's blessing will descend upon her head and upon her people. She will be happy in her marriage, and from her loins princes shall spring, who shall govern this realm wisely and well, and maintain it in the true faith."

"Heaven grant it may be so!" exclaimed the abbess, fervently. "As the old religion has been restored by the Queen, her most earnest desire is that it should be so firmly established that no fears need be entertained of a relapse into schism."

"Having read my treatise on the Punishment of Heretics, holy mother, you know the measures I recommend," replied Father de Castro. "To prevent the further spreading of this pestilence, it must be thoroughly rooted out."

"That will be a work of much time and difficulty, Father," replied the abbess, with a sigh. "But I do not despair of its full accomplishment."

"An Auto-da-Fé, such as we have in Spain, of frequent occurrence, would soon sweep off the tainted," observed the Bishop of Cuença. "I trust to see the Holy Inquisition established in this country."

"That can never be, my lord," replied the abbess.

"Wherefore not, good sister?" demanded the bishop.

"Because Englishmen would never submit to it," rejoined the abbess. "Such an attempt would cause a rebellion which nothing could put down. On this point, Romanists and Protestants would unite. The throne would not be secure, and in the confusion heresy might again become triumphant. Heaven avert such a contingency? But there is nothing to apprehend. The Queen will never yield to such counsels."

"You appear to be in Her Majesty's confidence, holy mother," observed the bishop, drily.

"I am so far in her confidence, my lord," replied the abbess, "that I know her to be decidedly adverse to the Inquisition, and that she will never authorise its introduction in her kingdom."

"Possibly the Prince her husband may incline her to different views," remarked the bishop.

"No, my lord," replied the abbess; "the Queen is not accustomed to change her mind, and will never act contrary to her judgment."

The bishop looked surprised at the vivacity of the abbess, but Philip hastened to interpose, and said, "The lady abbess is right, my lord. I shall never seek to influence her Majesty's opinions in aught that concerns her kingdom. That I have sworn—and by my oath I shall abide."

"Unless his Holiness shall grant you absolution," muttered the bishop.

Philip then briefly explained to the bishop and to his confessor why he had sent for them, and had just made an end, when Count D'Egmont entered, and said that M. de Noailles was without, and besought a moment's audience of his Highness.

"What! the perfidious assassin! how dares he approach me? But he shall rue his temerity," cried Philip, placing his hand on his sword. Then instantly becoming calm, he added, "but he could not have come more opportunely for my purpose. Admit him, D'Egmont. Once within this chamber, he is my prisoner. Place a guard at the door, and let him not go forth without my order."

"No harm must be done him," said the abbess, in a low, deep voice.

"I have not sent for him," rejoined Philip. "If he rushes to his own destruction it is not my fault."

"It was madness in him to come here at all," said

D'Egmont. "The Duke of Alva, who has heard of the attempt, and suspects De Noailles of its contrivance, is in the ante-chamber."

"I am glad to hear it," replied Philip. "The Duke will know how to act," he added, with a significant glance at D'Egmont.

"If any injury be done the ambassador, there will be war with France," observed the abbess, in the same low, deep tone as before.

"No harm shall befal him, if he be not proved guilty of this foul plot," rejoined Philip. "But, if it be his contrivance, he shall not escape the punishment he merits. Admit him, Count."

CHAPTER XV.

THE FRENCH AMBASSADOR.

D'EGMONT withdrew, and almost instantly re-appeared with the French ambassador.

M. de Noailles made a very gallant appearance, being splendidly attired in white and silver. He removed his plumed and jewelled cap as he entered the room, and advanced with a very smiling and confident air towards Philip. While he was being presented to the Prince by the Count D'Egmont, the Duke of Alva entered the room. At the same time, two Spanish halberdiers stationed themselves near the door.

Philip received the ambassador with freezing politeness.

"Considering the relations unfortunately subsisting between my father, the Emperor, and the King, your master, I scarcely expected this visit from your excellency," he said.

"I do not appear before your Highness in my quality of ambassador, but as a simple gentleman," replied De Noailles. "I could not hear of the felon attack made upon you last night without desiring to offer my congratulations on your escape; but I might have hesitated to do so if rumour, with its customary malice, had not sought to fix the contrivance of the dark deed on me."

"No one who knows your excellency could for a moment suspect you of planning such an affair," rejoined Philip. "You would never strike a dishonourable and cowardly blow. Others may suspect you—I do not,"

"He does not suspect him, because he is sure of his guilt," muttered Alva.

"Having received this most gratifying assurance from your Highness, I will retire," said De Noailles, slightly alarmed, "entreating you to believe that though placed by circumstances in an inimical position, I rejoice in your auspicious arrival in this country, and trust that Heaven may guard you from all ill, and shed its blessings upon you and her Majesty."

"Perfidious villain! I marvel that lies of such magnitude choke him not," exclaimed the Duke of Alva, involuntarily clutching his poniard.

"I thank your excellency for your good wishes, which I am convinced are as sincere as your vehement denial of all complicity in this black affair," rejoined Philip. "But I must detain you a few minutes longer. You have come most à *propos.* I am about to interrogate one of my assailants, and shall be glad that you should be present during the examination."

"The villain, as I have heard, is confined in the dungeon of the Bar-gate," replied De Noailles. "I will attend there whenever your Highness may desire."

"He is uneasy, and would fain get away," muttered Alva, who was watching the ambassador narrowly.

"I shall not need to give you that trouble," remarked Philip. "The examination will take place here."

"In this chamber," exclaimed De Noailles, startled. "I thought the man was desperately wounded and like to die."

"It is true he is badly hurt, but he hath life enough in him to speak, as your excellency will find. He will be here anon," observed Philip.

"But the scene will be disagreeable to me," cried the ambassador. "I must crave your permission to withdraw."

And without waiting for consent, he turned to depart; but D'Egmont and Alva planted themselves in his way.

"A prisoner," he ejaculated, in consternation.

"Ay, a prisoner at his Highness's pleasure," rejoined Alva.

"I protest against such violation of my privilege," cried De Noailles, with mingled terror and anger.

"You can claim no privilege," rejoined the Duke, sternly.

"You stated expressly that you came here as a private gentleman, and not as an ambassador. Back Sir, at your peril."

Seeing there was no possibility of escape, De Noailles tried to assume a bold and unconcerned demeanour ; but his nerves sustained another and yet severer shock as the door was thrown open, and a litter, the curtains of which were closely drawn, was borne into the room, under the conduct of Osbert Clinton. In attendance upon the wounded man was Malwood, the chirurgeon.

Behind the litter came Rodomont Bittern, and the four bearers were Rodomont's friends, who had voluntarily undertaken the office, in order to be present at the examination.

CHAPTER XVI.

THE EXAMINATION.

AFTER consulting the Prince by a look, Osbert caused the litter to be set down in the middle of the chamber. As the curtains were drawn aside by Rodomont, and the livid features of Derrick Carver were fully revealed to view, Philip narrowly watched the effect of the ghastly spectacle on De Noailles ; but he stood the ordeal firmly.

"Raise thyself, Carver," cried Rodomont to the prisoner.

"Where am I ?" groaned the wretched man.

"In the presence of the Prince of Spain," rejoined Rodomont. "Art thou prepared to answer his interrogations ?"

"I am too feeble to talk," replied Derrick Carver, sinking backwards.

"I have a potent elixir with me which will restore his natural forces," said Malwood.

"Give me the phial. I will administer the dose," cried Rodomont, pouring a few drops down the prisoner's throat.

"Enough !—enough !" exclaimed Malwood, staying his hand.

"By the girdle of Saint Francis ! it acts like magic," cried Rodomont. "The colour is coming to his cheeks, and his eyes look brighter."

"His pulse begins to beat firmly," said Malwood. "He is now able to answer any question your Highness may desire to put to him," he added to the Prince,

At a sign from Philip, Father de Castro here approached the litter.

"Who art thou?" demanded Derrick Carver, slightly raising himself, and regarding the priest sternly.

"I am the confessor of the Prince of Spain," replied the other; "and lost as thou now art, steeped in sin, it will gladden me to reconcile thee to Heaven. Dire as is thine offence, and justly as it calls for condign punishment, I will strive to intercede for thee with his Highness, provided thou wilt make clean thy breast and recant thine errors."

"Think not to move me," replied Derrick Carver. "I have the stuff in me of which martyrs are made, as you will find. If I be doomed to a death of torture, Heaven will give me constancy to bear it. I grieve not for myself, but for my fellow countrymen, who have much bitter persecution to endure."

"Pity is wasted on him, Father," said Rodomont.

"No, my son," rejoined De Castro. "Our Church is never without commiseration for the most hardened sinner, who may be received into its bosom even at the last hour."

"You prate of pity, yet would enforce obedience to your doctrines by torture and burnings," said Derrick Carver. "If I mistake not, you are the ruthless Father de Castro, who hath written and preached on the punishment of heretics, and hath been the means of consigning many true believers in the Gospel to the flames."

"I am he you suppose, unhappy man," replied De Castro. "I am a physicion to those who are sick of soul. If the only remedy for their disease be fire, ought I to hesitate to prescribe it?"

"Then treat me as thou hast treated others, merciless priest," rejoined Derrick Carver. "Thou wilt see what will ensue. Cast abroad my ashes to the winds, and they will cause a tempest which will crush thee and the Prince thy master."

"Hold thy peace, thou crazy fellow! Thou ravest," cried Rodomont.

"Not at thy bidding, base hireling of Spain," rejoined Derrick Carver. "I hold thee in utter contempt. I am an Englishman, and will bend to no foreign yoke—a Protestant, and will never abandon my faith. I give my life for my country and my religion. Wilt thou give thy dog's life for either?"

"My patriotism and religious zeal do not lead me to turn assassin, Carver," rejoined Rodomont. "Neither doth it become thee, who hath sold thyself for French gold, to talk of subserviency. I am a loyal subject to the Queen, and a foe to traitors, of whom thou, Derrick, art the vilest."

"Thou accusest me falsely," rejoined Carver. "No French gold has ever touched my hand."

"Answer the question I am about to put," said the Prince, approaching; "and beware! for thy life depends upon thy truthfulness. It is useless to deny that thou wert hired for this deed. Name thy employer, and I will obtain thy pardon from the Queen. I promise it on my royal word."

"You will not credit what I say," rejoined Carver. "Why, therefore, should I speak?"

"Look round this assembly," pursued Philip, "and say whether anyone within it is known to thee."

"I see none but Spanish nobles and priests," rejoined Carver, in accents of contempt.

"Look again, Derrick," said Rodomont. "They are not all Spaniards. There is a Frenchman among them."

"It may be," replied the wounded man. "What is that to me?"

"Much," replied Rodomont.

"I pray your excellency to approach the litter," said Philip to the French ambassador.

"Readily," replied De Noailles, advancing. "Have you ever beheld me before?" he said to the prisoner.

"Equivocate not, but answer plainly, Derrick," said Rodomont. "Have you ever beheld his excellency before?"

"I have," replied the prisoner. "I saw him last night, in a house near the West-gate."

"You are mistaken, Sirrah; you cannot have seen me!" cried De Noailles.

"Truth only will avail you," said the Prince to the prisoner. "What passed between you and his excellency?"

"Not a word—not a look. I do not think he even noticed me," rejoined Carver,

But there were others with you whom he did notice?" said the Prince. "Trifle not with me. It imports me to know who they were, and what occurred."

"The villain's statement respecting me is utterly false," cried De Noailles. "I did not stir from my lodgings last night."

"Your excellency must needs be in error there," remarked Rodomont, "since you were seen and recognised in the High Street, about half an hour before this murtherous attack took place, thus allowing ample time for its concoction. Moreover, this letter found on the body of the ruffian slain by the Prince, may serve to prove your share in the dark transaction."

"I deny the charge altogether," cried De Noailles. "'Tis a device of my enemies. When the matter is regularly investigated, and before a competent tribunal, I can easily clear myself."

"Justice shall be done you, Sir, of that you need not doubt," said Philip, sternly. "As to you, fellow," he added to the prisoner, "little as you deserve it, you shall have a pardon. But understand. You owe life and freedom to Mistress Constance Tyrrell—not to me."

"Are no conditions annexed to the pardon?" inquired Derrick Carver.

"None; it is unconditional," replied the Prince. "Here is her Majesty's order," he added, giving Rodomont the paper, signed by the abbess. "Are you content?" he added to Constance, who had approached at the moment.

"I am," she replied, with a look of unutterable gratitude.

"With your Highness's permission," said Rodomont, "the prisoner shall be taken to the hospital of the Domus Dei, where he can remain till his wounds be healed, and if there be a spark of gratitude in his breast, the residue of his life will be devoted to extolling your Highness's clemency."

"I trust he may become a good Catholic through your instrumentality," said the Prince to Constance. "Take him away," he added to Rodomont.

Upon this Rodomont directed the bearers to remove the litter, and making a profound obeisance to the Prince, he followed it out of the room.

"My part in this strange performance is now over, I presume," observed De Noailles to the Prince.

"Your excellency is at liberty to depart," rejoined Philip, coldly. "Attend him," he added, glancing at Alva and D'Egmont.

The look was so significant that it did not escape the ambassador, and caused him to pause.

"No treachery, I trust, is intended?" he said. "Your Highness will bear in mind that my person is sacred."

"So is mine," rejoined Philip, sternly. "Yet that circumstance did not save me from attack."

"Your Highness would not insinuate ——"

"I insinuate nothing," said Philip. "Go, Sir, Heaven go with you!"

Seriously alarmed, the ambassador did not dare to stir a step. The terrible looks of the Duke of Alva froze the blood in his veins. While he stood irresolute, the lady abbess went up to him, and said, "I will go with you."

"It seems, then, that I am really in danger," stammered De Noailles.

"Without me you will never quit this place alive," replied the abbess.

And signing to Constance to follow her, she left the room with the ambassador, the Duke of Alva and the Count D'Egmont having gone out before them.

As De Noailles and the two ladies entered the antechamber, they found it full of armed men, while both the Duke and D'Egmont had drawn their swords.

"Pass on, holy mother, and take your charge with you," said Alva to the abbess and Constance. "We must have a word with his excellency."

"I will not affect to misunderstand your purpose, my lord Duke," said the abbess, "but it must not be. I forbid it."

"You, holy mother!"

"Yes, I, the Queen!" she rejoined.

"The Queen!" exclaimed Alva, sheathing his sword. "Nay, then, we must needs obey. Your excellency will excuse this momentary interruption. Pray pass on."

As may be supposed, the ambassador was not slow to avail himself of the permission.

BOOK II.

THE ROYAL NUPTIALS.

CHAPTER I.

OLD WINCHESTER FROM SAINT CATHERINE'S HILL.

KNOW you the fair hill, crowned by a clump of trees, with a zone around its waist, and a carpet of smooth turf spread out upon its banks, arising from the well-wooded and well-watered meads in the immediate vicinity of the ancient city of Winchester? If you are a Wykehamist, you know it well. Graven on the brow of the hill is a labyrinth, or maze, the work of a poor student, who, being debarred from the delights of home during the holiday season, occupied his weary hours in this strange task, while his heart-sickness found relief in a ditty, still sung by his successors at Wykeham's famous school. The legend goes on to relate that the hapless youth, who thus carved a memorial on the hill, pined away and died beneath one of the trees on its summit. If so, his gentle spirit must still haunt the spot! Lower down, an entrenchment, deeply cut in the chalk, and attributed to the Dane, encompasses the hill. The base of the mount is washed by the silver Itchen—a stream dear to old Izaak Walton, whose remains have rested, ever since his "ninety

years and more" were told, in the adjacent cathedral.
Other hills there are hard by—as Saint Giles's, whereon the
greatest fair in England was annually held from the period
of the Conquest to the reign of Henry VI.; and Saint
Mary Magdalene's, on which the Empress Maud and the
valorous prelate Henry de Blois, brother of King Stephen,
met to treat—but neither of these eminences are comparable
in beauty of form, or in charm of situation, to fair Saint
Catherine's Hill.

If you are a Wykehamist, we repeat, you well know
Saint Catherine's Hill. Oft, in happy, bygone days—far too
soon flown—have you wended, with a joyous band of your
schoolfellows, across the meadows and by the brink of the
meandering Itchen towards your favourite hill. Oft, in
summer-tide, have you plunged into the deep pool hard by
the mill—oft have you thrown the line upon the glassy
water and dragged forth the speckled trout—oft have you
lingered on the rustic bridge and watched the light skiff,
rowed by a comrade, shoot swiftly under it—oft have you
joined the merry groups seated on the banks at the foot of
the hill, or started in the mimic chase with the fleetest
runners of the crew—oft have you climbed the steep sides
of the eminence, have tracked its circling trench, threaded
the intricacies of its maze, or, reclining beneath the shade of
its tree, enjoyed the glorious prospect of the ancient city
commanded from the point, Oft thence have you gazed
upon the turrets and crocketed pinnacles of the venerable
pile, erected by your benefactor, the revered William of
Wykeham. Deep is the debt you owe him. Nobler seat of
learning there cannot be than Winchester College; second
only in architectural beauty to regal Eton, Well-nigh five
hundred years has your famous school endured. May it last
five hundred more!

Beautiful, most beautiful, is, now-a-days, the view from
Saint Catherine's Hill; but in the middle of the 16th century, when we must now regard it, it was infinitely more so.
From this height, the fine old city, skirted on the south by
lordly trees, was beheld in its highest perfection. Thronged
with convents, colleges, hospitals, churches, and other buildings of ancient date, and great beauty of architecture, and
boasting one of the grandest cathedrals in the kingdom,

Winchester had then a grave, monastic air—something of
which it yet retains, despite the many and grievous changes
it has undergone.   True, its religious communities and
charitable establishments had been suppressed by Henry
VIII., and their revenues seized upon, but the spoiler had
spared the edifices.   Most of these monasteries and convents were restored by Mary, and the long exiled monks
and nuns had just got back to their old abodes.

The aspect of Winchester, however, at the epoch in
question, was martial, as well as monastic.   Besides well-
fortified walls, flanked by numerous towers, and defended
by bastions, the city possessed two large castles, one of
which, built by William the Conqueror, occupied a commanding position on the south-west, and covered a vast
area with its works and outworks.   This fine old Norman
castle, eventually demolished by Cromwell, was besieged
and taken by the Dauphin of France in the reign of John,
but it held out gallantly against Simon de Montfort and the
barons in the days of Henry III.   In Mary's time it was
in good repair, and well supplied with ordnance and men.

Wolvesey Castle, as the other fortress was called, stood
in the lower part of the city, to the south-east of the
cathedral.   Though less advantageously situated than the
upper strong-hold, it rivalled it in magnitude.   The two
giants tried their strength in the time of the warlike Henry
de Blois, but were too well matched for any decided result
to ensue.   Wolvesey Castle was built by the valiant prelate
we have just mentioned on the site of the old Saxon
palace wherein Egbert, Alfred, Edgar, and Canute had
dwelt, and derived its name from the tribute of wolves'
heads exacted from the Welsh princes by Edgar, and paid
at the palace gates.   Soon after the completion of Wolvesey
by De Blois, it was attacked by the Empress Maud, who
had possession of the upper fortress, and was invested at
the same time by the Earl of Gloucester, and David, King
of Scotland, but it held out against all its assailants.
During this conflict the city suffered much from the con-
tending parties, but especially from the adherents of
Stephen.   Fire-balls thrown from Wolvesey Castle caused a
tremendous conflagration, whereby the Abbey of Saint
Mary, the royal palace, the suburb of Hyde, with its superb

monastery of Saint Grimbald, commenced by Alfred the Great, and a multitude of churches were destroyed. Dismantled by Henry II., who dreaded its strength, Wolvesey was restored and refortified at a later period, and afforded shelter from the barons to the half-brothers of Henry III. During all this time, and for upwards of another century, Wolvesey was occupied by bishops, who belonging to the church militant, kept it in a good state of defence. Later on, it became less of a fortress, and more of an episcopal palace, and such it was at the period of our history, for though none of its fortifications were destroyed, and its walls, towers, and donjon were still standing, the buildings were devoted to pacific purposes. Great trees were allowed to grow up in its courts, and fair gardens were laid out beneath its walls. The principal apartments were in the keep, and here Mary was now lodged, while her large retinue found ample accommodation in the numerous towers and out-buildings. Gardiner had fitted up the palace splendidly for his royal mistress's reception. During her stay at Wolvesey, unbounded hospitality reigned there; and never at any time—not even in 1522, when Henry VIII. feasted the Emperor Charles V. in its halls—had greater profusion been displayed within the castle. Of this vast and stately pile, demolished by Cromwell, some picturesque ruins, o'ergrown with ivy, are still left, attesting its former extent and grandeur.

Wolvesey Castle was connected by a subterranean passage with the cathedral, so that communication could be kept up with that edifice during a seige. Opposite the gate-tower was the noble entrance to Wykeham's College. Near at hand was another college, founded by John de Pontissara, and still nearer, the hospital called " La Carité," appertaining to the cathedral. Tall trees sheltered these edifices, and added to their beauty. Indeed, this part of the city was so densely planted with timber, that it looked like a grove.

The most striking object in old Winchester, as in the existing city, was the cathedral. This ancient and splendid structure demands a far more lengthened description than we are able to afford it. The scene of many highly important events, it has been the place of coronation of our

8

earlier kings, and their mausoleum. Egbert, Edmund the son of Alfred the Great, Edred, Canute, and Hardicanute, found here a sepulchre. Alfred's honoured remains, temporarily deposited within the cathedral, were afterwards removed to the adjacent abbey of Hyde, which he commenced, but did not live to complete. Here, amongst other holy personages, Saint Swithun, Bishop of Winchester in the ninth century, the patron saint of the city and the cathedral, found a grave. Here, also, lie the bones of many an illustrious prelate—Bishops Walkelin, Edyngton, and Wykeham; Bishops de Blois and Waynflete, Cardinal Beaufort, Prior Silkstede, Bishop Fox, and Gardiner himself, of whom our story treats. Built at different epochs, Winchester Cathedral offers examples of various styles of architecture, which, though dissimilar, produce a magnificent whole. Upon its site stood a more ancient church, reared by the Saxon king, Kenewalch, which was partially pulled down in the 11th century, when the present edifice was commenced by Bishop Walkelin, who preserved such portions of the original fabric as suited his design. The greater part of the east end of the existing structure, including the massive central tower, is Walkelin's work; and that tower, though somewhat heavy, is a noble specimen of Norman architecture. Considerable alterations were next made, towards the close of the 12th century, by Bishop Godfrey de Lucy, who rebuilt the Lady Chapel. About 1350, a new nave was commenced by Bishop Edyngton, and the work was continued by the illustrious William of Wykeham, and after him by Cardinal Beaufort, and brought to a completion by Bishop Waynflete. The vast and lofty columns on either side of the nave, each pillar being about twelve feet in diameter, produce a grand effect, and the *coup d'œil* of the interior from the great western portal is superb beyond description. The transepts, wherein may still be seen the huge round pillars and vast circular arches, piled one upon another to the roof — the original work of Walkelin — constitute, perhaps, the most interesting part of the edifice.

Brief allusion can only be made to the marvels of the choir; to its elaborately carved stalls with their *misereres,* canopies, pinnacles, and other ornaments; to the magnificent carved screen behind the altar-piece; to the glories of the great east and west windows; to the superb chantries of Cardinal Beaufort, Bishop Waynflete, and Bishop Fox, all of extraordinary beauty and richness. On the south side of the nave, and exhibiting infinite richness of ornament and extreme delicacy of carving, is the mortuary chapel of William of Wykeham, in which may be seen a recumbent marble statue of that venerated personage, his head supported by angels, and three kneeling figures at his feet. In the north aisle, near the presbytery, is the mortuary chapel of Bishop Gardiner. In the Silkstede Chapel, in the south transept, will be found the lowly grave of gentle Izaak Walton.

And now a word in regard to the city itself. The early history of Venta, Caer Gwent, or the White City, as Winchester was originally called, is lost in obscurity, but the remote antiquity of the place is unquestionable. The Celt, the Roman, the Saxon, the Dane, and the Norman, have successively occupied the spot. Whether good King Arthur held his court in the White City, and banqueted his peerless knights at the Round Table, still preserved in the castle hall, may be doubted. But it is certain that, as the residence of our great Saxon kings, and the seat of their government, Winchester was the most important city in the island. In the days of Cerdic it was the capital of the West Saxons, and, on the dissolution of the Heptarchy, it became the metropolis of England. The most illustrious name connected with Winchester is that of Alfred the Great. Compelled to abandon the city for a while to the Danes, this great monarch and lawgiver retook it, restored it to its pristine splendour, and dwelt within it to his latest day. Canute also had his palace in Winchester, and died there. From Egbert to Edward the Confessor—a period of two hundred and forty years—all our old Saxon kings were crowned within the cathedral, and most of them found graves in its vaults. William the Conqueror loved Winchester, and strengthened it by the proud castle on the hill. William Rufus was buried in the cathedral, and the saints deposited there, resenting the intrusion of so impious a monarch upon their resting-place, caused the great tower to fall down. During the usurpation of Stephen, Winchester became, as we have shown, the scene of dire conflicts between the Empress Maud and Bishop de Blois. Henry III., surnamed of Winchester, was born within the city; and so was Arthur, eldest son of Henry VII., but the latter died too young to do credit to his birth-place. Edward I. held divers parliaments in the city, and partially restored its consequence. Great feasting occurred in Wolvesey Castle, with jousting and triumphs, when the Emperor Charles V., as we have previously related, was for a week the guest of Henry VIII. Of the crushing effect produced upon the city by the Reformation we have already spoken. It was now just recovering from the blow. Modern Winchester comes not within our scope. But the city is still beautiful, still picturesque. Though reft of more than half of its olden attractions, it still boasts its grand cathedral, its famous college, and its exquisite and unique hospital of Saint Croix. Retaining these, the city of Egbert, of Alfred, and Canute, must ever be one of the most interesting in the kingdom.

CHAPTER II.

SAINT CATHERINE'S CHAPEL.

AT the period of our history the finishing-point to the beauty of Saint Catherine's Hill was given by an exquisite Gothic chapel placed upon its summit. Erected in the 13th century, this little temple was much resorted to by the devout on account of the reliques it contained of Saints Birinus, Swithun, and Ethelwold. Within in might also be seen a ploughshare which, while red hot, had been trodden upon without injury by the beautiful Queen Emma, mother of Edward the Confessor. Constant pilgrimages were made to the shrine, and on the festival of Saint Catherine, to whom the chapel was dedicated, a long procession of religious personages of both sexes, headed by the Bishop of Winchester, and accompanied by an immense concourse, came forth from the city and ascended the hill, when the Bishop and those with him entering the chapel, placed rich gifts upon the altar. At such times, the spectacle of the vast assemblage kneeling around the little fane, or raising the choral hymn to heaven, must have been highly impressive. Formerly, Saint Catherine's Chapel had been well endowed, but its revenues were appropriated by Wolsey to his "twins of learning," Ipswich and Oxford. From this time, until the return to the old worship under Mary, the place was completely neglected. Restored by Gardiner, an aged priest, Father Jerome, who had officiated within it in former days, was appointed to its care. At the

same time its precious reliques were brought back. Luckily,
during the season of its desecration, it had sustained no
material injury—its extraordinary reputation for sanctity
having probably saved it—and it was now nearly as beautiful
as ever. As least, its custodian, good Father Jerome,
thought so.

In the olden time, it had been customary with devotees,
after early immersion in the clear waters of the Itchen, to
repair to Saint Catherine's Chapel, hear matins, and perform
other devotional exercises. This practice, healthful alike to
body and soul, was now revived. Welcome to Father
Jerome were all who came there to pray.

At an early hour· on the morning of the third day after
the Prince of Spain's public entry into Southampton, a remarkably handsome young gallant—tall, graceful in figure
and deportment, and very becomingly attired in a doublet of
green velvet, slashed with white silk, and wearing a small
velvet beret of the some colour, adorned with a white plume,
on his head—issued from the south gate of Winchester, and
passing through the grove of stately elms, colonised by
rooks, then environing this side of the ancient city, struck
across the charming valley watered by the Itchen.

The morning was lovely enough to have tempted the
veriest sluggard to quit his couch, and our handsome young
galliard seemed fully alive to its beauties. The sun had but
just o'ertopped sweet Saint Catherine's Hill. The grass was
heavy with dew, and a thin haze hung in some parts of the
valley, but this quickly disappeared. All nature looked
bright and smiling. The warblers of the grove carolled
blithely, the larks soared aloft rejoicingly, and a cloud of
clamorous rooks, quitting the tall trees near the city, winged
their way towards the marsh lands further south. Scared
by the young man's approach, the stately heron started from
the river in which he was fishing, while other aquatic fowl
dived beneath the green water-weeds and disappeared.

At no time are we so susceptible to Nature's beauties as
at early morn. Our senses of delight are quicker then than
at any other season, and invigorated by the freshness of the
atmosphere, we find something to charm in every object we
behold. So it was with the young gallant in question. He
was familiar with the scene around him, yet he discovered

beauties in it of which he had been hitherto unconscious. His eye ranged along the valley through which strayed the winding Itchen, pleased with all it encountered, until his gaze settled on the secluded hospital of Saint Croix.

Never before, it seemed to him, had the ancient edifice looked so lovely, so sequestered, as it did now. Though partially screened by trees, enough was visible to evidence its size and architectural beauty—the lofty gateway, the roofs of the quadrangular courts, and the square tower of the reverend church. A slight mist, enveloping but not hiding the outline of the pile, gave it a dreamlike character.

The hospital of Saint Croix was even then more than three hundred years old, having been erected in 1136 by Bishop Henry de Blois, of whom previous mention has been made. It was subsequently enlarged by Cardinal Beaufort, and is still, we are happy to say, in an admirable state of preservation. Here the hospitality of monkish times is still practised on a small scale. Like many other similar institutions in Winchester and elsewhere, Saint Croix was deprived of its rents and revenues by Henry VIII., but sufficient was fortunately saved from the spoiler's grasp to preserve it from utter extinction. New life was communicated to the decaying old hospital by Mary, and it was the thought of its unexpected revival that gave it special interest in the eyes of the young man who now gazed upon it. Contrasting its present condition with the past, he rejoiced that a fabric so lovely, and designed for such benevolent purposes, should have escaped destruction.

After indulging in these reflections for a brief space, he walked on, bestowing a glance as he crossed the wooden bridge over the Itchen at the trout shooting through the clear stream. He had now reached the foot of Saint Catherine's Hill, whither, apparently, he was bound, and disdaining to take the easy but circuitous path conducting to the little chapel, he speeded up the steepest part of the acclivity, across the Danish entrenchment, and did not halt for a moment till he gained the summit of the hill. He then turned to enjoy the splendid prospect commanded from the spot of the ancient city and its environs, which we have already endeavoured to bring before the reader.

While he was thus occupied, the door of the little chapel

was opened by a priest of venerable and benevolent aspect, who stepped towards him, bade him a kindly good morrow, and bestowed a benison upon him.

"What brings Master Osbert Clinton to Saint Catherine's Hill so early?" inquired the old priest.

"Nothing more than to hear matins in your chapel, good Father Jerome," replied Osbert. "I trust I am in time."

"You are in ample time, my son," replied the old priest, smiling. "Matins have not yet been said, and will not commence for half an hour. Except myself, you are the first on Saint Catherine's Hill this blessed morning. Indeed, I marvel to see you here so soon. That a young gallant like Master Osbert Clinton, engaged in all the gaieties of court, should have come to this little chapel to pray at so early an hour, argues a strength of devotion for which, I own, I scarcely give him credit."

"I will not attempt to deceive you, good father," returned Osbert. "It is not merely the desire to pray within your chapel that has brought me here, but the hope of meeting a fair maiden ——"

"Dare you make such an avowal to me, young Sir?" interrupted Father Jerome, in a tone of stern rebuke.

"Nay Father, be not angry with me," said Osbert. "You will pardon me, I am sure, when you know my motive. My object is to caution the damsel, and this is the only opportunity I may have of doing so."

"Methinks I know the damsel you allude to, my son," returned Father Jerome. "Mistress Constance Tyrrell, is it not? She was here yesterday, and after performing her devotions, poured forth the secrets of her heart to me, and besought my counsel."

"You are aware, then, of the perilous position in which she is placed, and of the necessity of extricating her from it without delay?"

"I know she is beloved by some exalted personage, and that she is full of apprehension ——"

"Well may she be so, holy Father," said Osbert. "I dare not tell you by whom she is beloved. Suffice it, that her position at court is fraught with peril. But it shall be my business to guard her."

"You love her, then, my son?" observed Father Jerome.

"Passionately," replied Osbert. "But I have not yet ventured to tell her of my love."

"You are encouraging a hopeless passion, my son, and I beseech you to check it while you can. But what tidings do you bring of the Prince of Spain? When comes he from Southampton?"

"This very day," returned Osbert. "I am to form part of the train which will escort his Highness hither. We shall set forth at noon, at which hour the Prince, with a large cavalcade, will leave Southampton, so we shall meet him midway."

"I am told he is a well-favoured Prince, but haughty and reserved of manner," remarked Father Jerome.

"I have not found him so," replied Osbert. "To me he has been singularly condescending, and, indeed, he is gracious to all."

"I am right glad to hear it. That speaks well for him. Long and earnestly have I prayed that our good Queen's union may be happy. Much does our holy Church owe her. Look down upon that city, my son. Regard those monasteries, convents, and hospitals. They have all been restored by her. Once more within yon noble cathedral mass is celebrated, and all the rites of the Romish Church performed. To Queen Mary we owe this blessed change. By her Saint Croix has likewise been restored, and it is to her benign influence that this little chapel has been again opened for worship—that the reliques of the saints have been brought back to it—and that I, myself, am enabled to officiate within it. By Queen Mary heresy and schism have been overthrown, and our holy Church delivered from bondage. May Heaven long preserve her! She is our hope and strength— our pillar and defence."

"I cry 'Amen' to that prayer with all my heart," said Osbert. "Heaven grant the Prince may prove a good husband to her!"

"You speak as if you doubted it, my son," rejoined Father Jerome. "But I cannot tarry for further converse. I must leave you now. The hour for matins is at hand. After prayers, if you have aught further to say to me, I shall be at your service."

With this, he re-entered the chapel, and presently a bell began to ring. Many persons, chiefly country-folk, obeyed the summons, coming from different parts of the valley, and entered the chapel, the door of which now stood open.

Osbert, however, did not enter with them, as he had caught sight of two female devotees slowly ascending the hill, in whom he recognised Constance Tyrrell and her old attendant, Dorcas. He waited till they gained the brow of the eminence, and then advancing towards the damsel, respectfully saluted her. Her appearance surprised and distressed him. She looked sad and pale, and traces of recent tears were on her cheeks. Scarcely returning his salutation, she entered the chapel, followed by old Dorcas, who appeared to be as full of affliction as her young mistress. Osbert went in after them, and knelt down by the side of Constance at the altar. But she did not once look towards him, and, indeed, seemed wholly unconscious of his presence.

At the close of the service, Osbert quitted the chapel with the country-folk, and waited outside, thinking Constance would soon come forth. But he was doomed to disappointment. More than an hour elapsed, and she did not appear. At the expiration of that time the chapel door was opened by Father Jerome, who looked very grave. Addressing Osbert, the old priest said, "Do not tarry here longer, my son. Mistress Constance Tyrrell has much to say to me, and seeks my ghostly counsel."

"But I will wait for her, good Father," cried Osbert. "I care not how long I stay. I *must* speak with her."

"Impossible! my son," replied Father Jerome, "I enjoin you to depart. Constance does not desire to see you. Stifle the unfortunate passion you have conceived for her. It can never be requited."

"In Heaven's name what has happened, good Father? Tell me, I adjure you?" cried Osbert.

"Question me not, but go!" said Father Jerome, authoritatively. "Constance will not come forth while you remain here. I myself will accompany her to Winchester."

"But will you tell me nothing more? Will you not give me a hope?" ejaculated Osbert, despairingly.

The old priest shook his head, and, with a compassionate glance at him, closed the door, and bolted it inside.

Osbert was half inclined to force an entrance into the chapel, but feeling the impropriety of such a proceeding, he tore himself away, and rushed wildly down the hill, scarcely knowing whither he went.

CHAPTER III.

HOW THE PRINCE OF SPAIN RODE FROM SOUTHAMPTON
TO WINCHESTER; HOW HE HEARD HIGH MASS AT THE
CATHEDRAL, AND VISITED THE QUEEN PRIVATELY AT
WOLVESEY CASTLE.

PHILIP prolonged his stay at Southampton from Friday, the 20th of July, 1554, the day on which he made his public entry into the town, till the following Monday. Before leaving, he dismissed his fleet, which set sail for Cadiz, under the command of the Admiral of Castile. The Flemish squadron also departed at the same time. Nothing was allowed to transpire publicly in regard to the Queen's secret visit to Southampton. After protecting the French ambassador from the Prince's vengeance, in the manner previously related, Mary returned to Winchester, taking Constance Tyrrell with her. Next day, the Count D'Egmont, attended by Osbert Clinton, brought her Majesty a set of diamonds, of inestimable value, as a present from Philip. Somewhat later in the same day, the noble Spanish dames, the Duchess of Medina Celi, the Marchionesses Pescara, de Farria, and del Valle, the Countesses Olivares, de Saldana, and de Modica, with several other gentlewomen, who had accompanied their consorts to be present at the approaching solemnity, arrived at Wolvesey Castle in magnificent chariots and litters provided for them by the Queen.

Meantime, Southampton continued in a fever of excitement, nothing being thought of in the town but revelry and rejoicing. On Sunday, Philip heard mass in Saint Michael's Church, and rode forth afterwards with his train to Netley Abbey, then in possession of the Marquis of Winchester, Lord High Treasurer, to whom it had been granted on the dissolution of the monasteries, and after being sumptuously entertained by his noble host, he returned, in the cool of a most delicious evening, by water to Southampton.

About noon on Monday, the 22nd, the Prince quitted Southampton, attended by a magnificent escort, comprising, in addition to his own suite, the Duke of Norfolk, the Marquis of Winchester, the Earls of Arundel, Derby, Worcester, Bedford, Rutland, Pembroke, and Surrey; with the Lords Clinton, Cobham, Darcie, Matravers, Talbot, and many others, numbering, with their gentlemen and esquires, upwards of two thousand horse. Never before had such a vast and splendid cavalcade passed through the Bar-gate. Stationed at the gate were Sir Bevis, with the Princess Josyan seated behind him on the broad back of Arundel, Ascapart, Canute, and Xit—the latter mounted on his little piebald horse—and when the royal *cortége* had passed by, these personages followed it at a short distance. Hundreds of persons on foot accompanied the cavalcade, which proceeded at a slow pace, half way to Winchester, when it encountered another large company of noblemen and gentlemen sent to meet it by the Queen. Amongst these were the Count D'Egmont and Osbert Clinton. Swelled by this addition, the cavalcade, which had now assumed the proportions of an army, pursued its course towards Winchester, the trees by which the valley of the Itchen was shaded affording protection from the scorching sunbeams. Ere long Philip came upon the hospital of Saint Croix, the secluded beauty of which might have attracted more of his attention had not Winchester itself, at the same moment, burst upon his view. Cries of admiration broke from the Spaniards as they caught sight of the ancient and picturesque city.

From Saint Croix to the South-gate the road was lined on either side by well-dressed spectators of both sexes, who cheered the Prince loudly as he rode by on his Andalusian barb. A roar of artillery from the castle batteries announced his entrance into the city to the Queen.

Philip was now close to the cathedral, which rose before him in all its majesty. Passing through a gateway, he reached the great western entrance, in the wide place in front of which some fifteen hundred horsemen were now drawn up, forming a most imposing spectacle.

Beneath the central portico, with its noble arch supported by clustered columns, and its tabernacles containing statues of the saints Peter and Paul, stood Gardiner, in his full pontificals, mitre, stole, chasuble, rochet, alb, and amice. His crosier was borne by a priest, who stood behind him. Beetle-browed, swarthy of complexion, hook-nosed, and harsh of feature, Gardiner, notwithstanding his forbidding looks and stern, searching glances, which seemed to read the hearts of those he looked upon, and inspired more dread than love, had a countenance replete with intelligence, while his imperious looks and manner, untamed by reverse of fortune, showed the confidence he felt in his own mental powers and resources. With Gardiner were Bonner, Bishop of London, Tonstal, Bishop of Durham, Day, Bishop of Chichester, Thirlby, Bishop of Ely, Heath, Bishop of Worcester, and other prelates, all in mitres and copes. Behind the bishops were the clergy belonging to the cathedral in their vestments.

As Philip dismounted before the porch, and bent the knee to Gardiner, who advanced to meet him, the bishop spread his arms over him, pronouncing a solemn benediction upon his head.

After bowing with profound respect to the other prelates, all of whom reverently returned his salutation, the Prince entered the cathedral and proceeded towards the choir, Gardiner and the other bishops leading the way. Ere many minutes, the nave was half filled by the nobles and gentlemen composing Philip's retinue. The furthest stall on the right of the choir was assigned to the Prince by Gardiner. Every other stall had a noble occupant; the one next to Philip being tenanted by the Duke of Norfolk.

High mass was then celebrated, Gardiner and the bishops officiating at the altar. After *Te Deum* had been solemnly sung, Philip retired into the sacristy adjoining the Silkstede Chapel with Gardiner, where a brief, but very kindly, conference took place between them. To the Prince's inquiries as to when he might be permitted to see the Queen, Gardiner replied, that the public presentation could not, according to court etiquette, take place till the morrow, but that he would engage to procure his Highness a private interview with her Majesty that evening.

On quitting the cathedral, the Prince was ceremoniously conducted by the Earl of Arundel to the deanery, which had been prepared for his reception. Here a grand banquet was subsequently served, at which the Lord Chancellor and all the principal English and Spanish nobles sat down.

In the evening, while Philip was alone, the Earl of Arundel and the Grand Chamberlain, Sir John Gage, were introduced, and informed him that they were enjoined by her Majesty to conduct him to her presence. Expressing the liveliest satisfaction, the Prince said he was ready to accompany them at once, and, immediately arising, he went forth with them into the deanery garden, whence, by a private way, he was brought to a postern in the walls of Wolvesey Castle. Of this postern Sir John Gage possessed the key, and the door being unlocked, gave them admittance to the gardens of the castle.

After tracking a long arcade of formally clipped yew-trees, they came upon a wide glass-plot, soft as velvet to the foot, laid out in front of the keep-tower, wherein, as we have already stated, were the Queen's apartments. Close to this charming lawn were parterres, embellished with knots of flowers, in the taste of the period. At the farther end stood the stately donjon reared by stout Henry de Blois, between which and the grass-plot lay a broad terrace-walk. This scene, beautiful at all times, was now rendered doubly beautiful by the light of a full summer moon hanging right above the keep, and flooding the place with radiance.

As the Prince and his attendants entered this fairy region, three persons were walking upon the grass-plot. These were the Queen, Gardiner, and one of her Majesty's ladies—the latter, however, being at some distance from the other two.

"There is her Majesty," observed the Lord Chamberlain. "Shall I announce your Highness?"

Receiving Philip's prompt assent, Sir John Gage advanced towards Mary, and after an instant's consultation with her,

Philip was formally presented—the Lord Chamberlain withdrawing as soon as he had performed his office. Gardiner also retired with the lady in attendance, and the royal pair were left alone together. Mary was very richly attired, and, viewed by this witching light, really looked attractive. Some excuse may therefore be found for the impassioned admiration which Philip expressed on beholding her features, now for the first time revealed to his gaze.

Mary was small of stature, with beautiful hands and feet. Her person was well made, but too thin, and her carriage, though majestic, was exceedingly stiff, and lacked the grace which ease alone can impart. In her younger days she had been accounted good-looking, but she could scarcely be considered so now. Her eyes were large and grey, and her glances keen and steady. Her face was round, her tresses inclining to red, if they did not even actually attain that hue; and the nose too flat and large. Her lips, too, were thin and compressed. Altogether, there was a hardness and severity about her face that destroyed its pleasing character, while premature wrinkles about the eyes and brow gave her age.

If Mary did not inherit the beauty either of her father or mother, she had many of the qualities by which both were characterised. She had the courage, firmness, and obstinacy of Henry VIII., and she had all the virtues belonging to the unfortunate Katherine of Aragon. Her conduct under the trials to which she was exposed was most exemplary, and even her enemies could find no fault with it. Firmly attached to the principles of the Catholic religion, in which she had been brought up, she never wavered for a moment in her adherence to her faith, but would have suffered martyrdom rather than renounce it. When commanded by the council under Edward VI., to desist from the performance of mass, she still continued to celebrate it in private.

Mary spoke well in public, and possessed a voice so sonorous that she could be distinctly heard by a large assemblage. Her stirring address to the citizens at Guildhall gave the *coup de grace* to Wyat's formidable rebellion. She also possessed many accomplishments, playing so well upon the lute and spinet as to astonish and delight professed musicians by her skill. She also greatly excelled in embroidery, and in other female work. Her intellectual accomplishments were of a high order, though they did not excite so much astonishment in those days of learned ladies as they would in our own. She spoke French and Spanish perfectly, and read Italian with ease, though she did not speak it. She was also mistress of Latin. At the request of Catherine Parr, she translated into English Erasmus's Paraphrase of the Gospel of St. John. Since her accession to the throne, all her time, except the hours of devotion, had been given to affairs of state. She arose at daybreak, performed her religious duties, heard mass, and thenceforward devoted herself to public business, being easy of access to all who desired to approach her. Bigoted Mary was, intolerant and severe towards those who differed with her on points of faith; but she had many redeeming qualities, which should have saved her from the obloquy to which she has been subjected.

Such was Mary when she met her affianced husband on that lovely moonlight night in the garden of Wolvesey Castle—a night ever after cherished in her memory as the happiest of her existence. Blissful, indeed, were her feelings as she paced to and fro upon that soft sward with her royal lover, listening to the vows he breathed in low and passionate tones, and believing all he said. Philip felt his power, and exercised it. From that moment to the latest of her existence, she fondly loved him. Ingrate that he was, he but poorly requited her affection.

We shall not record the words he uttered. Idle words were they, such as feigned passion has ever at command, but they produced the effect designed. Suspicious as Mary was by nature, she had no suspicion now. She persuaded herself that Heaven had rewarded her at last for all her sufferings by bestowing upon her a fond and faithful spouse.

Two hours elapsed before their moonlight walk was over— two happy, happy hours to the Queen. Then she re-entered the keep, while Philip, attended by the Earl of Arundel and Sir John Gage, returned to the deanery.

CHAPTER IV.

OF THE PUBLIC MEETING BETWEEN THE ROYAL PAIR.

IT having been arranged that the public meeting between the royal pair should take place on the following day, six richly carved and gilt chariots, covered with cloth of gold, drawn by horses trapped in white velvet embroidered with silver lions, and ridden by pages of honour attired in the royal liveries, were sent to convey the Prince and his suite to Wolvesey Castle. Attendant upon the chariots were a number of henchmen, likewise habited in the royal liveries, and mounted on richly-caparisoned horses, and besides these there was a guard of two hundred arquebusiers, fully equipped.

Precisely at noon Philip came forth from the deanery, attended by all his grandees, gorgeously attired, and glittering with jewels, and entered the chariot appointed for him. The Dukes of Alva and Medina Celi had places beside him. Preceded by mounted trumpeters and kettle-drums, making a loud bruit, the train moved towards Wolvesey Castle, the Prince being everywhere greeted by acclamations from those who witnessed his progress. At the noble gateway of Wykeham's College were stationed the warden and fellows in their gowns, and ranged by the side of the walls in files two deep stood the scholars, who shouted lustily and waved their caps as the Prince passed by. The young Wykehamists were still vociferating as the chariot containing the Prince passed beneath the arched gate-tower then forming the main entrance to Wolvesey Castle. At this gate, above which floated the royal standard, stood Og, Gog, and Magog, towering by the head and shoulders above the other halberdiers. The giants had now resumed their ordinary garb of yeomen of the guard, but were instantly recognised by the Prince.

Before the principal entrance of the keep stood a vast number of gentlemen, esquires, and pages, all splendidly apparelled, and, as Philip's chariot drew up, Sir John Gage, Grand Chamberlain, with Sir Henry Jerningham, Vice-Chamberlain, bearing their wands of office, came forth to assist his Highness to alight. The entrance-hall was filled with noble personages, amongst whom were the Lord Chancellor, the Duke of Norfolk, the Earls of Arundel and Derby, Sir Edward Hastings, Master of the Horse, the Earl of Bedford, Lord Privy Seal, the Lord Paget and Sir William Petre, both Secretaries of State, with many others. Bowing graciously as he passed through this splendid throng, the Prince was conducted by Gardiner to the great hall, where he found the Queen surrounded by a bevy of lovely dames. Mingled with the English ladies and contrasting strongly with them, from their rich Southern complexion, dark eyes and jet-black tresses, were the noble Spanish dames, making altogether a most dazzling group. At the further end of the hall, which was hung with costly arras, and otherwise gorgeously decorated, was a cloth of estate, embroidered with the arms of England and Spain. Under it were two velvet fauteuils.

On perceiving the Queen, Philip flew towards her, and, without tarrying for a formal presentation by Sir John Gage, embraced her, kissing her lovingly, to the amusement of all the ladies around, and then, taking her hand, led her towards the canopy at the further end of the hall, no one presuming to follow them. As the royal pair seated themselves on the fauteuils, and entered into tender converse, many a curious eye was directed towards them. However, they heeded not observation, but seemed entirely engrossed by each other.

Thus they continued discoursing for more than an hour. The Queen then rose, and the Prince rising likewise, Sir John Gage and Sir Henry Jerningham marshalled them into an adjoining chamber, where a grand banquet was laid out. Here they both sat down at the high table, and were waited upon by Gardiner; the rest of the company occupying the lower tables. Near the royal pair stood a cupboard filled with splendid salvers, flagons, and other vessels of gold and silver. In the course of the banquet, a goblet of wine being filled for the Queen by Gardiner, she drank from it to Philip; after which, the Prince pledged her in return from the same loving cup. At the close of the banquet, the Queen and Prince, attended by all the company, adjourned to the grass plot, where they walked for some time, enjoying the cool air. A concert in the great hall, at which many skilful musicians and singers assisted, brought the evening to an end. Attended by his grandees, Philip then returned to the deanery.

No meeting took place between the royal pair next day, the Queen being occupied in preparations for the marriage ceremonial, which was appointed for the morrow.

Philip passed his time in visiting several places in and about the city. At Wykeham's College, whither he first repaired, he was received by the warden and fellows, and shown over the ancient structure, appearing to be much struck by the great hall, the beautiful chapel, the cloisters, and the refectory. In the hall the whole of the students were assembled, and a Latin address was recited to him by the senior scholar. On his departure, the Prince ordered the contents of a well filled purse to be distributed amongst the youths, and the walls of the old quadrangle resounded with the joyous shouts of the recipients of the gift.

Accompanied by the Bishop of Cuença and Father de Castro, Philip next visited " La Carité," with several other religious establishments and hospitals, and left large presents behind him. This done, at the head of a brilliant retinue, consisting of the chief English and Spanish nobles, he rode up to William the Conqueror's Castle, and examined it throughout, mounting to the top of the donjon, whence he beheld Southampton, and the Isle of Wight in the far distance. In the great hall of the fortress he was shown King Arthur's Round Table, at which his august sire, the Emperor Charles V., had sat when he was the guest of Henry VIII.

" I was honoured with a seat at the Round Table on that ever-memorable occasion, your Highness," observed the old

Duke of Norfolk. " Seldom hath such a party assembled—not perhaps since the days of good King Arthur himself. Both your royal father and my late gracious master—whose soul God preserve !—played the boon companion, and bandied so many merry jests, that we could scarce contain ourselves for laughter. And yet they were nowise displeased, for state was banished from the Round Table, no one being able to say who sat above the other. On yonder wall, I mind me, was inscribed this distich in letters of gold:

> ' Carolus, Henricus vivant; defensor uterque,
> Henricus fidei, Carolus ecclesiæ.' "

"You describe an enviable banquet, my lord Duke," replied Philip; "and I marvel not it lives in your memory. But you shall sit again at that board, and as my guest; and though I cannot hope to rival my father, or your late royal master, as a boon companion, I will put no constraint upon your mirth."

The Duke of Norfolk bowed his thanks, and they quitted the hall. From the castle, Philip rode with his train to the Hospital of Saint Croix, with the beautiful and secluded situation of which he had been much struck as he approached Winchester. Passing through the ancient gateway, he dismounted in the court, where were drawn up the brotherhood in their long dark gowns, adorned with a silver cross—vestments and badges still retained by the fraternity. After examining the Hundred Men's Hall, and noting the statue of Cardinal Beaufort in a niche in the upper part of the chamber, Philip proceeded to the venerable church, where he heard mass. Well pleased with his visit, he caused a piece of gold to be given to each of the brethren.

On quitting Saint Croix, the Prince did not return at once to Winchester, but crossing the valley, and fording the Itchen at a place pointed out to him by Osbert Clinton, who acted as his guide, he rode up Saint Catherine's Hill. Good Father Jerome, who had watched the train ascending the mount, advanced to meet him. Courteously saluting the old priest, Philip put several questions to him respecting the chapel.

"Will it please your Highness to alight and view the reliques ?" said Father Jerome,

Readily assenting, Philip dismounted, Osbert holding his bridle the while.

The Prince then entered the chapel with Father Jerome, leaving all his suite outside to contemplate the magnificent prospect of the city. His first act was to prostrate himself before the altar, and in this pious posture he remained for several minutes, fervently occupied in prayer.

"Apparently he is devout," thought Father Jerome, as he stood behind him, with his hands meekly folded upon his breast. "And yet unholy passions rule his heart."

When Philip had concluded his devotions, Father Jerome unlocked a casket, and exhibited the various saintly reliques it contained, which the Prince regarded with due reverence. The old priest next displayed the wonderful ploughshare which had proved harmless to Queen Emma, and related the legend connected with it. While looking about the chapel, Philip noticed upon the credence-table near the altar a little tablet of gold, with an agate on either side, garnished with rubies, and having a large pearl pendant.

"How came this trinket here, father?" he inquired, fixing a stedfast look on the old priest. "It was my gift to a damsel who preserved my life."

"I know it, Highness," replied Father Jerome. "But the maiden felt she could not keep the tablet, and hath left it as an offering to Saint Catherine's shrine. In my humble mind she has done well."

"Has she confessed to you, father?" demanded Philip.

"I am not bound to answer that question, even to your Highness," replied Father Jerome. "Nevertheless, I will answer it. She has confessed."

"Then you know all?"

"All, Highness. And I pity her from my soul."

"And you blame me?"

"I said not so, Highness," replied the priest, somewhat evasively.

"Where is she?" asked Philip, after a pause, and in tones of deep emotion.

"Highness," replied Father Jerome, "she has returned to Southampton, where she is about to bury her woes in a convent. I applaud her determination,"

"Father, this step must be prevented," rejoined Philip. "She must not take the vows."

"I do not think she will yield to any persuasions to the contrary," replied Father Jerome. "Her resolution is taken."

"Make the attempt—I command you," cried Philip, imperiously. "See her without delay. Use all the arguments you can employ. If you succeed, count on my gratitude."

"Your Highness shall be obeyed, although I confess I like not the task," said Father Jerome, bowing his reverend head.

"And as an earnest of my good will, take this purse, and employ its contents as you list."

"I take it, only to bestow its contents on the poor," said the priest, as Philip quitted the chapel.

Philip then mounted his jennet, and rode down the hill with his train. The changed expression of his countenance did not escape notice, but no one ventured to remark upon it. Under the guidance of Osbert Clinton, the prince made his way along the banks of the Itchen, to the old stone bridge, said to be the work of St. Swithun, and crossing it, re-entered the city by the eastern gate, and proceeded to the deanery, halting by the way to examine the ancient City Cross.

While Philip was making the various visits we have described, most of the inhabitants had opportunities of beholding him, and all were favourably impressed by his youth, his handsome person, his proud yet affable deportment, and, above all, by the grace and skill with which he managed his fiery Andalusian barb.

That evening, the Prince had a long conference with Simon Renard, the Spanish ambassador, and Don Juan de Figueroa, Regent of the Council of Aragon, a nobleman much in the Emperor's confidence, and who had been sent to England, charged with a most important mission, which he had hitherto kept secret, but which he now proceeded to disclose to the Prince. The revelation then made seemed to yield Philip extraordinary satisfaction.

CHAPTER V.

HOW THE ROYAL NUPTIALS WERE CELEBRATED IN WINCHESTER CATHEDRAL.

SAINT JAMES'S DAY had been appointed for the marriage, that saint being the patron of Spain. Brighter or more beautiful morning never rose on Winchester than on this auspicious day. Magnificent preparations had been made for the event. Two triumphal arches spanned the High-street, and all the houses were hung with cloths of gold and silver, velvet and arras, while minstrels were everywhere engaged. The pinnacles of the graceful Cross, which belongs to the time of Henry VI., and still adorns the city, were hung with garlands of flowers, and the statue of Saint Lawrence, placed under its exquisite canopied niche, was garnished with beads, chains, and other articles of goldsmith's work. The conduits ran with white and red wines. All the poor were publicly feasted ; and at night great bon-fires were lighted on the adjacent hills.

The city was fuller of strangers than it had ever been known. Not only were the hostels crowded to overflowing, but the religious houses and colleges were thronged with guests. At an early hour of the day thousands of persons, who had travelled all night, began to arrive from various quarters—from Southampton, from Bishop's Waltham, from Alresford, from Stockbridge, from Romsey, and even from Salisbury—in short, from every place within a circuit of

twenty miles.   These new comers found scant accomoda-
tion, but booths were erected on Saint Giles's Hill, and on
Saint Mary Magdalene's Hill, as during fair-time, to which
they resorted.

Loud reports of ordnance were continually heard from
the batteries of the castle, and the bells of all the churches
pealed joyfully.   As the hour appointed for the ceremony
approached, a grand procession began to enter the cathedral.
First came the mayor and aldermen of Winchester, in
scarlet gowns, followed by the officers of the city, apparelled
in velvet and silk, carrying long staves.   Then, after a short
pause, came thirty gentlemen belonging to the Spanish
ambassadors, clad in doublets of yellow velvet striped with
red.   These were followed by Simon Renard and Don Juan
de Figueroa, both sumptuously apparelled.   Then came a
numerous body of sergeants and officers of arms, and after
them gentlemen, esquires, and knights, all richly attired,
and ranged according to their degrees.   On reaching the
steps leading to the choir, all these passed into the north
transept, which, ere long, was completely filled.   Then came
another long train of gentlemen and esquires belonging to
various noblemen, all in rich liveries of divers colours, and
making a splendid show.   Then came the Duke of Norfolk,
the Earls of Arundel, Sussex, Huntingdon, Shrewsbury,
Pembroke, and Derby, in their robes of estate of crimson
velvet furred with ermine, and powdered according to their
degrees.   All such as were Knights of the Garter wore the
collar and the lesser badge of the order.   These were
followed by the lords of the council in robes of scarlet.
After them came the choir of the cathedral, solemnly singing
as they passed along; then the clergy, in their copes and
gowns; then came the incense-bearers, with great silver
thuribles, censing the way.   Then followed the Bishops of
London, Durham, Ely, Lincoln, Chichester, and other
prelates, in copes and mitres.   After them came two priests,
each bearing a large silver cross, followed by another priest
with a crosier.   Next came Gardiner himself, in his full
pontificals.

Before proceeding, let us cast an eye around the interior
of the cathedral, and note the extraordinary splendour of
its decorations.   The mighty pillars lining each side of the

broad nave were covered to the height of twelve feet with crimson velvet, entwined with golden wreaths, while the intercolumniations were filled up with arras and rich hangings. Every pillar was further decked with flags and pennons. The aisles and transepts were likewise adorned with hangings, and the Lady Chapel, wherein the marriage ceremony was about to be solemnised, was hung with cloth of gold. Along the nave, as far as the choir, was stretched a cloth of ray, with rails on either side. Over the high altar was reared an immense silver cross, and the altar itself glittered with silver and gems. From an early hour in the morning, all portions of the cathedral allotted to the public were thronged to excess. Some thousands were present on the occasion. The precincts of the sacred pile were equally crowded, and the wide area in front of the grand western portal presented a dense mass of human beings.

At ten o'clock the royal bridegroom left the deanery, attended by the whole of his grandees, whose gorgeous habiliments glittered with priceless jewels. Cloth of ray had been laid down from the deanery to the great western entrance of the cathedral, and on this Philip and his nobles walked. Their path was further protected by rails, outside of which archers and halberdiers were stationed.

Philip's bridal attire was magnificent, and attracted universal admiration. His doublet and hose were of white satin, richly embroidered with gold, and over all he wore a gorgeous mantle of cloth of gold, presented to him by the Queen, and thickly covered with pearls and precious stones. His white velvet cap was studded with diamonds, rubies, and emeralds. Over his shoulders he wore the collar of the Garter, while the lesser badge of the order encircled his knee. Splendid, however, as was his attire, it hardly outshone the habiliments of his grandees, all of whom wore the collar of the Golden Fleece, or the insignia of some other order.

As Philip entered the cathedral with his train, trumpets were loudly sounded, and the martial bruit continued as he advanced along the nave. Midway he was met by the Earl of Arundel and other nobles, and ceremoniously conducted to a traverse, prepared for him in the south transept, where he awaited the Queen's arrival.

This was not long delayed. A peal of artillery, accompanied by reiterated shouts, announced that her Majesty had reached the precincts of the cathedral. Already, indeed, the foremost of her immediate attendants were passing through the grand portal. First came Garter King at Arms in his gorgeous tabard, followed by the other heralds, and attended by a band of trumpeters, with their silver clarions at their lips. Then came the Grand Chamberlain, Sir John Gage, his lofty figure seen to great advantage in a scarlet robe open before, and edged with ermine. Sir John Gage had the collar of the Garter round his neck, and carried his wand of office in his hand. He was accompanied by the Vice-Chamberlain, Sir Henry Jerningham, likewise in his robes of office, and bearing a white wand. Then followed a long train of pages attired in liveries of white and blue satin, which had a charming effect. Then followed the three gigantic yeomen of the guard, in scarlet, with the royal badge embroidered at the front and back of their doublets.

Fresh acclamations from without, continued by the crowd within the cathedral, proclaimed the entrance of the Queen. Mary walked beneath a canopy of cloth of gold, the gilt staves of which were borne by four knights, chosen for the purpose from their goodly presence, attired in crimson satin, with points of blue and red on their sleeves.

The Queen was arrayed in a gown of white cloth of tissue, the stomacher of which was encrusted with diamonds and precious stones, and her mantle of crimson velvet, bordered with ermine, and embroidered with gold, was borne by six noble dames, all magnificently attired. Her hair was unbound, as was then the custom of brides—and a beautiful custom it was—and on her head she wore a coif, encircled with gold, and studded with orient pearls and gems. Mary marched with a firm step along the nave, and really presented a very majestic appearance. She was followed by a long train of ladies, whose sweeping velvet mantles, furred and embroidered, were borne by pages in rich liveries.

As the Queen advanced along the body of the cathedral, Philip, who had been apprised of her coming, and, indeed, could not be unaware of it from the braying of trumpets and shouting, came from the traverse with his retinue, and met her just as she reached the steps of the choir. Saluting her with a warm demonstration of affection that savoured little of ceremony, he took her hand, and they ascended the steps together, Sir John Gage and the Vice-Chamberlain preceding them.

At this moment Gardiner and the other prelates came forth from the choir, and while the royal pair were standing there with the Bishop of Winchester, in full view of the immense assemblage, Don Juan de Figueroa, attended by Simon Renard, came towards them, and, bending the knee to Philip, presented a scroll to him.

"What means this, your excellency?" demanded the Prince, with a well-feigned look of astonishment.

"It means, your Highness," replied Figueroa, as he arose, "that your august sire, the Emperor, deeming it beneath the dignity of so high and mighty a sovereign as the Queen of England to wed with one of rank inferior to her own, has by this act resigned to your Highness the crown of Naples and Sicily, with the Duchy of Milan, and divers other seats and signories. From this moment, Sire, you are King of Naples, and as such her Majesty's equal."

"A right noble and gracious act, and worthy of my great father!" exclaimed Philip. "Does not your Majesty think so?"

"Nobly done, indeed, Sire!" cried Mary. "I joy that you are King of Naples, but you could not be dearer to me than as Prince of Spain."

"The Emperor's great and generous act must be made known to the entire assemblage," said Gardiner.

"Be that task mine," rejoined Simon Renard.

Whereupon silence being called by sound of trumpet, the Spanish ambassador advanced towards the edge of the steps, and in a loud voice, distinctly heard by the thousands congregated within the nave, announced what the Emperor had done for his son.

Tremendous acclamations followed, and the roof resounded with cries of "Long live the Emperor! Long live the King of Naples!"

No sooner had Simon Renard retired than Garter King at Arms advanced with a couple of trumpeters, and proclaimed the styles and titles of the two sovereigns in the following formula :—

" Philip and Mary, by the grace of God, King and Queen of England, France, Naples, Jerusalem, and Ireland; Defenders of the Faith; Princes of Spain and Sicily; Archdukes of Austria; Dukes of Milan, Burgundy, and Brabant; Counts of Hagsburg, Flanders, and Tyrol."

This proclamation being made, the trumpets were sounded, and the acclamations of the assemblage were renewed.

Preceded by Gardiner and the other prelates, ceremoniously marshalled by the Grand Chamberlain and Vice-Chamberlain, and attended by the principal nobles, English and Spanish, forming an assemblage of unrivalled splendour, the royal pair—now equals in dignity—marched hand in hand to the beautiful Lady Chapel built by Bishop Godfrey de Lucy, where the marriage was solemnised by Gardiner, assisted by the other prelates, the royal bride being given away in the name of the realm by the Marquis of Winchester and the Earls of Pembroke and Derby.

In all respects the ceremony was admirably performed. The prelates gathered round the richly-decked altar, the royal couple kneeling before it on velvet faldstools, the grand assemblage of English and Spanish nobles grouped around, the proud dames of both nations filling the galleries on either side of the chapel—all constituted a superb picture.

The solemnity ended, the royal couple returned to the choir, where a cloth of estate had been prepared for them, beneath which they sat while *Te Deum* was solemnly sung. Here the picture was even grander than that exhibited in the Lady Chapel, because it comprehended so much more of the cathedral. Fortunately, it could be seen by the vast crowd in the nave.

All being concluded, the royal couple quitted the sacred edifice, walking hand in hand beneath the canopy. Before them marched the Earls of Pembroke and Derby, each bearing a sword of state.

In this manner, amid the thunder of artillery, the sounding of trumpets, and the shouts of the crowd, they returned to Wolvesey Castle, where a grand banquet was given, followed by a state ball.

CHAPTER VI.

HOW PHILIP, WITH FOUR-AND-TWENTY NOBLE GUESTS,
DINED AT ARTHUR'S ROUND TABLE IN WINCHESTER
CASTLE; AND HOW THE FEAST ENDED.

THE royal couple sojourned at Wolvesey Castle for
a week, and during that time a series of grand
entertainments were given to all the nobility who
had attended the marriage ceremony. Pageants
were exhibited in the city, and in the pleasant meads
beyond the South-gate sports and pastimes of various kinds
took place—to wit, archery, horse-races, foot-races, throwing
of heavy weights, wrestling, rowing and swimming matches
in the Itchen, bear-baiting, badger-baiting, bull-running, cock-
fighting, duck-hunting in the river, and other diversions, in
which our ancestors delighted. These sports, many of
which were novel to them, afforded much amusement to
Philip and the Spanish nobles.

Mindful of his promise to the Duke of Norfolk to feast
his grace at Arthur's Round Table in Winchester Castle,
Philip appointed the day before his departure for the
banquet. Twenty-four guests were invited, half of whom
were English nobles, and the other half Spanish grandees.

In the midst of the great hall of the castle, which was
more than a hundred and fifty feet long, and with a lofty
roof of open rafters, richly sculptured, was placed

"——the pride of warlike years,
Old Arthur's board—"

in other words, the famous Round table, at whick King Arthur and his illustrious knights had often feasted.

Framed by Uter Pendragon, Arthur's royal sire, who flourished early in the 6th century, or more than twelve hundred years ago, this wondrous table was given by him to King Leodegraunce of Camelyard, who held it in high esteem. When Leodegraunce bestowed his fair daughter, the lovely but erring Guenever, upon Arthur, he sent him at the same time, as the richest present he could bestow, the royal table, causing it to be conveyed by a hundred knights. Enchanted with the gift, Arthur forthwith instituted the order of the Round Table (the earliest military order of knighthood), and had the places appointed for himself and his twenty-four knights blessed by the Archbishop of Canterbury. So runs the legend. But by whomsoever fashioned, the Round Table was at least remarkable for antiquity in the time of Henry VIII., who had it fresh painted for use at the banquet given by him to the Emperor Charles V. It still exists, as we have already intimated, and is constructed of stout oaken planks, painted in parti-coloured rays, on the borders of which

> "Some British pen has sketched the names renowned,
> In marks obscure, of Arthur's deathless peers."

Obscure as are the characters, the names of Sir Tristram, Sir Launcelot, Sir Galahad, Sir Percival, Sir Gawaine, Sir Ector, Sir Bors, and other peerless knights, may be read upon this scroll of fame. In Cromwell's time the Round Table narrowly escaped destruction from the parliamentary soldiers, who never lost an opportunity of committing sacrilege of some kind. They set it up as a target, and perforated it with bullets. In the centre of the board is the Tudor rose, and the sovereign's place is indicated by a full-length portrait of Henry VIII., seated under a canopy with an ermine mantle over his shoulders, and holding the orb and sword.

The great hall in which the Round Table was set was hung with ancient and somewhat faded arras, representing in one place the interview of the twelve Roman knights with Arthur, and in another the renowned British king receiving his sword Excalibur from the Lady of the Lake.

Five-and-twenty suits of armour of colossal size were
placed on stands against the walls, while the intervals were
filled with trophies composed of shields, spears, swords,
battle-axes, maces, and other weapons. The cushion of
each chair was embroidered in letters of gold with the name
of its occupant. A curiously carved oak chair, in which
bluff King Hal had sat was assigned to Philip. On his
right sat the Lord Chancellor, and on the left the Duke of
Norfolk. The place next to Gardiner was allotted to the
Duke of Alva, while Norfolk's neighbour was the Duke of
Medina Celi. In this wise were the twenty-four guests
disposed—English and Spanish nobles alternately.

No diaper covered the capacious board. But it was loaded
with salvers, dishes, goblets, and plates of gold and silver.
Sideboards, also, glittering with plate and drinking vessels,
were ranged around the hall. A multitude of pages, esquires,
and gentlemen were in attendance. The banquet consisted
of five courses, and comprised calvered salmon, stewed
lampries, slices of sturgeon, a porpoise in armour, soused
pike and bream, trout from the Itchen—pronounced delicious
—roast cygnets, a roast heron, wild-boar pie, a roast haunch
of venison, a roast kid, ruffs, dotterels, bitterns, and many
other good things. No restraint was placed upon his guests
by the King, who, by his easy and jovial deportment, seemed
to invite familiarity. The Spanish grandees declared they
had never before seen their royal master so full of mirth,
and the Duke of Norfolk vowed that he equalled the Emperor
in good fellowship. Certes, his Majesty jested as much, and
laughed as heartily as the rest of the company. So infectious
was the merriment, that even the stern features of the Duke
of Alva relaxed into a smile.

At the close of the repast, and as soon as the chargers
and other dishes had been removed, an immense silver bowl,
covered by a lid, was placed upon the table by the three
gigantic yeomen of the guard, Og, Gog, and Magog—a task
not accomplished without some difficulty — amidst the
laughter of the guests, who eyed the stupendous vessel with
astonishment.

"If that bowl be filled with hippocras, Sire," exclaimed
the Duke of Norfolk, "there must be enough liquor within
it to drown us all, or to float a man-of-war."

Before any reply could be made, the attention of the company was attracted by a ringing sound proceeding from the vessel.

All the guests looked towards their royal host as if for explanation.

"I know not what it means," said the King, who appeared as much surprised as the rest. "Take off the lid, and let us see."

The order was obeyed by Og, whose countenance wore a broad grin, and as he raised the cover, the cause of the strange sounds became manifest. In the midst of a sea of hippocras floated a silver boat, in which was seated Xit, in the guise of the Enchanter Merlin, and holding in his hand a silver ladle, with which he had struck the sides of the bowl, to intimate his presence. Raising himself carefully, so as not to upset the frail barque in which he was placed, the dwarf bowed as gracefully as circumstances would permit, to Philip, and said, "Doubtless your Majesty is surprised to see me here, but I trust I shall not incur your sovereign displeasure when I say that my desire to be present at your banquet led me to adopt this expedient to gain admittance. Besides, I may be useful," he added, flourishing the ladle.

"Thou art welcome, thou sprightly imp," replied Philip, laughing. "Keep our goblets filled, that is all we require from thee."

"Gramercy, Sire, I will endeavour to perform the office of butler to your entire satisfaction," replied Xit, filling the cup extended to him by the King.

After all the guests had been served with great expedition and skill, Philip said to the dwarf, "Now, Sirrah, a toast."

"I am greatly honoured by the command, Sire," replied Xit. "My toast, I am well assured, will be drunk with enthusiasm, both by your Majesty and your illustrious guests. I will give your royal consort, and our most gracious mistress, the Queen. May Heaven shed its choicest blessings upon her!"

"Well said, thou merry knave!" cried Philip. "No toast could be more agreeable to us. My lords, we will dedicate this cup to the Queen."

The toast was rapturously drunk by the assemblage, but just as the goblets were emptied an unexpected incident

10

occurred. In the excitement of the moment, and while waving the ladle, Xit lost his balance, and plunged head-foremost into the vinous flood beneath him. As he emerged the next moment, his half-drowned appearance caused shouts of laughter from the company, which were echoed by all the pages, esquires, and other attendants.

"Marry, thou hast had a bath such as few men have enjoyed," observed Philip, laughing.

"I would rather it had been water, Sire," spluttered Xit. "I shall never enjoy the flavour of hippocras again. I pray you let me be taken hence."

"There is no hurry," cried the Duke of Norfolk, laughing immoderately. "We cannot let thee go yet. Make the most of thy position, and quaff thy fill. The wine is spoiled for all but thee."

"Were I to quaff more than I have already done, I should become a sorry spectacle, your grace, and might offend this noble company," observed Xit. "I have no desire to die the death of the Duke of Clarence."

"Take him hence," said Philip, who thought the jest had lasted long enough; "but let him not out of the bowl till its contents be emptied."

On this, the three giants, lifting the mighty bowl from the table, conveyed it to another part of the hall, where they set it down. The King's commands were scrupulously obeyed. Notwithstanding Xit's piteous entreaties to be set free, he was detained a prisoner till the whole of the hippocras had been drunk. To this end the giants lent their best assistance, but before it could be fully accomplished, the King and his noble guests had departed. So ended the banquet at Arthur's Round Table.

Next day Philip and Mary, attended by their whole court, and by the Spanish grandees, quitted Winchester, and proceeded by easy stages to Windsor.

CHAPTER VII.

THE court had not been long at Windsor Castle, ere most of the Spanish grandees who had accompanied Philip, finding that owing to the terms of the marriage-treaty, which were strictly enforced by Gardiner and the council, no posts could be given them in the government, quitted England in disgust. As the Duke of Alva took leave of the King, he observed, " I am loth to leave your Majesty with this people, but as you have no present need of my services, while I may be of use to the Emperor, I deem it best to go."

" Have no fears for me, my lord Duke," replied Philip. " I am perfectly secure. I have paid a heavy price for the support of the English nobles—but I think I can count upon it."

" Do not trust them, Sire. The English nobles are treacherous as corrupt, and will fall off when most needed. Had your Majesty but listened to me, and pursued the bold course I suggested, you might now be King of England— not in name, merely, but in reality. It is not yet too late. Say the word and I remain."

" No ; you must go, Alva. I grieve to part with you, as with my other nobles, but your presence here is prejudicial to my plans."

" I see not how that can be, Sire. You yield too much to English prejudices. Pardon me for saying so, but you ought to be lord and master in your own house, and not subject to your wife—albeit she is a Queen."

"Why so I am, Alva," replied the King, smiling. "Her Majesty refuses me nothing."

"Except the matrimonial crown, Sire," said the Duke, bluntly. "She will not give you that. Neither will she place the supreme power of government in your hands, nor cause you to be declared presumptive heir to the crown."

"She dare not do so, Alva," observed Philip, coldly.

"I know not that," said the Duke. "For such a result all should be dared."

"Her Majesty will accede to my wishes in due time," said the King. "Should there be an heir to the throne, all difficulties will be removed."

"Ay, if there should—but the event may never occur," cried Alva, impatiently. "Again I say, why wait? With such a prize within your grasp, why hesitate to seize it? Oh! that your Majesty would leave the work to me."

"I could not trust you," said the King. "You would ruin all by precipitancy. My plan is slow, but sure. Farewell, my lord Duke. The saints give you a good journey to Brussels. Commend me in all love and duty to the Emperor, and say that in due time I trust he will have a grandson."

"Would I could add that heresy were completely extirpated from the realm, and the papal supremacy re-established," observed Alva.

"That will follow immediately on the arrival of Cardinal Pole," said Philip. "Most of the English nobles and men of wealth, as you know, have shared in the monstrous spoliation of the Church that occurred during the two previous reigns, and these persons will never acknowledge the supreme authority of the Pontiff, unless their ill-gotten possessions are secured to them. Until this point be conceded by his Holiness, the Lord Chancellor assures me it will be futile and even dangerous to propose the measure. Mauriquez has been dispatched to Rome to argue the matter with the Pope, and, till the question be decided, Cardinal Pole must be detained at Brussels. This you will explain to the Emperor."

"Humph!" exclaimed Alva. "I half hope the Pope

may refuse your Majesty's request, and then you will be compelled to have recourse to me to force these robbers to disgorge their plunder. 'Tis a dreadful wrong to the Church."

"I feel the injustice as keenly as you can do, Alva," rejoined the King; "but since the grievance cannot be redressed, it must be borne in patience."

"Well, we must hope for better days, when these plunderers will meet their deserts on the scaffold and the gibbet," said Alva. "I now take my leave of your Majesty." So saying, he departed.

That any assumption of regal power on the part of Philip would be resisted, was shown by a slight incident which occurred shortly afterwards. On the King's installation as a Knight of the Garter, in order to give greater importance to the proceeding, the royal arms of England were taken down in St. George's Chapel by the chief herald, at the instance of Simon Renard, and the arms of Castile and Aragon set up in their stead. But as soon as the change was discovered by the Earl of Arundel and Sir John Gage, they sharply reprimanded the herald, and, at the risk of offending Philip, caused the Spanish arms to be forthwith taken down and those of England restored.

Philip had many secret enemies, but none so active or so dangerous as the French ambassador. Notwithstanding the ill success of his previous plot, and the narrow escape he had run, De Noailles continued his intrigues among the factious and discontented. As Mary could not refuse to receive him at court without embroiling herself with France, he had opportunities of carrying out a design which he had conceived, of occasioning a rupture between the King and Queen. Aware of Philip's infidelities, and of the Queen's jealousy of disposition, he did not despair of accomplishing this project. By means of spies, who were well paid for the service, he kept a strict watch over the King's proceedings, hoping to make some discovery that might serve his purpose.

From a cause which we shall proceed to explain, Philip began to lose the popularity he had acquired on his first arrival. Though he continued extremely affable and condescending to the English nobles—far more so than he was to those of his own nation—and though he made them large gifts, in the hope of securing their friendship, he never could overcome their distrust, which was kept alive by the subtle practices of the French ambassador. Moreover, Spanish usages began to prevail at court, and these were highly distasteful to the English. Greater etiquette and formality were observed. The doors were not thrown open as they used to be, and those who desired an audience of their Majesties, even on matters of urgency, were detained long in the ante-chambers. So that although the King did not meddle with the government—at all events not directly—it was soon felt that the court was absolutely under his control. None but those high in his favour were admitted to him without much form and ceremony, which was especially irksome to the older English nobles, who had enjoyed easy access to the sovereign in the reign of Henry VIII. And there was every appearance that this strictness would increase rather than diminish.

Philip's public entry into London was not made until the latter end of August. Preparatory to the ceremony, the royal pair removed to Richmond Palace, where they stayed for two or three days, and then proceeded by water in a state barge, attended by all their retinue in other barges, to the Bishop of Winchester's palace at Southwark. They were received with great ceremony by Gardiner, and passed the night under his roof.

Next day, accompanied by a numerous and magnificent *cortége*, comprising all the chief officers of the court, together with many of the nobility, the royal pair passed over London Bridge into the City. The Queen, whose splendid attire of cloth of gold blazed with jewels of inestimable value, sat in a gilt chariot, drawn by six horses in housings of white satin, embroidered with gold, ridden by pages of honour in crimson satin. Her Majesty was accompanied by three of her principal ladies. Mounted on his fiery Andalusian barb, which was trapped with black taffetas, guarded with silver lace, Philip appeared to great advantage in his black velvet doublet, short mantle bordered with pearls, and berret with black and white plumes. He was attended by fifty horsemen in trappings of crimson velvet, with the arms of Spain embroidered on them in gold, with edges of silk and gold, and fringe of the same. Besides these, there were fifty pages in liveries of carnation satin, passmented with silver and black lace, and black silk caps, adorned with carnation and black plumes. A troop of halberdiers in full equipments formed the vanguard of the royal procession, and another brought up the rear. In front of the *cortége* rode a large band of musicians, consisting of trumpets, clarions, kettle-drums, and other martial instruments. These musicians were accoutred in scarlet mandillions, guarded with gold, and had the royal badge on the front and at the back. The pennons of the trumpets and clarions were likewise embroidered with the royal arms, and all the horses were caparisoned in scarlet satin, guarded with gold lace. As the procession passed over London Bridge, a loud peal of ordnance burst from the Tower batteries, and was continued by the guns of all the ships moored off the wharves.

At the gate then defending the entrance to the City from the bridge, the three gigantic yeomen of the guard were stationed, who reverently saluted the King and Queen as they passed by, and at the conduit of Gracechurch Street, which had been newly decorated for the occasion, was a large painting representing the nine Worthies. Noticeable amongst these august personages was Henry VIII., who was portrayed in armour. The idea of the artist had been to depict the great Defender of the Faith in the act of presenting the Bible to his son and successor, Edward VI., the sacred volume being inscribed in large characters *Verbum Dei;* but the device gave great offence to Gardiner, who ordered the limner, on pain of losing his ears, to obliterate this part of the picture, which he accomplished more effectually than tastefully, by brushing out the King's right hand.

In Cheapside there was another large picture, representing the " Five Philips "—namely, Philip of Macedon, Philip the Emperor, Philip the Bold, Philip the Good, and Philip, Prince of Spain and King of England.

Many pageants were exhibited to the King and Queen on their way through the City. All the houses were decorated with cloth of gold and silver, arras and velvet, while thousands flocked forth to welcome the Queen and her royal consort. Owing to the frequent stoppages, the progress of

intelligence, and directed that Constance should be brought to Hampton Court, where her Majesty was then sojourning, in order that she might confer with the unhappy maiden in person, and see how far the mischief had proceeded, and what could be done for its cure.

Constance accordingly was summoned from Southampton, and had several private interviews with the Queen, who soon discovered that Derrick Carver had succeeded in effecting her conversion. By the advice of her Majesty's confessor, who felt sure he could bring back the stray lamb to the fold, Constance was detained for a time within the palace.

No mention having been made of this proceeding to Philip, it was only by accident that he became aware that Constance was an inmate of the palace. On making the discovery, he went, wholly unattended, to the apartments wherein he had ascertained she was lodged. On entering the ante-chamber, he found old Dorcas, who appeared terrified at the sight of him, and who, without stopping to be questioned, exclaimed that her young mistress was unable to see his Majesty.

"But I must see her," rejoined Philip, authoritatively. "Go in at once, mistress, and tell her I am here."

Seeing from the King's manner that remonstrance would be useless, the old woman complied, and drawing aside a piece of tapestry, entered the inner room. In another moment she returned, and prayed his Majesty to step in.

Passing through the tapestry, Philip entered the room, where he found Constance alone. She was attired in black, and looked pale as death, and was evidently greatly agitated. She made the King a profound reverence, but did not raise her eyes towards him.

"So you have been here for some days, I find," cried Philip, "and have allowed me to remain in ignorance of your presence, though you know how anxious I have been to behold you again. I began to fear I had lost you for ever, and that you had really carried your threat into execution, and buried your charms in a convent."

"A great change has come over me, Sire," rejoined Constance. "I have wholly abandoned that intention."

"I rejoice to hear it," cried the King. "I dispatched

Father Jerome to you, and I suppose his arguments prevailed?"

"No, Sire," rejoined Constance. "I have been turned aside from my purpose by better arguments than any Father Jerome could employ."

"Nay, I care not who dissuaded you," replied Philip, "I am content with the resolution you have taken. I have been wretched—most wretched, since we parted, Constance."

"Your Majesty cannot have been half so wretched as I have been," she rejoined. "However, I have in some degree recovered my peace of mind, and I beseech you not to plunge me into misery again."

"I must tell you how passionately I adore you," exclaimed the King. "The love which you kindled in my breast when I first beheld you burns fiercer than ever, and cannot be extinguished. By my hopes of Paradise, fair Constance, I love you—only you."

"Cease, Sire, cease!" cried Constance. "I cannot listen to you—I must not."

"But you must—you shall listen to me," cried Philip, still more passionately. "You *shall* hear how constantly I have thought of you. Your image has been ever before me. I have tried to stifle my love, but without success. It has mastered me, as it masters me now. Behold me at your feet, sweet Constance!" he added, prostrating himself before her; "not the King—but your suppliant—your slave!"

"Rise, Sire, I intreat you, from this unworthy posture," cried Constance. "Think of your duty to the Queen—all your love should be given to her."

"Such love as I bear for you, sweet Constance, I cannot give to her Majesty," rejoined Philip, "for as I have just declared, you have sole possession of my heart. You need fear no rival in the Queen."

"Oh! hush, Sire—hush!" exclaimed Constance, with the utmost alarm. "You are overheard! ha!—her Majesty!"

"The Queen here!" exclaimed Philip, springing to his feet.

And turning, he perceived that the Queen was pushing aside the hangings, and about to enter the room. Close behind her Majesty, whose looks proclaimed the depth of her indignation, came Sir John Gage. For a moment, Philip seemed embarrassed, but he quickly recovered himself. Mary regarded her faithless consort with flashing eyes, but repressed the bitter reproaches that rose to her lips, though her heart swelled almost to bursting, and the veins on her brow distended with rage.

It was an awful moment, and Sir John Gage looked greatly troubled. The silence was broken by Constance, who flung herself at the Queen's feet, exclaiming :

"Do not judge me harshly, gracious Madam. Do not suppose that I have failed in duty to your Majesty. Do not deem that I have been a consenting party to this meeting. On my soul I have not. The King will confirm my assertion. Speak, Sire, speak ! "

Unable to resist this appeal, Philip said, "It is the truth, Madam. I alone am to blame."

"You hear, gracious Madam," cried Constance, "his Majesty acquits me. My sole crime is, that I have unhappily attracted his attention."

"And that is crime enough, minion," said Mary, regarding her fiercely. "You shall expiate the offence with your life. I will show you no mercy. Call in the guard, Sir John," she added to Gage.

"Take heed how you obey that order, Sir John," interposed Philip. "I am equal in authority here, and I forbid you. Your Majesty will do well to pause," he added, with stern significance, to the Queen, "ere a breach be made between us that cannot be closed."

"Oh ! do not let me be the cause of misunderstanding between yourself and the King your consort, gracious Madam," cried Constance. "I am not worth it. If my life will restore the peace I have unhappily disturbed, take it. I will lay it down freely."

"It will be best to let her go, Madam," observed Sir John Gage in a low tone.

There was a pause, during which it was evident that Mary was struggling hard with her feelings. Constance, who still remained in a kneeling posture, watched her countenance with the keenest anxiety. Folding his arms on his breast, Philip looked on coldly. Mary at length spoke.

"You have said truly, minion," she observed. "You are not worth a quarrel between the King and myself. His Majesty has sought to screen you, by taking all blame upon himself, but I am not to be deceived. If nothing more, you have been indiscreet."

"Indiscretion is a very venial fault," rejoined Philip. "But even that cannot justly be laid to this damsel's charge. Since her presence annoys you, let her leave the palace and return to her family."

"She *shall* leave the palace, and that without delay," rejoined Mary. "But she will be more secure in some religious house than with her family."

"I pray you let me return to my father," implored Constance, who had risen to her feet. "I will die rather than give you further cause of anxiety. But, as your Majesty is aware, I have quitted the Church of Rome."

"A heretic!" exclaimed Philip, aghast at the unexpected declaration. "To what is this sad change attributable? When I first beheld you, you were zealous and devout."

"I am zealous and devout still, I trust, Sire," rejoined Constance. "But my eyes have been opened, and I reject as idolatrous and superstitious the worship which I formerly practised."

"I lament to hear it," replied Philip, with a look of pious horror. My confessor, Father Alfonso, shall take you in hand. He will convince you of your errors."

"Nothing will shake me," said Constance. "My belief is fixed. I would rather endure martyrdom than peril my salvation."

"Your firmness may be put to the test," observed the Queen severely. "Your Majesty, methinks," she added to Philip, "will scarcely attempt to defend her now."

"I am horror-stricken!" exclaimed the King. "I could not have believed in so sudden and sad a defection. Who is the author of this evil work? To whose baneful counsel have you listened? Is it from the would-be assassin, Derrick Carver, that you have imbibed these pernicious opinions?"

"I have heard the truth from his lips, Sire," returned Constance.

"I guessed as much," said Philip; "and it is from this

polluted source that you expect the water of life to flow. I did not believe you capable of such weakness. I can no longer oppose her Majesty's design of placing you in some religious house, where discipline and good counsel may bring you back to the faith from which you have swerved."

"If mild measures prove ineffectual, others must be adopted," observed Mary.

"Do with me as you will," said Constance, resignedly. "I am in your Majesty's hands, and am prepared to seal my faith with my blood."

"Were anything wanting to convince me of the necessity of utterly extirpating heresy from the realm, I should now be satisfied," remarked Mary. "An example shall be made of this mischievous Derrick Carver. He shall be delivered over to the religious tribunals, to be dealt with according to his deserts. Prepare for immediate departure," she added to Constance. "I myself will give instructions respecting you."

Constance bowed submissively.

By this time the Queen's anger towards her consort had somewhat subsided, and she said to him in a somewhat kindlier tone, "Your Majesty can have no further business here. I will pray you to accompany me."

Philip bowed. As he quitted the chamber with the Queen, he cast a parting glance at Constance, who remained in the same humble attitude, with her eyes fixed upon the ground.

CHAPTER IX.

IN WHAT MANNER CONSTANCE FLED FROM HAMPTON COURT
PALACE.

THE unhappy girl was still alone in the chamber, having scarcely moved since the departure of the royal pair, when the fold of tapestry that masked the doorway was drawn quickly aside, and Osbert Clinton stood before her, pale and agitated.

"I have come to save you," he cried, abruptly. "I know what has occurred. The Queen designs to send you to a convent."

"True," she rejoined, sadly. "Her Majesty may deal with me as she thinks fit. But all efforts to compel me to return to the faith I have abjured will prove ineffectual."

"But this is not the real danger by which you are threatened," he continued. "The King will not permit her Majesty's intentions to be carried out, and has ordered me to convey you away privately to a secure retreat, where there will be no risk of discovery by his jealous consort. You will escape the convent, but only to encounter a worse fate."

"I will die rather than submit," she cried, despairingly. "Pity me, kind Heaven! pity me!"

"Hear me, Constance," he cried. "The avowal I am about to make is wrung from me by the circumstances in which you are placed. I love you to desperation, and would plunge my sword in Philip's heart rather than you should fall a sacrifice to him. Dismiss all doubts, and trust yourself with me. I will lay down my life for you."

"If I consent, whither would you take me?" she demanded. "But no! I cannot—dare not fly with you."

"You wrong me by these suspicions, Constance," he cried, half reproachfully. "Loving you as I do, could I do aught to injure you?"

"But the King himself professes to love me ——"

"He loves you not — his vows are false," interrupted Osbert, bitterly. "Shun him as you would shame and dishonour. If you have any love for him, tear it from your breast—no matter what the pang!—it can only lead to guilt and remorse."

"I have no love for him now," she rejoined; "and if for a moment I yielded credence to his vows and passionate declarations, I have expiated the offence by tears and contrition. My constant prayer has been never to behold him more."

"All further peril may be averted if you will confide in me. Give me a husband's right to defend you, and not all the world shall tear you from me. You cannot return to your father. He would not dare to give you shelter. And to enable me to watch over and protect you without damage to your fair fame, we must be bound together by sacred ties."

"Speak of this hereafter," she rejoined. "You have convinced me of your sincerity, and I will trust you. Take me hence—whither I care not—so I am freed from the King."

"Come then," rejoined Osbert. "No one will stay us. I have an order from the King, which will prevent all hindrance."

"But you will endanger yourself by the step you are about to take," she said, hesitating.

"Heed not that," he rejoined. "I am prepared for the worst. Come!"

They were about to quit the chamber, when they were stopped by old Dorcas, to whom her mistress hastily explained the necessity of flight.

"I can help you in this extremity," exclaimed the old woman. "I will show you a ready means of leaving the palace without traversing the corridor. While lifting the hangings against yon wall, I discovered a secret door opening upon a starcase, which I had the curiosity to examine, and found it led through a small postern to the garden. I meant to tell you of my discovery."

"You could not have reserved it for a better moment," said Osbert. "Adopt this plan, it will be safest," he added to Constance.

"Heaven be praised!" she exclaimed. "I can now escape without imperilling you!"

"Think not of me," he rejoined. "Pass through the secret door at once, but do not enter the garden till night, when I will meet you in the yew-tree alley. Meanwhile, I will make preparations for your conveyance to a place of safety. Delay not, I beseech you. Each moment is precious."

Thus urged, Constance snatched up a mantle and a few other articles, and declared she was ready to depart; whereupon Osbert drew back the hangings, while old Dorcas touched the spring of the secret door, which was artfully contrived in the oak panels. Casting a grateful look at her preserver, Constance disappeared with her old attendant.

Another minute and it would have been too late. Scarcely had the tapestry fallen to its place, when sounds proclaimed that several persons had entered the ante-chamber, and the next moment Sir John Gage presented himself, accompanied by Father Alfonso. They both looked surprised on finding Osbert alone.

"You are too late, Sir John!" cried the young man, forcing a laugh. "The bird has flown."

"Flown! not out of the window, I presume; though I see not how she can otherwise have escaped," rejoined Gage. "She cannot have passed through the corridor, or we must have met her. Where can she be?"

"Nay, I can give you no information, Sir John," rejoined Osbert. "On my arrival here a few moments ago, I found the room vacant, that is all I know."

"She appears to have taken her old attendant with her," said Gage. "However, we shall easily discover her hiding-place. She cannot have quitted the palace."

"Stay! is there no closet in the room?" said Father Alfonso, peering round. "Ha! here is one—but it is empty," he added, on opening it.

"We must seek her elsewhere," observed Gage. "I shall

not be sorry if she has got away altogether," he added in a low tone to Osbert, as they quitted the room, followed by Father Alfonso. "But what will her Majesty say to it?"

"Rather, what will the King say," rejoined Osbert. "He will be furious."

"It may be his contrivance," remarked Gage. "I suspect you know more about the matter than you choose to tell, and could find the damsel if you thought proper."

All search for the fugitives proved fruitless. The secret staircase was not detected.

When Constance's disappearance was reported to the Queen, her Majesty was greatly irritated, and her suspicions fell upon the King. Philip was equally angry, and equally at fault, attributing Constance's evasion to the Queen's agency, and believing that her Majesty had had recourse to this stratagem to baffle his designs.

Not until after midnight, and when all was still within the palace, did Osbert Clinton venture into the garden. Fortunately the night was dark and cloudy. On hearing his footsteps, Constance and her attendant came from out the alley in which they were hidden, and followed him noiselessly along various grassy paths to a gate opening upon the park.

In a few moments more the party had reached the banks of the Thames, when Osbert gave a signal. Immediately the plash of oars was heard on the other side of the river, and a wherry, rowed by two men, could be descried through the gloom, pulling towards them.

Constance and her old attendant were quickly placed within the boat by Osbert, and this was no sooner accomplished, than the boatman, without a moment's delay, pushed off, and dashed swiftly down the stream.

Osbert listened till the sound of the oars could no longer be heard, and then returned with a light heart to the palace, entering it as secretly as he had come forth.

As Osbert had foreseen, messengers were dispatched by the Queen to Southampton, to ascertain whether Constance had sought refuge with her father. If so, she was instantly to be brought back. After three days' absence, the messengers returned, bringing with them Master Tyrrell. He could give no account of his daughter, but pledged himself to deliver her up at once to the Queen in case she might reappear. On this understanding he was immediately released.

Another circumstance which occurred at this juncture contributed to heighten the Queen's displeasure. She had instructed the messengers sent to Southampton to arrest Derrick Carver; but on the very day before their arrival, the enthusiast, who by this time had recovered from his wounds, had quitted the hospital of the Domus Dei, and, it was thought, had passed over to France, as a vessel had just sailed thither from the port. In whatever way it was accomplished, Carver's escape was a source of vexation to the Queen.

CHAPTER X.

WHERE CONSTANCE FOUND A PLACE OF REFUGE.

AN old habitation situated on the banks of the river between the gardens of Durham-place and the Savoy Hospital, then recently restored by Mary, served Constance as an asylum. Thither she had been brought, after remaining a few days in a little hostel near Richmond.

The house had been long uninhabited, and was in a very dilapidated state. At the back there was a tolerably extensive garden, facing the river, and containing several fine trees, but, like the house to which it appertained, it was much neglected. Three or four back rooms, looking upon the garden, had been hastily furnished; but no change was made in the front of the habitation, for fear of exciting suspicion. Luckily, the garden was not overlooked, being bounded on the west by the high walls of Durham-place.

Though shut out from the world, Constance was far from finding her present mode of existence wearisome. Her time was fully employed either in her devotions, in reading, or in some feminine occupation. She never ventured forth except into the garden, and only took exercise there at night.

Of necessity, Osbert's visits were rare, and stealthily paid. As the safest course, he approached the house by water, landed in a wherry at the stairs of Durham-place, and then scaled the garden wall. These short and stolen visits, which were always paid at night, could not be otherwise than agreeable to Constance, and she looked forward to his coming with interest; and if, as sometimes chanced, he did not appear at the usual hour, she retired sadly.

Under such circumstances, it will not appear surprising that the gratitude felt by the damsel for her preserver should ripen into a warmer feeling. After the first ardent declaration of his passion made to her, Osbert refrained for a while from renewing his suit; but at length, emboldened by the evident change in her manner, he ventured again, with as much impassioned earnestness as before, to pour forth his protestations of affection, coupled with entreaties to her consent to a speedy union.

To these oft-repeated solicitations she at last replied that she would not attempt to disguise her feelings, but would frankly own that he was now absolute master of her heart, yet still there was a serious obstacle to their marriage.

"An obstacle?" exclaimed Osbert. "Of what nature? Can it not be overcome? Speak! speak!"

"Herein, then, it lies," she rejoined. "Our creeds are different. I have abjured the errors and idolatries of Rome, while you still cling to them."

"Granted," replied Osbert; "but this need be no hindrance to our union. I shall not quarrel with you on account of your religion. Who knows," he added lightly, "but that in due time you may convert me?"

"Heaven grant me power to do so!" she exclaimed, fervently. "Oh! that I could withdraw you from the paths of error, and bring you to those of truth. But much as I love you—much as I owe you—till you are converted, I never can be yours. I have scruples of conscience which cannot be overcome. I should not be happy if I felt there was a barrier between us which neither could pass. Better far we should never come together than be hereafter estranged. I could not respect you—could not love you with my whole heart, if you continued a papist."

"But I have said I may possibly be converted," said Osbert.

"Your conversion must take place before our marriage," rejoined Constance. "On that condition alone will I consent."

"Well, then, commence the good work," he said. "I promise to be a patient listener, and will strive to profit by your exhortations."

Gladly she obeyed, and proceeded to employ the arguments which had proved so prevailing in her own case, and with every prospect of success, her influence over her hearer being unbounded.

But though this difficulty was overcome, another arose. Constance declared that her father's sanction to her marriage was indispensable. In vain Osbert remonstrated. She remained firm, and finding she could not be moved, he at last set out for Southampton, to see Master Tyrrell on the subject.

The old merchant was indisposed to listen to him. He was deeply offended with his daughter. He bewailed her apostacy, and declared he would neither receive her under his roof, nor hold any intercourse with her, so long as she entertained heretical opinions. If she returned, he should deliver her to the Queen, in fulfilment of his pledge. As a staunch Romanist, he could not conscientiously support a heretic, even though she were his own flesh and blood. Let Constance recant the religious opinions she had so imprudently adopted, and he would receive her with open arms. Till such time, she must not come near him. He concluded his tirade by refusing consent to the marriage.

Deeply disappointed at his want of success, Osbert returned to London. On seeking Constance's place of shelter, he found to his surprise, that there was a guest in the house. This was Derrick Carver, who it will be remembered, disappeared from Southampton just before the order for his arrest arrived, and had escaped, as was supposed, to France. Instead of flying his country, however, Carver had proceeded along the coast to his native place, Brightelmstone, where he remained for a short time, but, fearing discovery, he removed to Lewes, and thence to London.

Being nearly destitute, he had endured great hardship, and was driven almost to extremity, when he accidentally met old Dorcas, who was purchasing provisions, and following her, made himself known, as soon as he could do so with safety. Touched by his miserable condition, the kind-hearted old dame took him home with her. He was joyfully received by Constance, and offered an asylum, which he gratefully accepted.

Such a guest, it will be easily conceived, was by no means

agreeable to Osbert, and he would gladly have got rid of him, had it been possible. Carver's presence introduced a new element of danger by increasing the chances of discovery, while his society had a very perceptible effect upon Constance's spirits and manner. Before his arrival, she had quite regained her serenity. But the sternness and austerity of the religious fanatic had cast a gloom over her, which could not be dispelled. The greater part of her time was passed in prayer, in the perusal of godly books, or in listening to Carver's exhortations.

Osbert was obliged to inform her that he had failed in obtaining her father's consent, but he earnestly besought her to fulfil her promise, and make him happy by becoming his bride.

Before assenting, she consulted Derrick Carver, who at once decided that under such circumstances the marriage could not take place. She must perforce wait. The enthusiast's aim seemed to be to alienate her thoughts from things of this world, and wean her, as he said, from all carnal affections. No wonder Osbert regarded him with dislike.

But the unhappy lover had another and more serious cause of disquietude. He had trusted that distractions of various kinds would efface Constance's image from the King's breast. But he was deceived. Though constantly engaged in some little affair of gallantry, concerning which he made no secret to Osbert, Philip often spoke of her, and in terms showing that his passion was unabated. Osbert's jealous rage at these confidences well-nigh caused him to betray himself, and his anger was not lessened when the King expressed his firm conviction that Constance must sooner or later fall into his power. Though Osbert deemed such a mischance improbable, the apprehension of it filled him with uneasiness.

One day Philip, who treated him with great familiarity, jestingly remarked :—

"So you have got some secret love affair on hand, I hear, and nightly visit your inamorata."

"Who can have told your Majesty this absurd story?" rejoined Osbert, trying to hide his confusion by a laugh.

" No matter how I learnt it," said Philip. "Your manner convinces me it is true. But why should you be ashamed to confess the affair? Most of the young court gallants plume themselves upon their successes, and talk openly of them."

" I am not one of those senseless boasters," observed Osbert, gravely.

" Now, by my faith, you take the matter so seriously, that I am satisfied there is more in it than I supposed," cried the King. "My curiosity is piqued. I must know who has thus enslaved you. Does she belong to the city or the court?"

" Your Majesty will pardon me, but I cannot answer these questions."

" As you please, Sir. I will press you no further. But take care. I shall find out the lady. Nothing escapes me, as you well know. Had you told me who she is, I should have been satisfied, but since you attempt concealment, look to yourself—ha! ha!"

Though Philip laughed while saying this, there was a half-menace in his tone that increased Osbert's alarm.

Apprehensive that his movements might be watched, Osbert refrained that night from his customary visit to Constance, but embarking as usual, instead of proceeding to Durham-place, crossed to the other side of the river. That he had acted wisely, was proved by the fact of another boat following him; and it soon became evident that he was watched. Next night he acted with like caution, but nothing occurred to excite his suspicions.

On the following night, therefore, he ventured to repair to Constance's hiding-place. But, instead of proceeding thither by water, he took a circuitous route, so as to mislead those who watched him, if any such there were.

Constance, who had been extremely uneasy at his unwonted absence, was yet more alarmed when she learned the cause of it; but he succeeded in allaying her fears, by telling her he would speedily find her another and yet more secure asylum, where she would be free from all risk of molestation.

" Methinks you magnify the peril," observed Derrick Carver, " Howbeit, if Mistress Constance elects to quit this house, and seek another place of refuge, I will go with her. You may trust her to my care."

"I am content to do so," replied Osbert. "The danger is greater than you seem to imagine. After what has occurred, I do not think she can tarry longer in London; but by to-morrow night I will have arranged some definite plan, and, meantime, you must prepare for departure."

"I am ready at any moment," cried Constance. "Now—if you deem it expedient."

"Nay, there is no such haste," rejoined Osbert. "By flying without due preparation, you would incur yet greater risk. Two days hence you shall be in perfect safety."

"Alas!" exclaimed Constance, "my mind misgives me, and I fear some dire calamity is in store for me."

"If it be so, you must bear it with fortitude," said Derrick Carver. "It has been my earnest endeavour to strengthen you for such an hour, and I trust my efforts have not been in vain, but that you may be equal to whatever trial you are subjected. Nay, even should you be called upon to attest your devotion to the Gospel by enduring fiery torments, I am assured your courage will not forsake you, but that you will earn a crown of martyrdom."

"Heaven, in its mercy, grant she may be spared any such terrible trial!" exclaimed Osbert, shuddering.

"Rather than deny my faith, and return to that which I have abjured, I will suffer death in any shape," said Constance, "even accompanied by the most cruel torments."

"Your words fill me with joy, daughter," rejoined Carver, "and prove that my teaching has not been thrown away. Thus prepared, you need have no fear."

"I am resigned to whatever may happen," said Constance.

"Self-preservation is as much a duty as any other," said Osbert, "and ought not to be neglected. Though prepared for the worst, you must not expose yourself to needless risk."

"I have said I am ready to depart whenever you may

enjoin me to do so," replied Constance, "and will go wheresoever you may direct."

"I neither oppose her going, nor counsel her tarrying here," said Derrick Carver. "Act as we may, Heaven's designs will be fulfilled."

After some further discourse to the like effect, Osbert took leave, promising to return at the same hour on the following night.

CHAPTER XI.

HOW CONSTANCE'S RETREAT WAS DISCOVERED.

THE next day passed as usual with Constance. At night she was alone in the room, the windows of which have been described as opening upon the garden, and anxiously expecting Osbert's coming. She was seated at a small table, perusing by the light of a single taper, which dimly illuminated the large but scantily-furnished apartment, one of the controversial tracts of the day, and essaying, but in vain, to fix her thoughts on what she read. Ever and anon she arose, and, going to the window, looked forth. The night was profoundly dark, and nothing was discernible except the trees skirting the lawn.

"He is later than usual," she thought, as time went on. "Will he not come?"

Scarcely had she asked herself the question, when she distinctly heard footsteps without, and, concluding it must be Osbert, she passed through the window, and flew to meet him. She could just descry a figure wrapped in a mantle, advancing towards her from beneath a tree.

In another moment this person, whom she took to be her lover, reached her, and seized her hand. Startled by the proceeding, she involuntarily exclaimed, "Is it you?"

"Yes, 'tis I—Osbert," rejoined the other, under his breath.

"I had almost given you up," she returned. "I feared something had occurred to prevent your coming."

The person she addressed made no reply. He had

recognised her voice, and mentally ejaculated, "Can it be possible that it is Constance Tyrrell !"

"You do not answer," she said, after a pause, "and your manner seems strange—very strange."

"'Tis she, by all the saints !" muttered the other. "Let us go in !" he added, drawing her through the open window into the room.

No sooner were they within the influence of the light than the countenance of him she most dreaded on earth was revealed to Constance.

"The King !" she exclaimed, in accents of affright.

"Ay, the King," rejoined Philip, regarding her with fierce exultation. "So, I have found you at last, and where I looked for you least. Little did I deem you were the beauty secluded with such jealous care by Osbert Clinton. Little did I expect, when I took the trouble to ascertain who he kept concealed, that I should be so richly rewarded. Never for a moment did I suppose that he would dare to rob me of my chief treasure. But he shall pay dearly for his audacity and treachery."

"Be not unjust towards him, Sire," rejoined Constance. "In Osbert's place, you would have acted as he has acted. He loved me, and seeing the peril in which I stood, did not hesitate to deliver me."

"And you have not proved ungrateful for the service," retorted Philip, bitterly. "You have requited his devotion. The love refused to me has been bestowed freely on him."

"Osbert's love for me was not dishonourable, Sire," she replied, "and in requiting it I committed no crime. I could not return your Majesty's love without guilt. By this time the passion I was unhappy enough to inspire you with must have subsided, and you will view my conduct less harshly."

"You are mistaken, Madam," rejoined Philip, sternly. "I have never ceased to love you. I cannot regard you with indifference—even though you deserve that I should do so. You are necessary to my happiness. You must— you shall be mine."

"Never !" exclaimed Constance, energetically.

"Hear me," pursued the King; "you are now wholly in

my power. Having found you, be assured I shall not part with you again. I am willing to excuse your conduct—to pardon your lover's disobedience and deceit—nay, more, to continue my favour towards him—but this consideration on my part must be met by complaisance on yours."

"I reject the proposal without a moment's hesitation, Sire," cried Constance, with scorn.

"Then mark what I have to say further," rejoined Philip. "I repeat, you are wholly in my power. Nothing can deliver you. On your decision hangs your lover's life. You—you will cause his immediate arrest—his imprisonment, torture—ay, torture—and death."

"Oh, say not so, Sire!" she cried, all her firmness deserting her. "What has he done to deserve such barbarous treatment?"

"He has dared to disobey me," rejoined Philip. "He has stepped between me and the object of my desires. But for your sake I am content to forego revenge—nay, to heap greater favours on his head. Will you cast him into a dungeon? Will you doom him to torture and death?"

"I cannot save him by the sacrifice you propose, Sire," she rejoined, in tones of anguish. "Neither would he consent to be so saved."

"You have avouched the truth, Constance," exclaimed Osbert, springing through the open window, and placing himself between her and the King. "A thousand deaths rather than such a sacrifice."

"My clemency, I find, is thrown away," said Philip, haughtily. "Yet I will give you a few minutes for reflection. Perhaps your resolution may change." And he moved towards the window.

"It is needless, Sire," rejoined Osbert. "Our determination is taken."

"Then prepare to part for ever," said Philip, sternly. "As to you, audacious and insensate traitor, you shall learn whose anger you have braved. It will be small alleviation, methinks, to your imprisonment to know that your mistress is in my power."

"Fear not the threat, Osbert," said Constance. "I will never yield to him."

"I do not ask your consent," rejoined Philip, derisively. "You are caught in a net from which there is no escape."

"Sooner than this shall be, my sword shall free the country from a tyrant," cried Osbert, plucking his rapier from its sheath.

"Ha! do you dare to raise your hand against me, traitor?" exclaimed Philip, stepping towards him, while Constance flung her arms about her lover, so as to prevent any movement on his part.

"Let him go," continued the King, after a pause, during which he sternly regarded the pair. "He wants the courage to play the assassin."

"You are right, Sire," rejoined Osbert. "Draw, and defend your life."

"Peace, madman!" cried Philip, disdainfully. "Think you I will deign to cross swords with you?"

"Heaven grant me patience, I am driven to the verge of frenzy!" ejaculated Osbert, distractedly.

"At last you are beginning to comprehend your true position," observed Philip, in a taunting tone, "and perceive that you are utterly without help."

"Not utterly," cried a deep voice. And Derrick Carver strode into the room. "Heaven will not desert them in their need. Thou hast uttered threats against them which thou wilt never live to execute. Thou has ventured into this dwelling, but wilt never return from it. My hand failed me when I first struck at thee, but it will not fail me now."

"Make the attempt, then, if thou think'st so, assassin!" cried Philip, keeping his eye steadily upon him.

"Hold!" exclaimed Osbert. "His life is sacred."

"Not in my eyes," rejoined Carver. "It were a crime to my country and to my religion to spare their deadliest foe. He shall die by my hand."

"I say it must not be," cried Osbert. "No harm must be done him. Persist, and I come to his defence."

"Fool! you destroy yourself, and her who should be dearer to you than life, by this mistimed weakness," rejoined Derrick Carver. "Leave him to me."

"Again I say, forbear?" cried Osbert.

"I owe you no obedience, and will show none," retorted

Carver, fiercely. "Have at thy heart, tyrant!" he exclaimed, drawing his sword.

But ere he could make the meditated attack, Philip placed a silver whistle to his lips, and sounding it, Rodomont Bittern, with his sword drawn in his hand, and followed by half a dozen halberdiers, entered through the window. The party instantly fell upon Derrick Carver, and, after a brief struggle, disarmed him.

"By Saint Thomas!" exclaimed Rodomont, regarding the enthusiast with surprise, "this is the murtherous villain whom we caught at Southampton. I cannot be mistaken in his ill-favoured visage."

"I will not deny myself," rejoined the other. "I am Derrick Carver. Heaven has permitted thee to thwart my righteous purpose for the second time."

"A plain proof that thy purpose is damnable, and that Heaven is against thee, thou bloodthirsty villain," rejoined Rodomont. "What is your Majesty's pleasure concerning him?" he asked of the King.

"Take him to the Tower," said Philip.

"It shall be done, Sire. Have you any further commands?"

"Ay," replied Philip. "An hour ago I would not have believed that Osbert Clinton would raise his hand against me, but he has done so, and his life is forfeit. Take him also with you."

"Here is my sword, Sir," said Osbert, delivering it to Rodomont. "I am ready to attend you."

Seating himself at the table, on which writing materials were placed, Philip took a paper from his doublet and proceeded to sign it. Just as he was about to consign the warrant to Rodomont, Constance, who had appeared transfixed with terror, rushed forward and threw herself at his feet.

"Have mercy on him, Sire!" she cried. "Full well I know what will be his fate if sent to the Tower. Oh spare him! spare him!"

"I cannot listen to your entreaties," rejoined Philip, coldly. "He has been guilty of high treason, and must pay the penalty of his offence."

"Do not intercede for me, Constance," said Osbert. "It is useless; he has no pity in his nature."

"I have none for those who deceive me," rejoined Philip, sternly. "Take him hence, Sir," he added to Rodomont. "Here is your warrant."

"Oh no! let him not go thus!" shrieked Constance, starting to her feet, and falling into her lover's arms, "You will not separate us, Sire?"

"Wherefore not?" demanded Philip. "Is he your husband?"

"Ay, in the eyes of Heaven. I am affianced to him," she replied.

"Even were you wedded to him you could not accompany him," rejoined the King. "But no marriage will ever take place between you. Bid him a lasting farewell. You will meet no more on earth."

"No more! You cannot mean it, Sire. Oh, unsay those terrible words!" shrieked Constance.

Philip remained inflexible.

"Calm yourself, Constance," said Osbert. "I heed not what may happen to myself. My sole distress is in leaving you."

"Fear nothing on my account," she rejoined, in a low tone. "Heaven will protect me. Yet I will make one last effort to save you. Oh, Sire," she added, approaching the King, "as you are great and powerful, be generous and merciful. Forgive him. He will offend no more. I am the cause of his disobedience. When I am gone he will be faithful as ever."

"On one condition I will spare him," said Philip, in a low tone.

"I dare not ask your Majesty what that condition is?" rejoined Constance, trembling.

"You may easily guess it," returned Philip. "Be mine."

"Then all hope is over," sighed Constance. "I will die rather than assent."

"So you think now," muttered Philip; "but I will find means to shake your stubbornness. Take hence the prisoners," he added aloud to Rodomont.

"I am equally guilty—if guilt there be," cried Constance, with a loud voice. "I take all present to witness that I utterly reject the doctrines of the Romish Church, and hold its ceremonies to be vain, superfluous, superstitious, and abominable."

" Be silent, imprudent girl," cried Philip.

"Be not afraid to speak out, daughter," cried Derrick Carver. " Truly you have profited by my exhortations."

" I will never forsake my opinions," cried Constance, firmly, "but will maintain them at any tribunal before which I may be brought. After this declaration and confession, your Majesty must send me with the other prisoners."

" You have indeed put it out of my power to befriend you," rejoined Philip, angrily. " Since you ask to be brought before a religious tribunal, you shall have your wish."

" I have succeeded in my design," whispered Constance to Osbert. " I shall not be separated from you. Your Majesty has conferred a boon upon me by this decision," she added to the King, "and I humbly thank you for it. Now, Sir," to Rodomont, "you can take me to the Tower with my friends."

" Is such your Majesty's pleasure ? " demanded Rodomont.

" No," replied Philip. " Let her be conveyed to some place of imprisonment, but not to the Tower."

" An please your Majesty, there is the Lollards' Tower at Lambeth Palace, where heretics are oft confined," observed Rodomont. " No better prison lodgings can be found than the cells therein."

" Are the cells strong and secure ? " demanded the King.

" Marry, as strong and secure as the dungeons of the Tower, Sire," replied Rodomont.

" I have heard of those prison chambers in the Lollards' Tower," rejoined Philip, "but did not bethink me of them at the moment. Take Mistress Constance Tyrrell forthwith to Lambeth Palace, and see her safely bestowed—safely, I say, but with all comfort and convenience that the prison will admit of—d'ye heed ? Take Derrick Carver also thither, and let him be securely lodged. The ecclesiastical court shall deal with him. No intercourse whatever must be allowed between the prisoners."

12

"Your injunctions shall be strictly obeyed, Sire," replied Rodomont.

"I have changed my mind in regard to Osbert Clinton," pursued Philip. "In consideration of the important services he has heretofore rendered me, I am disposed to overlook the grave offence he has committed. He is pardoned."

There was a brief pause, but no word of gratitude escaped Osbert.

"Do you not hear, Sir?" said Rodomont, as he gave back the sword to Osbert. "Have you no thanks for the grace vouchsafed you by his Majesty?"

"The grace is unsolicited by me, and claims no thanks," rejoined Osbert, almost fiercely.

"Leave him alone," said Philip; "his mind is disordered. When the fit has passed, and he is become calm, he will think differently. Away at once to Lambeth Palace with the prisoners."

"Constance!" exclaimed Osbert, rushing towards her.

"Farewell for ever!" she rejoined. "Do not grieve for me. Now I know you are free, I can bear any sufferings that may be inflicted upon me."

"My freedom shall be employed for your preservation," he whispered. "I will accomplish your liberation, or perish in the attempt."

"I forbid it," she returned. "Henceforward I shall strive to shake off all earthly ties, and fix my thoughts entirely upon Heaven. Farewell for ever!"

With this she disengaged herself from him, and passed forth from the room with Derrick Carver, attended by the guard, and followed by Rodomont. Two armed attendants, stationed near the window, remained with the King.

"A word before I go," said Philip, approaching Osbert, and speaking in a tone so low and deep as to be inaudible by the attendants. "On peril of your life, I charge you to hold no further intercourse of any kind with Constance. Look upon her as dead—for dead she is to you. Return to your duty, and I will think no more of what has just occurred."

So saying, he quitted the room with his attendants, leaving Osbert overwhelmed by despair.

While Philip returned in his barque to Whitehall Palace, a barge conveyed the two prisoners to Lambeth Palace.

On arriving there, they were detained for a short time in the guard-room of the ancient gateway, and as soon as all had been made ready, they were lodged in the prison chambers assigned them in the Lollards' Tower.

End of the Second Book.

BOOK III.

LAMBETH PALACE.

CHAPTER I.

HOW CARDINAL POLE ARRIVED IN ENGLAND, AND HOW HE WAS WELCOMED BY THE KING AND QUEEN.

THE court returned to Whitehall in November, Parliament being about to meet in the middle of that month.

One morning, as the royal pair were walking together in the west gallery overlooking the garden, the Lord Chancellor presented himself with a despatch in his hand. It was easy to perceive, from the joyous expression of his countenance, that he brought good tidings.

"Welcome, my good lord," said Mary. "I see you have satisfactory intelligence to communicate. Have you heard from Rome?"

"I have just received this transcript of the decree which has been sent to Cardinal Pole by the Pope," replied Gardiner, "in which his Holiness, after due deliberation, has agreed to extend the privileges of the Legate, so as to enable him to act on all occasions with the same plentitude of power as the Pope himself. In regard to church revenues and goods, his Holiness fully recognises the great difficulty of the question, feeling it to be the main obstacle to the nation's recognition of the Papal supremacy, and he therefore invests his Eminence with the most ample power to agree and compound with the present owners ; to assure to them their possessions, on whatever title they may hold them ; and to exempt them from any duty of restitution."

"This is glad news indeed !" exclaimed the Queen. " Parliament meets in a few days. Your first business must be to repeal the attainder of the Cardinal, who will then be free to return to his own country, and aid us with his counsels. Hasten his arrival, I pray you, my lord, by all means in your power. I shall not feel perfectly happy till I behold him ! "

" There shall not be a moment's needless delay, rely upon it, gracious Madam," replied Gardiner. " The repeal of the attainder may be considered as already accomplished, since no opposition will now be made to the measure. Meantime, an escort shall be immediately despatched to Brussels to bring over his Eminence with all honour to this country."

Having nothing more to lay before their Majesties, he then bowed and withdrew.

Parliament was opened by the King and Queen in person, a sword of state and a cap of maintenance being borne before each of them as they went in state to the House of Lords. Everything proceeded as satisfactorily as had been anticipated by Gardiner. The first bill brought before the Lords was that for reversing Pole's attainder, which, being quickly passed, was sent down to the Commons, and read thrice in one day ; after which it received the royal assent, the impression of the great seal being taken off in gold.

Meantime, in confident anticipation of this event, a brilliant escort, comprising Lord Paget, Sir Edward Hastings, Sir William Cecil, and forty gentlemen of good birth, had been despatched to Brussels, to bring back the illustrious exile to his own country. As soon as intimation was received by Pole that he was free to return, he took leave of the Emperor, and set out with his escort for England.

Among the Cardinal's suite was one of whom some account may be necessary. Years ago, while studying at the celebrated university of Padua, Pole contracted a friendship with Ludovico Priuli, a young Venetian noble, distinguished for his personal accomplishments, refined manners, and love of learning. From this date the two friends became inseparable. Possessed of an ample fortune, Priuli, from his position, might have filled the highest offices in the Venetian Republic, but he preferred sharing Pole's labours, and proved a most valuable coadjutor to him. Chosen as successor to the Bishop of Brescia by Pope Julius III., Priuli declined to exercise his functions, and even refused the purple rather than quit his friend. He had remained with Pole during his retirement at the convent of Maguzano, had attended him to Brussels and to Paris, whither the Cardinal went to negotiate terms of peace between Spain and France, and of course accompanied him to England. Besides the Lord Priuli, Pole was attended by his secretary, Floribello, an excellent scholar, together with the Signori Stella and Rollo, both men of learning and piety, though somewhat advanced in years.

Owing to the infirm state of his health, the Cardinal was unable to proceed far without resting, and after a week's slow travel he reached Calais (then, it need scarcely be said, in possession of England, though soon afterwards lost), where he was received by the governor with a distinction rarely shown to any other than a crowned head.

Pole attended high mass at the cathedral, and the populace clad in holiday attire, flocked thither to receive his blessing. One circumstance occurred which was regarded as a most favourable omen. For more than a week strong adverse winds had prevailed in the Channel, but a favourable change suddenly took place, promising a swift and pleasant passage to the Cardinal.

A royal vessel awaited him, in which he embarked with his train, and escorted by six men-of-war, well armed, and under the command of the Lord High Admiral, he sailed on a bright sunny day for England, and, impelled by a fresh wind, arrived in a few hours at Dover.

A royal salute was fired from the guns of the castle as the Cardinal landed, and he was received by his nephew, Lord Montague, son of his elder brother, who had been put to death by Henry VIII. With Lord Montague were several other noblemen and gentlemen, amongst whom were the mayor and the town authorities, and besides these there was a vast miscellaneous concourse.

No sooner did the Cardinal set foot on the mole, closely followed by his other nephew, Sir Edward Hastings, and Lord Priuli, than the whole assemblage prostrated themselves before him. Spreading his arms over them, Pole gave them his solemn benediction. All eyes were fixed on the venerable and majestic figure before them—all ears were strained to catch his words. The noble cast of the Cardinal's countenance, proclaiming his royal descent—his reverend air, increased by the long grey beard that descended to his waist—the benignity and sweetness of his looks—the stateliness of his deportment—all produced an indescribable effect on the spectators. Lofty of stature, and spare of person—the result of frequent fastings—Pole, notwithstanding the ailments under which he laboured, carried himself erect, and ever maintained a most dignified deportment. To complete the picture we desire to present, it may be necessary to say that his garments were those proper to his eminent ecclesiastical rank, namely, a scarlet soutane, rochet, and short purple mantle. His silk gloves and hose were scarlet in hue, and from his broad red hat depended on either side long cords, terminating in tassels of two knots each. These garments became him well, and heightened the imposing effect of his presence.

Behind him stood his friend, Lord Priuli, who was nearly of his own age, though he looked full ten years younger, and appeared scarcely past the prime of life. The noble Venetian had a countenance which Titian would have delighted to paint, so handsome was it, so grave and full of thought. Priuli was attired in black taffetas, over which he wore a long silk gown of the same colour, and had a black skull-cap on his head.

Signor Floribello, Pole's secretary, was a Roman, and had a massive and antique cast of countenance, which might have become one of his predecessors of the Augustan age. He had a grave, scholar-like aspect, and was attired in dark habiliments. With him were the Cardinal's other attendants, Stella and Rolla, neither of whom merit special description. The former was the Cardinal's steward, and the latter his comptroller, and each wore a gold chain around his neck.

Lord Montague was a very goodly personage, and bore such a remarkable resemblance to his ill-fated father, that Pole exclaimed, as he tenderly embraced him, " I could almost fancy that my long-lost and much-lamented brother had come to life again. I doubt not you possess your father's excellent qualities of head and heart, as well as his good looks."

" I trust I am no degenerate son, dear and venerated uncle," replied Montague. " But I would my father had lived to see this day, and to welcome you back to the land from which you have been so long and so unjustly exiled."

" Heaven's will be done!" ejaculated Pole, fervently. " I do not repine, though I have never ceased to lament the calamities and afflictions I have brought upon my family."

" Think not of them now, dear uncle," rejoined Lord Montague " They are passed and gone. The tyrant who inflicted these injuries is in his grave. Happier days have dawned upon us. Your brother yet lives in me, to honour and serve you. Perchance your martyred mother now looks down from that heaven which her destroyer shall never enter, and joys at her son's return."

" It may be," replied the Cardinal, glancing upwards, "and ere long I hope to join her, for my sojourn in this Vale of Tears is nearly ended ; but I have much to do while I tarry here. Oh! my good nephew! what mixed emotions of joy and sorrow agitate my breast—joy at returning to the country of my birth — sorrow for the relatives and friends I have lost. Many a time and oft, during my long banishment, have I besought Heaven to allow me to return and lay my bones in my native land; and now that my prayers have been granted, I tremble and am sad, for I feel like a stranger."

" You will not be a stranger long, dear uncle," returned Lord Montague. " There is not one of this throng who does not feel that Heaven has sent you to us to give us a blessing, of which we have so long been deprived."

As he spoke, the crowd, which had been pressing on

them, could no longer be kept back, but completely surrounded the Cardinal; those nearest him throwing themselves at his feet, kissing his garments, trying to embrace his knees, and making every possible demonstration of reverence. Little children were held up to him; old men struggled to approach him; and it was long before he could extricate himself from the throng, which he did with great gentleness and consideration.

Graciously declining the hospitality proffered by the mayor, the Cardinal proceeded with his suite to the Priory of Saint Martin, where he tarried for the night.

On the next day, attended by an immense *cortége*, and having two great silver crosses, two massive silver pillars, and two silver pole-axes borne before him, as emblems of his Legantine authority, he journeyed to Canterbury. Here he heard mass in the magnificent cathedral, of which he was so soon to become head, and rested at the palace.

On the second day he proceeded to Rochester, his escort increasing as he went on; and on the third day he reached Gravesend, where he was met by the Bishop of Durham, the Earl of Shrewsbury, and other important personages, who had been dispatched by their Majesties to offer him their congratulations on his safe arrival in England, and at the same time to present him with a copy of the act by which his attainder was reversed.

At Gravesend he again tarried for the night, and next morning entered a royal barge, richly decorated, lined with tapestry, and containing a throne covered with gold brocade. At the prow of this barge a silver cross was fixed, which attracted universal attention as he passed up the river, attended by several other gorgeous barges conveying his retinue.

As the Cardinal approached the metropolis, the river swarmed with boats filled with persons of all ranks eager to welcome him, while crowds collected on the banks to gaze at his barge with the great silver cross at the prow.

While passing the Tower, and gazing at the gloomy fortress where the terrible tragedies connected with his family had been enacted, the Cardinal became a prey to saddening thoughts. But these were dispelled as he approached London Bridge, and heard the shouts of the spectators, who greeted him from the windows of the lofty habitations. The next objects that attracted his attention were Baynard's Castle and Saint Paul's, and he uttered aloud his thanksgivings that the ancient rites of worship were again performed in the cathedral.

Sweeping up the then clear river, past the old palace of Bridewell, Somerset House—built in the preceding reign by the Lord Protector, and which the Cardinal had never before seen—past Durham-place and York House, attended by hundreds of barques, he at length approached the palace of Whitehall, and was taken to the privy stairs.

At the head of the stairs stood Gardiner, ready to receive him, and after they had interchanged a most amicable greeting, and Pole had presented his friend Priuli, Gardiner conducted the Cardinal through two lines of attendants apparelled in the royal liveries, all of whom bowed reverentially as Pole passed on to the principal entrance of the palace, where the King, with the chief personages of his court, awaited his coming.

As the Lord Legate slowly approached, supported by Gardiner, Philip advanced to meet him, and, embracing him affectionately, bade him welcome, saying how anxiously both the Queen and himself had looked for his coming. To these gracious expressions Pole replied :

" I have rejoiced at the union her Majesty has formed, Sire, because I regard it as a presage of my country's future felicity. Inasmuch as a nuptial disagreement between an English monarch and a Spanish queen led to a most lamentable breach with the Holy See, so the marriage of a Spanish king and an English princess will serve to heal the breach. Most assuredly my countrymen will reap the benefit of this auspicious alliance, and so far from finding any yoke placed upon them, as they once apprehended, will recognise the difference between your Majesty and that Prince who chastised them with so heavy a rod."

" With the aid of your Eminence in all spiritual matters, and with that of the Lord Chancellor in temporal affairs," replied Philip, " I doubt not I shall be able, through the Queen's Highness, to contribute to the welfare and prosperity of the realm. Such has been my constant endeavour since I have been here. And now suffer me to lead you to her Majesty, who is all impatience to behold you."

Hereupon they ascended the grand staircase, the King graciously giving his arm to the Lord Legate. At the head of the staircase they found the Queen, who exhibited the liveliest marks of delight on seeing the Cardinal, and gave him a most affectionate greeting.

Pole could not fail to be deeply moved by so much kindness, and with streaming eyes, and in broken accents, sought to express his gratitude. He soon, however, regained his customary serenity, and attended the Queen to the privy-chamber, whither they were followed by the King and the Lord Chancellor. He then delivered his credentials to her Majesty, and they had a long discourse together, in which both the King and the Lord Chancellor took part.

Before withdrawing, Pole besought permission to present his friend Lord Priuli, and Mary kindly assenting, the noble and learned Venetian was introduced to their Majesties, and very graciously received by both. After this the Cardinal took leave, and, attended by Gardiner, re-entered his barge, and was conveyed in it to Lambeth Palace, which had been prepared for his residence.

On the same day a grand banquet was given at Whitehall in honour of the Lord Legate, at which all the nobles vied with each other in paying him attention. Indeed, since Wolsey's palmiest days no such distinction had been shown to an ecclesiastic. Priuli, also, came in for some share of the tribute of respect paid to his illustrious friend.

On the following day, in order to celebrate Pole's arrival publicly, a grand tournament was held in the court of the palace, where galleries were erected, adorned with rich hangings, having two canopies of crimson cloth of silver, embroidered with the royal arms, prepared for their Majesties—a chair for the Cardinal being set near that of the Queen. Precisely at two o'clock her Majesty issued from the palace in company with the Cardinal, attended by her ladies, and took her place beneath the canopy, Pole seating himself beside her. The galleries on either side presented a magnificent sight, being thronged with all the beauty and chivalry of the court—high-born dames and noble gallants, all richly apparelled.

The lists were under the governance of the Lord Chamberlain, Sir John Gage, who was clad in russet armour, and
mounted on a powerful and richly-caparisoned steed ; and as
soon as the Queen and the Cardinal had taken their places,
loud fanfares were blown by a bevy of trumpeters stationed
on the opposite side of the court.

At this summons two champions immediately rode into
the ring, attracting great attention. One of them was the
King. He was clad in a suit of richly chased armour inlaid
with gold, and his helm was adorned with a panache of
red ostrich plumes. His courser was trapped with purple
satin, broached with gold. As he rode round the tilt-yard
and saluted the Queen, a buzz of applause followed his
course.

His opponent was Osbert Clinton, whom his Majesty had
challenged to a trial of skill. Osbert wore a suit of black
armour, with a white plume, and was mounted on a powerful charger, with bases and bards of black cloth of gold of
damask.

As soon as the champions had taken their places, the
signal was given by Sir John Gage, and dashing vigorously
against each other, they met in mid-career, both their lances
being shivered by the shock. As no advantage had been
gained on either side, fresh lances were brought, and they
immediately ran another course. In this encounter, Osbert
had the best of it, for he succeeded in striking off the King's
helmet, and was consequently proclaimed the victor, and received a costly owche as a prize from the hands of the Queen.

Other courses were then run, and spears broken, all the
combatants demeaning themselves valiantly and like men of
prowess. Amongst the Spaniards, those who most distinguished themselves were Don Ruy Gomez de Silva, Don
Frederic de Toledo, and Don Adrian Garcias ; whilst amongst
the Englishmen the best knights were accounted the Lord
Admiral and Sir John Perrot. The King was more fortunate in other courses than in those he had run with Osbert
Clinton, and received a diamond ring from her Majesty, amid
the loud plaudits of the spectators.

After this, Sir John Gage called upon them to disarm, the
trumpets sounded, and graciously bowing to the assemblage,
the Queen withdrew with the Cardinal.

CHAPTER II.

OF THE RECONCILIATION OF THE REALM WITH THE SEE OF ROME.

A few days afterwards, in consequence of the Queen's indisposition, which, however, was not supposed to be of a nature to inspire uneasiness, both Houses of Parliament were summoned to the palace of Whitehall, and assembled in the presence-chamber. Mary, who was so weak at the time that she had to be carried to her throne, was placed on a hautpas, beneath a rich canopy embroidered with the royal arms in gold.

On her left hand was seated the King, attired in black velvet, over which he wore a robe of black cloth of gold, bordered with pearls and diamonds. The collar of the Garter was round his neck, and the lesser badge studded with gems, beneath his knee.

On the Queen's right, and on the haut-pas, but not beneath the canopy, sat Cardinal Pole. His robes were of the richest scarlet, and he wore a mantle of fine sables about his neck. He was attended by four gentleman ushers, all richly clad, and having heavy chains of gold round their necks. Two of these carried the large silver crosses, and the other two bore the silver pillars. Behind the Queen stood Sir John Gage, in his robes of office as Grand Chamberlain, and holding a white wand, and with him were the Vice-Chamberlain and other officers of the royal household. All the Queen's ladies were likewise grouped around the throne.

Near to the Lord Legate stood Gardiner, and as soon as all

were in their places, and the doors had been closed by the ushers, he addressed both Houses, informing them that the Right Reverend Father in God, the Lord Cardinal Pole, legate *a latere,* who was now present before them, had come as ambassador from Pope Julius III. to the King and Queen's Majesties on a matter of the utmost importance, not only to their Highnesses, but to the whole realm. As representatives of the nation, they were called there to listen to the declaration about to be made to them by the Lord Legate.

When Gardiner concluded his address and retired, every eye was fixed upon the Cardinal, and a hush of expectation fell upon the assemblage. After a moment's pause, Pole arose, and with a dignified bow to their Majesties, commenced his address, in tones that vibrated through every breast.

"Long excluded from this assembly," he said, "and exiled from my native country by laws upon the severity and injustice of which I will not dwell, I have most heartily to thank you, my Lords of the Upper House, and you, good Sirs, of the Nether House, for reversing the sentence pronounced upon me, and enabling me to appear before you once more. I rejoice that I am able to requite the great service you have rendered me. You have restored me to my country and to my place amongst the highest nobility upon earth. I can restore you to a heavenly kingdom, and to a Christian greatness, which you have unhappily forfeited by renouncing a fealty annexed to the true Church. Bethink you of the many evils that have occurred to this land since its lamentable defection. Estimate aright the great boon now offered you. Until the late most unhappy schism, the English nation ever stood foremost in the regard of the See of Rome, abundant proofs of which I can offer you. While reminding you of your past errors, let me exhort you to a sincere repentance, and to receive with a deep and holy joy the reconciliation with the Church of Rome, which I, as Legate, am empowered to impart to you. To reap this great blessing it only needs that you should repeal whatever you have enacted against the Holy See, and those laws by which you have severed yourselves from the body of the faithful."

Delivered in tones of mellifluous sweetness and persuasion, this discourse was listened to with profound attention, and produced an unmistakeable effect upon the auditors. As the Cardinal resumed his seat, Gardiner advanced towards him.

"I thank your Eminence," he said, " in the name of their Majesties and the Parliament, for the good offices you have rendered the nation. The members of both Houses will at once deliberate upon what you have proposed, and will speedily acquaint you with their determination, which, I nothing doubt, will be favourable to the cause of our holy religion."

Upon this, the Lord Legate arose and retired with his attendants into an adjoining chamber, there to await the decision of the Parliament.

As soon as he was gone, Gardiner again addressed the assemblage in these terms : " Heaven hath spoken to you by the lips of the holy man to whom you have just listened. I can confirm the truth of all he has uttered. I acknowledge myself to be a great delinquent, but I have deeply and sincerely repented of my errors, and I beseech you to do so likewise. Rise from your fallen estate, and dispose yourselves to a complete reconciliation with the Catholic Church, and a return to its communion. Are ye all agreed to this ? "

"We are all agreed," replied the whole assemblage, without a moment's hesitation.

"I rejoice to hear it," replied Gardiner. "If you have erred, you at least make amends for your error."

The promptitude and unanimity of this decision gave great satisfaction to their Majesties, and the King, calling Gardiner to him, held a brief conference with him, after which Sir John Gage, with the Earl of Arundel, six knights of the Garter, and the like number of bishops, were sent to summon the Lord Legate. As Pole again entered the presence-chamber, the whole of the assemblage arose. The Cardinal having resumed his seat, Gardiner called out, in a loud voice,—

"I again ask you, in the presence of the Lord Legate, whether you sincerely desire to return to the unity of the Church, and the obedience due to her chief pastor ? "

"We do !—we do !" cried the entire assemblage.

A radiant smile passed over Pole's benign countenance at these exclamations, and he raised up his hands in thankfulness to Heaven.

"This moment repays me for all I have suffered," he murmured.

Then Gardiner turned towards the King and Queen, and, making a profound obeisance to them, said :—

"On behalf of the members of both Houses of Parliament, representatives of the whole realm, I have to express to your Majesties their sorrow for the former schism, and for whatever they have enacted against the See of Rome and the Catholic religion, all which they now annul ; and would humbly beseech you to obtain from the Lord Legate pardon and restoration to that body from which they had separated themselves by their misdeeds."

"We pray your Eminence to grant the pardon and reconciliation thus humbly sued for ?" said Philip, turning towards the Cardinal.

"Right joyfully will I accede to your Majesty's request," replied Pole.

The Cardinal's assent having been communicated to the assemblage by Gardiner, they all advanced towards Pole, who arose as they approached, and said :—

"Thanks are due to Divine goodness for granting you this opportunity of cancelling your past offences. If your repentance be answerable to the importance of the occasion and the heinousness of the fault, great, indeed, must be the joy of the saints at your conversion."

It being now evident that the Cardinal was about to pronounce the absolution, the whole assemblage, with the exception of the King and Queen, fell upon their knees. Extending his arms over them, Pole, in a clear and distinct voice, said :—

"As representative of Christ's Vicegerent, I here absolve all those present, and the whole nation, and the whole dominion thereof, from all heresy and schism, and all judgments, censures, for that cause incurred, and restore them to the communion of the Holy Church, in the name of the Father, Son, and Holy Ghost."

To this the whole assemblage responded "Amen !"

Nothing could be more solemn and impressive than the

Cardinal's manner while pronouncing this absolution, and his words penetrated all hearts. The Queen and most of her ladies shed tears. As the assembly rose from their kneeling posture, they embraced each other, and gave utterance to their satisfaction.

The King and Queen, with their attendants, then proceeded to the royal chapel to return thanks, and were followed by the Cardinal, Gardiner, and the entire assemblage. A solemn mass was then performed, and *Te Deum* sung.

CHAPTER III.

OF THE EVENTS THAT FOLLOWED THE RESTORATION OF THE PAPAL AUTHORITY.

NO sooner was the nation's reconciliation with the See of Rome completed, than an express was sent by Cardinal Pole to Pope Julius III., acquainting his Holiness with the joyful event. On receipt of the intelligence, public rejoicings on the grandest scale were held at Rome, religious processions paraded the streets, masses were performed in all the churches, and a solemn service was celebrated at Saint Peter's by the Pontiff in person. The event, indeed, was a signal triumph to the Pope, and in reply to Cardinal Pole he thanked him heartily for the great service he had rendered the Church, and warmly commended his zeal and diligence. Moreover, he issued a bull granting indulgences to all such persons as should openly manifest their satisfaction at the restoration of the Papal authority in England.

Public rejoicings also took place in London, and in other towns, but they were productive of mischief rather than good, as they led to many serious brawls and disturbances. Though compelled to submit to their opponents, who were now in the ascendant, the Reformers were far from subdued, but were quite ready for outbreak, should a favourable opportunity occur for attempting it. The triumphant demonstrations of the Romanists were abhorrent to them, and constant collisions, as we have said, took place between the more violent adherents of the opposing creeds. In these encounters, the Protestants, being the less numerous, got the worst of it, but they promised themselves revenge on a future day.

On the Sunday after the reconciliation, a sermon was preached by Gardiner at Paul's Cross, before the King and Cardinal Pole. A large crowd collected to hear him. On this occasion, in spite of the presence of a strong guard, some interruptions occurred, proving that there were dissentients among the auditors. Evidently there was a growing feeling of dislike to Philip and the Spaniards, fostered by the malcontents, and many a fierce glance was fixed upon the King, many a threat breathed against him, as, surrounded by a band of halberdiers, he listened to Gardiner's discourse.

But if Philip was hated even by the Romanists, who after all were as true lovers of their country as those of the adverse sect, and equally hostile to the Spaniards, the universal feeling was favourable to Cardinal Pole, whose benevolent countenance pleased the Reformers, as much as his dignified deportment commanded their respect. He and the King rode together to Saint Paul's, and after hearing the sermon, returned in the same way to Whitehall. Philip had the sword of state borne before him, but the Cardinal contented himself with the silver cross.

A few days afterwards, intimation was sent by the council to Bonner, Bishop of London, that the Queen was in a condition to become a mother. Command was given at the same time that there should be a solemn procession to Saint Paul's, in which the Lord Mayor, the aldermen, and all the City companies, in their liveries, should join, to offer up prayers for her Majesty's preservation during her time of travail, coupled with earnest supplications that the child might be a male.

This announcement, which, as may be supposed, was quickly bruited abroad throughout the City, gave great satisfaction to the Romanists, but it was anything but welcome or agreeable to the Reformers, who saw in it an extension of power to their enemies, and an increase of danger to themselves. If an heir to the throne should be born, Philip's authority in England would be absolute. Such was the general impression, and its correctness was confirmed by a petition made to the King by both Houses,

which prayed "that if it should happen otherwise than well
to the Queen, he would take upon himself the government
of the realm during the minority of her Majesty's issue."
As may be supposed, Philip readily assented, and an act
was immediately passed carrying out the provisions above
mentioned, and making it high treason to compass the
King's death, or attempt to remove him from the government and guardianship confided to him.

Under these circumstances the solemn procession to Saint
Paul's took place.   Vast crowds encumbered the streets
as the civic authorities proceeded from Guildhall to the
cathedral, headed by ten bishops in their robes, the pix
being borne before them under a canopy.   This gave such
offence, that had not a strong military force kept the
populace in awe, it is certain that the procession would have
been molested.   As it was, expressions of antipathy to
Philip could not be checked.   "England shall never be
ruled by the Spaniard," was the indignant outcry, which
found an echo in many a breast, whether of Romanist or
Reformer.

In spite of all these clamours, the procession reached
Saint Paul's in safety, and high mass was celebrated by
Bonner and the other bishops, after which prayers were
offered up for the Queen, in accordance with the council's
mandate.   The mass of the assemblage joined heartily in
these supplications, but there were some who refused to
recite them, and secretly prayed that Philip's hopes of an
heir might be frustrated.

The reader is already aware that Cardinal Pole, immediately on his arrival in London, had been put in possession
of Lambeth Palace.   This noble residence, with the
revenues of the Archbishopric of Canterbury, confiscated
on the condemnation of Cranmer for high treason, was
bestowed on the Cardinal by the King and Queen ; but
Pole could not be promoted to the archiepiscopal see while
Cranmer lived.

One of the Cardinal's first acts on taking possession of
the palace was to summon all the bishops and principal
clergy before him, and, after listening to their expressions
of penitence for the perjuries, heresies, and schisms they had
committed during the late reigns, he gave them absolution.

And now, before proceeding further, it may be desirable to give a brief description of the ancient edifice occupied by the Cardinal.

The present vast and irregular pile, known as Lambeth Palace, was preceded by a much smaller mansion, wherein the archbishops of Canterbury were lodged, and to which a chapel was attached. This building was pulled down in 1262 by the turbulent Archbishop Boniface, and a new and more important structure erected in its place. Of Boniface's palace little now remains save the chapel and crypt. So many additions were made to the palace by successive archbishops, and so much was it altered, that it may almost be said to have become another structure. A noble hall, subsequently destroyed in the time of the Commonwealth, was built by Archbishop Chichely, who flourished in the reign of Edward IV.; while the chief ornament of the existing pile, the gateway, was reared by Cardinal Archbishop Morton, towards the end of the 15th century. The Steward's Parlour, a chamber of large dimensions, was added by Cranmer, and a long gallery and other buildings were erected by Cardinal Pole.

Before entering the palace, let us pause to examine the gateway, a structure of almost unrivalled beauty, and consisting of two large square towers, built of fine brick, embattled, and edged with stone. The archway is pointed, and has a groined roof springing from four pillars, one in each corner. Spiral stone staircases lead to the upper chambers, and from the leads of the roof a wonderful prospect of the surrounding metropolis is obtained. Connected with the porter's lodge is a small prison-chamber, having a double door, and high, narrow-grated windows. The walls are cased with stone, and of prodigious thickness, while three heavy iron rings fixed in them attest the purpose to which the room was formerly applied.

Passing through the principal court, we enter the great hall, rebuilt by Archbishop Juxon on the exact model of the old hall, demolished during the Protectorate, so that it may be considered a counterpart of Archbishop Chichely's banqueting-chamber. Nearly a hundred feet in length, proportionately wide and lofty, this noble room has a superb pendant timber roof, enriched with elaborate carvings, and lighted by a louvre. In the great bay-window, amidst the relics of stained glass, recovered from the original hall, may be discerned the arms of Philip of Spain, painted by order of Cardinal Pole. At the present day the hall is used as the palace library, and its space is somewhat encroached upon by projecting bookcases, filled with works of divinity. At the upper end is the archbishop's seat.

From the great hall we may proceed to the gallery and guard-chamber, the latter of which was once used as the armoury of the palace. It has an ancient timber roof, with pendants, pointed arches, and pierced spandrels. Here are portraits of many of the archbishops of Canterbury, among which may be seen that of Cardinal Pole, copied from the original by Raffaelle, preserved in the Barberini Palace at Rome.

Pass we by the presence-chamber and other state-rooms, and let us enter the long gallery erected by Cardinal Pole —a noble room, lighted by windows enriched with stained glass.

Hence we will proceed to the chapel erected by Boniface. Lighted by three lancet-shaped windows on either side, and divided by an elaborately carved screen, on the inner side of which is the archiepiscopal stall, this chapel contains but little of its pristine character, and is disfigured by a flat-panelled ceiling, added by Archbishop Laud.

Beneath the chapel, and corresponding with it in size, is an ancient crypt, with a groined roof, once used as a place of worship. In this part of the palace is a large room built by Cranmer, and now called the Steward's Parlour, and close to it are the servants' hall and the great kitchen.

We now come to a part of the palace to which interest of a peculiar nature attaches. This is the Lollards' Tower, a large stone structure, erected by Archbishop Chichely, which derives its name from being used as a place of imprisonment for the followers of Wickliffe, called Lollards. This time-worn tower faces the river, and on its front is a small niche or tabernacle, formerly occupied by an image of Thomas à Becket.

In the lower part of the Lollard's Tower is a gloomy chamber of singular construction, the heavy timber roof being supported by a strong wooden pillar standing in the centre of the chamber, whence the place is called the Post Room. Tradition asserts that the unfortunate Lollards, confined in the chamber above, were tied to this pillar and scourged. The Post Room is lighted by three low pointed windows looking towards the Thames, and its flat-panelled ceiling is ornamented at the intersections with grotesque carvings.

Ascending by a narrow spiral stone staircase, we reach the prison-chamber just referred to, which is guarded by an inner and outer door of stout oak, studded with broad-headed nails. A strange, strong room, that cannot fail powerfully to impress the visitor. Wainscot, ceiling, floor, every part of the chamber is boarded with dark oak of great thickness. Fixed to the wainscot, breast-high from the ground, are eight massive rings. The boards adjoining them are covered with inscriptions—mementoes of the many unfortunates confined there. The prison-chamber is lighted by two small grated windows, narrowing outwardly, one of which looks upon the river.

Attached to the palace are a park and gardens of considerable extent, and in the olden time of great beauty. Within the gardens, up to the commencement of the present century, grew two singularly fine fig trees, planted by Cardinal Pole, and trained against that part of the palace which he erected.

Lambeth Palace came into Pole's hands in a very habitable condition, having been well kept up by his predecessor, Cranmer. So well pleased was the Cardinal with the mansion, that he not only embellished it in many ways, but enlarged it, as we have previously mentioned. He also took great delight in the gardens, and laid them out in the Italian style.

Unostentatious of character, and simple in his tastes and habits, Pole felt it due to his elevated position to maintain princely state in the residence assigned to him by their Majesties, and employ his large revenues in hospitality and charity. When complete, which it was within a month after his occupation of the Palace, Pole's household was as numerous and magnificent as Wolsey's, and comprised a high-chamberlain and vice-chamberlain, twelve gentlemen ushers, steward, treasurer, comptroller, cofferer, three marshals, two grooms, and an almoner. In his chapel he had a dean, a sub-dean, twelve singing-priests, and the like number of quiristers. Besides these, there were his cross-bearers, his pillar-bearers, and two yeomen to bear his poleaxes. The inferior officers were almost too numerous to particularise, comprehending purveyors, cooks, sewers, cup-bearers, yeomen of the larder, of the buttery, of the ewery, the cellar, the laundry, the bakehouse, the wardrobe, the chandry, the wood yard, and the garden. Of gardeners, indeed, there were several. Besides these, there were a multitude of pages and grooms, a sumpter-man, a muleteer, and sixteen grooms of the stable, each of whom had four horses. Then there were tall porters at the gate, yeomen of the chariot, and yeomen of the barge. Nor were these all. In addition to those previous enumerated, there were a physician, two chaplains, and two secretaries.

Such was the magnificent establishment maintained by Pole during his residence at Lambeth Palace. His hospitality may be judged of by the fact that three long tables were daily laid in the great hall, abundantly supplied with viands, and ever thronged with guests. At the upper table sat the Cardinal, generally surrounded by nobles or ecclesiastical dignitaries. A place at this table, not far from his illustrious friend, was always reserved for Lord Priuli.

Apartments in the palace were, of course, assigned to Priuli, who had likewise his own attendants. The entire control of the vast establishment devolved upon the noble Venetian, who undertook the office in order to relieve the Cardinal of a portion of his labours.

Amidst all this profusion the poor were not forgotten. Dole was daily distributed at the palace gate, under the personal superintendence of Pole and Priuli. The wants of the necessitous were relieved, and medicines were delivered to the sick. None who deserved assistance were ever sent empty-handed away by the Cardinal.

Amongst the Cardinal's officers were our old acquaintances Rodomont Bittern, Nick Simnel, and Jack Holiday, the first of whom had been recommended to Pole by the King himself. Rodomont was appointed captain of the palace guard, and his two friends were made lieutenants. On state occasions they formed part of the Cardinal's body-guard.

One fine morning, at an early hour, these three personages had scaled the lofty gate-tower, in order to enjoy the goodly prospect it commanded. Before them flowed the Thames, then a clear and unpolluted stream, its smooth surface speckled, even at that early hour, by many barques. A ferry-boat, laden with passengers and horses, was crossing at the time from Lambeth to Westminster. On the opposite side stood the ancient Abbey, with the Parliament House, the Star Chamber, the beautiful gates of Whitehall, designed by Holbein, the royal gardens, and the palace. Further on cold be observed the exquisite cross at Charing, subsequently destroyed by fanatical fury. Then following the course of the river, the eye lighted upon York-place, Durham-place, the Savoy, and the splendid mansion then but recently completed by the aspiring Duke of Somerset. Further on was the ancient palace of Bridewell, and beyond, Baynard's Castle, while above the clustering habitations of the City rose the massive tower and lofty spire of old Saint Paul's.

London at the period of wh'ch we treat was singularly picturesque and beautiful. The walls encircling it were well fortified and in good repair, and most of its oldest and most remarkable edifices were still standing, no terrible conflagra-tion having as yet touched them. Numberless towers, churches, and picturesque habitations, with high roofs and quaint gables, excited the admiration of those who stood that morn on the gateway of Lambeth Palace ; but perhaps the object that pleased them best was London-bridge, which, with its gates, its drawbridges, its church, and lofty habita-tions, proudly bestrode the Thames. Having gazed their fill at this wondrous structure, or rather collection of struc-tures, they turned towards the Surrey side of the river, and noted Saint Mary Overy's fine old church, the palace of the Bishop of Winchester, the Ring, at that time much fre-quented, in which bulls and bears were baited, and the adjacent theatre, wherein, at a later date, many of the plays of our immortal bard were represented. Content with this distant survey, they then looked nearer home, and allowed their gaze to wander over the park and gardens of the palace, and finally to settle upon the various courts, towers, and buildings composing the pile.

" By my faith, 'tis a stately edifice, this palace of Lambeth!" exclaimed Rodomont. "Our lord and master the Cardinal is as well lodged as the King and Queen at White-hall."

"Were it not for yonder ague-bringing marshes the palace would be a marvellous pleasant residence," observed Nick Simnel.

"Why should a sturdy fellow like you, Nick, fear ague?" cried Rodomont. "Lord Priuli tells me that his Eminence enjoys better health here than he has done since he left the Lago di Garda—a plain proof that the place cannot be insalubrious, as you would have it."

"Follow my example, Nick, and fortify yourself against the morning mists with a thimbleful of aqua vitæ," remarked Jack Holiday, with a laugh. "'Tis a sovereign remedy against ague. But see! yonder are the Cardinal and the Lord Priuli, taking an early walk in the garden. They seem engaged in earnest discourse."

"I warrant their discourse relates to the recusant Pro-testant divines, who have just been excommunicated by the ecclesiastical commissioners, and are to be burnt," observed Rodomont. "There will be rare doings at Smithfield ere long, if Gardiner and Bonner have their way. But our good lord the Cardinal is averse to persecution, and may succeed in checking it."

"Heaven grant he may!" exclaimed Jack Holiday. "If once the fires are lighted at Smithfield, there's no saying when they may be extinguished, or who may perish by them. 'Tis a marvel to me that the late occupant of this palace, Cranmer, has so long been spared. If the ecclesiastical commissioners desire to deal a heavy blow against the Reformers, why not strike their leader now they have him in their power?"

"I will tell you why," rejoined Rodomont. "In this high place none can overhear us, so we may talk freely. Gar-diner would fain be Archbishop of Canterbury, but he knows that if Cranmer be burnt, our lord the Cardinal will at once be appointed to the archiepiscopal see. Therefore Cranmer is allowed to live, in the hope that Pole may be recalled to Rome by his Holiness. But the crafty Bishop of Winchester will be disappointed, for the Cardinal is not likely to leave his native country again."

"I am rejoiced to hear it," said Simnel. "We could ill spare him. The Cardinal is the pillar of the Romish church in England."

" By our Lady, he is a pattern to all," cried Rodomont. "There lives not a better man than his Eminence. Even the Queen, they say, is governed by his advice. He has more influence with her than the King himself."

" Like enough," observed Jack Holiday, "for they do say that the royal couple, like other married folk, have an occasional quarrel. Her Majesty is plaguily jealous."

" And not without reason," said Rodomont, with a laugh. "It was not to be expected that the King, who is of an amorous complexion, as all the world knows, should continue faithful to a woman eleven years older than himself, and ill-favoured into the bargain. He wants something younger and better-looking."

" Like poor Constance Tyrrell," said Nick Simnel; " she who is shut up yonder," he added, pointing to the Lollard's Tower.

" Ay, and she will never get out unless she yields to the King's wishes," observed Jack Holiday.

" Don't be too sure of that," rejoined Rodomont. " It will be her own fault if she remains here another twenty-four hours."

" How so ?—who will unlock the door for her ?—not her gaoler ?" said Holiday.

" Not her gaoler, fool," rejoined Rodomont, "but her lover, Osbert Clinton. Since he can't unlock the door, he will unbar the window. You are both too generous to betray him, I know, and therefore I'll e'en tell you what occurred last night. While making my rounds, a little after midnight, I entered the outer court, and was standing near the Water Tower, when looking up, I espied a head above yon ivied wall, which divides the court from the river. In another moment a body became visible as well as a head, and before I could count twenty a man dropped from the top of the wall into the court. It was Osbert Clinton. I recognised him even in that imperfect light, or I should have challenged him. Guessing his purpose, I retired, placing myself so that I could watch his movements without being perceived. As I expected, his errand was to the Lollard's Tower, though how he hoped to gain admittance to Constance's cell passed my comprehension."

"And did he gain admittance to her?" inquired Holiday.

"You shall hear," replied Rodomont. "Yon small grated window in the upper part of the tower belongs to her cell. How, think you, he contrived to reach it?"

"Nay, I can't say," replied Holiday. "He could scarcely climb up to it."

"Climb up a tower! No, I should think not. But for the ivy, he would never have got over yonder wall. He reached the window by means of a rope-ladder which he had brought with him. How the plan had been preconcerted is more than I can tell you, but it was evident Constance expected him. A slight cough served to announce her lover's presence to her. At the signal, a cord was immediately let down from the window of the cell, and as soon as it came within Osbert's reach, he caught it, and fastening the rope-ladder to it, the cord was quickly drawn up again, taking the ladder with it. In another minute the ladder was made fast to the bars of the window, and this done, up sprang Osbert, and was soon only separated from the object of his affections by the grating."

"A pize upon the grating!" exclaimed Holiday. "I would there had been no envious bars between them."

"That was exactly my feeling," said Rodomont. "Their discourse was in whispers, but I heard enough to learn that Osbert proposed some means of escape to her, but judged from his expressions of disappointment that she would not consent to the plan. Fear of discovery compelled him to cut short the interview, however he might have desired to prolong it, but before descending he promised to come again to-night. The ladder being unfastened, he was quickly over the wall, and in another minute must have regained the boat, which I conclude was waiting for him. Now, what say you, my masters? Shall we not aid him in his efforts to get this poor girl away?"

"I will gladly do so," replied Holiday.

"So will I," said Simnel.

"Then we will forthwith set our wits to work, and something must come of it," rejoined Rodomont. "If she remains here, she is lost. But see ! the poor folk are beginning to crowd round the gate in expectation of their dole. How many, think you, are daily fed by the Cardinal ? "

" Fifty or sixty, it may be," replied Simnel.

"Upwards of a hundred," said Rodomont. " Yonder comes his Emminence, with Lord Priuli. Let us go down. This keen morning has given me a rare appetite, and I propose that we hie to the great hall, and break our fast with a cold chine and a flagon of humming ale."

" Agreed," replied the others.

Whereupon they descended to the court, and bowing reverentially to the Cardinal and Lord Priuli as they passed them, proceeded to the banqueting-chamber, where preparations were already made for a substantial repast. Sitting down at a side-table, they fell to work with right good will.

CHAPTER IV.

ON the same day, at a late hour, in a large room of the palace, panelled with dark oak, and lighted by a deep bay-window filled with stained glass, beside a table covered with books and papers, sat Cardinal Pole and Lord Priuli. They were engaged in conversation. Pole wore his scarlet soutane and lawn rochet, and had a red silk calotte on his head. Priuli was in black velvet, which set off his noble figure to great advantage.

"An embassy is about to be dispatched in a few days to Rome," observed Pole. "It will consist of my nephew, Lord Montague, the Bishop of Ely, and Sir Edward Carne. If you have any desire to return to your beloved Italy, you can do so in their company. Do not let any consideration for me weigh with you, I entreat. I am not without misgiving that this chill climate, and, above all, the exhalations from the marshes near the Palace, may be prejudicial to your health. I need not say how greatly I shall miss you, but I shall be reconciled to the deprivation by feeling that you are better off than with me."

"If I can serve you by accompanying this embassy to Rome, I will readily do so, dear friend," rejoined Priuli; "but I have no desire to return to Italy. It would be idle to say that I do not prefer sunshine and an exhilarating

atmosphere to a cold and brumous climate like that of England. Undoubtedly, I would rather dwell in Rome than in
London, but, deprived of your society, Italy, with its blue
sky and noble monuments, would be a blank to me. I am
happier here than I should be at the Vatican without you.
Say no more, therefore, to me on that head, I beseech you.
But you yourself may be compelled to return to Rome. Not
improbably you may be elected to the Pontifical Throne!"

"Should it be so, I should decline the dignity," replied
the Cardinal. "You, my good friend, who know my sentiments perfectly, are aware that I have little ambition, and
that all my exertions have been directed to the welfare of
our holy Church. This cause I can best serve by remaining
here, and I trust Heaven may spare me for the complete
fulfilment of my task. I do not delude myself with any
false hopes. I shall never behold Rome again, and it is
from this conviction that I would not hinder your return."

"I will remain with you to the last," rejoined Priuli.
"My life is linked with yours. Nothing but death can
divide us."

At this juncture an usher announced the Lord Chancellor,
and the next moment Gardiner entered the room. Both the
Cardinal and Priuli rose to receive him. After courteous
but grave salutations had passed between them, Gardiner
remarked, "Your Eminence desires to speak to me about
those recusants who were yesterday excommunicated by the
ecclesiastical tribunal, and delivered to the secular power.
I may as well state at once that nothing can be advanced in
arrest of the judgment certain to be passed upon them.
They obstinately persisted in their heresy, and firmly refused
to subscribe to the doctrines of the Church."

"I grieve to hear it," replied Pole. "Yet I trust they
will not be severely dealt with."

"They will be dealt with as they deserve—they will be
burnt at the stake," rejoined Gardiner.

"But not without time allowed them for reflection, I trust,
my lord," said the Cardinal. "Undue severity will injure
our cause rather than serve it. These men will be accounted
martyrs, and held up as an example to others. Policy,
therefore, would dictate milder measures."

"Mild measures have been tried, and have proved ineffectual," rejoined Gardiner. "We must now make a terrible example of these obstinate and dangerous heretics."

Again the usher entered, and this time to inform the Cardinal that their Majesties had arrived at the palace, and were already in the courtyard. Hereupon Pole instantly arose, and followed by Priuli, repaired to the ante-chamber. Scarcely had he entered it, when the royal pair, preceded by Sir John Gage, and attended by several officers of the court, appeared at the outer door. The Cardinal immediately hurried forward to bid them welcome, and thank them for the distinguished honour conferred upon him by the visit.

"Had I been aware of your coming, gracious Madam," he said to the Queen, "I would have been at the gate to receive you."

"It is not a visit of ceremony," replied Mary, "therefore we did not deem it necessary to send intimation of our design. If your Eminence is at leisure, the King and myself will gladly pass an hour in your society, and profit by your counsels."

"I am entirely at your Majesty's disposal," replied the Cardinal, bowing. "I pray you enter. And you, too, Sire," he added, conducting them to the inner room.

Mary looked ill and lauguid, and moved slowly and with difficulty, requiring the King's support. But her illness being attributed to her condition, occasioned no alarm.

On reaching the inner room, the Queen seated herself on a high, carved oak chair proffered her by the Cardinal, while Philip occupied a fauteuil on her left. As their Majesties would not allow the Cardinal to remain standing, he took a seat on the other side of the Queen. At a little distance from the royal pair stood Gardiner, Priuli, and Sir John Gage. All the other attendants withdrew.

"I did not expect to find you here, my lord," the Queen observed to Gardiner, after bowing to him and Priuli.

"I was sent for, gracious Madam," replied the Lord Chancellor. "The Cardinal desired to confer with me on an important matter connected with the maintenance of the Established Church, in which his Eminence and myself differ in opinion. In most matters I should readily defer to his Eminence's better judgment. But I cannot do so in this instance. I am glad your Majesty has come, as I feel certain you will support my views."

"Whence arises this difference of opinion?" demanded Mary. "I should have thought your lordship and the Cardinal must infallibly agree on all points touching the welfare of the Church."

"The question between us, gracious Madam," said Pole, "is whether, on the score of humanity and policy, it would not be better to deal leniently rather than severely with those who profess heretical opinions. I allude particularly to the ministers of the Reformed Church who have just been excommunicated and degraded, and delivered over to the secular power, and who, unless mercy be shown them, will suffer a dreadful death."

Mary's brow darkened.

"Surely your Eminence would not pardon them if they persist in their heresies?" she cried.

"I would not put them to death," rejoined Pole, "but would endeavour to convince them of their errors by argument and instruction. Failing in this, I would resort to such measures as might be deemed best adapted to meet the exigencies of the case—but those measures should be tempered with mercy."

"I did not expect such opinions as these from your Eminence," observed Mary. "The enemies of our faith must be destroyed, or they will destroy us. A single diseased sheep will taint the whole flock. If you have an unsound limb, the surgeon will tell you that for the safety of the body it must be cut off. The preservation, therefore, of the Catholic Church requires that these tares amidst the corn be rooted up and cast into the fire."

"These false brethren are seditious as well as heretical," said Philip sternly; "rebels against the Queen, and enemies to the Church. No mercy ought to be shown them."

"Your Eminence perceives that their Majesties are of my opinion," said Gardiner to the Cardinal. "But has not our Church deep wrongs to avenge? Have we not suffered stripes and persecution from these heretics when they were in power? Have not I myself been deprived of my revenues, and imprisoned within the Tower, with the sentence of death

14

hanging over my head, for years, until happily released by her Majesty ? "

"At least your life was spared," observed Pole.

"It was spared more from fear than favour," retorted Gardener. "But had King Edward lived another year, nay, a few months longer, I should not have been here now to protest against leniency towards such bitter enemies. One of the latest acts of Cranmer was to frame a sanguinary code against the professors of the ancient faith, which had it been put in force, would have been fraught with fearful consequences; but ere that code became law, King Edward died, and the weapon sharpened for our destruction fell from the maker's hands."

"To strike off his own head," cried Philip, fiercely. "Your Eminence would scarcely extend your clemency to this arch-offender ?" he added to the Cardinal.

"I would pardon him, if he recanted," replied Pole.

"What, pardon Cranmer, the apostate and heretic !" exclaimed Gardiner. "Pardon him who betrayed and enslaved the Church of which he ought to have been the protector !—who manifested the most abject compliance with the will of his royal master, flattering his passions, and humouring his caprices ! Pardon him who shamefully promoted and pronounced the divorce between the King and her Majesty's royal mother, casting thereby a blemish on their daughter ! Would you pardon him whose life has been one of dissimulation, and who professed and practised what in his secret heart he disbelieved and abhorred ? Would you pardon a Reformer, who subscribed the terrible Six Articles, though they were directed chiefly against his own sect, and who would have subscribed any other articles enjoined by his royal master—who on King Edward's accession declared himself in favour of the principles of Zuinglius and Calvin— who abolished the ancient worship—attacked every article of our Church—denied its traditions—stigmatised its rites— brought over foreign sectaries, however anti-Christian their tenets, as Martin Bucer, Paul Fagius, Peter Martyr, Ochinus, and others, procured them churches, and recommended them to royal favour—and who filled up the measure of his guilt by supporting the treasonable projects of Northumberland, helping him to place a usurper on the throne, and preaching against the rightful claims of our sovereign mistress? Would you spare this hypocrite, this apostate, this heretic, this double-dyed traitor?"

"His crimes are many and indefensible, but I would leave their punishment to Heaven," rejoined Pole.

"I could forgive him every injury he has done me, except the divorce pronounced against my sainted mother," said Mary, her cheek flushing, and her eyes kindling as she spoke. "In pronouncing that unjust sentence, he uttered his own condemnation. His fate is sealed."

"Why has the punishment he so richly merits been so long delayed?" demanded Philip.

"His offences, Sire, are of so heinous a nature," responded Gardiner, "and so fraught with injury to our holy religion in its most vital part, that it has been necessary to refer them to that supreme tribunal before which such inquests can only properly be held. His case has been laid before the Pope, who has appointed the Bishop of Gloucester and a commission to try him. On their report, judgment will be pronounced in solemn consistory by his Holiness. What that judgment will be, cannot for a moment be doubted. Cranmer will be excommunicated and anathematised, deprived of the archbishopric of Canterbury, and of all ecclesiastical privileges. Furthermore he will be degraded and delivered to the secular power, and your Majesties will be required by his Holiness to proceed towards him as the law directs."

"For his offences the law prescribes death by fire, and by that death he shall die," said Mary.

"Alas, that it should be so!" muttered Pole. "When will the true spirit of the Gospel, which inculcates toleration, charity, and forgiveness of injuries, be understood, and its principles practised? I would make a last appeal to your Majesties in behalf of those unfortunates," he added to the Queen.

Before replying, Mary consulted the King by a look. His stern expression of countenance confirmed her.

"It is in vain," she replied. "My heart is steeled against them."

CHAPTER V.

BISHOP BONNER.

SHORTLY afterwards, the Bishop of London was announced by the usher. A brief preliminary description of this remarkable prelate may be necessary.

Edmond Bonner, Bishop of London, whose severity towards the Protestants has caused his memory to be justly detested, was by no means the savage-looking or repulsive personage generally supposed. Of middle height, stout, and of fresh complexion, he had rather a jovial countenance, being fond of good cheer, and his features, except when inflamed by passion, as they not unfrequently were, had a pleasant expression. But he was exceedingly hot-tempered, and when excited, lost all control of himself, and became perfectly furious. Neither did his anger, though easily roused, quickly subside. In some respects he resembled his royal master, Henry VIII. His disposition was cruel and vindictive, and he never forgot or forgave an injury. To the Reformers, whom he bitterly hated, he proved, as is well known, a terrible scourge.

Born towards the close of the 15th century, Bonner was now near upon sixty, but though he had undergone many hardships, and had endured more than four years' imprisonment in the Marshalsea, his spirit was unbroken, and his health unimpaired. During his long captivity he had been supported by the conviction that the ancient worship would be restored, and his enemies be delivered into his hands.

What he had hoped for, and prayed for, having come to pass, he promised himself ample compensation for the afflictions he had endured. Learned and acute, Bonner had early attracted the attention of Wolsey, by whom he was much employed; and being subsequently appointed chaplain to Henry VIII., he rose rapidly in favour, as he accommodated himself without scruple to the King's caprices. Instrumental in furthering the divorce with Katherine of Aragon, Bonner co-operated in the religious changes accomplished by his royal master, and was also entrusted by him with several missions of great delicacy, which he fulfilled very satisfactorily, rendering himself altogether so useful, and continuing so subservient, that, though often rebuffed by the monarch—as who was not?—he never entirely lost his good graces.

But when Edward VI. mounted the throne, all was changed. Opposed to the Reformation, though he did not dare openly to manifest his hostility to it, Bonner was regarded with suspicion and dislike by the chiefs of the Protestant party, who determined upon his overthrow. Cited before an ecclesiastical commission, of which Cranmer was the head, notwithstanding an energetic defence, appeals to the King against the illegality of the tribunal, and the injustice of his sentence, Bonner, at that time Bishop of London, was deprived of his see and benefices, and imprisoned in the Marshalsea, whence he was only liberated on Mary's accession. Restored to his diocese, and reinstated in power, he burned to avenge himself on his enemies, chief amongst whom he reckoned Cranmer, Ridley, and Latimer. But now that they were safe in prison, he was content to wait. The cup of vengeance was too sweet to be hastily drained.

Bonner's appearance at this juncture was hailed with satisfaction by Gardiner, who could count upon his support against Pole, and he therefore remarked, after the bishop had made his obeisance to their Majesties, " My associate in the ecclesiastical commission concurs with me that no mercy whatever should be shown to heretics."

" Mercy to heretics !" exclaimed Bonner, surprised. " It were mistaken clemency to spare such dangerous offenders. Rigorous measures will alone check the spread of the pestilence by which your kingdom is unhappily affected, gracious Madam," he added to the Queen. "Now is the time to strike terror into the hearts of these false brethren—to exterminate them by fire and sword."

"The Lord Cardinal does not think so," rejoined Mary. "He is of opinion that those convicted of heretical pravity should be leniently dealt with."

"You amaze me, Madam," cried Bonner.

"The object your Majesty has in view," said Pole, "being to bring back those who have strayed from the paths of truth, and not to drive them yet further off, gentleness, and not force, should be employed. By severity you will increase the evil instead of curing it. Fear will make hypocrites, not converts."

"No matter," cried Bonner. "Let the sacramentarians conform outwardly. We care not to search their hearts. Enough for us if they profess themselves Catholics."

"I grieve to hear you say so, my lord," rejoined the Cardinal. "It is better to have an open enemy than a false friend. Our Church does not desire to encourage dissimulation, put to eradicate error and schism. I beseech your Majesty to pause before you proceed further in a course which I foresee is fraught with danger. Hitherto, all has gone well. Your enemies are confounded. Your people are loving and loyal, willing to make any sacrifices for you, save those of conscience. The faith of your forefathers is restored in its integrity. Your kingdom is reconciled to the Holy See. Is this an opportune moment for persecution? Would you sully the snowy banner of the Church with blood? Would you destroy a tithe of your subjects by fire and sword—by burning and massacre? Yet this must be done if persecution once commences. Such means of conversion are as unwarrantable as impolitic—contrary to the will of Heaven, and likely to provoke its wrath. I defy the advocates of severity towards heretics to produce a single passage from the Gospel that would authorise Christians to burn their fellow-men for questions purely of conscience. As, therefore, such rigour cannot be sustained by appeal to Holy Writ, neither can it be upheld by any other consideration. It will increase the evil complained of, rather than mitigate it."

"Your Eminence forgets how much we have suffered from the Reformers," remarked Bonner.

"If they have done ill, ought we to imitate them in ill-doing?" rejoined Pole. "Let us prove to them that we are better Christians than they are. Your Majesty may trust me, that the true way to convert the Protestants is to reform our own clergy, whose ill-regulated conduct has led to heresy and backsliding. Better this remedy than the stake."

"All this shall to the Pope," observed Gardiner, in a low tone, to Bonner. "His Eminence will be speedily recalled."

"It is high time he should be recalled, if he entertains these opinions," rejoined the other, in the same tone.

"Nothing that has been urged will shake my purpose," said Mary. "I will free my kingdom from the curse that has so long afflicted it, even though I inundate the land with blood. But I agree with your Eminence that much reform is needful in our own clergy, whose manners provoke scandal, and encourage infidelity. I will address myself to the task. To you, my Lord Chancellor, and to you, my Lord Bishop," she added to Gardiner and Bonner, "I commit the extirpation of heresy. Relax not in your efforts."

"Rest assured we will not, gracious Madam," replied Gardiner.

"Your Eminence seems to think," observed Bonner to the Cardinal, "that the Lord Chancellor and myself have not used proper means of weaning back these misguided men from their errors. As there are two prisoners confined within the Lollards' Tower for religious offences, may I venture to inquire whether you have succeeded in accomplishing their conversion?"

"Not as yet," replied Pole; "but I do not despair of ultimate success."

"What prisoners do you refer to?" demanded Mary. "I have not heard of them."

The Cardinal was about to reply, when a look from the King stopped him.

"Who are they, I repeat?" cried Mary, somewhat sharply, surprised at Pole's disinclination to answer.

"One of them is the unhappy Constance Tyrrell, and the

other the half-crazed fanatic, Derrick Carver," replied the Cardinal.

"Indeed!" exclaimed Mary. "Was your Majesty aware that these persons are confined here?" she added to the King.

"They were sent hither by my orders," rejoined Philip, coldly.

"And why was I not informed of the matter?" asked Mary.

"Because I did not deem it needful," replied the King.

"Not needful!" exclaimed Mary. "By my soul, but it was needful! 'Twas a strange step to take without my knowledge or privity."

"You heat yourself unnecessarily, Madam," interrupted Philip. "'Twas to spare you annoyance that I kept the matter secret from you."

"How so?" demanded Mary. "The unaccountable disappearance of this girl troubled me, as you know, and Carver's supposed escape was equally displeasing to me."

"You would have been informed of all in good time," said Philip. "How I discovered their hiding-place, and why I sent them hither, shall be explained anon."

"I trust the explanation will prove satisfactory," replied Mary. "Meantime, I will see the prisoners myself, and interrogate them."

"Shall they be brought before you?" inquired Pole.

"No," returned the Queen; "I will proceed to the Lollards' Tower. Your Eminence will attend me thither."

"'Twere better not, Madam," said Philip. "Be ruled by me, and let alone this visit."

"You have some motive," rejoined Mary, in a low tone— "some powerful motive for wishing me not to see Constance Tyrrell. I will see her. I will question her. I will learn the truth."

"Well, then, learn the truth, Madam," said Philip. "If you are pained by it, it is not my fault."

"You have deceived me," continued Mary—"shamefully deceived me. Of that I am convinced."

"Reserve these remarks for a more fitting opportunity, Madam," said the King. "Since you are bent upon going to the Lollards' Tower, I will not interfere to prevent you.

But at least put some guard upon yourself, and breed not scandal by your causeless suspicions."

Without making any reply, Mary arose. The King offered his arm, but she rejected it, saying she needed not support. Philip, however, was determined to accompany her, and they went forth together, attended by the Cardinal. No one else ventured to follow them, and Gardiner and Bonner, fearing the King might be offended with them, thought it best to retreat, and hastily quitted the palace.

CHAPTER VI.

HOW CONSTANCE TYRRELL WAS BROUGHT BEFORE THE QUEEN IN THE LOLLARDS' TOWER.

PRECEDED by Rodomont Bittern and others of the guard, and attended by the Cardinal, their Majesties crossed the court to the Lollards' Tower. As the Queen was slowly ascending the steps leading to the entrance, a sudden faintness seized her, and she paused.

"Better turn back, gracious Madam, if you feel ill," observed the Cardinal, noticing her extreme paleness.

"No, it will pass in a moment," she replied.

Resolved not to give way, she went on; but the effort was too much for her, and she had no sooner gained the Post Room than she sank on a chair completely exhausted.

"What place is this?" she asked, in a feeble voice, and glancing around.

"It is called the Post Room, Madam, from that wooden pillar in the centre," replied Pole.

"It looks like a torture-chamber," observed Philip.

"It has been put to a similar purpose, I fear," said the Cardinal. "Yon pillar has not served merely to support the roof."

"Where is Constance Tyrrell?" demanded Mary.

"In the prison-chamber overhead," replied Pole. "The staircase is steep and difficult. 'Twould be hazardous to your Majesty to mount it."

"Let her be brought down," said the Queen.

Upon this, Rodomont Bittern, who, with Simon Mallet, keeper of the tower, stood waiting for orders, immediately disappeared through an arched doorway at the further end of the sombre apartment. Shortly afterwards they returned, bringing with them Constance Tyrrell. This done, they retired.

Constance looked thin and pale, but her colour heightened as she beheld Philip seated near the Queen. The blush, however, quickly faded away, and was succeeded by a death-like pallor, but she did not lose her self-possession. Advancing towards her, the Cardinal said, in a low tone,—

"Kneel to her Majesty. Peradventure, you may move her compassion."

Constance did as she was bidden, and threw herself at the Queen's feet, crying,—

"If I have offended your Majesty, I implore your forgiveness."

"What have I to forgive you, minion?—what have you done?" said Mary, fixing a searching look upon her. "I know nothing of your proceedings since you fled from Hampton Court. Where have you hidden yourself? Why were you brought here? Speak!"

"It is a long story to tell, Madam," cried Constance, troubled by the stern gaze of the King.

"On peril of your life, I command you to conceal nothing from me!" cried Mary, with a burst of uncontrollable fury. "Confess your guilt, or I will wrest the avowal of it from you by torture. Speak out, and you have nothing to fear —but hesitate, equivocate, palter with me, and you are lost."

"As I hope for salvation, Madam," rejoined Constance, "I have nothing to confess."

"It is false!" cried the Queen, with increasing fury. "I read your guilt in your looks. You cannot regard me in the face, and declare you have not injured me."

"I can look Heaven itself in the face, and declare I am innocent of all offence towards your Majesty," rejoined Constance.

"The King, no doubt, will confirm your assertions," observed Mary, bitterly.

"If I did not, I should belie the truth," replied Philip.

"By whose contrivance did you fly from Hampton Court?" demanded Mary.

"Not by the King's, Madam. I fled with Osbert Clinton."

"Tut! Osbert Clinton was merely a tool," exclaimed Mary, incredulously. "Did his Majesty know of your hiding-place?"

"Assuredly not, Madam," replied Constance. "He it was I dreaded most."

"Ha! we are coming to it now," cried Mary. "Why did you dread him?"

"Nay, Madam, persist not in these inquiries, I entreat you," interposed the Cardinal. "You will gain nothing by them, and will only torture yourself."

"Though each word should wound me to the quick, I will have it," said Mary. "Why did you fear the King?"

"Oh! bid me not answer that question, Madam—I cannot do it."

"I will answer it for you," said Mary. "Contradict me if you can. You thought that the King loved you, and would pursue you."

"If she believed so, her flight was justifiable, and merits not reproach from your Majesty," observed the Cardinal. "Pardon me if I say you are unjust towards this maiden. I am satisfied you have no real ground of complaint against her."

"At least, she has been the cause of much trouble to me," cried Mary.

"The innocent cause," said Pole.

"Ay, truly so," said Constance. "I have never wronged your Majesty in act or thought. Beset by dangers, I fled from them, and, if I did wrong, it was from error in judgment, and not from ill intent. Had I stayed —— But I will not dwell upon what might have happened. Your Majesty's reproaches cut me to the soul. I do not deserve them. Rather, indeed, am I an object of pity than reproach. Six months ago I was happy. My life was unclouded—but a change came suddenly, and since then all has been darkness and misery."

"You could not expect happiness, since you have fallen from your faith," said the Queen, severely. "You have justly provoked the wrath of Heaven, and cannot wonder that you have felt the effects of its displeasure. From what you have said, and from what his Eminence has urged in your behalf, I do not believe you have been culpable towards me. But you have cost me many a pang," she added, placing her hand upon her breast.

"Yield to the pitying emotions which I can see sway your breast, gracious Madam," interceded Pole, "and forgive her."

"For the affliction she has caused I do forgive her," replied the Queen, with an effort; "but if her conduct towards myself is free from blame, as you represent it, in other respects it is reprehensible. She was nurtured in the true faith, and was once a model of piety—nay, even contemplated devoting herself to a religious life. But she has listened to the baneful exhortations of one of these teachers of heresy, and has become a proselyte to the new doctrines. What shall be done with her ?"

"Leave her to me, Madam," rejoined the Cardinal. "I do not despair of accomplishing her cure. My hand shall lead you back," he added to Constance. "My voice shall direct you. It cannot be that one of a devout nature like yourself, imbued from childhood in the principles of our Holy Church, familiar with its rites and worship, can efface its doctrines from your breast, and abandon them for another creed. Your conscience must be troubled. The sure way to regain serenity is to abjure your errors."

"Time was when every word uttered by your Eminence would have found a response in my breast," rejoined Constance. "But the rites I formerly practised seem to me idolatrous, and the doctrines then taught me unwarranted by the Gospel. I cannot go back to the faith of Rome."

"You shall be forced back, Mistress, if you continue perverse," cried the Queen, sharply.

"Hold, Madam !" exclaimed Pole. "In this instance let me have my way. I would win back this maiden by gentleness, and not by coercion. I would appeal to her reason and judgment, and not to her fears. Her cure may be the work of time, because the disorder under which she labours is obstinate, but I do not think it will baffle my skill."

"If I could be persuaded by anyone to return to the faith I have abjured, it would be by your Eminence," said Constance, yielding to the kindly influence of his manner.

"You see, Madam, I have already made some little impression," observed Pole to the Queen. "Mildness is more efficacious than violence. As she was enticed from the fold, so must she be lured back to it."

"Well, have your way with her," replied Mary. "Where is the other prisoner, Derrick Carver?"

"In a dungeon beneath this room," replied Pole. "He was placed there in order that no communication should take place between him and Constance Tyrrell. They have not seen each other since they were brought to the Lollards' Tower."

"Such were my orders," observed Philip.

"It is well," rejoined the Queen. "They shall see each other now. Let him be brought before me."

CHAPTER VII.

AN ACCUSER.

ON being brought into the room by Rodomont and Mallet, Derrick Carver made a profound reverence to the Queen, but none to Philip and the Cardinal.

Then addressing himself to Constance, he said, "Welcome, daughter! is the time come for our deliverance from bondage?"

"Not yet," she replied.

"How long, O Lord! wilt thou suffer thy saints to be persecuted?" exclaimed the enthusiast. "It would be glad tidings to me to learn that the end of my weary pilgrimage was near at hand."

"Are you prepared to meet the death you seem to covet?" asked Pole.

"I trust so," replied Carver. "I have prayed long and deeply."

"And repented of your sins—of your murtherous designs against the life of his Majesty?" pursued Pole.

"I do not regard that design as sinful," said Carver. "Repentance, therefore, is uncalled for."

"And you believe yourself to be religious, mistaken man," rejoined Pole. "I tell you, if you die in this impenitent state, you will perish everlastingly. You are so blinded by pride and vain-glory that you cannot discern evil from good, and persuade yourself that you are actuated by high and noble motives, when in reality your motives are sinful and damnable. You are nothing more than an execrable assassin; so hardened in guilt that your heart 'is inaccessible to virtuous and honourable feelings. True religion you have none. You profess to believe in the tenets of the Gospel, yet practise them not. Our blessed Saviour would never number you among his followers, but would cast you off as an unprofitable and faithless servant. You reject truths you do not understand, treat sacred rites as superstitious, and revile those who differ from you in opinion. Go to! you ask for death, and yet you are unfit to die."

"It is not for you to pass sentence upon me," said Carver. "Heaven, to whom my secret motives are known, will judge me."

"And condemn you, if you repent not," said Pole, "for your soul is charged with heavy offences. As I am informed by those who have heard you, you have prayed for her Majesty's destruction."

"I have prayed Heaven to touch her heart, so as to cause her to abandon idolatry, or to abridge her days," rejoined Carver. "Better she be removed than false gods be set up in our temples."

"And know you not that by giving utterance to such a prayer you incur the doom of a traitor?" said Pole. "Your offences are so rank and monstrous, that unless you exhibit some penitence, I cannot intercede in your behalf with her Majesty."

"I ask for no grace from her, and expect none," replied Carver. "Had I twenty lives, I would lay them down for my religion and for my country. We have been delivered to a foreign yoke. But it will not bind us long."

"Peace!" cried Rodomont. "Knowest thou not that thou art in the presence of the King?"

"I know it well, and therefore I speak out," rejoined Carver. "I tell this proud Prince of Spain that England will never submit to his hateful and tyrannous rule. The country will rise up against him, and cast him off. He persuades himself that a son will be born to him, and that through that son he will govern. But he is puffed up with vain hopes. Heaven will refuse him issue."

"Ha! this passes all endurance," cried Philip.

"Have I touched thee, tyrant?" pursued Carver, exultingly. "Heaven, I repeat, will refuse thee issue. The support on which thou countest will be taken from thee. Didst thou dare make the attempt, the accursed Inquisition would at this moment be established amongst us. Thou hast it in reserve for a future day, but ere that day arrives thy perfidy will be discovered. False to thy oaths, faithless to thy Queen, treacherous to all, thou shalt meet thy just reward."

"Faithless to me!" exclaimed Mary. "What wouldst thou dare insinuate, thou foul-mouthed villain?"

"That which I will dare maintain," rejoined Carver— "that the consort you have chosen and have placed on the throne beside you is false to his marriage vows."

"Away with him!" cried Philip, furiously.

"Stay!" exclaimed Mary. "I would question him further."

"Forbear, I beseech you, Madam," interposed Pole. "You only give him power to level his poisonous shafts against you."

"His tongue ought to be torn from his throat for giving utterance to the lies his black heart has conceived!" cried Philip.

"My tongue has uttered no lies," said Carver. "I have shown the Queen how she has been deceived."

"Thou hast simply proved thine own wickedness and malevolence," said Pole. "Her Majesty despises thy slander."

"But it cannot pass unpunished," said Philip. "Let the false villain instantly retract the calumnies he has uttered, or he shall be tied to yon post and scourged till he shall confess himself a liar and a slanderer. Let him be forced to recite the prayer for her Majesty's safe deliverance, on pain of further torture. And, until he manifest contrition for his offences, let his chastisement be daily repeated."

"I will do none of these things," rejoined Carver, reso-

lutely. "Scourge me to death, and I will not retract a
single word I have uttered. I will not pray that the
Queen, whom thou hast deceived and wronged, may bear
thee a son, and so confirm thine authority. But I will pray
to the last that my country may be delivered from oppression, that the Papal power may be overthrown, and the
Protestant religion be re-established."

"Thy resolution shall be tested," said Philip.

"Your Majesty is justly incensed against this miserable
man," said Pole to the King. "Yet would I step between
him and your anger, and entreat you to spare him the
chastisement you have ordered to be inflicted upon him. I
do not seek to extenuate his offences, they are many and
heinous, and he must bear their punishment. But spare
him additional suffering. Spare him the scourge and the
rack."

"I will spare him nothing unless he retract," replied
Philip, sternly.

"I would accept no grace procured by thee," said Carver
to Pole. "As the representative of Antichrist, I regard
thee with loathing and detestation, and will take nothing
from thee."

"Were not thy mind distraught, thou couldst have no
antipathy to one who would befriend thee," replied the
Cardinal. "My religion teaches me to bless those that
curse us, to pray for them that use us despitefully. Be
assured I shall not forget thee in my prayers."

Carver regarded him steadily, but made no answer.

"I shall pray that thy heart may be softened," pursued
Pole, "that thou mayst understand thy sinfulness, and truly
repent of it ere it be too late. Once more I beseech your
Majesty to spare him the torture."

"Be it as you will. I can refuse your Eminence nothing,"
replied Philip.

"This is all the revenge I would take," said Pole, turning
to Carver. "You have declared that you hate me—that
you regard me as the representative of Antichrist. You
profess yourself to be a believer in the Gospel. My
practice is, at least, more conformable to its precepts than
yours."

Carver made no reply, but his lip slightly quivered.

"Miserable man," continued Pole, looking at him com‚ passionately, "I pity you, and would save you if I could. I see the struggle going on in your breast. Wrestle with the demon who would gain the mastery over your soul, and cast him from you. Pride stifles the better emotions of your heart. Do not restrain them."

"If I listen to him much longer, my resolution will fail me," murmured Carver. "I cannot resist his influence."

"Ere long you will be in a better frame of mind," continued Pole, "and more accessible to the arguments I would employ."

"Think it not," interrupted Carver, at once recovering his sternness. "You will never convert me to Popery and idolatry."

"I may at least make you sensible of your errors, and lead you to repentance," said Pole. "The rest lies with Heaven."

"He shall remain in your Eminence's charge during a short space," said Mary, "in the hope that you may be able to bring him to a full sense of his enormities, and prepare him for his end. His life is forfeited."

"So the death to which I am doomed be the same as that wherewith the staunchest adherents of our faith are menaced, I am content," said Carver.

"Thou shall have thy wish," rejoined Mary. "Thy death shall be by fire."

"Then I shall gain my crown of martyrdom," cried Carver, exultingly.

"Fire will not purge out your sins," said the Cardinal. "Those will cling to the soul, which is indestructible. Therefore repent."

"And speedily," added Mary, "for thy time is short."

Hereupon her Majesty arose, and, quitting the Post Room, proceeded to the chapel, to which, as we have previously intimated, there was access from the lower part of the Lollards' Tower.

Here mass was performed, and, by the Queen's express orders, both Constance Tyrrell and Derrick Carver were brought into the chapel during the service. At its close

15—2

they were taken to the cells, while the royal pair proceeded with the Cardinal to the banquetting chamber, where a collation was prepared.

The Queen, however, declined to partake of the repast, saying she felt faint and ill, and two ladies who had accompanied her to the palace being hastily summoned, she retired with them.

CHAPTER VIII.

HOW THE QUEEN CONFIDED HER GRIEFS TO THE CARDINAL.

PHILIP, who exhibited little uneasiness at the Queen's indisposition, was still seated at table with Pole, when the Cardinal's physician, Doctor Forest, came in, and informed his Eminence that her Majesty desired instant speech with him.

"The Queen is not seriously ill, I trust, Sir?" said Philip, alarmed by the physician's grave looks.

"She appears to have received a severe shock, Sire," replied Forest, "but I trust no ill consequences may ensue. Her Majesty wishes to see your Eminence—alone," he added to the Cardinal.

"Go to her at once," said Philip. "If my hopes of succession should be blighted, it will be grievous indeed. But you have no such fears, Sir?" he added quickly to the physician.

"I shall have no fear if her Majesty's mind can be tranquilised," replied Forest—"and that, I trust, his Eminence will be able to accomplish."

"My reliance, then, is upon you," said Philip to the Cardinal. "A few words from your lips will not fail to calm her."

Thereupon Pole hastened to the apartment where the Queen had been conveyed. On entering it, he found her reclining on a couch, and attended by her ladies, who, on his appearance, immediately withdrew.

"I am much concerned to see your Majesty thus," observed Pole. "It will be a real affliction if your visit to me should be productive of ill consequences to yourself."

"I am sorry I came," replied Mary. "The words of that malignant heretic have sunk deep into my breast. He said that I shall never be a mother."

"Let not his words trouble you for a moment, gracious Madam," said Pole. "They are of no account. He but gave utterance to the evil wishes of his heart—nothing more. Dismiss all fears from your breast, and look joyfully and confidently forward to the moment which will crown a nation's satisfaction in your marriage by giving it a prince."

"Your words are comforting," replied Mary, faintly ; "but I cannot shake off my fears. Something whispers in mine ear that the fond hopes I have indulged will prove vain. And what will happen then ?" she continued, with a shudder. "I shall lose my husband."

"Oh ! think not so, gracious Madam—think not so !" cried Pole. "If the consummation you dread were to happen—which Heaven, in its goodness, avert !—and fill the land with sorrow—the King, your husband, would be more devoted to you than ever."

"Hear me, my Lord Cardinal," said Mary, grasping his arm convulsively. "I have already lost my husband's love, if I ever possessed it, which I more than doubt. Were I to disappoint his expectations now, he would leave me."

"Leave you, gracious Madam ! Impossible !"

"I say he would," rejoined the Queen. "This is the only tie that binds us together. I cannot give him my kingdom, and if I fail to give him an heir, through whom he may exercise the sovereignty, he will return to Spain."

"I cannot believe him so ungrateful," cried Pole. "Your Majesty does him injustice."

"His conduct towards me leaves no doubt as to his intentions," rejoined Mary. "On our first meeting he vowed he loved me, but his vows were false. I am not blind to my defects. I know that I have few charms of person to attract him—that I have neither youth nor beauty. But I gave him a deep, true love. Moreover, I gave him a kingdom. How has he requited me ?—by neglect, by harshness, by infidelity."

"Oh! Madam, I would willingly discredit what I hear," cried Pole. "If it be as you represent, I pity you from the bottom of my heart."

"My sainted mother, Queen Katharine of Aragon, was most unhappy," pursued Mary; "but I am little less unhappy. Neglected, injured, scorned as I am by my husband, I cannot, despite the efforts I make, shake off the love I bear him. I summon pride to my aid, but in vain. My heart is wrung with jealousy, but I hide my torments. What shall I do if I lose him?"

"You will not lose him, gracious Madam—fear it not," exclaimed Pole. "I will remonstrate with him. I will convince him of the wickedness of his conduct."

"Proceed with caution, or you will only make matters worse," said Mary. "Were I to lose him, I should die."

"Do not distress yourself thus, Madam," said Pole. "Exalted as is your station, it does not exempt you from the ordinary sufferings of humanity—nay, it exposes you to greater ills than fall to the lot of those less loftily placed. The King is unworthy of your love, I grant, but I counsel you not to resent his neglect, nor to reproach him. Bear yourself ever gently towards him, ever maintaining your own dignity, and if you win not back his love, you are certain to gain his esteem."

"Perchance I have reproached him overmuch," cried Mary. "But, as I have already said, my heart has been wrung by jealousy."

"Crush all such feelings, at whatever cost," rejoined Pole. "Give him no grounds of complaint."

"But his unkindness makes me wretched," cried Mary. "Would I could hate him—despise him!"

"It is sad that love like yours should meet so poor a return," sighed Pole; "and the King is blind to his own happiness that he does not estimate the treasure he casts away, to set up worthless baubles in its place. Pray constantly and fervently to Heaven to bless you with a son, and if your prayers are granted, you will be happy."

"But if Heaven should deny me the blessing?"

"Heaven will compassionate you," said the Cardinal. 'It will not be deaf to prayers like yours."

"Yet my mother's prayers were unheard, though her

wrongs and sufferings were greater than mine. She died neglected, heart-broken. Such may be my fate."

"The indulgence of these thoughts is like to bring about the very calamity you would avert, Madam," said Pole. "You know and feel how much depends upon the event we so much desire, and your physician will tell you that to a favourable issue freedom from agitation and anxiety are essential. You will undo all the good if you harass yourself thus unnecessarily."

"I will try to follow your counsel," replied Mary. "And now, my good Lord Cardinal, answer me one question. Have I wrongfully suspected Constance Tyrrell?"

"Madam, I truly think so," replied Pole.

"Then send for her instantly, that I may repair the wrong I have done," cried Mary.

The Cardinal readily complied, and ere long Constance made her appearance.

"Come hither, child," said the Queen, in a kind voice, on seeing her. "I have done you injustice. But I will make amends. You told me that you fled from Hampton Court with Osbert Clinton. Why did you trust him?"

"I trusted him because—because he loved me, gracious Madam," replied Constance. "Since then we have been affianced."

"Is the King aware of your betrothal?" inquired Mary.

"He is, Madam," replied Constance. "But he has forbidden Osbert, on pain of death, to see me again."

"Indeed!" exclaimed Mary. "Then I cannot aid you as I should wish to do. You must think of Osbert no more."

"I cannot obey you in that respect, Madam," replied Constance. "He is never absent from my thoughts."

"Poor child!" exclaimed Mary. "Your fate is as sad as my own. We are both doomed to unhappiness."

"But it is in your Majesty's power to make me happy— to make Osbert happy," cried Constance.

"Alas! child, you give me credit for more power than I possess," rejoined Mary. "I dare not oppose the King in this matter. Osbert must not see you again. Should he do so, I cannot save him from the King's resentment. But I will do all I can for you. You shall be released from confinement, but you must remain for a time with the good Cardinal, who, I am sure, will be a father to you."

"I will willingly take charge of her," said Pole. "She shall have free range of the palace."

"But she must not quit it without my consent," said Mary. "Neither must she see Osbert Clinton."

"I will answer for her," rejoined the Cardinal.

"Nay, I will answer for myself," cried Constance. "I thank your Majesty from the bottom of my heart, and will faithfully obey your injunctions."

"It will be a period of probation, that is all," said the Queen. "You will be better and happier for it in the end— at least, I trust so. And now, child, you may retire. Remember what I have said about Osbert Clinton."

"I shall not fail, gracious Madam," she replied. And kissing the hand extended to her by the Queen, she withdrew.

Some further conversation then took place between Mary and the Cardinal, which had the effect of restoring the Queen to comparative cheerfulness, and she declared that she now felt quite able to return to Whitehall. By her desire, Pole then summoned her ladies, and, on their appearance, quitted her to communicate the glad intelligence of her recovery to the King.

CHAPTER IX.

THE FRANCISCAN.

PHILIP remained for some little time in the banqueting-chamber, expecting the Cardinal's return, but as Pole did not appear, the King at last sallied forth into the court, where several of the Cardinal's retinue were assembled. Perceiving Rodomont Bittern among them, he signed to him to approach, and then walking apart with him, said, with a certain significance—

"Since Constance Tyrrell has been imprisoned in the Lollards' Tower, no communication has passed between her and Osbert Clinton?—ha!"

"Access to her while shut up in yon tower were impossible without consent of the keeper, Sire," replied Rodomont; "and he is faithful."

"Difficult it may be, but not impossible," rejoined the King. "Yon ivied wall would not be difficult to scale. Her prison-chamber has a window which might be reached by a rope ladder."

"Can he suspect?" thought Rodomont, uneasily.

"Such plans are common enough in Spain, where walls, bolts, and bars, and even watchful gaolers, cannot shut out lovers," pursued Philip. "Osbert Clinton is rash enough—enamoured enough to attempt anything."

"Your Majesty is a better judge of such matters than I can pretend to be," said Rodomont; "but I would risk life and limb for no woman, were she twice as lovely as Constance Tyrrell. The danger of the enterprise would effec-

tually cool my ardour. Osbert Clinton well knows that he
would incur your Majesty's severe displeasure were he to
make any such attempt."

"Danger, I repeat, will not deter him," said the King.
"It is not enough that Constance is shut up in yon tower—
that the doors of her cell are locked, and the windows
barred. I tell you, he will find a way to her—if he has not
done so already."

"I dare not contradict your Majesty," replied Rodomont.
"It may be as you suspect. What more would you have
done?"

"That tower must be strictly watched at night," said
Philip, "and you must be the watcher."

"I am ready to obey your Majesty," replied Rodomont;
"but such an office will somewhat interfere with my duties
to the Cardinal."

"Heed not that!" said Philip. "I will hold you excused with his Eminence. You will commence the watch
to-night."

"To-night, Sire?"

"Should Osbert Clinton venture hither, arrest him, and
keep him in close confinement till you learn my pleasure."

"May I make bold to inquire if your Majesty has any
reason to suspect that he will come?" said Rodomont.

"It matters not what I suspect. Do as I command you."

"Your injunctions shall be obeyed, Sire," returned Rodomont. "And for his own sake I hope Master Osbert Clinton
may keep away."

At this moment a tall Franciscan friar, with the cowl of
his grey robe drawn over his head, was seen marching
slowly along the court-yard. He directed his steps towards
the Lollards' Tower, and on reaching it stayed at the doorway, where he remained in converse with Mallet, the keeper.

"Who is yon monk, and what is his errand?" demanded
the King, who had been watching him with some curiosity.

"I know him not, Sire—he is a stranger," replied Rodomont. "Apparently he is seeking admittance to one of the
prisoners, which Mallet, the keeper, is unwilling to grant.
Perchance, it may be Mistress Constance Tyrrell whom he
desires to see."

"Bring him before me, I will question him." said Philip.

Rodomont instantly obeyed, and shortly afterwards returned with the friar and Mallet. The Franciscan made
a humble obeisance to the King, but did not attempt to
raise his hood.

"An please your Majesty, this holy man is from Winchester," said Mallet. "He is charged by Father Jerome
of Saint Catherine's Chapel on the Hill, with a message to
Mistress Constance Tyrrell. Is it not so?" he added to the
monk.

The Franciscan bowed his head.

"Is Father Jerome aware that she to whom he has sent
you has lapsed from the faith?" said the King.

"He is, Sire," replied the monk, in tones that sounded
strangely hollow, "but he hopes she may still be reclaimed.
With the design of rendering some aid in the good work, I
have come hither. Great success has hitherto attended my
efforts; and therefore it is that good Father Jerome, who is
deeply interested in Mistress Constance's spiritual welfare,
hath selected me for the office."

"An opportunity shall be afforded you of making the
attempt," said the King. "There can be no reason why
this holy man should not be admitted to her," he added to
Mallet. "Take him to her cell."

"Mistress Constance is not in her cell at present, Sire,"
observed Mallet.

"Where is she, then?" cried the King, sharply.

"She is with her Majesty, Sire," replied Mallet.

"With the Queen?" exclaimed Philip, surprised. "Go
into the tower, good father, and await her return."

"Ha, here comes Mistress Constance," exclaimed Rodomont, as the damsel, escorted by Simnel and Holiday, issued
from the palace, and made her way towards the Lollards'
Tower. Bowing humbly to the King, she would have
passed on, had he not stopped her.

"You have been with her Majesty, as I understand?" he
said. "How fares it with her now?"

"As well as you could desire, Sire," she replied. "Her
Majesty has quite recovered."

"I would fain reward you for your good tidings," said
Philip. "It rests with yourself whether your imprisonment
in this tower shall be prolonged."

"My term of durance is at an end, Sire," she rejoined. "I am a prisoner, it is true, but only restricted to the limits of the palace. I desire no greater freedom. The Queen has conferred this grace upon me."

"Her Majesty has only anticipated my intentions," said Philip. "It grieved me to think you should have been confined within that dreary cell. But why did you not appeal to me, when you well knew that a word would have procured you full liberty?"

"But I could not utter that word, Sire," she rejoined, coldly.

"Tarry a moment," said the King, checking her departure. "This holy man has been sent by Father Jerome, to whose ghostly counsels you once gave heed, in the hope that he may restore you to the Catholic Church."

"I am much beholden to Father Jerome for his kindly concern in my behalf," she rejoined; "and it pains me to dismiss the good friar he has sent without a hearing. But a conference would be profitable to neither of us, and I must therefore decline it."

"How know you that such a conference would be unprofitable, daughter?" said the friar, in tones that trembled with emotion. "I pray you send me not away unheard."

At the sound of his voice Constance started, and was seized with a trepidation which she could hardly conceal.

"Can he have ventured here in this disguise?" she murmured. "Imprudent that he is, he will sacrifice himself by his rashness! No, no," she added aloud, "I cannot consent to a conference with you without the Cardinal's sanction. I am under his charge."

"'If that be all, his Eminence's sanction can be readily procured, for here he comes," said Philip.

"The Cardinal here, then he is lost!" mentally ejaculated Constance. "You have come on a vain errand," she added, to the monk.

"Nay, let us hear what his Eminence has to say to the matter," observed Philip. And, as Pole came up at the moment, he told him what had occurred.

"'Father Jerome must have much confidence in this friar if he imagines he will succeed where we have failed," remarked Pole. "I will question him, and judge of his fitness for the task. Bring him to me anon," he added to Rodo-mont.

"I do not desire to confer with him," cried Constance, distractedly. "Send him away!—Send him away!"

"What means this strange emotion?" thought the Cardinal. "A word with you, daughter," he added, taking her aside. "Who is this monk? I must know the truth. Attempt to deceive me, and I will compel him to raise his hood."

"In mercy spare him," she rejoined. "If the King beholds his features he is lost."

"Then it is Osbert Clinton," said the Cardinal. "I will not betray him, but you must promise to hold no converse with him."

"I do—I do," she rejoined.

"Control yourself, or you will excite the King's suspicions," pursued the Cardinal. "I am glad I made this discovery in time. I shall warn this rash youth not to come here again. If he does, he must not count on my protection. And now," he added, so as to be heard by the King, "retire to your cell till a chamber can be prepared for you in the palace. I will speak with this friar anon, and act as may seem best to me in regard to him."

Thanking him for his goodness, and making an obeisance to the King, Constance withdrew.

Philip and the Cardinal then hastened to the Queen, and shortly afterwards the royal pair embarked in the barge awaiting them, and returned to Whitehall.

CHAPTER X.

OF THE COUNSEL GIVEN TO OSBERT CLINTON BY THE CARDINAL.

THEIR Majesties had not long quitted Lambeth Palace, when the Franciscan friar was summoned by Rodomont to the presence of the Cardinal.

While crossing the court with the monk, Rodomont paused for a moment, and directed his companion's attention to the Lollards' Tower.

"You would imagine the prisoners must be secure in that tower, holy father," he remarked.

"Unquestionably so, my son," replied the friar.

"His Majesty, however, is not of that opinion," rejoined Rodomont. "He is under the impression that a certain young gallant, whose brain seems turned by love, would be rash enough to climb, by means of a rope-ladder, to the window of the cell wherein his mistress is confined."

"Does the King suspect this?" inquired the monk, uneasily.

"So shrewdly, that he has ordered me to keep strict watch to-night, and to arrest the love-sick gallant should he appear. The task is not to my liking, but I must obey his Majesty's orders. Some men will run any risk for those they love—but you, father, cannot understand such matters. You would reprove Osbert Clinton—for so the gallant is named—for his rashness and folly."

"I should pity him, rather than blame him," said the friar.

"And you would not deem it wrong if I were to aid him, eh, father? Certes, I should be loth to betray him—but he is so imprudent that he might betray himself. 'Tis a miracle that he 'scaped detection by the King just now."

" What mean you, my son ? " cried the monk, alarmed.

" I mean that Master Osbert Clinton has been rash enough to venture hither," said Rodomont ; " and though luckily his Majesty did not see through his disguise, I was not equally blind."

" You knew me, then ? " said Osbert Clinton.

" My suspicions of the truth were roused from the first, and were speedily changed to certainty," rejoined Rodomont. " 'Twas marvellous, I repeat, that you imposed upon the quick-sighted King, but I do not think the Cardinal was deceived. However, you have not much to fear from his Eminence, who is too kind-hearted to do more than chide you for your indiscretion. Had things continued as they were. and Mistress Constance been kept a prisoner in yon tower, I would have helped you to liberate her. But a change for the better has occurred. The doors of her cell are opened, and she is free to go where she lists within the palace. Let that content you. And now I must bring you before his Eminence."

With this they entered the palace, and after passing though the vestibule, where a number of persons belonging to the household were collected, they proceeded to a spacious chamber, with a carved oak ceiling, windows filled with painted glass, and walls furnished with book-shelves stored with goodly tomes, where they found the Cardinal seated at a table. He was writing at the moment, and only suspended his task to look up, and then resumed it. When he had finished his letter and sealed it, he delivered it to Rodomont, bidding him give it to Lord Montague's messenger, who was waiting to receive it. As soon as they were alone, he turned to Osbert, and assuming a grave and severe expression of countenance, ordered him to throw back his hood ; and, as the young man complied, he said, "'Tis as I suspected. You are Osbert Clinton."

" Yes, I am he," replied the other. " It was my intention to avow myself to your Eminence—to explain my motives in coming hither, and to crave your pardon."

" It is needless to explain your motives," said Pole ; " I am fully aware of them. Neither, though I blame your rashness, shall I refuse you pardon. But this indiscretion must not be repeated. If you come here again, you must take the con-

sequences of your folly. You are free to go as you came—
but again I say, you must not return."

"Ere I go, your Eminence's goodness emboldens me to
ask your permission for a brief interview with Constance
Tyrrell."

"I cannot grant your request," replied the Cardinal,
"though it pains me to refuse it. I pity both you and Constance, but I cannot aid you in the dilemma in which you are
placed. Patience is difficult, especially to a young and ardent
lover; but you must perforce practise it. Be not cast down.
If Fortune refuses to smile on you now, she may do so hereafter. Be hopeful, be courageous, be trustful; and if your
love survives these trials, you will be rewarded in due season.
Rashness and precipitancy will destroy all. Constance will
be safe with me—safe as with her own father; nay, safer,
for I have more power than he can possess. If I cannot
give her to you—if I cannot even allow you to approach her
—I can protect her. Seek not then to disturb her, or to
plunge yourself into difficulties from which none can extricate you. I shall employ the same arguments with Constance. I will tell her that your enforced separation will
only be for a time—that she must not despair, but may confidently look forward to to a meeting with you on some future
day."

"I am fully sensible of the wisdom of your Eminence's
counsel, and will endeavour to profit by it," said Osbert.
"Though the separation will be hard to bear, it will be shorn
of much of its anguish by the reflection that she has found a
sanctuary with you."

"And such, in truth, it is, for she will be protected from
all danger," rejoined Pole. "Henceforth you may picture
her, not as the inmate of a narrow cell, condemned to pass
her hours in seclusion, but as my guest, free to go where she
will within this mansion; not coerced in matters of religion,
though I shall try by all proper means to lead her back to
her former faith; subject to no harsh discipline or regula-
tions; not compelled to perform any severe penance, but left
to her own free will—such will be the course I shall pursue
with her, and I trust it may tend to her comfort and benefit."

"It cannot fail," said Osbert. "Under your Eminence's
benignant influence she must be happy."

"She will at least find a refuge from the terrible storm which is at hand, and which might overwhelm her as it will many others," said the Cardinal. "Be thankful, therefore, that she is not exposed to this great peril, and is not likely to be numbered amongst the victims of the religious persecution, which, I fear, is at hand. And now fare you well, Sir. Take my blessing with you. No words of gratitude are needed. You shall thank me hereafter, when I restore Constance to you."

With this, he struck a small silver bell which stood upon the table beside him. Before the summons could be answered, Osbert had drawn the cowl over his head.

"Conduct this monk to the gate," said the Cardinal to Rodomont, as the latter entered the room, "and suffer him not to talk with anyone by the way."

"It shall be done as your Eminence enjoins," said Rodomont. "Come, Father!"

And he quitted the room with Osbert.

CHAPTER XI.

HE good Cardinal acted up to his promise in regard to Constance. An apartment was assigned her in a wing of the palace overlooking the garden, and that nothing might be wanting to her comfort, search was made for her old attendant, Dorcas, whose retreat being discovered, without much difficulty, by Rodomont, she was brought to the palace, and reinstated in her former position with her young mistress.

Ever since the night when Constance had been carried off to the Lollards' Tower, the poor old woman had been inconsolable. Her joy, therefore, on finding her young mistress again, may be imagined. She strained her to her breast with all a mother's affection, wept over her, and could scarcely cease her demonstrations of regard. The Cardinal, who witnessed the meeting, was much touched by it, but at last deemed it proper to moderate the old woman's transports of delight. But this only turned the tide of her gratitude upon him. She fell down at his feet, embraced his knees, and prayed that his goodness might be rewarded.

Treated with paternal kindness and consideration by the Cardinal, Constance could not but feel profound gratitude towards him ; and as the virtues of his character became more fully revealed to her, she began to regard him with feelings akin to veneration.

They had frequent discourses together on points of faith,

16—2

and, though Constance's adherence to the new doctrines remained unshaken, she listened with attention to the Cardinal's able and profound exposition of the tenets of the Church of Rome. The differences between their respective creeds appeared slighter than she had at first supposed, and if all Romish priests and prelates were like the Cardinal, lived as he lived, and taught as he taught, she felt that there might, indeed, be one universal Church.

The calmness of Pole's manner, the clearness of his judgment, his profound theological learning, contrasted strongly with the fanaticism and fiery zeal of Derrick Carver, who had as little toleration for the Romanists as they had for him. Her mind, over-excited by the stimulative discourses of the enthusiast, acquired a healthier tone from the exhortations of the Cardinal, and she felt like one who had recovered from a fever.

Perfectly resigned to her position, strengthened in all her good resolutions by Pole, and allowed the free exercise of her own religious opinions, she became composed and cheerful, and, if not quite happy, was at least free from despondency. Her personal appearance improved in the same ratio, and, ere many weeks had flown, she had quite recovered her beauty. Her life might appear dull and monotonous, but its very monotony was not without a charm to her, who from early years had meditated the seclusion of a convent. Caring little for the world, or its pleasures and vanities, she was well content with her present existence, and scarcely desired to change it. Not that the Cardinal's palace, with its princely establishment, its numerous and important guests, was devoid of the stir and bustle of active life, but in this she took no part. She did not mingle with the household, and was never seen by the Cardinal's numerous guests.

The garden was open to her, with its long terraces, its alleys and groves, and therein she took her walks at morn. At such times she often met Pole and Priuli, and discoursed with them. In argument Priuli displayed the same moderation and clearness of judgment as his friend, though he did not equal him in profundity of intellect or learning. Perhaps Pole was disappointed that he did not produce a more sensible impression upon his pupil, and bring her to express contrition for her errors, and a desire for reconciliation with the Church of Rome, but he did not manifest any impatience; still less did he employ harshness or threats. Attendance at the chapel at matins or evensong, or during the celebration of mass, was not compulsory on Constance, nor was she forced to assist at any of the rites or observances of the Church of Rome.

Not unfrequently the Cardinal spoke to her of Osbert Clinton, and held out to her, as he had done to her lover, the hope of a meeting at some future day.

Shortly after Constance's partial restoration to freedom, the Cardinal dispatched Rodomont to Southampton to acquaint Master Tyrrell with the steps he had taken in his daughter's behalf, and inviting him to come and see her.

Rodomont would fain have brought the old merchant back with him, but Tyrrell declined. His anger against Constance had not yet abated. Unless she renounced her errors, she need not hope to see him again, he declared. He left her entirely in the Lord Cardinal's hands, satisfied that if her conversion could be accomplished it would be by his Eminence. The old merchant, it was clear, was so apprehensive of being implicated with his daughter, and suspected of heretical pravity himself, that he was resolved not to go near her.

Rodomont seized the opportunity of ascertaining his sentiments in regard to her union with Osbert Clinton. But on this point the old merchant was equally obstinate. "I will not consent to her marriage—I will not give her my blessing —I will not see her till she recants, and returns to the faith of her forefathers," he cried. "Then she shall be my daughter once more."

"It is well for her that she has found a father in the Cardinal, since her own father deserts her in her need," observed Rodomont.

"Why, what would you have me do?" cried Tyrrell.

"Go see her! comfort her! persuade her to conform," rejoined Rodomont.

"And be suspected of heresy, and cited before the ecclesiastical commissioners—mayhap burnt before my own door," said Tyrrell. "No, I thank you. I mean to keep out of harm's way."

"Well, if you can reconcile such conduct to your conscience, I have no more to say," observed Rodomont; "except, that if you escape burning in this world, you stand a good chance of burning in the next. So you positively decline to go back with me to Lambeth Palace—eh ?"

"Positively," replied Tyrrell. "As a good Catholic, the Cardinal will applaud my conduct."

"There you are mistaken," rejoined Rodomont. "You little understand his Eminence, if you suppose him dead to the feelings of human nature, as you appear to be. He can but entertain one opinion of your conduct—disgust." So saying he left him.

On his return to Lambeth Palace, Rodomont informed the Cardinal what had passed between himself and Master Tyrrell. Pole could scarcely credit the relation, so astounded was he at the old merchant's extraordinary indifference to his daughter. However, the effect produced upon him by Tyrrell's stoical conduct, was to increase the fatherly concern he already felt in Constance, and make him more anxious than ever for her conversion.

How he prospered in his efforts we have already seen.

BUT there was another person besides Osbert Clinton in whom Constance took deep interest, and whose perilous position occasioned her profound anxiety. This was Derrick Carver. True, since her intercourse with Pole, her admiration of the enthusiast had somewhat abated, but she could not forget the benefits he had conferred upon her. All that she could learn respecting Carver was, that he had been removed from the underground dungeon to the prison-chamber in the Lollards' Tower, which she herself had occupied, and that he was still confined there. She also ascertained, by means of old Dorcas, that he had been several times examined by Bonner, and had been severely handled by them for his contumacy. Fain would she have obtained an interview with him—fain would she have prayed with him and consoled him—but this was not permitted. Pole, who considered the fanatic's influence over her to be most pernicious, refused her solicitations, and in a manner that did not allow her to renew the request. The Cardinal declared that, finding Carver impracticable, he had surrendered him to the ecclesiastical commissioners, and he was now entirely in their hands.

Constance, therefore, had no hope of beholding the enthusiast again in this world. Strange to say, she did not altogether deplore his fate, but in moments of exaltation almost envied him the martyrdom which it appeared certain he would have to endure.

Throughout this time of trial, Carver's resolution had never deserted him—had never even wavered. The prison chamber to which he had been removed was a great improvement upon the dismal dungeon wherein he had been previously immured. In fact, as his movements were not restrained, and he was allowed writing materials, with a Bible and a book of prayer, he was well enough content with his lodging. To the mementoes of the many sufferers for conscience' sake who had preceded him in this cell, and had carved their names on the stout oak panels lining the walls, he added his own name, with these words: "APPROVED BY STRIPES, IMPRISONMENT, AND DEATH."

His cell was by no means gloomy. Through the narrow grated window looking upon the Thames, and at which Osbert had conversed with Constance, he obtained a glimpse of the river, and of some structures on its opposite banks, while he could hear the dash of oars in the water, and the cheerful voices of the boatmen. But the stern enthusiast bestowed but little thought on the external world. His time was now entirely occupied in preparation for eternity, and in fortifying himself for the fiery ordeal by which his faith was to be approved.

On several occasions, as we have already stated, he had been interrogated by Bonner, but neither promises of grace, nor threats of torture, could move him. He resolutely refused to subscribe the recantation proffered him by the bishop; and when the latter, exasperated by his obstinacy, had him taken to the Post Room, stripped to the girdle, tied to the wooden pillar in the centre of the chamber, and severely scourged, he uttered no cry, but persisted in his refusal.

Determined to try the effect of greater severity, and having means and appliances at hand, Bonner ordered him to be chained to the walls of his cell till he should show signs of submission.

This was done. The unfortunate captive was fastened to two of the ponderous iron rings which may still be seen in the walls of the prison, and kept in such a position that he could neither lie down nor stand erect.

In this woful plight he remained for three days and three nights, debarred of his chief solace, the Bible, and unable to kneel in prayer without putting himself to excruciating agony, but his constancy was unsubdued, and when Bonner again visited him, thinking he must needs be overcome, he found him unyielding as ever.

What further barbarities might have been practised by the savage prelate upon the unfortunate captive can only be imagined, but happily his victim was snatched from his clutches by Pole. Made aware how severely the prisoner had been treated, the Cardinal instantly interfered, caused the poor wretch's chains to be taken off, and interdicted any further application of torture. Bonner sullenly acquiesced, as indeed he was obliged to do, but he promised himself to report the Cardinal's culpable leniency —for such he esteemed it—to their Majesties, and also to the Pope.

"His Eminence is an abettor of heresy, instead of an up-rooter of it," muttered the bishop. "If he be not recalled by the Pope, he will undo all we have done."

Not altogether satisfied with the report he had received of the prisoner's condition, Pole resolved to visit him in his cell, and was accompanied in the errand of mercy by Priuli. The ascent of the narrow spiral stone staircase leading from the Post Room to the prison-chamber was somewhat painful to the Cardinal, and he was compelled to pause for a few moments to recover himself as he reached the arched entrance of the cell. This gave him an opportunity of examining the double doors, which we have already described as of oak, bound with iron, and studded with broad-headed nails ; and he pointed out the immense thickness of the planks to Priuli.

Neither of them had been before in the upper part of the Lollards' Tower, and, as they entered the prison-chamber, they looked around it with melancholy interest. The oak panels, dark almost as ebony, the black boarded roof, the black boarded floor, the small grated windows, the ponderous iron rings fastened in the walls, the prisoner seated on a stool at a table of similar material and similar hue to the panels, all constituted a picture that powerfully impressed them.

Derrick Carver was engaged in reading the Bible, and so profoundly engrossed, that he did not raise his eyes on their entrance. The Cardinal signed to Mallet, by whom they were attended, not to disturb him. The rugged features and gaunt frame of the fanatic had undergone little change, but his beard was grizzled, and his locks had become snow white.

The Cardinal and Priuli contemplated him for some time with profound interest, and in perfect silence, but at last an observation made by the latter, though uttered in a low tone, reached the ears of the prisoner, and caused him to look up. When he perceived who were in his cell, he tried to rise, but was compelled by pain and weakness to relinquish the attempt.

"The man is really too feeble to stand," remarked Mallet. "Shall I bring your Eminence a chair?"

Pole declined the offer, saying he could stand well enough.

"Leave the room, and remain without till you are summoned," he added to Mallet, who immediately obeyed the injunction, closing the door after him as he went out.

"You are weak and ill, my poor friend," said Pole, in a sympathetic tone. "Wine and nourishing food shall be sent to recruit your strength."

"I do not need them," replied Carver. "Herein I find new life and vigour," he added, pointing to the Bible. "For three days and three nights, while fastened to yon wall, was I deprived of this consolation, and I account it the worst part of my suffering. I lack nothing now."

"I am sorry you have been treated with so much severity," observed the Cardinal.

"I do not complain," replied Carver. "I may not have been lawfully punished with the scourge, or lawfully fastened to yon iron rings, but there is little law or justice in England now, since we are under Spanish rule."

"You are mistaken, friend," replied Pole. "The statutes against heresy and schism, which were in force when this prison-chamber was built by Archbishop Chicheley, in the time of Henry IV, more than a hundred years ago, have been revived, and though your punishment has been severe, t has not been contrary to law."

"I have said I do not complain," rejoined Carver. "We have provoked Divine displeasure, and must endure our merited chastisement till the wrath of Heaven be appeased. Were I called upon to suffer all the persecutions endured by holy Paul, I would cheerfully bear them for the sake of the Gospel."

"I admire your resolution, friend," said Pole; "but I beseech you to consider well whether you may not be in error."

"I cannot be in error, when I rely solely on the truths of Scripture," rejoined Carver.

"But there are doctrinal points upon which men are not agreed," said the Cardinal.

"There are," replied Carver, "and my principles are those of the Reformed Church. I abominate the Church of Rome, and regard it as the synagogue of Satan, and the very sink of all heresy, superstition, and idolatry. I will have no masses, no auricular confession with penance, no image-worship. I deny the real presence in the sacrament. And I also deny that the Pope is the head of the Christian Church, and utterly reject his authority."

"But if I can prove to you that you are wrong," said Pole; "if I can convince you that the Pope's authority is derived from Saint Peter, and through him from our Saviour himself, will you not admit that you have formed erroneous conclusions?"

"I believe the Romish faith to be anti-Christian and naught," rejoined Carver. "I cannot worship at its altars, and were I to do so I should place my soul in jeopardy. It is in vain to argue with me. Threats or fair promises will be alike ineffectual. I am not be moved."

"But if you obstinately close your ears, how can you ever learn the truth?" said the Cardinal.

"I *have* learnt the truth," rejoined Carver, "and am proof against fallacy and delusion. I have enough regard for your Eminence to wish you were of my mind."

"Well, try to convince me. Let me hear what you have to say in defence of your faith," observed Pole.

"'Twere to show him too much indulgence," said Priuli.

"I could say much in defence of my faith," observed Carver, "but I know you would not listen to me, and I should therefore only throw away my time. But let me not appear ungrateful. I am assured that your Eminence is actuated by a sincere desire for my welfare."

"I would save you, if possible, from the terrible death by which you are menaced," said the Cardinal. "Conform, and I will obtain your pardon. Reflect on what I have said."

"I need no reflection," rejoined the other. "I could not conform with hypocrisy, and I will never belie my conscience."

"Have you no ties that bind you to earth?—none for whom you desire to live?" said the Cardinal.

"I have a wife and children, and an aged mother," replied Carver; but I gave up all when I entered the service of my Heavenly Master."

"And would you leave them without a protector?" said Pole.

"Heaven will watch over them," rejoined the other.

"This man appears callous to all human emotions and sympathies," observed Priuli.

"There you do not judge me rightly," said Carver. "My breast is not devoid of affection. I love my wife and children—I love my mother—dearly—very dearly. But I am a soldier of Christ, and having been summoned to the fight, must obey the call. If I die in His cause, those dear to me will not be deserted. You cannot touch me. There is no weak part in my armour."

"Then you do not desire to confer with me further?" said Pole. "You have nothing to ask of me?"

"There is one favour I would solicit," said Carver. "Before I am taken hence I would fain have a last interview with Constance Tyrrell."

"I cannot grant it," replied Pole. "I hope to accomplish her conversion, and your influence might counteract my efforts."

"But she continues stedfast in her faith?—Tell me that?" cried Carver, anxiously.

"I cannot answer the question," returned Pole; "would not, if I could."

"She does!—I am sure she does!" exclaimed the enthusiast. "She is my spiritual daughter. Her conversion was my work, and I glory in it. Having opened her eyes to the light, she will not relapse into darkness—never. No; I have no misgivings about Constance."

"Be not too confident," rejoined Pole. "My hope is to bring her back to the fold from which she has strayed. You have preferred a request to me which I am compelled to refuse, but I will grant you a favour which you have not solicited. I desire to benefit you as far as I can, and will lighten the irksomeness of your confinement. In a few days you will have recovered your strength, and will be able to go forth. Pledge me your word to return early in the evening, and you shall be allowed liberty during the daytime."

"What is this I hear?" cried Carver, astounded. "Is it possible that your Eminence will allow me to go where I list during the daytime?"

"You shall go forth wholly unattended on your promise to return," rejoined the Cardinal.

"I never looked for such indulgence as this," said Carver, much affected. "When I have heard the voices of the boatmen on the river, and other gladsome sounds, I have longed to join my fellow-men, but I have checked the feeling, knowing it could not be gratified. But now your Eminence offers me this great boon—a boon I should not have dared to ask —and with no conditions annexed to it."

"None save that I mentioned," replied Pole. "You shall be free to go forth, but you must come back to your cell at eventide."

For a few moments Carver covered his face with his hands, and tears trickled down his rugged cheeks. After a while he looked up and, in broken accents, said, "I did not think to weep again either for joy or grief. But your Eminence's goodness has touched me to the heart, and opened fountains which I deemed fast sealed. You shall not find me unworthy of the confidence reposed in me. The promise you exact shall be religiously fulfilled. If I am suffered to go abroad, I will assuredly return."

"Is it safe to let him out?" observed Priuli. "He is seditious and perilous."

"I will trust him," replied Pole.

Upon this he called in Mallet, and informed him of the permission he had granted the prisoner.

"But, your Eminence," remonstrated the keeper, "I am responsible for his safe custody to Bishop Bonner. If this unheard-of license be granted him, the man will never come back."

"Set your mind at ease on that score, good friend," observed Carver. "I have plighted my word to the Lord Cardinal, and I will die rather than break it."

"But what am I to say to the bishop? I shall never be able to face him."

"Say that you act by my orders," returned the Cardinal. "Refer the bishop to me."

"Such a thing was never done before," said Mallet. "As well let loose a ravening wolf among a flock of sheep as liberate this man."

"Let my bidding be done," said Pole. "If blame there be, it will rest on my head.—Farewell, friend," he added to Carver, "do not abuse the license given you."

"Your Eminence shall have no cause to repent your trust in me," said Carver.

On this the Cardinal and Priuli quitted the cell.

"Methinks you have shown too much consideration to this man," observed Priuli. "He does not deserve your kindness."

"Time will show," replied Pole. "I have faith in him— hope in his conversion."

CHAPTER XIII.

HOW DERRICK CARVER FULFILLED HIS PROMISE.

THREE days afterwards, Derrick Carver, upon whom the Cardinal's goodness had operated like a sovereign cordial, giving him new life and energy, announced that he was strong enough to avail himself of the permission he had received, and, accordingly, the door of his cell was unlocked by Mallet, who accompanied him to the palace gates, and there let him go, never expecting, as he frankly avowed, to behold him again.

"It may be well to follow him and see what he is about," observed Rodomont, who was standing by.

"Nay, his Eminence has strictly forbidden that," said Mallet. "The man is to be left to his own devices. If he come back, I shall esteem him a greater fool than heretic."

"Tut, he will return," said Rodomont. "His Eminence understands him better than you do."

"Well, we shall see," rejoined the other.

On that very day, it chanced that Bishop Bonner came to Lambeth Palace, and proceeding straightway to the Lollards' Tower, inquired for the prisoner. On learning that he had been allowed to go forth, he flew into a violent passion, and declared he would have the keeper punished for his gross breach of duty. Mallet excused himself, and referred the infuriated bishop to the Cardinal, but Bonner could not obtain an audience till his rage had had time to subside. Pole listened to his complaints and then replied, calmly,—

"It is true, I have let the man go on his promise to return in the evening."

"But what is the promise of such a false knave worth?" cried Bonner, contemptuously. "He will infallibly break it."

"I do not think so," rejoined the Cardinal. "But tarry with me till eventide, and you will see."

Bonner agreed, dined with the Cardinal in the banqueting-hall, and, as there were many other important guests that day, he made merry, and thought no more about the prisoner. While he was sitting, however, with his host and Priuli, Rodomont Bittern entered, and, bowing to the Cardinal said,—

"Your Eminence desired to be informed when Derrick Carver came back. As the clock struck five, he returned to his cell."

Pole smiled, and, turning to the Bishop, observed,—

"I was right in my judgment of him, you perceive."

"I cannot deny it," replied Bonner. "Nevertheless, I would advise your Eminence to recall your permission. Most assuredly he will do much mischief out of doors."

"If it turn out so, he shall be kept within his cell," rejoined Pole.

Shortly after this, Bonner took leave of the Cardinal, but, before quitting the palace, he satisfied himself, by personal inspection, that Carver was safe in his cell. He found him, as usual, reading the Bible, and, if he had dared, would have vented his rage upon him by causing him to be tied to the whipping-post in the chamber beneath and scourged.

"I will have him burnt as soon as possible," he observed to Mallet. "It is monstrous that such a vile wretch should be treated with so much leniency. And what of the Cardinal's other cade-lamb, Mistress Constance Tyrrell? Has she been brought back from her apostasy?"

"I cannot say, in sooth, my lord," replied Mallet. "But I incline to think not, seeing she doth not attend mass."

"Not attend mass! Then she is still defiled by heresy," cried Bonner. "We will have her at Smithfield in spite of the Cardinal." And with this amiable resolve he departed.

Next morning Carver went forth again, returning punctually at five o'clock in the evening, and he pursued the same course for nearly a week, rather anticipating his time than staying beyond it. One evening, however, he did not appear as usual. Three hours more went by, and still he came not, and then Mallet thought it right to acquaint the Cardinal with his prolonged absence. The information caused Pole to look grave.

"Something must have happened to him," he said. "I do not believe he would have stayed away of his own accord, still less do I deem he has any design of evasion. Send Rodomont Bittern to me."

On Rodomont's arrival, the Cardinal ordered him to make immediate inquiries after the prisoner, and to take any persons with him who might aid in the quest.

"My own opinion is that the man has fallen into a snare." Pole said. "But I leave it to your shrewdness to discover what has become of him."

"In obedience to your Eminence's injunctions, his movements have not been watched," replied Rodomont, "so that we have no clue to guide us. Nevertheless, I will essay to find him."

"About the business forthwith, and with a good heart," said the Cardinal. "You are quick-witted, and your penetration will put you on the right track."

Taking with him his lieutenants, Jack Holiday and Nick Simnel, Rodomont set out on his mission. Revolving what the Cardinal had said while dismissing him, he came to the conclusion that he should get on the right track by going to Bonner, who, he suspected, had a strong motive for keeping the prisoner out of the way.

Accordingly, he entered the Cardinal's barge with his friends, bidding the oarsmen row them with all possible dispatch to the stairs at Paul's chain, where, landing, they made the best of their way to the palace of the Bishop of London—a large edifice, which then stood on the north-west side of the cathedral.

From the porter at the palace gate they ascertained that Bonner was attending vespers in Saint Paul's, where they could speak with him on the conclusion of the service. Rodomont then inquired from the porter whether any heretics had been arrested that day. The man replied that several had been taken at a conventicle in Foster-lane, and

17

that the chief sacramentary, who had been holding forth to the others, was detained in a strong-room in the gate till the lord bishop should decide what was to be done with him.

Rodomont then explained to the porter that he was an officer in Cardinal Pole's household, and with his companions was in search of an heretical prisoner named Derrick Carver, and this perchance might be he.

" Marry, 'tis the very man," replied the porter.

Whereupon, he unlocked the door of the strong-room, and showed them Carver within it, seated on a bench, with his hands tied behind his back with cords. Rodomont would fain have carried him off at once, but this the porter would not permit, saying they must tarry till the bishop returned from Saint Paul's.

Half an hour elapsed before Bonner made his appearance, and when he found Rodomont and his comrades there he was exceedingly wroth, and refused to give up the prisoner.

"The knave was taken at a conventicle in Foster-Lane," ne said, "where he was preaching heretical doctrines, praying against her Majesty, and giving the communion according to the prohibited book of service. I greatly marvel that the Cardinal should allow such a pestilent wretch to go forth to spread contagion abroad. Depart now, and tell his Eminence that I will bring back the man to him to morrow. He is safe here, as ye can bear witness."

" Our orders are to bring him back wherever we may find nim," rejoined Rodomont, "and those we must obey."

"What!" cried Bonner. "Will ye take him from me by force ? "

"We trust your lordship will not drive us to that extremity," replied Rodomont. "We claim this man as the Lord Cardinal's prisoner, and we require your lordship to deliver him up to us. If you resist, the fault will rest with you."

"E'en take him, then," rejoined Bonner furiously. "But ye may rest assured I will not be robbed of my prey. He is a preacher of heresy and sedition, a blasphemer and traitor, and I will burn him in spite of the Cardinal. It shall go hard if I burn not Mistress Constance Tyrrell at the same time."

Rodomont and his comrades stayed to hear no more, but carried off the prisoner, and placing him in the barge, conveyed him to Lambeth Palace. On arriving there they took him at once before the Cardinal, and Rodomont explained what had occurred.

"Your Eminence will perceive that I was forcibly detained," said Carver. "Had it not been so, I should have returned at the appointed hour."

"I sent you not forth to propagate heresy and sedition," said Pole, severely. "You have broken the compact between us, and abused my confidence. You can go forth no more."

Carver bowed his head in submission, and was taken to his cell in the Lollards' tower.

End of the Third Book.

BOOK IV.

SMITHFIELD.

CHAPTER I.

HOW A SOLEMN PROCESSION WAS FORMED AT SAINT PAUL'S,
AND SET FORTH TOWARDS SMITHFIELD.

FIVE Protestant divines, amongst whom were Hooper, the deprived Bishop of Gloucester, and Rogers, a prebend of Saint Paul's, having been excommunciated and delivered to the sheriffs, and continuing firm in the maintenance of their opinions, they were doomed to death at the stake. It was appointed that Hooper should suffer at Gloucester, and Rogers at Smithfield, and it was furthermore appointed that Rogers should be the first to die. Rogers, we may mention, was one of the first theological scholars of the age, and had assisted Tyndal in translating the Bible in the time of Henry VIII.

At the earnest solicitation of Gardiner and Bonner, the King consented to be present at the celebration of this act of faith but Cardinal Pole refused to attend it, stating that he would not countenance such a proceeding. Enraged at his opposition, the two prelates took the only revenge in their power, and procured a warrant from the Queen, authorising them to compel the attendance at the terrible ceremonial of any heretical prisoners they might designate.

Armed with this warrant, on the night previous to the execution they gave notice to the Cardinal that they should send for Derrick Carver and Constance Tyrrell at an early hour on the morrow.

That night, as enjoined by the Cardinal, and as her own feelings would have prompted without the injunction, Constance never sought her couch, but spent the hours in prayer and meditation. Before daybreak she awoke old Dorcas, who was slumbering tranquilly, and with her aid attired herself carefully in dark habiliments, and, thus prepared, patiently awaited the anticipated summons. Ere long, a gentle tap was heard without, and the door being opened by Dorcas, the Cardinal entered.

" I have come to see you before you set out, daughter," he said. " My own heart is sad. I have passed the night in vigil and prayer, yet I do not feel comforted. I cannot divest myself of the dread that this day will be prejudicial to our religion. A just man is about to be sacrificed, and his blood will cry out for vengeance. But here come the guard," he added, as Rodomont and his companions appeared at the doorway. "Are you ready ? "

" Quite ready," she replied. " But before I leave, let me crave a blessing from your Eminence."

" You have it, daughter," he replied, extending his arms over her. " May Heaven sustain you during the awful scene you will be compelled to witness ! "

Quitting the room, she followed Rodomont and the others to the outer court. At the Lollards' Tower they were joined by Derrick Carver, who was brought forth by Mallet. On beholding Constance, the enthusiast uttered a joyful exclamation, but he was not permitted to converse with her, and the party proceeded in silence to the wharf without the palace gate, where lay a barge, which had been sent for the prisoners by Bonner.

Within this vessel were two Dominicans, an officer of the guard, and a couple of halberdiers. At the prow was displayed a black banner, on which was inscribed the words : EXURGE, DOMINE, ET JUDICA CAUSAM TUAM, ET DISSIPENTUR INIMICI FIDEI.

The prisoners having entered the barge with Rodomont Bittern, who had been enjoined by the Cardinal to attend them, the vessel was pushed off, and moved down the stream.

The morning was dark and raw. A fog hung over the river, partly concealing the objects on its banks. Officers and men maintained a moody silence, and the only sound heard was a doleful hymn chanted by the Dominicans, and taken up by the occupants of some skiffs that had accompanied the barge from Lambeth.

At Paul's Wharf the prisoners were landed, and conducted thence up Bennet's Hill and Paul's Chain to the Cathedral.

Matins were just over, and within the broad nave of the noble fane a great number of priests, attired in their robes, were assembled, prior to marching in solemn procession to Smithfield.

In the aisles, guarded by halberdiers, were collected groups of recusants of both sexes, brought thither to give effect to the ceremonial. Apart from these, but likewise brought from prison to grace the procession, were several deprived divines of the Protestant Church, some of whom afterwards testified to their faith at the stake, while others were starved in their cells, or died from ill treatment. Many who then met on that melancholy morn, and exchanged a friendly greeting, or a few words of comfort, saw each other for the last time on earth. But in the faces of these stout-hearted champions of the Protestant Church no traces of doubt or discouragement could be discerned. They were evidently prepared to meet their fate with resolution. Neither did they manifest sorrow for the brother about to suffer, regarding him as one whose trials were well-nigh over, and who was certain of meeting his reward.

Within the nave and aisles were congregated a vast number of spectators of the solemn scene.

Close to one of the enormous columns lining the south aisle of the magnificent fane stood Constance. She was looking with a wistful eye at the deprived Protestant divines, when her own name was breathed in her ear by some one close behind.

Not doubting who spoke, she partly turned her head, and perceived Osbert Clinton, who, screened from the guard by the pillar, had contrived to approach her. The only person who noticed the manœuvre was Rodomont, but the kind-hearted fellow looked another way, and tried not to hear what was passing.

Not much was said—but the few words spoke of the young man's wretchedness at the protracted separation from her he loved.

"Be patient," she said. "All will be well in the end."

"Talk not to me of patience," he rejoined. "I am unable to practice it. My heart will burst in the effort. I cannot live without you, Constance. Commit yourself to me, and I will free you. You will be gone before the guard can notice your absence; and once mingled with the throng, you will be safe. Come!"

"I cannot—dare not go," she replied. "What would the good Cardinal think of me if I complied?"

"Heed him not, but think of me, whom you doom to misery by hesitation. Do not throw away this chance. Another may not occur."

"Pass if you will," interposed the friendly Rodomont, in a low voice. "I shall hear and see nothing."

Squeezing his arm by way of thanks, Osbert renewed his entreaties to Constance.

"No, I cannot do it," she rejoined. "My word to the Queen restrains me."

"What? not gone!" exclaimed Rodomont, looking round. "Peste! it is now too late."

Just then a movement took place in the nave, and the attention of the guard was drawn to the prisoners.

Clad in his full robes, wearing his mitre, and carrying his crosier, Bonner issued from the sacristy. Before him were borne two large silver crosses, and the pix under a rich canopy. At the same time, the procession was marshalled by the priests. Long wax tapers were lighted and distributed among the recusants, who were compelled to carry them; the Protestant divines being alone exempted from this degrading office.

As soon as the procession was formed, the halberdiers at the head of it marched through the great western portal of the cathedral, and were followed by a long line of recusants, men and women, bearing lighted tapers. Amongst these were Constance and Derrick Carver.

Then came the deprived Protestant clergy, walking two

and two. They were succeeded by monks and friars in the habits of their orders. Then came priests in their robes, and lastly Bonner himself, attired as we have described, and preceded by the large silver crosses and the pix. On either side of the sacramentaries were halberdiers to keep off the crowd. Nor was this the only precaution taken. Outside the cathedral there was a detachment of mounted arquebusiers to clear the way for the train, while a band of archers brought up the rear.

As the procession issued forth from Saint Paul's, the bells of Saint Martin's, Ludgate, and other churches on the line of way, began to toll slowly and solemnly.

CHAPTER II.

THE HALT AT NEWGATE.

IT was a day of triumph to Bonner, and his heart swelled with pride and gratified vengeance as he marched along. The precincts of the cathedral were crowded with spectators, as indeed were all the streets traversed by the *cortége* on its way to Smithfield. The majority of the beholders being Romanists, they prostrated themselves devoutly as the host went by, while the priests accompanying the bishop sprinkled them with holy water.

However, there were many who refused to kneel, and who were only restrained by fear from giving utterance to their abhorrence of the ceremony. As the train was passing through Ludgate, a man called out in a stentorian voice, "So, my masters, at last we have got the Inquisition in England !" But scarcely had the words escaped him, when he was seized and dragged off.

Arrived at Newgate, where Prebend Rogers had been kept since his condemnation, the *cortége* came to a halt, and, after a short delay, the prisoner was brought forth. He was a man of middle age, tall of stature, thin, but well-built, dark-complexioned, and possessing a grave, intelligent countenance.

He looked perfectly composed, and remarked, as he noticed the extent of the *cortége*, "Ye make as great a show as if ye were about to conduct me to a festival, and not to the stake."

While the sheriffs, who had charge of the doomed man, and who wore their robes and chains, were mounting their horses, a painful incident occurred. With loud cries, that ought to have moved every breast, a woman, having a young child in her arms, and with several other terrified children clinging to her, burst through the ranks of the halberdiers, exclaiming, "For Christ our Saviour's sake, let me bid a last farewell to my husband!"

"Get hence, importunate and troublesome woman!" cried one of the sheriffs, named Woodrooffe, in loud and harsh tones. "This man is not thy husband."

"I protest to you he is, Sir," she rejoined, in extremity of anguish, "my lawful husband, and these are our children."

"Spawn of the devil!" shouted Woodrooffe. "Away with all thy brood of Satan, or the men shall drive you hence with their halberds. You ought to know that a priest cannot marry."

"We have been married these fourteen years, Sir," said Rogers. "I pray you suffer her to come to me. 'Twill be a comfort to her and to the children to say farewell, and receive my blessing, Our parting will be short. If you are a husband and a father yourself, you will not be deaf to my appeal."

"I am both, yet will I not suffer her or her base-born brats to come near thee," roared Woodrooffe. "Push them away with your pikes if they will not retire peaceably," he added to the guard.

"Heaven forgive you!" exclaimed Rogers, as his wife and children were thrust aside. "'Twas the sole consolation I asked, and that is denied me."

Shortly after this interruption, the *cortége* moved forward again, the condemned, closely attended by the sheriffs and their officers, following next after Bonner.

On either side of the doomed man walked a priest with a crucifix in his hand, one or other of whom was constantly dinning exhortations to repentance into his ears. To these he would not listen, but recited aloud the *Miserere.* His firm deportment and serene countenance—for he speedily recovered his composure—produced a strong effect upon the beholders.

The bell of Saint Sepulchre's tolled solemnly as the procession wended its way along Giltspur Street, and the bells of the two churches dedicated to Saint Bartholomew filled the air with the like dismal clangour, as the head of the cavalcade rode into Smithfield.

CHAPTER III.

SMITHFIELD IN THE SIXTEENTH CENTURY.

NO part of London is richer in historical recollections of various kinds than Smithfield. In this enclosure, which in old times was a broad and pleasant field, lying without the City walls on the north-west, were held jousts and tournaments on the most splendid scale, and attended by kings, foreign potentates and ambassadors, nobles, knights, and dames of the highest rank and peerless beauty. Barriers were frequently set up in Smithfield by Edward III., and here a grand tournament, which lasted for a week, was given by the same monarch, in the latter part of his reign, in honour of the beautiful Alice Perrars, by whose charms he was bewitched. Another grand tournament was held here by Richard II., on which occasion sixty knights on richly-caparisoned coursers, and each attended by a lady of honour mounted upon a palfrey, rode from the Tower to Smithfield, where, in the presence of the King and Queen and chief nobles, many commendable courses were run. In the same reign, the Earl of Mar came from Scotland to challenge the Earl of Nottingham, and the trial of skill took place at Smithfield, resulting in the overthrow of Mar, who was so severely hurt by his opponent that he died on the way back. In the time of Henry IV., the Earl of Somerset, Sir John Cornwall, Sir Richard Arundel, and others, tilted with certain Frenchmen ; and in the same reign a duel took place between Gloucester and Arthur, which would have terminated fatally but for the King's interference. In the succeeding reign, Sir Robert

Carey fought an Aragonese knight at Smithfield, and slew him. Several desperate combats occurred here in the reign of Henry VI., but we cannot dwell upon them, and must conclude our brief summary by allusion to the famous encounter between Lord Scales and the Bastard of Burgundy, held before Edward IV., at which the English noble had the advantage, both mounted and on foot, with poleaxe as well as with spear.

Many judicial combats were likewise fought at Smithfield, and here it was that the armourer was slain by his false servant—a picturesque incident introduced with admirable effect by Shakespeare in the Second Part of "Henry VI." Other occurrences of a yet more tragical character are not wanting to deepen the interest of the spot. At the north of the field, and between a large pool and a track of marshy land, grew some gigantic elms, and amidst these stately trees stood a permanent gallows, at which the great Scottish hero, William Wallace, was barbarously hanged, and, while yet breathing, disembowelled and quartered. In the centre of the field the Lollards were burnt, and on the same spot, at a later date, numberless victims of the tyrant Henry's rage perished in the same fearful manner.

The darkest page, however, in the annals of Smithfield, belongs to the period under consideration.

But Smithfield has lively as well as sombre traditions. Here the famous Bartholomew Fair was held, the humours of which have been painted by Ben Jonson. Though the amusements of this annual City carnival might scandalise the present decorous generation, they suited our forefathers, who had no objection to a little riotous excess. In the last century, when Bartholomew Fair was at its zenith, excellent theatrical representations were given there, and Fielding himself had a booth at Smithfield.* However, tastes changed. Bartholomew Fair lost its attraction, was voted a nuisance, and finally abolished, though it lingered on till within the last few years.

At the period of our history, Smithfield retained most of its original features. It was still an open field without the

---

* See Mr. Morley's "Memoirs of Bartholomew Fair"—a work full of curious research and delightfully written.

walls, resorted to by the citizens for purposes of recreation, and was constantly used, as at an earlier date, for grand military displays and for public executions. The grove of giant elms, with the gallows in the midst, was still standing near the pool, and no part of the broad enclosure had as yet been encroached upon.

On the east side of the area, partially screened by a large mansion, stood the Priory of Saint Bartholomew, a noble religious institution, founded in the time of Henry I., by Rahere, the King's minstrel, and which flourished until the dissolution of the monasteries, when it was granted by Henry VIII. to his Attorney-General, Sir Richard Rich. The size and importance of the priory will be understood, when it is stated that in addition to the abode and dormitories of the prior and monks, the establishment comprised a large conventual church, refectory, hall, cloisters, courts, and numerous offices, together with extensive gardens— among which was a mulberry-garden. The splendid church was partially pulled down, and the materials sold, but, on the accession of Queen Mary, the remnant of the sacred pile, together with other portions of the monastery, were restored to the brotherhood of Black Canons, from whom they had been wrested, and continued in their hands till the time of Elizabeth, when the fraternity was ejected.

In front of the priory, as above stated, was a large and picturesque mansion, which delighted the eye with its high pointed roof, carved gables, richly-sculptured portals, and mullioned windows. Adjacent to this habitation was an ancient gateway, leading to the conventual church, over the pointed arch of which was a tabernacle containing a statue of Saint Bartholomew holding a knife. On the north of the priory ran a long narrow lane, with detached houses and gardens on either side of it, communicating with Aldersgate Street.

On the south side of Smithfield stood the old hospital belonging to the priory, at the rear of which was the church of Saint Bartholomew the Less. On the west of the area were a few scattered habitations, amongst which were three renowned hostels, the Saint Catherine's Wheel, the King's Head, and the Rose. Here another narrow lane, skirted by small tenements, ran down to Holborn.

The best view of Smithfield was from the ground near the old elm-trees. Standing there, and looking towards the City, the prospect was exceedingly striking. On the left was the priory, surmounted by the square tower of the conventual church, and contiguous to it the ancient hospital—a highly picturesque structure. Further on was Saint Sepulchre's. The north-western angle of the ancient City walls, with its ramparts and battlements, was seen to great advantage from this point. Hundreds of lofty and slender spires, graceful steeples, crocketed pinnacles, and embattled towers, long since destroyed, met the gaze. But the grand object of all was the venerable Gothic cathedral, with its spire, upwards of five hundred feet in height, which could here be surveyed in all its majesty and beauty.

CHAPTER IV.

WHAT PASSED IN SAINT BARTHOLOMEW'S CHURCH.

 GREAT crowd had assembled in Smithfield to witness the sad spectacle, but a circular space was kept clear in the centre of the area exactly opposite the ancient gateway leading to the priory.

Within this ring, which was guarded by a double line of halberdiers, stood a stout square oak post, about nine feet high, driven securely into the ground, and having a heavy iron chain attached to it by a staple. Hard by was an immense pile of fagots, with some blocks of wood. A little further off there was another pile, consisting of bundles of dried reeds.

Close by the stake stood three men, of savage and repulsive aspect, clothed in leathern jerkins and tight-fitting hose of blood-red hue, having long iron prongs in their hands.

As the *cortége* entered Smithfield, and the intended martyr was descried, a murmur of commiseration rose from those who sympathised with him, but it was instantly drowned by a hurricane of fierce and exulting yells from the Romanists.

Meantime, the mounted arquebusiers having cleared a passage through the crowd, the long line of priests with their banners and crosses, the recusants with the tapers, the deprived Protestant divines, Bonner and the condemned, passed through the gateway, and, traversing the court, proceeded to the ancient conventual church, the bell of which sounded dolefully the while.

At the portal they were met by the prior of the Black Canons, with several of the brethren in their sable robes, and conducted to the places appointed for them in the sacred edifice.

The recusants were ranged on one side, and the Protestant divines on the other, while the Romish priests proceeded to the presbytery. A chair opposite the pulpit was assigned to the doomed man, on which he sat down, with two halber-diers standing behind him.

On a faldstool near the altar sat Philip, who had come there quite privately, and was only attended by his confessor, Father Alfonso de Castro. In the choir sat Gardiner, with some members of the council.

Beneath a circular arch, resting on massive cylindrical pillars, near the north transept, stood Osbert Clinton, who, having accompanied the *cortége* from Saint Paul's, had entered the church at the same time with it, and stationed himself where he could best see Constance without being observed by the King. She soon became aware of his presence, but only ventured occasionally to look towards him, and then her glances yielded him little comfort.

After a brief delay, Bonner ascended the pulpit, and taking for his text Saint Paul's words to the Galatians, "*I would they were cut off that trouble you,*" he preached a violent sermon on the necessity of punishing heretics and false brethren with death, citing many authorities in favour of his views, and asserting that to maintain that heresy ought to go unpunished would be to maintain that the worst crimes should be unchastised. "Heresy," he said, "being treason against Heaven, deserves the punishment of treason. As such a traitor," he added, turning to Rogers, "thou wilt be consigned to a fire, which will be to thee a foretaste of the flames in which thou shalt burn everlast-ingly. Thy fate will be a terrible lesson to all who think with thee."

"It will be a lesson to them how to testify to their faith," rejoined the prebend.

Bonner having descended from the pulpit, a votive mass for taking away schism was performed by Gardiner, who solemnly pronounced the oration :—*Deus qui errata corrigis, et dispersa congregas, et congregata conservas ; quæsumus, super populum Christianum tuæ unionis gratiam clementer infunde : ut divisione rejecta, vero Pastori Ecclesiæ tuæ se venies, tibi dignè valeat famulari.*

Mass ended, the *Dies Iræ* was sung by the choir of the Black Canons, and, while this was proceeding, the *cortége* began to move, passing slowly before the altar, preparatory to quitting the church.

As before, a long array of priests with banners walked with noiseless tread, bowing reverently as they passed the altar. Then came the recusants, carrying their lighted tapers, but not a knee was bent amongst them, not a head inclined.

Last amongst these walked Constance, alone. She had to pass close by Philip, who was seated on the faldstool, with Gardiner and Father Alfonso beside him, and as she approached him, her strength began to fail, and her knees tottered. She tried to summon all her energies, but in vain. In another moment she felt she must sink. Philip's gaze was fixed steadily upon her. A desperate effort to pass deprived her of the little strength left, and with a cry she let fall the taper, and would have sunk upon the pavement if the King himself had not caught her.

" Oh that I could die ! " she gasped.

" No, you must live for me, Constance," whispered Philip, passionately.

She looked at him for a moment with mingled fear and aversion, and then closed her eyes.

"She has swooned," said the King, consigning her to Rodomont, who had been marching behind her. " Take her where she can be tended."

In obedience to the injunction, Rodomont bore her to the sacristy, where restoratives were applied by a monk, who acted as physician to the brotherhood of the Black Canons.

This incident, as may be supposed, had not passed unnoticed by Osbert Clinton, whose eyes had never quitted Constance for a moment. As she tottered and fell into the King's arms, his agony became almost insupportable ; and when she was borne to the sacristy by Rodomont, he would have flown instantly to her assistance if he had dared.

Meanwhile the *cortége* continued to pass slowly by the King. The Protestant divines made him an obeisance as they passed, but sedulously abstained from bowing to the altar. Lastly came the intended martyr, who walked with a firm step, and head erect.

As he came near, Gardiner commanded him to stop, and thus addressed him: "John Rogers, somewhile priest, but now an excommunicate person, we have striven to convert thee, and by wholesome admonitions to reduce thee again unto the true faith and unity of the universal Catholic Church, but we have found thee obstinate and stiff-necked, stedfastly continuing in thy damnable opinions and heresies, and refusing to return to the lap of the holy mother church. Wherefore, not being willing that thou shouldst infect the Lord's flock with thine heresy, we have cast thee out from the Church as an obstinate, impenitent sinner, and have left thee to the judgment of the secular power, by whom thou hast been justly condemned to perish by fire. The punishment is inflicted upon thee for the salvation of thine own soul, and as a step towards the extirpation of heresy."

"What consequences may follow my punishment, my lord, none of us can tell," rejoined Rogers; "but I am fully prepared to die."

"Sinner as thou art, wilt thou be converted and live?" cried Gardiner. "Here is her Majesty's pardon," he added, showing him a scroll.

"I reject it," said Rogers, stoutly. "I maintain that the Catholic Church of Rome is the Church of Antichrist. Item, that in the sacrament of the altar ——"

"A truce to thy blasphemies," interrupted Gardiner, furiously. "Away with him to the stake!"

"I am ready," said Rogers. "I bid you all to my funeral pile. You shall see how a true believer can die. If I blench, proclaim me a renegade."

Hereupon, the Protestant divines, who had listened with great satisfaction, moved on, and Rogers followed them with a firm step.

While this occurred, Osbert Clinton had contrived to steal unperceived to the sacristy. Constance had just recovered from her swoon. Luckily, no one was with her but

18—2

Rodomont, the monk who had tended her having just quitted the chamber.

"Why have you come here, Sir?" cried Rodomont. "Matters were bad enough before, but your imprudence will make them ten times worse. If the King discovers you, you are lost."

"I care not what happens to me," replied Osbert. "I could not keep away. Fear nothing, Constance," he added, "I will not quit you more."

"This is madness," cried Rodomont. "The King is certain to come hither, and then you will be arrested. Hide yourself in this cupboad," he added, opening the door of a large oak ambry reared against the wall. "It only contains a few priestly vestments, and you can stand upright within it."

But Osbert refused to move.

"Do as he recommends, I implore you," said Constance to him. "You will throw away your life by staying with me."

"To be sure he will," rejoined Rodomont, dragging him away, and forcing him into the ambry, the door of which he shut.

The step was only just taken in time. In another moment, the King came into the sacristy, and seeing that Constance had recovered, he signed to Rodomont to leave the chamber.

"I have much to say to you, Constance," he began, "but this is not the moment for it. Are you still in the same mood as when I saw you last. Has no change been wrought in your sentiments?"

"None, Sire," she replied. "I am quite happy in the life I lead with the good Cardinal, and only pray it may continue."

"But you still maintain your heretical opinions?" said the King.

"Firmly as ever, Sire."

"And does not this awful ceremonial shake you?"

"On the contrary, it strengthens my convictions."

"All heretics are alike—all obstinate and contumacious," muttered Philip. "Constance, you cannot go back to the Cardinal. He is much too lenient to you. I shall deliver you to Bishop Bonner, who will treat you very differently."

"Oh! Sire, do not deliver me to that cruel man. Let me go back to the good Cardinal, who has been as a father to me. Have compassion upon me."

"You have no compassion upon me, Constance," rejoined Philip. "You care not for my sufferings. Relent towards me, and I will be less rigorous towards you."

"It cannot be, Sire," she rejoined.

"Be not hasty. Reflect. If I consign you to Bonner, your fate is certain. After the execution, the sight of which I will spare you, I will return for your answer. A guard will be placed at the door to prevent your exit, but no one shall disturb you. Again, I say, reflect. On your own decision hangs your fate."

So saying, he quitted the sacristy, the door of which was locked outside.

CHAPTER V.

THE solemn proceedings we have described as taking place in the conventual church of Saint Bartholomew occupied more than an hour, and during this time the concourse within Smithfield had considerably increased. Every available inch of ground commanding a view of the place of execution was by this time occupied. The roofs and windows of all the habitations overlooking the enclosure were filled, and the giant elm-trees near the pool had hundreds among their branches. Romanists and Protestants could be readily distinguished from each other by their looks—the countenances of the former being fierce and exulting in expression, while those of the other bespoke sorrow and indignation.

On the left of the gangway leading to the priory and opposite the stake, a large scaffold had been erected. It was covered with black cloth, and in front was an immense cross embroidered in silver, underneath which was inscribed, UNUS DOMINUS, UNA FIDES, UNUM BAPTISMA. This scaffold was intended for the recusants and Protestant divines, and was guarded by mounted arquebusiers.

On the right of the gateway was reared a long covered gallery, hung with crimson cloth of gold, and emblazoned with the royal arms. This gallery was approached from the upper windows of the mansion against which it was set, and was reserved for the King, the bishops, and the council. It was likewise guarded by mounted men-at-arms.

The patience of the densely-packed crowd, eager for the exciting spectacle it had come to witness, was well-nigh exhausted, when the solemn tolling of the bell of the conventual church announced that, at last, the intended martyr was coming forth.   Then all noise and tumult suddenly ceased, and deep silence fell upon the throng.

In the midst of this hush the doleful hymn chanted by the monks could be distinctly heard.   Every eye was then directed towards the gateway.   Presently the priests emerged, carrying the crucifixes and banners, and mounting the scaffold, they ranged themselves in front of it.   They were followed by the recusants with lighted torches, who were placed at the back of the scaffold, while the middle seats were allotted to the Protestant divines.

All these proceedings were watched with deep interest by the spectators.   Many an eye was then cast towards the royal gallery, but it was still vacant.

As yet nothing had been seen of the doomed man, but now the sheriffs rode forth from the gateway, and in another moment Rogers came after them, still maintaining his firmness of deportment.   He was preceded by half-a-dozen halberdiers, and followed by two officers, with drawn swords in their hands.

At this moment Philip came forth, and sat down in the fauteuil prepared for him in the centre of the gallery.   Close behind him stood Father Alfonso, while on his right were Gardiner and Bonner, and other prelates, and on his left the principal members of the council.

As Philip appeared, a half-suppressed murmur arose among the spectators, and had not their attention been diverted by what was going on below, stronger manifestations of dislike might have been made.   Philip frowned as these murmurs greeted him, but made no remark.

Meanwhile, Rogers continued to march resolutely towards the place of execution—some of the spectators pitying and comforting him, others flouting and reviling him.   His firmness, however, was exposed to a sore trial at the last.   His unhappy and half-distracted wife having followed him with her children to Smithfield, had managed to force her way close up to the ring of halberdiers encircling the stake; and as he came up, aided by some charitable persons near her, who drew aside to let her pass, she burst forth, and ere she could be prevented, flung herself into his arms, and was strained to his breast, while his children clung to his knees.

But this agonising scene, which moved most of those who beheld it, whatever their religious opinions might be, was of brief duration. Seeing what had occurred, Sheriff Woodrooffe turned fiercely round, and roared out, "What! here again, thou pestilent woman! Pluck her from him, and take her and her children from the ground."

"Go, dear wife and children," cried Rogers. "We shall meet again in a better world, where none will trouble us. Farewell for a little while—only a little while! My blessing be upon you!"

"I will not leave you. I will die with you," shrieked his unhappy wife.

"Let these cruel men kill us also," cried one of the younger children—a little girl. "We do not desire to live."

"Pluck them away instantly, I say," roared Woodrooffe. "Why do you hesitate? Do you sympathise with these heretics?"

"Gently Sirs, gently," said Rogers. "See ye not she faints. Farewell, dear wife," he continued, kissing her marble cheek. "You can take her now. She will not struggle more. Be of good cheer, my children. We shall meet again in heaven. Once more, farewell."

As his swooning wife and weeping children were taken away, he covered his face with his hands, and wept aloud, but, roused by the angry voice of the sheriff, he lifted up his head, and, brushing the tears from his eyes, marched with firm footsteps into the ring, in the midst of which was planted the stake. No sooner had he come there than a priest advanced towards him, and, holding up a crucifix, besought him to repent.

But Rogers pushed him aside, and, turning to the assemblage, called out with a loud voice,—

"Good people, having taught you nothing but God's holy word, and such lessons as I have learnt from His blessed book, the Holy Bible, I am come hither to seal my faith with my blood."

"Have done, thou false knave!" cried Woodrooffe, "or I

will have thy lying tongue torn from thy throat. Make ready. Thou hast detained us long enough."

"Nay, treat him not thus harshly," interposed the priest. Again, I implore you to renounce your errors."

"You waste time with him, good father," cried the sheriff.

"Not so," rejoined the priest. "Perchance, even now, Heaven may soften his heart."

"I pray you let me be," said Rogers, taking a Prayer-book from his breast, and turning the leaves.

"Thou shalt not read that book," cried the sheriff, snatching it from him. "I will cast it into the fire with thee. Make ready, I say."

On this Rogers went up to the stake, and pressing his lips fervently to it, exclaimed, "Welcome the cross of Christ! Welcome eternal life!"

On turning round, he would have addressed a few more words to the people, but the sheriff, perceiving his design, authoritatively forbade him.

Then one of the men standing near the stake came up and besought his forgiveness.

"Forgiveness for what?" rejoined Rogers. "Thou hast done me no injury that I know of."

"I am one of those appointed to burn you," replied the man.

"Nay, then, I freely forgive thee, good fellow," replied Rogers. "And I will give thee thanks also, if thou wilt heap plenty of wood about me."

With that he took off his gown and doublet, and bestowed them upon the man. Then, kneeling down by the stake, he passed a few moments in deep and earnest prayer; after which he arose, and said, in a firm voice, "I am ready."

Thereupon, a smith and his man, who were in attendance with the sheriffs, stepped forward, and putting the chain around him, fastened it at the back of the stake. An iron hoop was likewise passed around his body, and nailed to the post.

Then the men with the prongs began to pile the faggots around him, mingling them with bundles of reeds.

"Are your fagots dry?" he inquired, as they were thus engaged.

"Ay, marry are they," replied the man to whom he had

given his cloak and doublet. "You shall not be long a-burning, I'll warrant you."

When sufficient fagots had been heaped around him, Sheriff Woodrooffe called for torches, which were brought, but ere they could be applied, the priest again interposed.

"Hold yet a moment," he exclaimed.

Then advancing towards the martyr, who, chained to the stake and half covered by the fagots, regarded him steadily, he displayed a warrant to him, and said, "Here is the Queen's pardon. Recant, I conjure thee, and thou shalt be spared."

"Away with thee, tempter!" exclaimed Rogers. "I take you all to witness," he added, with a loud voice, "that I die in the Protestant faith."

"Kindle the pile instantly!" vociferated the sheriff.

Three blazing torches were then applied to the bundles of reeds, and the next moment the flames leaped up and enveloped the martyr.

Many of the beholders shouted and exulted at the terrific spectacle, but groans and lamentations burst from others.

Then the flame fell for a moment, and the serene countenance of the martyr could be descried, his lips moving in prayer. But not a groan or a cry escaped him.

The fagots now began to crackle and blaze. The flames mounted higher and higher, and again wrapt the martyr from view.

At this moment the sheriff threw the Prayer-book into the fire, commanding the assistants to heap on fresh fagots as fast as the others were consumed; and this was continued till the sufferer was reduced to ashes.

Thus died the Proto-martyr of the Protestant Church.

End of the Fourth Book.

BOOK V.

THE INSURRECTION.

CHAPTER I.

WHAT PASSED BETWEEN OSBERT AND CONSTANCE IN THE
SACRISTY.

N the King's departure from the sacristy, as previously narrated, Constance immediately released
Osbert from the ambry, and the unhappy lovers,
rushing into each other's arms, forgot for a short
space the perilous position in which they were placed. At
last, Osbert, partially disengaging himself from the mistress
of his heart, exclaimed with bitterness,—

"What have we done that we should suffer thus severely?
Heaven seems never weary of persecuting us. Yet we have
committed no fault save that of loving each other."

"Alas!" cried Constance, "it would seem that we are
never to be united on earth, since we meet only for a moment, to be torn asunder. We must look for happiness
beyond the grave."

"That is but cold comfort, Constance," cried Osbert. "I
cling to life and hope. I yet hope to make you my bride,
and to spend years in your society—happy, happy years,
which shall make amends for all the misery we have undergone."

"It would indeed be bliss to dwell together as you say," replied Constance ; "but fate opposes us, and to struggle against our destiny would be vain. The trials we experience are given us for our benefit, and ought to be borne cheerfully. At this very moment, within a short distance of us, a martyr is purchasing, by a cruel death, a crown of glory and a place in heaven. Hark to those cries !" she exclaimed, as shouts were heard without ; "perchance he is now bound to the stake. I am thankful to be spared the frightful spectacle, but I can pray for him here."

And she knelt down on the pavement, and prayed aloud.

While she was thus engaged, Osbert glanced anxiously around in search of some means of escape, but could discover none. The sacristy was lighted by two lancet-shaped windows, but they were narrow, and barred outside.

"Despair !" he exclaimed, in half-frenzied accents, as his search concluded. "Flight is impossible. We are lost."

But Constance's thoughts were with the martyr in Smithfield, and the appalling scene seemed to be passing before her eyes. Suddenly she shrieked out, "The fire is kindled. I can see the red reflection of the flames through yonder windows. Oh, it is horrible. Would I were back with the good Cardinal !"

"Would you were !" ejaculated Osbert. "But I fear you will never behold him more. The King will be here presently, and will require an answer. What will you say to him ?"

"Say ! What shall I say ?" cried Constance, bewildered.

"Ask me not," rejoined Osbert, in a sombre voice. "Take this dagger," he added, placing a poignard in her hand. "Conceal it about your person. You may need it."

"This dagger !" she cried, regarding the weapon. "What am I to do with it ?"

"Should the worst befall, plunge it in the King's heart, or your own," he rejoined.

"I cannot," she replied, letting the poignard fall upon the pavement. "I will not commit a crime that would doom me to perdition. Were I, in a moment of desperation, to do as you suggest, all hope of our reunion in a better world would be over. Then, indeed, I should be lost to you for ever."

"But this inexorable demon will be here anon," cried

Osbert, picking up the dagger. "The thought drives me mad. Would that these strong walls would crack asunder to let us pass, or the floor yawn and swallow us up. Anything to avoid him."

"Fresh shouts! more light against yon windows! They are adding fuel to the fire!" cried Constance. "'Twill be over soon."

"And then the King will come hither," said Osbert. "Are you prepared for him?"

"Fully prepared," she rejoined. "Return to your place of concealment, lest he should appear suddenly."

"No, I will remain here, and brave his anger," said Osbert.

"Oh, do not act thus rashly!" she exclaimed. "You can render me no aid, and will only place yourself in needless peril."

"I have no desire to live. Let the tyrant wreak his utmost vengeance upon me if he will. Ha! he comes," he cried, as the key grated in the lock, and the door opened.

It was not the King, however, but Rodomont Bittern who entered.

"Just as I expected!" exclaimed Rodomont. "Prudence is not to be looked for in a lover. I was certain I should find you talking to your mistress, and therefore I came to warn you that the King will be here directly. Back to the ambry at once."

"No more hiding for me," returned Osbert. "I shall remain where I am."

"And be sent to the Tower, and have your head chopped off for your pains," observed Rodomont. "What service will that do to Mistress Constance?"

"It will only tend to make me more wretched," she rejoined. "If you love me," she added to Osbert, "you will not expose yourself to this great danger."

"There, you cannot resist that!" cried Rodomont. "Back to the ambry at once," he continued, pushing him towards it. "And as you value your head, do not stir till the coast is clear."

"I cannot answer for myself," remarked Osbert, as he got into the cupboard. "A word from the King will bring me forth."

"Then I'll answer for you," said Rodomont, locking the ambry, and taking away the key. "That's the only chance of keeping him out of harm's way. Be not cast down, fair mistress," he added to Constance. "The Cardinal will protect you."

"Were I with him, I should have no fear," she replied. "He would shield me against all wrong; but I am now in the King's power, and he has threatened to deliver me to Bishop Bonner."

"And if his Majesty should so dispose of you, 'twill be but a brief confinement, for the Cardinal will speedily have you back. So be of good cheer. But hist! there is a stir within the church. The dread ceremony is over. I must leave you, or the King will find me here. Keep up your courage, I say."

With this he quitted the chamber, and made fast the door outside.

CHAPTER II.

AFTER a brief interval, but which appeared like an age to Constance, the door was again thrown open, and Philip entered the sacristy. To judge by his looks, no one would have supposed that he was fresh from the terrible spectacle he had just witnessed.

"One would think that burning must be pleasant to those tainted with heresy," he observed. "The wretch who has just suffered for his contumely smiled as the pile was lighted. But it was not to speak of him that I came here, but of yourself, Constance. Have you reflected?"

"I did not need to reflect, Sire. My determination was instantly formed, and is unalterable."

"You will regret it, Constance—bitterly regret it. Consider what you sacrifice—life, and all that can render life attractive—for a solitary cell, and a fiery death in Smithfield."

"I require no consideration, Sire. I choose the dungeon and the stake."

"Yet a moment," urged Philip. "Bishop Bonner is without, but I am unwilling to summon him."

"Do not hesitate, Sire. I have said that my determination is unalterable."

After regarding her stedfastly for a few moments, and perceiving that she manifested no symptoms of relenting, Philip moved slowly towards the door, and, on reaching it, paused, and again looked at her fixedly. But, as she still continued firm, he summoned Bonner, who immediately afterwards entered with Father Alfonso. The bishop's features were flushed with triumph, but the Spanish friar appeared grave and sad, and his cheeks were almost livid in hue.

" Here is another obstinate heretic for you, my lord," said the King, pointing to Constance. " Take her, and see what you can do with her."

" If the Lord Cardinal and your Majesty have failed in bringing her to reason, I shall stand but a poor chance of doing so," replied Bonner. " Nevertheless, I will essay. You must not expect the same gentle treatment from me, mistress," he added, in a harsh voice, to Constance, " that you have lately experienced from the Cardinal."

" I do not expect it, my lord," she rejoined.

" He has been far too indulgent," pursued Bonner. " You have been free to roam about the palace gardens—have had your own attendants and your own chamber, as if you were the Cardinal's guest, and not his prisoner—have been exempted from mass, and other privileges, wholly inconsistent with your state. None of these immunities will you enjoy with me. You will have no garden to walk in, but a prison court with high walls—no dainty and luxurious chamber, but a close cell—no better fare than bread and water—no attendant save the gaoler—none to converse with except the priest. This is the plan I shall pursue with you. If it fails, and you continue obstinate, you need not be reminded of your doom."

For a moment there was a pause. Constance then addressed herself to the King, and, speaking with a spirit which she had never previously displayed before him, said, " I protest against this course, Sire. If I am a prisoner at all, I am the Lord Cardinal's prisoner. I was placed in his Eminence's charge by the Queen's Majesty, and I demand to be taken back to him. If I be not, but be illegally and unjustly detained by the bishop, let his lordship look to it, for assuredly he will have to render a strict account to the Cardinal. I have been brought hither in virtue of a warrant from her Majesty, which compels my attendance at this execution, but the warrant declares that I am to be taken back, and this the bishop engaged to do."

"Is this so?" demanded Philip.

"I cannot deny it," replied Bonner; "but your Majesty can overrule the order."

"The King will not follow such ill counsel," said Constance. "If I be not taken back in accordance with the warrant, both her Majesty and the Cardinal will be sore displeased."

"The damsel speaks boldly yet truthfully, Sire," interposed Father Alfonso, "and has right on her side. The bishop admits that she was brought here under her Majesty's warrant, and does not deny that he undertook to take her back to the Cardinal. If this be not done, his Eminence will have just ground of displeasure. Furthermore, since Mistress Constance was placed by the Queen under the Cardinal's charge, her Majesty's consent must be obtained ere she can be removed."

"But the King can set at nought the warrant," cried Bonner, "and can remove the damsel from the Cardinal's charge if he thinks fit."

"Doubtless his Majesty can act as he may deem meet," rejoined Father Alfonso; "but your lordship can scarce expect to escape blame in the affair. The Queen is certain to resent the disrespect shown to her authority, and the Cardinal will be equally indignant at the interference with him. Both will visit their displeasure on your head."

"But you will hold me harmless, Sire?" said Bonner.

"Nay, my lord, I care not to quarrel with the Cardinal," rejoined Philip. "You must bear the brunt of his anger."

"And also of the Queen's displeasure," remarked Father Alfonso. "Her Majesty takes great interest in this damsel, and had a special design in placing her under the Cardinal's care. If her plan be thwarted ——"

"Enough, good father, enough!" interrupted Bonner. "Unsupported by your Majesty, I dare not act in opposition to the Queen and the Cardinal, and consequently Mistress Constance must go back to Lambeth Palace."

"Thank Heaven I am saved!" exclaimed Constance, clasping her hands fervently.

"Be not too sure of that," muttered Bonner, with the growl of a tiger robbed of his prey.

"Your lordship is right," observed Philip, who for a

moment had been buried in thought. "Direct opposition to the Cardinal might be fraught with ill consequences. Let Mistress Constance go back to Lambeth Palace. But ere many days—perchance to-morrow—the Cardinal shall be compelled to yield her up to you. The Queen herself shall give you the order."

"I do not think her Majesty will sign such an order," observed Father Alfonso.

"Be content, my lord, you shall have it," said the King significantly to Bonner.

"There is another prisoner in the Lollards' Tower whom I would fain have, Sire," observed the bishop.

"You mean the crazy fanatic, Derrick Carver," rejoined Philip. "He shall be given up to you at the same time as Constance. Come to Whitehall betimes to-morrow, and I will procure you the warrant from her Majesty. Meanwhile, let Constance go back."

"Your injunctions shall be obeyed, Sire. Ere long, I hope to offer your Majesty a grand *auto-da-fé* at Smithfield."

"If his Majesty will be guided by me, he will not attend another such dreadful execution as we have this day witnessed," observed Father Alfonso.

"Why so, father?" demanded the King.

"Because you will infallibly lose your popularity with the nation, Sire," said Father Alfonso. "The odium of these executions will attach to you, instead of to their authors."

"There is something in this," observed Philip, thoughtfully. "We will talk of it anon. Farewell, my lord. To-morrow morning at Whitehall." And with a glance at Constance, he quitted the sacristy, attended by his confessor.

After addressing a few harsh words to Constance, for whom he seemed to have conceived an extraordinary antipathy, Bonner likewise quitted the chamber.

Shortly afterwards Rodomont entered, and hurrying to the ambry, unlocked it, and set Osbert free.

Again the unhappy lovers rushed into each other's arms, but Rodomont thought it necessary to interpose, saying there was no time for the indulgence of such transports now, but urging them to bid each other farewell.

"You heard what has passed just now," remarked Constance to Osbert; "I am to be taken back to the good Cardinal."

"True; but to-morrow he will be compelled to surrender you to Bonner," rejoined Osbert.

"Do not believe it, fair mistress," said Rodomont. "His Eminence will protect you. You have escaped many difficulties, and may be equally fortunate now. You are to return with the procession to Saint Paul's, after which you will be taken to Lambeth Palace."

"Farewell, Constance," said Osbert, straining her to his breast.

"Make haste!" cried Rodomont, impatiently, "or we shall have the guard here, and then there will be a fresh entanglement. Methinks I hear their footsteps. Quick! quick!"

"I come," rejoined Constance.

And tearing herself from her lover, she followed him out of the sacristy. The door being left open, Osbert allowed a brief interval to elapse, and then issued forth into the church, which by this time was well-nigh deserted.

CHAPTER III.

HOW OSBERT WAS INDUCED TO JOIN A CONSPIRACY.

AMONGST those who witnessed the burning of Rogers was the French ambassador. On quitting Smithfield, he repaired to the court adjoining the conventual church, and was watching the religious procession set out on its return to Saint Paul's, when he noticed Osbert Clinton, whose eyes were following the retreating figure of Constance. Approaching him, De Noailles said, in a low voice, "I am sorry to see poor Constance Tyrrell among those recusants. Has she been delivered over to Bonner's *chambre ardente?* "

"Not as yet," rejoined Osbert, in a troubled tone.

"I trust she never may be," said De Noailles, "for Bonner has no pity for a heretic. Youth and beauty weigh very little with him. 'Tis enough to drive one mad to think that so lovely a creature should be his victim !"

"She never shall be !" exclaimed Osbert, moodily.

"How will you hinder it?" said De Noailles. "Can you snatch her from his grasp if he once secures her? Can you unlock the prison in which she will be immured? Dare you even approach her now? How, then, will you be able to free her, when she is led to the stake, escorted by a guard as strong as that which accompanied the poor wretch who has just been sacrificed?"

"Torture me not thus!" cried Osbert. "I feel as though I could sell myself to perdition to accomplish her deliverance."

"You shall not need to do that," observed De Noailles, perceiving that Osbert was in the right frame of mind for his purpose. "Now listen to me. A plot is hatching, having for its object the overthrow of Philip, the deposition of Mary, and the restoration of the Protestant faith, as a guarantee for which the Princess Elizabeth is to be proclaimed Queen. With this movement all the heads of the Protestant party are connected, and only await a favourable moment for an outbreak. That moment is at hand. The execution which has just taken place is but the prelude to others equally dreadful. In a few days Bishop Hooper will be burnt at Gloucester, Saunders at Coventry, and Taylor at Hadley; and, ere the month be out, others will swell the fearful catalogue. Thoroughly alarmed, the Protestants feel that, if they do not offer prompt and effectual resistance, they will be exterminated. It is certain, therefore, that they will all rise when called upon, and, if well managed, the scheme cannot fail of success."

"What has this plot to do with Constance Tyrrell?" demanded Osbert.

"Much," replied the other. "Join us, and I will engage to procure her liberation."

"On those terms I will join you," said Osbert. "What would you have me do?"

"I cannot explain our plans now. But meet me to morrow, at midnight, in the cloisters of Westminster Abbey, and I will introduce you to the chief conspirators."

"I will be there at the hour appointed," said Osbert. "Till then, farewell!"

And moving away, he followed the procession to Saint Paul's, leaving De Noailles well satisfied with his manœuvre.

CHAPTER IV.

WHAT PHILIP HEARD WHILE CONCEALED BEHIND THE ARRAS.

EXT day in the forenoon, Bishop Bonner repaired to Whitehall Palace, and found the King in a cabinet communicating with the great gallery. Philip was seated at a table covered with dispatches, and near him stood Rodomont Bittern, with whom he was conversing.

"I am glad you are come, my lord," said the King to Bonner, as the latter entered the cabinet. "This gentleman is the bearer of a letter from the Lord Cardinal to her Majesty, in which his Eminence solicits an audience of her on a matter of importance. The Cardinal will be here at noon, and the important matter on which he comes relates to the delivery of Constance Tyrrell to your lordship. Is it not so, Sir?" he added to Rodomont.

"It is, my liege," replied the other. "His Eminence is unwilling to give up the maiden, and desires to ascertain the Queen's pleasure on the subject. As I have already told your Majesty, the Cardinal was much troubled on learning from Mistress Constance what had befallen her, and he declared that unless he had the Queen's positive commands to that effect he would not surrender her to the ecclesiastical commissioners. I do not think I ever saw him more moved."

"I make no doubt that his Eminence blamed me, Sir," remarked Bonner,

"To speak truth, my lord, he did," replied Rodomont; "and he said plainly to Lord Priuli that you should not have the damsel."

"Your Majesty hears that?" cried Bonner. "This proud Cardinal defies your authority."

"Nay, there was no defiance on his Eminence's part of the King's Highness," observed Rodomont, "but only of your lordship. The representative of his Holiness, he said, should not be insulted with impunity, and he added some words which I care not to repeat, but they spoke of reprimands, censures, and possible privation of dignity."

"His Eminence takes up the matter with great warmth," observed Bonner, uneasily.

"I have never known him so put out before," said Rodomont. "He paced to and fro within his chamber for an hour, and the Lord Priuli could scarce pacify him. This morning, after an interview with Mistress Constance, his anger broke out afresh, and he dispatched me with a letter to her Majesty, craving an audience at noon. This is all I have to state. I have thought it right to warn your lordship that if you think fit to persist in the matter, you may know what to expect."

"Enough, Sir," observed the King. "You may withdraw."

Rodomont bowed and retired, laughing in his sleeve at the fright he had given Bonner. "Heaven forgive me for making a bugbear of the good Cardinal," he muttered; "but the trick seems to have succeeded."

"So, the Cardinal is determined to try his strength with us," observed Philip, as soon as he and Bonner were left alone.

"I must beg to retire from the contest, Sire," replied the bishop. "Whoever wins, I am sure to lose by it."

"Tut! I will bear you harmless," rejoined the King. "But the Cardinal will be here anon. I must prepare the Queen for his arrival."

"I would your Majesty could be prevailed upon to abandon this design," observed Bonner. "It will lead to nothing save trouble and confusion. Ever after I shall have the Cardinal for an enemy."

"You alarm yourself needlessly," rejoined Philip. "That

knave purposely exaggerated his master's anger. The Cardinal knows full well that the act is mine, and not your
lordship's."

With this, he passed through a side-door, and, accompanied by the bishop, entered a large and magnificently
furnished apartment, embellished with portraits of Henry
VIII. and his family. No one was within this superb room,
and after traversing it, the King and Bonner reached an
ante-chamber, in which were assembled a number of pages,
esquires, and ushers in the royal livery.

On seeing the King, these personages drew up and bowed
reverently as he passed, while two gentleman ushers, each
bearing a white wand, marshalled him ceremoniously towards
the entrance of the Queen's apartments, before which stood
a couple of tall yeomen of the guard with halberds in their
hands.

As he approached this door, Sir John Gage came forth,
and Philip inquired if the Queen was alone. The Lord
Chamberlain replied in the affirmative, but added that Cardinal Pole was momentarily expected, and that he himself
had come forth to receive his Eminence.

"It is well," replied Philip. "When the Cardinal comes,
do not mention to him that I am with her Majesty. I pray
your Lordship to remain here till you are summoned," he
added to Bonner.

With this he passed through the door, which was thrown
open by the ushers, and entered the Queen's chamber—a
spacious apartment, richly furnished, hung with tapestry,
and adorned with many noble pictures, chief among which
were portraits of the Queen's ill-fated mother by Holbein,
and of her royal husband by Sir Antonio More.

Mary was seated at a table placed near a deep bay-
window. She occupied a large armed-chair, and was
reading a book of devotions. Her attire was of purple
velvet, and a coif set with precious stones adorned her head.
A smile lighted up her pallid countenance on the King's
entrance.

"I give your Majesty good-day," she said. "To what do
I owe the pleasure of this visit?"

"You expect the Cardinal," rejoined Philip, abruptly and
sternly. "Do you know what brings him here?"

"I do not," she answered, "But I shall be glad to see him, as I desire to consult him as to the restitution of the Church property vested in the crown during the King my father's reign."

"Reserve that for another occasion, Madam," said Philip. "The Cardinal's errand relates to Constance Tyrrell."

"Ha!" exclaimed Mary, startled. "What has he to say concerning her?"

"That you will learn on his arrival," rejoined Philip. "But it is my pleasure that she be removed from his custody and delivered to Bishop Bonner."

"Then his Eminence has failed to reclaim her?"

"Signally. Nothing remains but to try extreme rigour, and if that will not effect her conversion, the laws she has offended must deal with her."

"I pity this unhappy maiden, albeit she continues obstinate," said Mary. "Be not angry if I tell you that I designed to marry her to your secretary, Osbert Clinton, to whom she is betrothed."

"She shall never wed him," said Philip, harshly. "Why should you meddle in the matter? Has Osbert Clinton dared to prefer this request to you?"

"No, on my soul," replied Mary. "But I know the girl loves him tenderly, and, had she recanted, it was my design to reward her with the husband of her choice."

"But she does not recant, I tell you, Madam," cried Philip, "so it is idle to speculate on what might have been. It is my will that she be delivered up to Bonner. But the order must proceed from yourself, not from me. Thus, when the Cardinal comes, you will be prepared with an answer to him."

"But let me first hear what he has to urge," objected the Queen.

"No matter what he urges," rejoined Philip. "Lay your commands upon him, as I have intimated. Nay, I will be obeyed," he added, authoritatively.

Mary sighed, but made no further remonstrance.

"The Cardinal must be at hand," continued Philip. "By your leave, I will be an unseen witness of the interview."

And he stepped behind the arras, near which the Queen was seated.

"He distrusts me," murmured Mary; "and, in sooth, he has imposed a most painful task upon me."

Shortly afterwards, the Cardinal was announced, and, greeting him kindly, the Queen begged him to take a seat by her side.

"If your Majesty has heard what occurred yesterday in Saint Bartholomew's Church at Smithfield," premised Pole, "you will guess the object of my visit. Constance Tyrrell, whom you confided to my charge, and whom I yet hope to reclaim, is to be wrested from me. But I shall refuse to deliver her up."

"Your Eminence must needs comply with my order," said Mary.

"True, Madam," replied the Cardinal. "But I do not believe you will give any such order, when I say that in surrendering her I shall only be consigning her to infamy and dishonour."

"I pray your Eminence to explain yourself," said Mary.

"It is painful to me to speak out," replied Pole, "but I cannot allow this unhappy maiden to be sacrificed. She has opened her heart to me, and has confessed all. Blinded by an insane and wicked passion for her, the King, since his first accidental meeting with her at Southampton, has never ceased to persecute her with his dishonourable solicitations. Yesterday, during that dread ceremonial, when, terrified and fainting, she was borne into the sacristy of Saint Bartholomew's Church, he renewed his unholy suit, and bade her choose between his love and deliverance up to Bishop Bonner. I doubt not that she would sustain this trial, as she has sustained others. I do not think that imprisonment or torture would shake her. But why should she be exposed to such treatment. Madam, this is not the case of an heretical offender. Constance Tyrrell is to be imprisoned, is to be tortured, is perhaps to suffer a fiery death, not on account of her religious opinions, but because she has virtue enough to resist the King. Madam, such wrong shall not be, while I can raise my voice against it."

"It shall not be," said Mary. "Is Bonner a party to this foul transaction? If so, as I live, I will strip him of his priestly robes."

"No, Madam," replied Pole. "I must acquit Bonner of

any complicity in the affair. He merely looks for a victim."

" He shall not find one in Constance Tyrrell," said Mary, "My heart bleeds for her."

"Well it may, Madam," replied Pole. "A sad fatality has rested upon her ever since the King's arrival in South-ampton, when her marvellous beauty attracted his attention, and excited a passion which nothing apparently can subdue."

" He saw her before he beheld me, and loved her better than he loved me !" cried Mary, bitterly. "Something of this I suspected, but I thought I had removed her from his influence by taking her with me to Winchester."

" Ay, but the King contrived to obtain a secret interview with the damsel before your departure," said Pole, "and this is the only part of her conduct that deserves censure. Moved by his passionate words and captivating manner, which few could resist, she listened to him, and at last owned she loved him, or thought she loved him."

" Oh, I know his power !" cried Mary. "He exercised the same fascination over me."

" But withdrawn from his baneful influence, poor Con-stance bitterly repented of the error into which she had been led, and, by the advice of Father Jerome, the good priest of Saint Catherine's chapel at Winchester, to whom she con-fessed her fault, she left with him a tablet of gold, enriched with precious stones, which had been given her by the King as a gage of love. By Father Jerome's advice, also, she quitted Winchester and returned to her father at South-ampton, the good priest dreading lest, if she remained with your Majesty, she might be exposed to further temptation."

" Father Jerome did right," said Mary ; "and, perchance, he saved her from dishonour."

" Up to this time, Constance had been a zealous Catholic," pursued Pole ; "but, while attending Derrick Carver at the Hospital of the Domus Dei at Southampton, she imbibed his pernicious doctrines, and embraced the Reformed faith. This deplorable change, I fear, is attributable to the King."

" Methinks your Eminence is unjust there," observed Mary.

"My grounds for the opinion are these," replied Pole.
"Constance's nature is devout and impressionable. Full of
grief and remorse, she was thrown into the way of Carver,
who took advantage of her troubled state of mind to accomplish her conversion. Had I met her at that time she would
not have been lost to us, and I still trust she may be recovered. With the rest of her history your Majesty is
acquainted. It is a series of misfortunes ; neither does it
seem likely she will ever be wedded to him she loves.
Happy had it been for her that she had never excited the
King's love ! Happy had it been for her that her faith had
not been unsettled, and that she had been able to pass her
life in holy and tranquil retirement. But her destiny was
otherwise. She has abjured her religion—she has lost her
father's affection—she has endured imprisonment—but,
though sorely tempted, she has not sinned. Be it yours,
gracious Madam, to preserve her from further suffering—
from further temptation."

"What can I do ?" cried Mary. "I have promised the
King an order for her removal from your Eminence, and
deliverance up to Bonner."

"Madam, if that order be given and acted upon, I shall
resist it," replied Pole.

"Heaven aid me !" exclaimed the Queen. "I am sorely
perplexed, and know not how to act for the best."

"Consult the King, your husband, Madam," rejoined the
Cardinal. "Tell him what I have told you, and of my
resolution."

"I shall not need to be told," said Philip, coming from
behind the arras. "I have heard all that has passed between you and her Majesty."

"I shrink from nothing I have uttered, Sire," rejoined
Pole. "I should have spoken with equal freedom had you
stood before me. But I beseech you pursue not this matter
further. Consequences you may not foresee will flow from
it. You will array against you a force stronger than you
can resist. I may be compelled to yield, but my voice will
be heard, and its echoes may shake your throne to its
foundations."

"Your Eminence menaces me," cried Philip, sternly.

"No, Sire, I warn you," rejoined the Cardinal, with dignity. "You are on a perilous path, from which it were wise to turn back."

"Your Eminence seems to have forgotten your former experiences, and how you fared in your struggle with her Majesty's royal father," observed Philip. "In those days the priesthood received a lesson from the crown which it would be well if they remembered. The proudest of them, Wolsey, was hurled from his high place. I warn you, therefore of your danger before you enter upon a conflict with me. What Henry VIII. accomplished may be done again. If the priesthood wax insolent they may be crushed. The Papal authority has been just restored, but it can be easily shaken off again. Your Eminence has but recently returned from a long exile, and you may have to endure a second banishment."

"I shall do my duty without fear, Sire," replied Pole, firmly. "I well know what my resistance to the will of King Henry cost me. Because he could not reach me he struck at those most dear to me—at my sainted mother, the Countess of Salisbury, at my beloved brother, the Lord Montague, at my friends the Marquis of Exeter and Sir Edward Nevil, and at the young and gallant Earl of Surrey. On all these he wreaked the vengeance which ought to have alighted on my head. But I shall not fly now. I shall stay to answer for my acts in person."

"Pshaw!" exclaimed Philip, changing his tone. "Your Eminence takes the matter too seriously. I desire no quarrel with you, or with the Church. It would be idle to do so on an affair so trifling as the present."

"The affair is not trifling, Sire," rejoined Pole. "The liberty, the honour, the life of a poor damsel are at stake."

"That is your Eminence's version of the business," said Philip. "You are simply protecting a heretic. I counsel you to give up the girl peaceably. 'Twill be best."

"I have already stated my determination, Sire," rejoined Pole. "Madam, I take my leave."

"Stop, my Lord Cardinal," cried Mary. "Depart not thus, I beseech you. For my sake, tarry a few minutes longer. Perchance his Majesty may relent."

"I would tarry till midnight if I thought so," replied

Pole. "Oh, Sire," he added to Phillip, "let me make a final appeal to the latent generosity and goodness of your nature. You have many high and noble qualities, inherited from your august father. Let me sway you now. Be not governed by wild and unhallowed passions, the gratification of which will endanger your eternal welfare. If you sin, you must not hope to escape chastisement; and as your sin will be great, so will your chastisement be severe. Wrongs, such as you would inflict upon her Majesty, are visited with Heaven's direst wrath, and years of prayer and penance will not procure you pardon. Cast off these delusions and snares. You are fortunately united to a Queen as eminent for virtue as for rank, whose heart is entirely given to you, and who has just proved that she will obey you in all things. In every respect she is worthy of your love. She is your equal in birth, devout and pure, a loving wife, and a great Queen. To sacrifice her true and holy affection for lighter love would be unpardonable ingratitude. In all the highest qualifications of a woman, as purity, piety, judgment, discretion, dignity, none can surpass your consort, and you must be insensible indeed not to estimate her merits aright."

"I do estimate them—estimate them at their true worth," cried Philip. "Your Eminence has roused the better nature in me, and made me sensible of my faults, and ashamed of them. Forgive me, Madam," he added to Mary.

And as he spoke he approached the Queen, who threw her arms fondly about his neck, exclaiming, "Oh, my good Lord Cardinal, I owe this happiness to you."

"I am equally beholden to his Eminence," said Philip. "He has spoken the truth to me, and awakened me to a sense of my folly."

"I have called your Majesty's good feelings into play, that is all," rejoined Pole. "Henceforth, I trust that nothing will disturb the good understanding that ought to subsist between you and your royal consort. Pardon me if I press you further, Sire. Your heart being opened to kindly emotions, you will not refuse to listen to me. It is in your power to make ample amends to poor Constance Tyrrell for the misery she has endured, by giving your consent to her marriage with Osbert Clinton."

"I will add my entreaties to those of the Cardinal," said the Queen.   "Let it be so, I pray you."

"If your Eminence will reclaim her from heresy I will not refuse my consent," replied Philip.

"I ask no more," rejoined Pole; "and I trust their nuptials will not long be delayed."

"They shall never take place," mentally ejaculated Philip. "Your Majesty may desire some private converse with his Eminence," he added to the Queen.   "I will go and dismiss Bonner, who is waiting without.   He will not trouble your Eminence further."

And he quitted the chamber.

CHAPTER V.

PRAYING the Cardinal to resume his seat by her, Mary said, "There is a matter on which I desire to consult your Eminence. I cannot reconcile it to my conscience to retain the revenues arising from the Church lands, which were unlawfully vested in the crown during the late schism; but the Lord Chancellor, to whom I have spoken on the subject, seeks to dissuade me from my purpose, and declares that if I part with these large revenues, which amount to well-nigh a hundred thousand pounds a year, I shall not be able to maintain my dignity. To this objection, I replied in all sincerity, that I value my salvation more than ten crowns like that of England, and that I would not endanger my heavenly inheritance for all the wealth the world can offer. Still Gardiner opposes me, and says that the giving up of my revenues will be taken ill by those who are in possession of the abbey lands and other property of the Church, possession of which has been secured to them by the papal bull sent to your Eminence. But I see not why I should not set the holders of these ill-gotten treasures a good example. Peradventure some of them may follow it."

"I trust so, Madam," replied Pole; "and I applaud your resolution, for though you may impoverish your exchequer, yet you will lay up a far greater treasure for future enjoyment in heaven. The bull to which you refer was sent by the Pope at the solicitation of Gardiner, to prevent the opposition of certain nobles to reconciliation with the See of Rome, but his Holiness's real sentiments may be judged by another bull which he has just sent into Germany, excommunicating all who may keep any abbey or church lands, and placing under the like ban all princes, prelates and magistrates, who shall refuse to assist in the execution of the bull. Though the bull is addressed to Germany, it undoubtedly applies to this country as well, since his Holiness can never regard those with favour who have enriched themselves with the spoils of the Church. Moreover, the Church is poor, and some provision must be made for its wants."

"Provision *shall* be made for it," replied Mary. "I feel with horror that I myself may be excommunicated. But the load shall be removed from my soul. All the crown revenues, derived from the source I have mentioned, shall be relinquished, and placed at the disposal of your Eminence, to be applied in such manner as you may deem fit, for the benefit of the clergy, and the augmentation of small livings."

"Your Majesty will do a great and disinterested act, which will for ever redound to your credit, and secure you the prayers of the whole Church," said Pole. "I will take care that the revenues entrusted to me are properly applied."

"I would I could go still further," observed Mary, "and procure an act to compel the restoration of Church property, in whatever hands it may be. Think you it could be done?"

"I do not believe such an act could be procured, Madam," replied Pole. "Certain I am that it would not be prudent to attempt to obtain it at this juncture. Let us wait to see the effect of your own great action."

"I yield to your judgment," said Mary. "It is my intention to re-establish three monasteries dissolved by the King, my father—namely, the Grey Friars at Greenwich, the Carthusians at Sheen, and the Briggittines at Sion."

"Heaven has stirred your heart to much good work, Madam," said the Cardinal. "The Church will have cause to bless your name."

"Yet another matter," observed the Queen. "I desire to

20

have masses said for the repose of my father's soul, and would fain endow a church for that especial purpose."

"Alas! Madam, I cannot aid you there," replied Pole. "His Holiness will never permit the endowment of a church for the benefit of the soul of so determined a foe to the See of Rome as Henry VIII. No priest will pray for him."

"But I can pray for him, and do so daily," rejoined Mary. "I trust his heavily-laden soul is not beyond the reach of intercession. Since I may not endow a church to say masses for him, I will augment the revenues of the college he re-founded at Cambridge, in the hope that those who are taught there may pray for the soul of their benefactor."

"A pious act, Madam," said Pole, "and I trust it may be profitable to your father's soul."

"All these things I do, my Lord Cardinal," pursued Mary, "in preparation for my hour of travail, when I may be called away suddenly from this transitory life. If I should be, you will religiously fulfil my designs."

"By Heaven's grace, Madam, I will accomplish the work you confide to me," said the Cardinal. "The goods of the Church shall be restored to holy uses, and all other things done as you have appointed."

"One question more, and I have done," said Mary. "I am about to make my will, and propose to settle the crown on the King my husband, after my decease."

"Is his Majesty aware of your intention, Madam," inquired the Cardinal.

"It is his wish that I should do so," replied Mary.

"So I suspected," said Pole. "Madam, as your kinsman and faithful counsellor, as your loyal and loving subject, I implore you not to make the will you propose. Englishmen will never accept a Spaniard as their sovereign, and if you bequeath your kingdom to your husband, your will will assuredly be set aside."

"But the King has caused the will to be prepared," said Mary.

"Ha! has it gone so far as that?" cried Pole.

"It will be brought to me this very day for my signature," replied Mary.

"Have you consulted the Lord Chancellor and the council, Madam?" demanded Pole.

"I have consulted no one," she replied. "The King enjoined me not to do so. But I could not help confiding the matter to your Eminence, knowing your affection for me."

"By that affection, of which you know the depth and sincerity, I charge you not to execute that will, Madam," said Pole. "Your ministers, if consulted, will agree with me. This is no light question. The welfare of your kingdom is at stake."

At this moment a side-door opened, and Father Alfonso appeared at it, with a packet in his hand. On seeing the Cardinal, he would have retired, but the Queen signed to him to come forward, and he was compelled to obey.

"It is the will," she observed in an under tone to Pole.

"It is providential that I am here," he replied.

Meanwhile, Father Alfonso advanced, and, bowing reverently to the Queen and the Cardinal, laid the packet on the table.

"Here is the document for your Majesty's signature," he said. "The witnesses await your summons without."

"The scheme is carefully planned, but I will thwart it," mentally ejaculated Pole. "The witnesses may be dismissed. The Queen will not sign this document," he added, aloud.

"What do I hear, Madam," cried Father Alfonso. "His Majesty expects ——"

"I say the Queen will not sign it," interrupted Pole, taking up the will, "nor any other document to the like effect."

Making a profound obeisance to the Queen, he quitted the room, taking the packet with him.

CHAPTER VI.

OF THE MIDNIGHT MEETING IN THE CRYPT BENEATH THE CHAPTER-HOUSE.

IT was on the stroke of midnight that Osbert Clinton, muffled in a long black cloak, and armed with rapier and dagger, arrived at the place of rendezvous appointed by De Noailles. The night was bright and beautiful, and the moon, nearly at the full, and hanging above the north side of the noble Gothic fane, silvered its hoary battlements and buttresses, and glittered upon the tinted panes of the great pointed windows.

Passing through an arched doorway, he entered the cloisters, and marched slowly along the south ambulatory. No one was there. Having thus tracked one side of the square, and glanced down the alley on the left, he stood still and listened, but no sound reached his ears, until shortly afterwards the deep bell of the abbey tolled forth the hour of midnight. Then all again relapsed into solemn silence, and had there been even a light footfall on the pavement, Osbert must have heard it.

Again he moved slowly on. His thoughts were too much occupied with the business he had on hand, or he might have noted the vaulted and richly-ornamented ceiling overhead, or the pillared openings at the side, through which the moonlight streamed upon the pavement, but though he was not wholly unconscious of these architectural beauties, they produced little effect upon him, neither did the serene loveliness of the night, or the hushed tranquility of the spot, soothe his perturbed spirits.

He had reached another angle of the cloisters, and was proceeding along the alley, which was here plunged in gloom, when he fancied he discerned a dark figure advancing towards him, upon which he quickened his steps, and soon reached the person, who, on seeing him, remained stationary. It was De Noailles. Like Osbert he was muffled in a cloak, and his broad-leaved hat was pulled over his brows.

"You have not changed your mind, I perceive," observed De Noailles, "but are resolved to go on with the enterprise."

"I am," replied Osbert.

"Follow me, then," rejoined the French ambassador, "and I will introduce you to those in league with us."

Marching quickly but noiselessly along, he conducted Osbert towards the chapter-house. On reaching it, they descended a flight of stone steps which seemed to lead to a vault, but further progress was arrested by a door, against which De Noailles tapped gently. At this summons the door was cautiously opened by a man, who appeared to be well-armed, and they were admitted into a large subterranean chamber.

This crypt, for such it was, was dimly illumined by an iron lamp fixen to a pillar standing in the centre of the vault. The stone walls were of great solidity, in order to sustain the weight of the chapter-house, and the roof, which likewise formed the floor of the superstructure, was of stone, ribbed, and groined, and supported by the pillar to which the lamp was fixed.

In this crypt were assembled some eight or nine young men, all of good condition, judging from their attire and deportment. As De Noailles and Osbert entered the vault, a tall, richly-dressed man detached himself from the group with whom he was conversing, and advanced to meet them. As he advanced, Osbert instantly knew him to be Thomas Stafford, second son to Lord Stafford, and grandson of the Duke of Buckingham, a disaffected personage who had been engaged in Wyat's rebellion, but had escaped owing to want of proof of his complicity in the affair.

" Your excellency is welcome," said Stafford to the ambassador. " I am glad to find you bring us a recruit. What !
Osbert Clinton, is it you ? " he added, as the young man un-
muffled his countenance. " You are, indeed, an important
accession to our ranks. But you must take the oath of
fidelity. Our object is to deliver our country from the
tyranny of Spain, to depose Mary, to place Elizabeth on the
throne and wed her to Courtenay, and to restore the Protestant faith."

" I will be true to you to the death," replied Osbert emphatically, " and will aid you to the utmost of my power—
this I solemnly swear."

" Enough," replied Stafford ; " and now I will present you
to my associates in this great and holy cause. Some of them
you know."

" I know Sir Henry Dudley, Sir Anthony Kingston, and
Sir Nicholas Throckmorton," replied Osbert, saluting the
three persons he named, " but the rest are strangers to me."

" This is honest Master Udal, and this bold Master Staun-
ton, both good Protestants, and hearty haters of the Spaniard
and Popish idolatry," said Sir Henry Dudley. And after
salutations had passed by Osbert and the persons indicated,
he went on : " These gentlemen," bringing forward two
others, " are Masters Peckham and Werne. You have heard
of them, I make no doubt ? "

" Ay, marry have I, oftentimes," replied Osbert. " They
are officers to the Princess Elizabeth. I am glad to see
them here."

" They bring us messages from the Princess approving of
our design," said Dudley. " Her Highness will not write,
after the danger she incurred from her intercepted correspon-
dence with Wyat."

" Her Grace is very favourable to your cause, as I have
already stated, Sir Henry," observed Peckham, " and wishes
it all possible success."

" She has need to do," said Sir Anthony Kingston. " If
we succeed, we shall place the crown upon her head."

" There is yet another gentleman whom you have not made
known to me, Sir Henry," said Osbert, indicating a dark,
sinister-looking personage, in a philemot-coloured mantle
and doublet, who stood aloof from the others.

" Ha ! this is a very useful person," replied Dudley, " This is M. de Freitville, a secret agent of the King of France, who promises to aid our enterprise with men and money."

" I hope he will fulfil his promises better than those made by him to Wyat," remarked Osbert, regarding Freitville distrustfully.

" Had Wyat held out a few days longer, he would not have lacked support," rejoined Freitville. " My royal master afforded an asylum and gave pensions to all those implicated in the rebellion who fled to France. His Excellency M. de Noailles will tell you that his Majesty has ever been hostile to this Spanish alliance, and that, failing in preventing it, he is now determined to drive the Queen and her husband from the throne, and set up the Princess Elizabeth in their stead."

" Has he no other views ? " said Osbert.

" None averse to this country," said De Noailles, "that I can declare emphatically. It would be idle to assert that my royal master is influenced by the same motives that you are; but the end is the same. You both seek the dissolution of this marriage and the overthrow of Philip—he as the avowed enemy of Spain, you as suffering from the tyranny of Philip, and anxious to restore the Reformed religion. Our interests, therefore, are identical, and we make common cause together against the foe. For my own part, I have a personal antipathy to Philip. He has done me a grievous injury, and I will never rest till I requite him. Some day or other his life will be in my hands and then he shall feel my vengeance."

" My wrongs are greater than yours," cried Osbert. " I have thrown off all allegiance to him, and am henceforth his deadly foe. He has stepped between me and her whom I love dearer than life, and has sought to sacrifice her to his unhallowed desires. He is unworthy to be the Queen's consort—unworthy to govern Englishmen. I will shed my heart's blood in the attempt to drive him from the throne."

" Why not plunge a dagger in his breast," said Freitville, " and so rid the country of a tyrant ? "

" I am no assassin," replied Osbert. " Deeply as I hate him, I would not slay him save in fair fight. No, we must rouse our countrymen to a sense of their danger, and rise in arms against him, and put him justly to death, or drive him from the country."

"His design is to subjugate England, and reduce us to the condition of Flanders and Burgundy," cried Stafford. "If he is allowed to remain on the throne for another year, he will become absolute master of our liberties. The twelve strongest fortresses in England—the Tower itself included—are to be delivered up to him by the misguided and unworthy Queen, and garrisoned by twenty thousand Spaniards."

"I can scarce think the Queen would be thus false to her country," said Osbert.

"It is so, Sir, and I will tell you more," pursued Stafford. "Alva is to be governor of the Tower, and ere he has been there many months more noble English blood will drench the scaffold than ever dyed it in King Harry's days. The Inquisition, also, is to be established."

"It is already established among us," cried Sir Henry Dudley. "We had our *auto-da-fé* in Smithfield yesterday."

"The Queen is so infatuated by her love for the King," pursued Stafford, "that she can deny him nothing. You, Sir," he added to Osbert, "who have been in attendance upon him, must know how shamefully he abuses her regard, and the scandalous infidelities he practises."

"It is true," replied Osbert. "It is true, also, that her Majesty can refuse him nothing. He has incited her to settle her crown upon him by her will in the event of her decease during her time of travail."

"Can she be so blind as not to perceive that by making such a will she ensures her own death by poison?" observed De Noailles. "But her senseless passion deprives her of all judgment."

"Now is the time to strike," cried Stafford. "Men's minds are so excited that a single spark will set the whole city of London in a flame. All the Protestants are ripe for outbreak. Let us raise the standard of revolt in Smithfield, on the very spot where Rogers was martyred, proclaim the Princess Elizabeth Queen, the deposition of Philip and Mary, and restoration of the Reformed religion. We can only number a handful of men at first, but what matters that? Thousands will soon rally round us, and ere night we shall be masters of the City."

"The enterprise is desperate," said Osbert, "but the moment is propitious. I am with you."

"So are we all!" cried the others.

"Our cry shall be, 'Down with Philip and Mary! Down with the mass and idolatry! Long live Queen Elizabeth, the head and defender of the Protestant Church!'" said Stafford. "Every Protestant will respond to the call."

"If we fail, we throw away our lives in a righteous cause," rejoined Osbert.

"We shall not fail," cried Sir Henry Dudley. "I was at Smithfield yesterday, and spoke with hundreds, who are ready for an outbreak."

"So did I," added Sir Anthony Kingston. "I can vouch for the detestation with which the King is regarded. Let not the attempt be delayed."

"It shall be made to-morrow," said Stafford. "I can muster fifty well-armed men."

"And I half that number," said Dudley.

"And I twenty," said Kingston.

"I can bring no one with me," said Osbert. "But I will gain a thousand followers before the day is over."

"At what hour shall we meet to-morrow?" said Dudley.

"At noon," replied Stafford. "Give me your hand upon it, Osbert Clinton."

"Readily," rejoined the other, grasping the hand stretched out to him."

At this moment the lamp was suddenly thrown down, and the crypt plunged in darkness.

"Traitors, before to-morrow you shall be all clapped in the Tower!" cried a voice.

"'Tis the King!" mentally ejaculated Osbert Clinton. And he sprang towards the door.

"Perdition! we have a spy among us," cried Stafford. "Seize him and put him to death!"

And, as he spoke, swords were drawn by the conspirators.

"Let no one go forth, but let each man answer for himself. Where is Osbert Clinton?"

"Here," he replied, from the door.

"Where is Sir Henry Dudley?"

"Here," answered the person designated.

While Stafford was pursuing these inquiries, Osbert heard some one approaching, and stepped a little aside. It was well he did so, as otherwise a rapier would have transfixed him. As it was, the point of the weapon merely pierced the side of his doublet, without doing him any injury. But at the same moment Osbert seized the arm that had dealt the blow. After vainly struggling to free himself from the iron grasp in which he was held, the King (for it was he) whispered, "Release me, Sir, I command you."

"Your commands are of no weight here, Sire," replied Osbert. "But I will not see you assassinated. Save yourself!"

And letting go his hold as he spoke, the King instantly passed through the door, and made good his retreat.

At the noise occasioned by his exit, all was confusion and alarm among the conspirators. Amid fierce shouts and exclamations a general rush was made to the door, and had they not reached it quickly, the whole party would have been made prisoners without the possibility of escape, for some one was trying to lock them in.

Made aware of their approach by the noise, this person fled, without having accomplished his purpose, but, while hastily mounting the steps, he became entangled in his gown —for his garments were those of a monk—and fell. The first of the conspirators to issue from the crypt, were Stafford and Dudley, and on catching sight of the monk, who was getting up as quickly as he could, they recognised Father Alfonso de Castro.

"By Heaven! it is the King's confessor who has been playing the spy upon us," exclaimed Stafford.

"He shall not escape to tell the tale," roared Dudley. "My sword shall stop his preaching in future."

And they dashed up the steps. Ere they could reach him, however, Father Alfonso had regained his feet, and speeded across the court, shouting lustily for help.

His object was to gain a small tower, then standing near the cloisters, on the summit of which tower, under a wooden pent-house, hung the alarm-bell. As Father Alfonso was aware, the door of this building was always left open, and if he could only reach it, he would be safe. Fear lent him wings, and he had passed through the door, shut it, and barred it inside before his pursuers came up.

While they were venting their disappointment in maledictions, he ran up a narrow spiral stone staircase, and, reaching a small chamber, seized a rope that dangled from a hole in the ceiling, and began to ring the alarm-bell,

CHAPTER VII.

IN WHAT MANNER THE OUTBREAK COMMENCED.

MEANTIME, all the conspirators had come forth from the crypt, and were gathered together in the court, considering what should be done under the circumstances. The sudden and violent ringing of the alarm-bell seemed to leave them no alternative but flight.

"We must separate and beat a retreat," cried Stafford. "The meeting must not take place as appointed to-morrow at Smithfield, but must be deferred to some other opportunity. That cursed Spanish friar has overheard our plans, and will reveal them. You will all best consult your safety by keeping out of the way for the present. The great enterprise has been thwarted for the moment, but it will not be abandoned."

"Assuredly not," cried Dudley. "Would there were some means of silencing that infernal clatter."

"If it goes on it will rouse up half the town," cried Sir Anthony Kingston.

"Why should it not serve as the signal for the rising?" cried Osbert, who felt the necessity of immediate action. "Why should we not commence the great enterprise now? To-morrow we shall all be proscribed, and a price set upon our heads. Let us act to-night. That bell will spread alarm through all this quarter of the town, and the people will soon come flocking hither to learn its import. Let us tell them that a rising takes place this night against the Spanish domination."

"Agreed !" exclaimed several voices.

"I approve of the plan," said De Noailles, who was evidently much alarmed ; "but I cannot be seen in the matter. You know where to find me, gentlemen. Success attend you !"

And he hastily retired with Freitville.

Meanwhile, the alarm-bell continued to ring violently, and it was evident, from the shouts and noises heard without, that the people were roused, and were flocking towards the spot.

"I hear them. They are coming now," cried Stafford. "Let us forth to meet them. Ring that bell as loudly as thou canst, thou pestilent friar ! It shall bring those together who shall aid us to dethrone thy master."

And, as if in compliance with the request, the alarm-bell was run more violently than ever.

The conspirators then marched, sword in hand, into the Dean's-yard, where some of that dignitary's servants were collected, but on seeing them these persons immediately retreated. But the next moment there burst through the gateway a troop of citizens, hastily and imperfectly attired, and armed with various weapons, swords, pikes, and arquebuses.

"What ho, my masters !" shouted the foremost of these. "Why rings the alarm-bell ?"

"It rings to call you to arms," replied Osbert, "in defence of your liberties and religion. A rising is about to take place to depose Philip and Mary, place the Princess Elizabeth on the throne, and restore the Reformed Religion, as established by King Edward VI., of blessed memory."

"Hear you that, my masters ?" cried the man. "The mass is to be put down, and the Protestant faith restored."

It so chanced that the whole of the persons addressed were Protestants, so they cheered lustily, and shouted, "Down with the mass !"

Meanwhile, the bell never for a moment ceased its clamour, and numbers of other persons, armed like those who had first appeared, answered the summons. Many of these joined in the cries against Popery. but others being

Romanists, retorted furiously, and struggles immediately began to take place between the opposing sects. As the crowd was continually on the increase, the hubbub and disturbance grew louder and louder, and a general engagement was threatened.

Just then, a party of twenty-five or thirty men, armed with pikes and carrying lanterns, came up, shouting, "Down with the'mass! Down with Antichrist!" Thus reinforced, the Protestants laid about them stoutly, and soon drove off their opponents.

This victory gained, they began to shout lustily, and called out for a leader, whereupon Osbert Clinton leaped upon a stone bench, and waving his sword above his head, cried out in a loud voice, so as to be heard by all, "I am ready to lead you, and if you will stand firmly by me and my associates, we will deliver you from Spanish tyranny and oppression, and re-establish your religion. No more inquisitorial practices—no more ecclesiastical commissions— no more burnings at Smithfield. We will release all those imprisoned for heresy."

"We will release our preachers and pastors," cried Stafford, leaping upon the bench, "and punish their judges. We will hang Gardiner and Bonner."

Shouts and terrific yells responded to this proposition.

"Here come the arquebusiers!" shouting several voices, as the trampling of horses and the clanking of arms were heard.

"Close up, and stand firm!" cried Osbert, springing from the bench and making his way towards the head of the crowd, which now, in obedience to his commands, had formed itself into a compact mass.

The next moment a troop of arquebusiers galloped up, with their swords drawn, and drew up in front of the mob.

After commanding a halt, their captain rode up to the front ranks of the crowd, and called out, " In the Queen's name, as good and loyal subjects of her Majesty, I command you to disperse, and go peaceably to your homes."

A general refusal was the response.

"You had best not be obstinate," retorted the captain of the guard. "Mark what I say. You have got amongst you several traitors, who are conspiring against their Majesties and against the safety of the realm."

"We are all traitors and conspirators," cried several voices. "We have thrown off our allegiance to the Queen and the Pope. We will have no Spaniard for King."

"Hear me," shouted the officer. "If you do not instantly deliver to us Sir Henry Dudley, Sir Anthony Kingston, Thomas Stafford, Osbert Clinton, and other traitors and conspirators whom ye have among you, we will cut you to pieces, and take them."

"Make good your threat, Sir," rejoined Osbert. "I am one of those you have named. Advance and take me if you can."

The officer instantly pushed forward his horse, but at that moment a bullet from an arquebuse, fired behind Osbert, crashed into his brain, and he fell heavily to the ground.

On seeing their leader fall, the arquebusiers instantly charged the mob, cutting at them with their swords and hewing down a considerable number. Still, as the sturdy citizens, encouraged by their leaders, stood firm, and received their assailants on their pikes, less mischief was done them than might have been expected.

A dreadful *mêlée* now took place, which endured for nearly a quarter of an hour; and while it was going on fresh parties, both of Protestants and Romanists, arrived at the scene of strife, and at once engaged in the conflict.

At first, it seemed as if the insurgents must be speedily routed; but though the arquebusiers did great damage in the early part of the fray, they were completely discomfited in the end, most of their horses being killed under them.

During the fight, all the leaders of the outbreak distinguished themselves by their bravery. Osbert Clinton threw himself into the thickest of the fight, encouraged his followers by word and deed, struck down three of the horsemen, and mainly contributed to the victory eventually gained by the insurgents. In little more than a quarter of an hour after the commencement [of the conflict, the arquebusiers were dismounted and discomfited, and the Romanists driven off.

The alarm-bell, which had ceased during the raging of the conflict, began to ring again more violently than ever.

A brief consultation was then held among the leaders of
the outbreak as to the course that should next be pursued,
when it was agreed that they should march on past Charing
Cross and along the Strand, and if they received sufficient
accession to their forces, should break down Temple Bar,
enter the City, liberate the prisoners for religion from Newgate and the Marshalsea, and march on to the Tower.

"I will lead on this party," said Stafford.

"I will set free the prisoners from the Gate House here
at Westminster," said Sir Henry Dudley.

"I will crave to be allowed to pass over to Lambeth
Palace," said Osbert, "and set free Constance Tyrrell and
Derrick Carver. This done, I will cross London-bridge and
join you. Let me have fifty men for the enterprise."

"Take double that number," said Stafford. "We shall
find plenty of others as we march along. Harkye, my
masters!" he called out to the crowd. "I want a hundred
men to go to Lambeth Palace."

"What to do?" demanded a burly citizen. "Not to
harm Cardinal Pole. He is a just man, and against persecution. We will hang Bonner and Gardiner, and the rest of
the Romish prelates, but we won't hurt a hair of the good
Cardinal's head."

"Right, Master Rufford, we won't hurt Cardinal Pole,"
cried a man near him.

"I would not have him harmed," replied Osbert. "My
sole object is to liberate two Protestant prisoners—Constance
Tyrrell and Derrick Carver.

"Derrick Carver is confined in the Lollard's Tower," said
Rufford; "it was he who spoke to me of the Cardinal's
goodness. If it be merely to free him and Constance Tyrrell,
we are with you."

"Ay, any of us will go with you on that errand," cried
several voices.

"I also will go with you," said Udal.

A hundred men were then told quickly off, all of whom
were armed with pikes and other weapons.

"How are we to get across the river?" demanded
Rufford.

"We will make the best of our way to the Horseferry,
where we shall find boats enow," replied Osbert.

"Ay, to the Horseferry! to the Horseferry!" cried several voices.

"We shall meet again ere daybreak, if all go well," said Osbert to Stafford and the others.

Then, putting himself at the head of his party, he led them at a quick pace round the south-west precincts of the abbey, and quickly gaining the banks of the river, proceeded to the Horseferry.

Up to this time they had been unopposed. The occupants of the scattered habitations on the road opened their windows to watch them pass, but none came forth to join them. As Osbert expected, they found the large ferry-boat, two barges, and sufficent smaller craft to transport them across the river, and the whole party having embarked in these boats, they pushed off and began to row towards Lambeth.

Scarcely, however, had they got a bow-shot from the shore, when a band of mounted archers rode up to the ferry station, and finding they were too late, and that all the boats had been taken away by the insurgents, they fired a volley at them, but without doing them any injury. Without trying the effect of a second volley, the horsemen rode back to Westminster, probably to find boats to enable them to cross the river.

CHAPTER VIII.

MEANTIME, Osbert and his party were more than half across the Thames.

Before them rose the stately palace of Lambeth, with its towers and gateway, looking like a black mass relieved against the clear sky. The serene beauty of night, which contrasted forcibly with the agitating events that were taking place, was not without effect upon Osbert. As he stood at the prow of the barge, leaning upon his sword and contemplating the scene, its holy calmness insensibly softened him, and he began to feel compunction for what he had done. But it was now too late to recede. The step was taken, and he must go on. He must either perish as a traitor, or live as the liberator of his country. Stifling all remorseful feelings, he tried to fix his thoughts on the latter contingency.

As the insurgents approached Lambeth Palace, it was evident from the lights gleaming from the windows, and the sounds heard from the courts, that its inmates were alarmed and astir.

In another moment the little squadron reached the wharf. Osbert was the first to land, and leaped ashore sword in hand. Udal and Rufford followed him, but such expedition was used that only a few minutes elapsed before the whole party had disembarked.

Meantime, their movements were watched from the battlements of the gateway by Rodomont Bittern and his two lieutenants. As soon as the insurgents had landed, and were drawn up, Osbert marched at their head towards the gateway, but before he reached it, Rodomont called out in a loud voice :—

"Who are ye, Sirs, and what seek ye, that ye approach the palace of the Lord Cardinal in this hostile fashion ? State your business without parleying, that I may report it to his Eminence. But I warn you that you can have no admittance at this hour."

"We will obtain admittance for ourselves if our request be refused," replied Osbert. "We require Constance Tyrrell and Derrick Carver, both detained within the palace, to be delivered up to us."

"By whose warrant do you make this demand?" inquired Rodomont.

"By mine own," replied the other, "which thus backed, shall answer as well as any other, were it even the Queen's."

"None but her Majesty's own order will procure their liberation," rejoined Rodomont; "and since you possess not that, you are likely to go away empty-handed. Though I would fain disbelieve it, methinks it is Master Osbert Clinton who speaks to me."

"I am he you suppose," replied Osbert. "Use dispatch, good Rodomont, and convey my message to the Lord Cardinal."

"If you are turned rebel, as I suspect from the tone you adopt, and the armed rout at your heels," rejoined Rodomont, "I must pray you to cease all familiarity with me. But I will make your demand known to the Lord Cardinal."

"Fail not to add, that if they be not delivered up, we will enter the palace and take them," said Osbert.

"I will communicate your exact words," rejoined Rodomont, "but I warn you, that if you make the attempt you will assuredly be hanged."

With this he quitted the battlements.

While he was gone, Osbert employed the time in explaining to the insurgents what must be done in the event of the Cardinal's refusal.

After a brief delay, a wicket in the gate was opened, and Rodomont Bittern came forth.

" What answer bring you from the Lord Cardinal?" demanded Osbert, on seeing him."

" His Eminence will answer you in person," said Rodomont. " But if you will take the advice of one who was once your friend, and is still your well-wisher, you will pursue this matter no further."

"A truce to this," cried Osbert, sternly. " I must have the Cardinal's answer without delay, or I shall proceed to action. I have no time to waste."

" You are peremptory, Sir," observed Rodomont dryly.

" So peremptory, that I *will* have the prisoners," rejoined Osbert, fiercely.

" You must discuss that point with the Lord Cardinal himself," rejoined Rodomont.

As he spoke, the falling of heavy bars within side proclaimed that the gates were being unfastened, and in another moment the ponderous valves swung aside and disclosed the Cardinal standing beneath the archway.

Close behind him stood Priuli with Constance Tyrrell, habited in black, and looking deathly pale, and a little further removed was Derrick Carver, with Mallet, the keeper of the Lollard's Tower.

No guard was near the Cardinal; the only persons with him besides Simnel and Holiday being some half-dozen attendants bearing torches. Pole's features wore a grave and somewhat severe expression. He manifested no apprehension whatever, but fixed a searching though somewhat sorrowful glance upon Osbert and the insurgent crew drawn up behind him.

Seen by the light of the torches which gleamed upon the Cardinal's majestic figure, upon Constance's pallid but lovely features, upon Priuli's noble countenance, and Derrick Carver's rugged physiognomy—upon Osbert, who, sword in hand, confronted the Cardinal, and upon the insurgents with their pikes—the whole picture was exceedingly striking.

The conference was opened by Pole, who, eyeing Osbert severely, and speaking in a stern tone, said, " I have caused my gates to be thrown open to you, Sir, in order to show you that I have no fear. By what authority do you demand the liberation of the persons committed to my charge?"

" I have no authority for the demand I make," replied

Osbert, "but I have the power to enforce compliance, and that must suffice. You have done well in throwing open your gates to us, Lord Cardinal, for we design you no injury. Let Constance Tyrrell and Derrick Carver, both of whom I see with you, be delivered up to us, and we will trouble you no further."

"And what will you do if I refuse?" said the Cardinal, sternly.

"We will take them," rejoined Osbert. "But I beseech your Eminence not to compel us to have recourse to violence."

"Hear me, misguided man," said Pole; "and hear me all of ye," he continued, addressing the insurgents in a louder tone, "I will not affect to misunderstand the character in which you come. You are rebels and traitors to the Queen, and have risen in arms against her."

"None would be more loyal and devoted subjects of her Majesty than we, were our rights and liberties respected," said Osbert: "but we have thrown off our allegiance because we will not submit to be governed by a Spanish king. We will not suffer our preachers and pastors to be burnt at the stake as heretics and infidels, nor our country to be enslaved. But we have not come hither to make known our grievances to your Eminence, or to ask for redress, which we well know we cannot obtain from you. We have not come hither to do you injury of any sort, for we hold you in profound respect, and wish there were many of your creed like you. Our object is to liberate all prisoners for religion, and we therefore require the release of the two persons in your custody."

"Before you proceed to extremities," rejoined Pole, "let me counsel you to pause and consider what you are about. You are engaged in a rash enterprise, which will in no way benefit your cause, but will infallibly lead to your destruction. By this outbreak you will give your rulers a plea for further oppression. I do not hesitate to say that I am averse to religious persecution, and would gladly see an end put to it, but this is not the plan to pursue. In a few hours your outbreak will be crushed, and then the party you represent will be worse off than ever. To all such as are peaceably disposed among you, whose families are dear to them, and who would avoid bloodshed and ignominious death, I would say disperse quietly, go to your homes, and come not forth again on a like pretext. To you, Osbert Clinton, who have been unwise enough to place yourself at the head of this insurrection, I must hold other language. Your only safety is in flight. A price will be set on your head, and, if taken, you will die the death of a traitor."

"I am aware of it," replied Osbert. "But I have sworn to free my country and my religion, or perish in the attempt. I have no thoughts of flight, neither will my followers desert me. But we have talked long enough. You know our determination. Are we to have the prisoners peaceably, or must we take them by force?"

"I should be loth to provoke you to bloodshed," replied the Cardinal. "Here are the two prisoners, as you see. I will place no restraint upon them. If they choose to go with you, it is well. If not, you will depart without them."

"I readily agree to the terms, and thank your Eminence for sparing me the necessity of violence," replied Osbert. "I do not think they will hesitate. Derrick Carver, you have heard what has passed. We wait for you."

But, to Osbert's great surprise, the enthusiast did not move.

"I cannot go unless I am set free by the Cardinal," he said.

"How?" cried Osbert.

"His Eminence suffered me to go forth on my promise to return," replied Carver, "and I will now prove to him that I am to be relied on."

"I cannot prevent your departure," said Pole; "neither can I set you free."

"Then I stay," replied Carver.

"I am not disappointed in you," observed Pole, approvingly.

"If such be your determination when freedom is offered you, you must have taken leave of your senses," said Osbert. "Constance, I call upon you—and shall not, I am sure, call in vain."

"I cannot leave the good Cardinal, who has sheltered and protected me, without his consent, even at your bidding, Osbert," she replied.

"And my consent must be refused," said Pole. "Alas! misguided man," he continued to Osbert. "You little know what you have done. Just as the King has assented to your union with Constance, you yourself raise an insuperable obstacle to it. Now Constance is lost to you for ever."

"It is too true, Osbert!—it is too true," she cried. "Why did you come hither thus?"

"Ah! why?" he cried, striking his head with his clenched hand. "Perdition on my folly!"

"Save yourself by instant flight—that is the best advice I can give you," said the Cardinal.

"Desert my friends—never!" exclaimed Osbert. "The die is cast, and I must stand the issue. Constance, by all the love you profess to bear me, I implore you to come with me."

"Alas! alas! I cannot obey you," she rejoined.

"Then I will carry you off in spite of your resistance," cried Osbert. "Forward, friends, forward!"

Some few advanced at the summons, but the majority, upon whom the Cardinal's harangue, combined with subsequent circumstances, had produced a powerful impression, held back.

As Osbert stepped forward, Rodomont and his two comrades placed themselves in his way.

"Back, misguided man!" cried the Cardinal. "Another step, and you rush on certain destruction. The sanctity of this asylum shall not be violated with impunity."

Just then loud shouts were heard, and some of the insurgents rushing forth to see what was the matter, immediately returned to say that a large number of the royal guard were landing from boats, and that some of them were already on the wharf.

"What shall we do?" cried several voices.

"Give them battle," rejoined Osbert, in a loud voice. "Farewell, Constance," he added; "if I fall, think that I came to save you. Now, friends, to the wharf!—to the wharf!"

Hereupon, all the insurgents, headed by Osbert, rushed forth simultaneously from the archway, shouting, "Down with King Philip!—down with the Pope!"

As soon as they were gone, the gates were closed by order o. the Cardinal.

Some thirty or forty archers had already disembarked from the boats that had brought them, and others were leaping ashore, as Osbert and his partisans appeared on the wharf. Fierce shouts were raised on both sides, and in another instant a desperate conflict commenced. By a sudden dash, Osbert hoped to drive the enemy into the river; but the archers stood their ground well, and being quickly reinforced by their comrades from the boats, they not only repelled the attack made upon them, but forced the insurgents to retire.

It soon became evident to Rodomont and his lieutenants, who had mounted to the summit of the gateway to watch the conflict, that it must speedily terminate in favour of the archers, who were more than a match for their brave but undisciplined opponents. And so it turned out. In less than ten minutes the conflict was over, and the insurgents dispersed or made captive. Osbert fought desperately to the last, but finding it in vain to struggle longer, followed by three or four others, among whom were Udal and Rufford, he leaped into a boat, and, pushing off, was borne swiftly down the river.

Half-a-dozen other boats, manned by archers, instantly started in pursuit, and frequent shots were fired at the fugitives. Whether any of these took effect could not be ascertained by Rodomont and his comrades, who watched the chase with great interest from the battlements; but, at all events, the flying barque held on its course, and seemed to gain upon the others. At last, pursued and pursuers disappeared from view.

"As the Queen's loyal subject I ought not to wish well to a traitor and a rebel," remarked Rodomont, "and yet I cannot help hoping that Osbert Clinton has escaped."

In this wish both his comrades concurred.

End of the Fifth Book.

BOOK VI.

THE LEWES MARTYR.

CHAPTER I.

OF THE PARTING BETWEEN DERRICK CARVER AND CONSTANCE.

THE attempt made by the conspirators to cause a general rising proved completely abortive. Stafford and his party received some accessions to their numbers as they marched along, but before they reached Charing Cross they were attacked and dispersed by a troop of mounted arquebusiers, who issued from Whitehall. Several persons were arrested, among whom were the two officers of the Princess Elizabeth's household, Peckham and Werne, but the ringleaders managed to escape. Next day, Stafford, Dudley, Kingston, Udal, Osbert Clinton, and the rest of the party, were publicly proclaimed as outlaws, rebels, traitors, and disturbers of the peace, and a large reward offered for their capture.

Nothing, however, was said about the French ambassador. Only to Gardiner did Philip avow that he had been secretly present with Father de Castro at the meeting in the crypt, and the Chancellor counselled him not to allow this circumstance to transpire publicly, as they had proof enough against the conspirators without it ; above all, Gardiner was opposed to any proceedings being taken against De Noailles. Thus the wily ambassador escaped with impunity as on previous occasions. A strict watch, however, was kept upon his movements.

It was confidently anticipated, both by the King and Gardiner, that before many days all the chief conspirators would be arrested, but in this expectation they were disappointed. No traces of any of them could be discovered. Some doubts were entertained as to the fate of Osbert Clinton. Two persons were shot in the boat in which he escaped from Lambeth, and their bodies thrown into the Thames, and it was thought he was one of them ; but this was by no means clear.

While the search for the leaders of the outbreak was thus being actively, though unsuccessfully, prosecuted, Peckham and Werne were taken to the Tower and put to the torture, in order to compel them to accuse the Princess Elizabeth of complicity in the affair, but nothing could be wrung from them, and, with twenty other luckless personages who had been captured at the same time, they were hanged, drawn, and quartered, and their heads set upon the north gateway of London Bridge.

Meanwhile, the religious persecution continued with unabated rigour. Bishop Hooper, with two others, had undergone martyrdom at different places, and six more prisoners, excommunicated by Bonner, and delivered over to the civil power, were about to perish in the same manner.

Conscious of the odium attaching to these sanguinary measures, Gardiner prudently resigned his post at the ecclesiastical tribunal to Bonner, who thenceforward acted as supreme judge, and was undeterred by scruples of any sort.

A momentary check was, however, given to his severity from an unexpected quarter. From the various manifestations made towards him by the Protestant party, and from other circumstances, Philip could not fail to perceive that if he took any further part in these barbarous proceedings, he should raise up a host of determined enemies, so he caused Father Alfonso to preach publicly, before him and the court, a sermon strongly condemnatory of religious persecution. The plan completely answered the King's expectations, it being felt that such a sermon could not have been preached without his sanction, and it was argued, therefore, that he must disapprove of the course pursued by Bonner.

The effect of this remarkable discourse—remarkable, indeed, as emanating from one who had been designated "The Scourge of Heresy"—was to stay the bitter persecution for a while, but, though momentarily checked, it revived with a greater fury than before. The six unfortunate persons excommunicated by Bonner were consigned to the flames, and urged to greater activity by the Marquis of Winchester, and other members of the council, the zealous prelate looked out for fresh victims.

Bonner had long burned to wreak his vengeance upon Derrick Carver, and was at last able to gratify his desire. Having procured a warrant from the Queen for the deliverance up to him of the prisoner, who was still confined in the Lollards' Tower, he immediately acted upon it. Before he was taken away, Carver, by permission of the Cardinal, was allowed to bid farewell to Constance Tyrrell. The interview took place in the Post Room in the Lollards' Tower, and in order that there might be no check upon their freedom of discourse, they were left alone together.

"Daughter," said Carver, who appeared more subdued than usual, "I am about to win the crown of martyrdom for which I have so long striven, and to inscribe my name upon that scroll which shall hereafter be a guide to our Church. In quitting you for a while, I expect you to remain stedfast in the faith. Be not shaken by the arguments of the Cardinal, who, though a good man, has been brought up in superstition and idolatry, and cannot free himself from the errors of his creed."

"Have no fear for me," replied Constance. "I shall soon follow in the same path you are about to tread."

"Heaven forbid!" exclaimed Carver, with an irrepressible shudder. "Oh! Constance, while alone in my cell, I have communed with myself, sounding my breast to its depths, and weighing every thought and action, and I reproach myself that I have led you too far. I have kindled a holy fervour in your breast like that which animates my own, and which incites you to bear witness to your faith by death."

"True. But surely you should rejoice that you have kindled such a flame," she rejoined,

"No; I would quench it," he cried. "Seek not martyrdom. Rush not upon fiery torments—but live—live a godly life."

"These words are strange from you, who have so often painted the glories of martyrdom to me, and urged me to share them with you."

"I repent that I did so," he rejoined. "Were you to suffer with me, your torments would afflict me a thousand times more than my own. 'Twere terrible that a frame so fair as yours should be consumed by fire. It must not be. You are young and beautiful. You love, and are beloved. Live and be happy. Live for Osbert Clinton."

"Alas!" exclaimed Constance, "I know not if Osbert still lives. It is thought he perished on that fatal night when he came here to liberate us. He has not been heard of since. But if he lives, it is as a proscribed rebel, with a price set on his head, and if he be taken, his doom is certain. I have nothing left but to die."

"No, you must live," said Carver, solemnly. "Osbert Clinton is not dead. He did not perish on that disastrous night, as you suppose. I have seen and spoken with him at the window of my cell, which he reached as he did when you, dear daughter, were its occupant. He and his friends are not disheartened by the ill success of their enterprise. It was rash and precipitate, and failed in consequence. But they are planning another insurrection, and I pray Heaven to crown it with success, since it has for its aim the restoration of our religion and the downfall of Philip!"

"I rejoice to hear that Osbert still lives," said Constance; "but I fear these plots will eventually conduct him to the scaffold."

"If he should so perish, then seek for a martyr's crown, if you will," said Carver; "but while he lives, live for him. Something tells me you will yet be united."

"I dare not hope so," she rejoined.

"If my last prayers will avail to ensure your happiness, you shall have them," said Carver. "And now we must part. Once more I exhort you to continue stedfast in the faith. But be not influenced by the desire of vain-glory, which, perchance, may be my own besetting sin. And now receive my blessing!"

And as she bent before him, he spread his arms over her head, and pronounced a solemn benediction.

There was then a deep silence, broken only by Constance's sobs.

"Weep not, dear daughter," he said. "Our parting ought to be joyous rather than sad, seeing that my trials are well-nigh over, and I am about to reap my reward. Farewell!" he added, taking her hand, and pressing his lips to it. "Forget not what I have said to you."

"Fear me not!" she rejoined, sinking upon a bench. "Farewell!"

Carver cast a compassionate look at her, and then striding resolutely towards the door, he called out that he was ready, whereupon Mallet instantly appeared.

Without hazarding another glance at Constance, he then quitted the chamber, and was taken by Mallet to the gate, where he was delivered to the officers sent for him by Bonner.

A barge awaited him, and in this conveyance he was taken to Paul's Wharf. Thence he was escorted to the consistory at Saint Paul's, where Bonner was sitting in judgment with the Lord Mayor, the sheriffs, and several members of the council.

CHAPTER II.

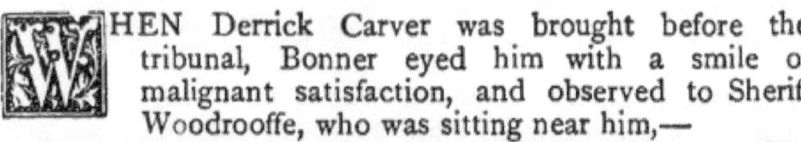HEN Derrick Carver was brought before the tribunal, Bonner eyed him with a smile of malignant satisfaction, and observed to Sheriff Woodrooffe, who was sitting near him,—

"At last I have got this pestilent fellow, whom the Cardinal has so long screened from justice. He shall not escape now. I will deal roundly with him."

On this, he caused the minutes of the prisoner's previous examinations to be read to him by an officer in the court, which being done, Bonner said, in a bitter and derisive tone,

"Such were the detestable and damnable opinions professed by thee, Derrick Carver, when thou wert last interrogated in the Lollards' Tower ; but doubtless the exhortations and persuasions of the Lord Cardinal have wrought a beneficial change, and thou art now willing to confess thine errors and abjure them."

"My op nions have undergone no change," replied Carver. "But if any Romanist could have converted me, it would be Cardinal Pole."

"Ah ! you admit so much," cried Bonner. "Why should Cardinal Pole prevail with you more than others? Hath he more zeal—more devotion—more theological learning than others have ?"

"I know not whether he hath more zeal and learning than your lordship, but he has more Christian charity," replied

Carver. "He understands the Gospel, and is guided by its precepts, which you are not."

"Belike you deem his Eminence less rigid, less orthodox than I am?" said Bonner.

"My tenets are not *his* tenets," replied Carver; "yet I hold him to be a good man, though, unhappily, blinded to the truth. Your lordship may be the more orthodox Catholic of the two, but you are the worse man."

"I thank thee for the admission, thou foul-mouthed knave," cried Bonner. "You all hear that he charges the Cardinal with unsoundness of opinion," he added to the court.

"I charge thee with attempting to pervert my words," retorted Carver. "I meant to say that Cardinal Pole is the chief living light and glory of the Church of Rome, whereas thou art its shame and reproach. In after times, when this bitter persecution of the faithful is spoken of, Reginald Pole will be remembered for mildness and toleration, while thou wilt be execrated as the 'bloody Bishop Bonner'—a name that shall cling to thee for ever!"

"I would rather have thy censure than thy commendation," rejoined Bonner. "Had the Cardinal treated thee with due severity, thou wouldst never have lauded his virtues. But thou hast said enough to convince us thou art obstinate and impenitent. Therefore I shall not take up the time of the court by questioning thee further. Down on thy knees while sentence of excommunication is pronounced upon thee."

"I kneel only to Heaven," replied the prisoner, firmly.

At a sign from the bishop, two officers seized him, and, in spite of his resistance, forced him upon his knees, detaining him in this posture while the sentence was read to him by Bonner. This done, he was permitted to rise, and the officers left him.

"Thou art now accursed," pursued Bonner, "and henceforward, if any man shall eat with thee, or drink with thee, or otherwise help thee or comfort thee, he will be a partaker in the curse."

"You have put me out of the communion of a Church which I have quitted of my own accord for these ten years," said Carver. "As to your anathemas, they affright me not. May they recoil with added strength on your own head."

gladsome to mine eyes as was Ramoth Gilead to the fugitives from Jordan.   There shall I be at rest."

"There will be a rare bonfire in that old town to-morrow," observed Captain Brand, in a jeering tone, to the prisoner— "a bonfire such as the townsfolk have seldom seen, and which they are likely long to recollect.   'Twill be a grand spectacle to those who look on," he added with stern significance.

"I had rather be the chief actor in the spectacle than a beholder of it," replied Carver; "and I trust those who witness it will long remember it."

On this, Brand rode on, and Father Josfrid resumed the exhortation which he had been obliged for the nonce to suspend.

CHAPTER III.

T the period of our history, Lewes, as we have just
intimated, was surrounded by walls built of stone,
and of considerable strength, though few traces of
these fortifications are now left. At the west
gate of the town the party was met by the high sheriff, Sir
Richard de Warren, and Master Piddinghoe, the headborough, attended by a large posse of men armed with
halberds. Besides these, there were many burgesses and
priests, who had come forth to see the prisoner. At this
place Derrick Carver was delivered over to the high sheriff
by Captain Brand, who at the same time handed to Sir
Richard the warrant for the prisoner's execution.

"All shall be ready for the ceremonial to-morrow morning," said De Warren. "We cannot lodge him in the castle,
but we will place him in a vault beneath the Star Inn, where
he will be perfectly secure."

"I have fulfilled mine office in delivering him into your
hands, Sir Richard," replied Brand. "But my orders from
Sheriff Woodrooffe are to tarry here till the sentence is
carried out."

"You will not be detained beyond to-morrow morning,
Sir," said De Warren.

On this the party passed through the gate, and began to
move slowly down the High Street, which formed a gradual
descent towards the centre of the town. On either side the

street were habitations of various sizes, but all of quaint and picturesque architecture. As the train advanced, the inhabitants came forth to see the prisoner, to many of whom he was personally known, and these loudly expressed their commiseration, and their abhorrence of his persecutors.

By the time the train had reached the massive Norman gate of the castle, so large a crowd had collected that the progress of the party was impeded, and the high sheriff's attendants had to use the poles of their halberds to effect a passage. In spite, however, of the exertions of the officers and men, the throng could not be kept back, but forced themselves up to the prisoner, and catching hold of his garments, and clinging to his horse, besought his blessing.

"Stand back!—touch him not!" cried Father Josfrid. "He is excommunicated."

Little attention however, was paid to the priest. In vain Carver besought those nearest him to retire—in vain the officers commanded them to stand back—they would not stir. At last, force was employed, they were thrust violently aside, and amid shrieks of terror and groans and yells of indignation, Carver was hurried along, and finally conveyed through a gateway into a large yard at the rear of the Star Inn. As soon as this had been accomplished the gate was shut, and a guard placed in front of it.

This ancient hostel, which still exists, though it has undergone many transformations, was then a large and substantial structure, capable of accommodating a great number of guests, and was managed by Dame Dunster, a buxom widow, whose boast it was that the best mutton in Sussex, the fattest capons, the most perfectly seasoned venison pasties, the most delicious stewed eels, and the brightest sack and claret, were to be had at the Star at Lewes. Besides these good things, and many others, those who lodged with Dame Dunster had the luxury of linen white as snow, and fragrant of lavender. Nothing, in short, was wanting at the Star—a comely and good-humoured landlady, young and not ill-favoured handmaidens, and active drawers—these for the guests, while for their steeds there were good stables and good provender.

Beneath the hostel there existed, and indeed still exists, a large vault, wherein, as the high sheriff had intimated to Captain Brand, it was intended to place Derrick Carver for the night. The subterranean chamber was of great strength, the roof high and arched, and the walls of solid stone. It was of great antiquity, and had originally belonged to a monastic edifice. On one side, at a considerable height from the ground, was an unglazed window or aperture, contrived for the admission of air and light. This aperture was placed on a level with the street, and was secured by stout iron bars, fixed horizontally and close together. This singular vault is still much in the same state as we have described it, though it is now used for other purposes than as a place of detention of prisoners, being, in fact, a very cool and commodious cellar.

When Derrick Carver was taken into the inn-yard, as already related, he became so faint that he was obliged to sit down on a horse-block for a few minutes to recover himself. Noticing his feeble condition, Dame Dunster who had come forth to look at him, kindly sent for a cup of sack, and offered it to him. But Father Josfrid again interposed, and bade her take the wine away, if she would not fall under the same ban as the miserable wretch before her. But the kind-hearted hostess persisted, whereupon the priest snatched the cup from her, and dashed its contents on the ground.

"You must have a heart utterly void of compassion, or you could not act thus," cried Dame Dunster to Father Josfrid. "You would see the poor man die, and not raise a hand to help him. It would be happy for him, indeed, if he were to die, as in that case he would escape further cruelty."

"I am better now," replied Derrick Carver, raising himself to his feet by a great effort. "I lack not the wine you would have given me to drink, but I thank you heartily for the kind intent, and invoke Heaven's blessings upon your house."

"Thy blessings will prove curses, thou outcast from Heaven," cried the priest.

"Be not troubled by his words, good sister," said Carver. "Be mindful of what I say to you. Avoid idolatry and superstition. Place your faith in the Gospel, and you shall live. Pray for me, sister, and I will pray for you."

Dame Dunster and her maidens turned away weeping, while Carver descended a flight of stone steps leading to the vault, the door of which being unlocked he was rudely thrust into the subterranean chamber. A few trusses of straw for a couch, with bread-and-water for sustenance, being supplied him, he was left alone, and the door locked outside.

After glancing round the vault, noting its size, and the solidity of its walls, Carver turned his attention to the barred opening, already described as being on a level with the street. Through this opening noises reached his ears, but no one was allowed to approach and hold converse with him, a guard being placed outside the inn.

Carver took a few turns in the vault, and then sitting down upon a wooden bench, which constituted its sole furniture, took out his Bible, which had been happily spared him, and began to read it. He had been occupied in this manner for some time, when the strokes of a pickaxe dealt upon the stones in the street disturbed him, and he raised his head to listen. By-and-by the clatter of a shovel was heard—then there was a great noise as if several men were carrying a heavy mass, which appeared to be plunged into a hole that had just been digged; and then there was a dull, dead, thumping sound, as if the earth were being beaten down by a ram.

Suspecting what was going forward, but desiring to know the truth, Carver placed the bench immediately below the window, and, mounting upon it, raised himself so that he could just look through the bars into the street. He then found that his conjectures were correct, and that the noises he had heard were caused by men who were planting the stake in the ground to which he was to be attached on the morrow. With a mournful curiosity he watched them at their work, and did not withdraw till the stake was firmly secured, and a heavy iron chain attached to it. He had just got down, when he heard Captain Brand, whose harsh voice he instantly recognised, giving directions to the men.

" Take care that plenty of fagots are provided," he said ; " and, furthermore, I must have an empty tar-barrel large enough to hold the prisoner. He boasts of his firmness," added Brand with a bitter laugh. " We will see whether we cannot shake it."

It would seem that he was likely to be disappointed in his expectation, for Carver heard the order given without the slightest feeling of dread, but calmly resumed the perusal of the sacred volume at the point where he had laid it aside. Neither did he desist until it grew dark, and he was unable to read longer.

He then knelt down and prayed fervently, continuing his vigils until long after midnight, when weariness overcame him, and flinging himself upon the straw, he presently fell asleep.

He was roused from his slumbers by a stone which fell upon the floor of the vault not far from where he was lying, and as he stirred he heard a voice calling to him from the barred window, and looking in that direction, he could just distinguish the figure of a man.

"Who speaks?" he demanded rising to his feet.

"A friend," replied the other. "Come nearer—quick!"

"The voice seems familiar to me," observed Carver, "and if I did not deem it impossible, I should say it was ——"

"It is he you suppose," interrupted the speaker. "Come as near me as you can, and come quickly, for I may be discovered."

Thus adjured, Carver mounted the bench, and was then only separated by the bars from the person outside, whom he now recognised as Osbert Clinton.

"Why have you incurred this danger on my account, oh, rash young man?" he cried.

"I have somewhat to impart," replied Osbert; "but I must be brief, for though the man on guard has quitted his post, he may return. In a word, then, I shall make an attempt to deliver you from these bloodthirsty tigers to-morrow. I have half a dozen friends with me, and when you are brought forth for execution, we will fall upon the guard and set you free."

"I forbid you to make the attempt, my son," replied Carver. "I am fully prepared to die, and would not accept a pardon from my enemies were it offered me. By freeing me as you propose, you would wrest from me the crown of martyrdom which I hope to win at yonder stake. My race is almost run, and the goal is at hand. I have done with the world, and would not be brought back to it. My last sufferings will be sharp, but they will be speedily over, and I rejoice that I am able to bear them. Again, I say, this attempt must not be made."

"Since you will have it so, I must needs obey," rejoined Osbert, in a mournful tone. "And yet I would try to move you."

"It would be in vain," said Carver. "Our moments are precious. Let them not be wasted in idle discussion. I will not fly from the death prepared for me. The stake is ready, and shall not want the victim. I know you will readily do me a service. Seek out my poor wife and children at Brightelmstone, and bid them farewell for me."

"I have already seen them," replied Osbert. "Your wife is ill—too ill to leave the house—and I enjoined her not to come here to-morrow."

"You did right—quite right," rejoined Carver. "What of my aged mother?" he demanded, in a voice of profound emotion.

"I ought to have no concealment from you now," said Osbert. "Your mother is no more."

"I thought so," replied Carver, after a pause. "She appeared to me just now during my slumber. Her countenance wore a heavenly smile, and methought her lips opened to address me, but I could not catch the words she uttered. Her spirit was still hovering nigh me when you woke me from the blissful dream."

There was a deep, solemn pause, after which Carver continued: "And now, Osbert Clinton, I have some counsel to give you. The success of the great enterprise on which you are engaged will depend on the prudence with which it is conducted. Be not rash. Wait for a favourable opportunity to strike the blow, and take heed that you do not place confidence in traitors."

"We expect men and money from France," said Osbert.

"France will play you false, as she has done before," replied Carver.

"But we are obliged to trust to that power, since we have now no other resources," said Osbert. "All our possessions have been seized and sequestered, and we have not wherewithal to pay the host we could raise. We have men, but not money. We lack as many chests of gold as were brought from Spain by Philip when he landed at Southampton."

"What became of that Spanish bullion?" demanded Carver.

"Part of it has been expended in bribes to our venal nobles," replied Osbert. "But the rest is deposited in the Tower."

"Is there much of the treasure left?" inquired Carver.

"Half is left, as I understand," replied Osbert.

"Why not seize upon it, then?" cried the other. "'Tis lawful spoil. Instead of being employed to corrupt mercenary nobles to enslave their country, let it be used to free the land from Spanish thraldom and Popish tyranny. Have no scruples. Seize upon it, I say. It was brought into England to forge golden fetters for our rulers, let it be turned into avenging swords."

"That treasure, indeed, would accomplish all we seek, if we could obtain possession of it," said Osbert. "But I have told you it is safely deposited in the Tower."

"And I say to you that it must be your business to get it thence," rejoined Carver.

"You would not have me lay siege to the Tower to obtain it?" said Osbert.

"By stratagem you may accomplish what you desire," returned Carver. "I have no plan to suggest; but if you weigh the matter carefully over, one is sure to occur to you."

"I will give it due consideration," said Osbert. "Have you aught more to say?"

"Only to wish you happiness with her you love," replied Carver. "My last words to Constance were to urge her to look forward confidently to the day when she will be united to you. For that day will come. It may not come so soon as you anticipate and desire, but come it will. One word more, and I have done. Should this insurrection prosper, and your enemies fall into your hands, let no harm befal Cardinal Pole. And now tarry no longer, my son. Take my blessing with you, and depart."

"It is time," replied Osbert. "I hear the footsteps of the guard. I shall be near you at the stake. Adieu!"

So saying, he disappeared, while Carver, descending from the bench, knelt down and prayed fervently.

His devotions ended, he arose, and bethinking him of

the vision he had seen during his slumber, he called out, "Spirit of her from whom I derived my being, if thou art indeed permitted to visit me, and art nigh me now, as I think, I adjure thee to manifest thyself to me in the same angelic form, and with the same angelic aspect, as I beheld thee in my dream. Appear before me in this celestial guise if thou canst, and cheer and comfort me with thy smile!"

At the close of this invocation, which he uttered with great fervour, he looked around, half hoping that the spirit would become visible, but nothing met his gaze except the gloomy walls of his prison. He fancied, however, that he heard something like a soft, low sigh, and felt a breath of cool air upon his brow.

"It may not be," he said. "Thou canst not reveal thyself to me, or mine eyes are unable to discern thee. But I must have patience. In a few short hours I shall be as thou art, and we can then hold the communion together which is denied us now."

He then resumed his devotions, and continued in earnest prayer till dawn glimmered through the bars of the window, and ere long filled the vault with light.

Then some slight stir began to be heard in the street, and by-and-by those on guard peered in at the bars of the window. They beheld the prisoner seated upon the bench, with the Bible open on his knee, profoundly occupied in its perusal.

CHAPTER IV.

THE PROCESSION TO THE CALVARY.

LOVELY morning dawned upon Lewes. The sun, which ere it reached its meridian was destined to shine upon a terrible ceremonial, rose brilliantly over Mount Caburn, glittering upon the brow of that majestic eminence, and on the smooth summits of the adjacent hill, and filling the wide valley, watered by the meandering Ouse, with radiance. Kingston Hill with the heights, enclosing the valley on the west, and extending to Newhaven, glowed with roseate lustre, as did lordly Mount Harry and his subject hills at the rear o. the town. The noble amphitheatre of downs, by which the town is surrounded, were seen in all their beauty, and no one unacquainted with what was passing, would have supposed that a morn so auspicious could usher in other than a joyous day.

At an early hour the bells of the different churches began to toll solemnly, announcing to the inhabitants that a sad ceremonial was about to take place, and shortly after six o'clock a religious procession, consisting of a number of Cluniac monks, with the clergy and authorities of the place, the high sheriff, the under-sheriffs, the chief burgesses, with the headborough and constables, assembled in the High Street, and proceeded to the Star Inn, where Derrick Carver was brought out, and ordered to join it. The train was headed by the Cluniac monks, who were attired in the habits of their order, and after them walked the prisoner, with Father Josfrid beside him. Next came the sheriff with Captain Brand, then the local clergy and authorities, while the head-borough and constables brought up the rear. The procession descended the steep street leading to the East Gate, through which it passed, and then, turning off on the right, and skirting the old walls, which were thronged with spectators, crossed the valley to Southover, and shaped its course towards the singular mount rising on the east of the ruined priory of St. Pancras. On the summit of this eminence, a large crucifix, with the figure of the Saviour nailed to it, was then reared, forming, from its commanding position, a conspicuous object for miles around.

On reaching the summit of the mount, the monks prostrated themselves at the foot of the cross, and began to recite a prayer, while the rest of the procession assumed an equally reverential posture. Derrick Carver, however, refused to kneel, and on this occasion his prejudices were respected. As he remained standing amidst the kneeling assemblage, he cast his eyes around, and surveyed the fair scene of which he was about to take leave for ever. To one less firmly constituted, it might have seemed hard to quit so lovely a world. But his thoughts were fixed on heaven, and though nature put on her most tempting aspect, she could not lure him back to earth.

Immediately beneath him lay the ruins of the once noble priory of St. Pancras, demolished by the Vicar-General Cromwell, in the reign of Henry VIII., and as he looked at the fragments of this vast and stately pile, Carver rejoiced in its destruction. Adjoining these ruins was an immense dovecot, built in the form of a cross, above which thousands of pigeons were circling or alighting on its roof. On his right, across a woody valley, climbing the side of a hill, and with its picturesque habitations intermingled with trees, was the town with whose annals his name was thenceforward to be associated. Beautiful it looked on that bright clear morning, and proudly towered its old Norman castle—grey walls, quaint houses, and church-towers, glittering in the sunbeams, and all seeming to claim attention; but Carver turned from them to gaze at the downs, and as his eye wandered over those fair hills, thoughts of other days rushed upon him.

Many and many a happy hour had he spent upon those downs. Familiar with all their beauties, his imagination carried him from point to point, till it brought him to the little fishing-town where he was born, and where the greater part of his life had been spent. For a moment only did he yield to the emotions awakened within his breast. They were sharp and poignant, but he instantly checked them, and resumed his former stoicism.

Just then, the monks having finished their prayer, arose, and began to chant a hymn to the blessed Virgin, in which all those with them joined. Many of the inhabitants of the town had followed the procession to the calvary, and by this time a large concourse had assembled on the sides and at the base of the mount. All these persons joined in the choral hymn; and the effect of so many voices linked together in harmony was inexpressibly fine.

At the conclusion of the hymn the monks began slowly to descend the mount, chanting lugubrious strains as they moved along. The others followed in the same order as before. As Derrick Carver marched on, many of the spectators expressed their sympathy for him, but no one was suffered to approach him, or exchange a word with him.

Amongst those who had followed the procession to the mount were some half-dozen young men on horseback, who had hitherto kept aloof from the crowd; but just as Derrick Carver reached the foot of the mount, one of them suddenly dismounted, and leaving his steed with his companions, forced himself into a front place amid the line of spectators.

The movement attracted the attention of the prisoner, who instantly recognised Osbert Clinton, and signified to him by his gestures that no change had taken place in his sentiments.

Osbert's imprudent movement, however, had not escaped the notice of Captain Brand, who, moreover, detected the glance of intelligence that passed between the young man and Carver. When Osbert shortly afterwards rejoined his

. . . . Brand directed the

sheriff's attention to the group, and inquired if he knew the young men.

De Warren replied in the negative, declaring they must be strangers.

"I am certain I have seen that young man before," observed Brand, "though I cannot, for the moment, give him a name. Ha! I have it!" he exclaimed, quickly. "It is Osbert Clinton."

"What! he who was engaged in the last rising?" cried the sheriff, surprised.

"The same," replied Brand. "I am sure of it. And now I look at the others, I cannot doubt but that they are the ringleaders in that treasonable affair. A heavy price is set on all their heads, and I must call upon you to aid me in their capture, Sir Richard."

"I will readily do so," replied De Warren; "but even supposing you are right in your suspicions, we must act with prudence. They are all well mounted, and on the slightest movement will be off, and easily baffle pursuit upon these downs. Alarm them not. They are following the procession. Once in the town, we can easily secure them."

"They are evidently come to witness the execution," said Brand, "and may design to rescue the prisoner."

"Fear nothing; we shall have them safe enough if we proceed with caution," rejoined the sheriff. "I will presently give instructions concerning them to Master Piddinghoe, the headborough."

"Leave the matter to me, I pray you, Sir Richard," said Brand. "I can manage it without the headborough's aid."

"You desire to obtain the whole reward, eh, Captain Brand?" observed De Warren. "Well, as you please."

The whole of this conversation had reached the ears of Derrick Carver, who marched in front of the speakers, and the danger incurred by Osbert and his friends caused him great uneasiness. Fain would he have warned them of their peril by look or gesture, but no opportunity of doing so occurred.

Meantime, the procession moved on, and, pursuing a

different course on its return, entered the town by the Water-gate, and then ascending the steep and narrow thoroughfare called Saint Mary's Lane, came forth into the High Street, exactly opposite the Star Inn. To his great satisfaction, Captain Brand remarked that Osbert Clinton and his companions had likewise passed through the Water-gate.

CHAPTER V.

HOW CAPTAIN BRAND SOUGHT TO CAPTURE THE CONSPIRATORS.

ON being brought back to the hostel, Derrick Carver was again conducted to the vault, there to remain till the hour appointed for his execution. He was so much troubled in spirit, owing to his anxiety for the safety of Osbert Clinton and his companions, that he could not address himself to prayer, and was pacing to and fro, when the door was unlocked, and the hostess entered. Her first business was to set down a little basket which she had concealed under her mantle, and she then informed Carver that she had brought him some wine and food. "I have prevailed on Master Piddinghoe to grant me admittance to you," she said, "and I have managed to bring in this basket unperceived by the guard. Eat, I pray you, if only a morsel, and drink a cup of wine. It will strengthen you."

"I thank you heartily, good mistress," replied Carver, "but I shall eat and drink no more. There is, however, one great service which you can render me, if you are so minded."

And he looked at her wistfully.

"What is it?" she replied. "Tell me, and I will do it. You may perfectly confide in me."

Carver then, in a few words, informed her of the danger of Osbert Clinton and his friends, and after describing their appearance, entreated her to warn them speedily.

"I will do your bidding without an instant's delay," she replied. "I have seen the gentlemen you describe, and will find them out, and urge them to instant flight. This accounts for the orders I heard given to Master Piddinghoe by Sir Richard de Warren, that all the town gates are to be closed, and no one allowed to go forth without a pass-word. Luckily, I overheard it, and will give it to your friends."

"You have removed a load of anxiety from my breast, good mistress," said Carver. "If they are safe, I shall die content."

"Then let no anxiety on their account trouble you fur-ther," she rejoined. "Ere many minutes they shall be out of Lewes. Farewell!"

"Farewell, sister; my blessing go with you."

Hereupon the hostess quitted the vault, and Carver, whose bosom was no longer oppressed, knelt down and resumed his devotions.

Meanwhile, Dame Dunster, quitting the hostel privily, went in search of Osbert and his companions; but she could discover nothing of them, and at last came to the conclusion that they had already flown. She ascertained, however, that in obedience to the sheriff's orders, all the town gates where shut and guarded.

The hour appointed for the execution was now at hand. The bell of Saint Michael's Church began to toll solemnly. A great crowd was already collected in front of the Star Inn, but a clear space was kept by the constables around the stake.

The din and confusion in the street, though it reached his ears, did not distract the prisoner from his devotions, and he continued in earnest prayer, until at last the door of his cell was thrown open, and the sheriff, with Captain Brand, Father Josfrid, and two officers provided with halberds, entered the vault. On seeing them, Derrick Carver imme-diately arose from his knees, and told them in a firm voice, that he was ready.

"I cannot hold out any hope of pardon to you," said De Warren, "but I would fain hope that you will not die impenitent."

"I shall die, Sir, as I have lived, in the faith I have pro-fessed and defended," replied Carver.

"Peradventure, you are of opinion that an attempt will be made to liberate you?" observed Brand. "It is well you should be undeceived. The dangerous rebels who have ventured here have fallen into a snare."

"Are they taken?" cried Carver.

"They soon will be," replied Brand. "Thou thyself mayst possibly behold their capture. We hold them in our hands. Their retreat is cut off. It will be my business to convey them to the Tower."

"Alas! why did they come hither?" groaned Carver.

"That is best know to themselves," rejoined Brand; "but they have done me a good turn by coming."

"Have you aught to confess or declare concerning them?" demanded the sheriff.

"An idle question," rejoined Carver. "Think you I would say aught to their detriment?"

Thereupon, the sheriff, bidding the officers bring forth the prisoner, quitted the cell, and was presently followed by the others. Several persons were assembled in the inn-yard, and amongst them were Dame Dunster and her handmaidens, weeping bitterly, to whom Carver bade an eternal adieu, bidding them be comforted.

The gates, which had been hitherto kept closed, were then thrown open, and the prisoner becoming visible to a portion of the vast assemblage collected in the street, loud cries arose.

The stake, as we have already mentioned, was planted in the middle of the High-street, exactly opposite the Star Inn, where the throughfare was widest. Around the place of execution a large circular space was kept clear by the constables and other officers armed with halberds, and within this ring was heaped up a great pile of fagots with bundles of dried gorse. In front of the stake stood the large empty tar-barrel, commanded by Captain Brand. It was reared on end, and the top had been staved in. Such were the preparations made for the terrible ceremonial.

Into this ring Derrick Carver marched with firm footstep, and his appearance was greeted with outcries of various kinds from the beholders. He was closely attended by Father Josfrid, who continued to press exhortations upon him, to which he refused to listen. At this juncture Captain

Brand came up to him, and said, "Thy life shall be spared for a few minutes, that thou mayst know the fate of thy friends." He then added to the officers : "Chain him not to the stake till you receive the sheriff's signal from yonder window."

And he pointed, as he spoke, to a large open window on the first floor of the inn, which, unlike all the other windows of the house, was destitute of spectators. Every spot, indeed, commanding a view of the place of execution was occupied. The entrance to St. Mary's-lane was blocked up by a small party of horsemen, who, it need scarcely be said, were Osbert Clinton and his friends. They had stationed themselves at this point in order to secure a retreat in case of need, but were wholly unaware that a party of armed men were slowly ascending the narrow throughfare in their rear.

On quitting Derrick Carver, Captain Brand returned to the inn-yard, where he had left his officers, and, putting himself at their head, was about to sally forth and make the arrest he meditated, when his plan was most unexpectedly thwarted by Dame Dunster, who, suddenly appearing at the open window which we have described as reserved for the high sheriff and his attendants, leaned from it, and waving a kerchief to attract the attention of Osbert and his friends, called out to them in a loud voice,—

"Save yourselves ! — save yourselves ! — you are be-trayed ! "

Thus warned, the horsemen turned instantly to ride down the hill, but at once perceived that their retreat in this direction was cut off. Osbert did not hesitate a moment, but calling out lustily to the crowd, "Make way, friends !— make way ! " a passage was instantly opened for him and his companions, and, ere any hindrance could be offered them, they were all within the ring, and close to the prisoner.

"You will not see this good man barbarously put to death, my masters," cried Osbert, "but will aid him to escape."

Several voices instantly answered the appeal, and a great tumult arose amid the crowd.

"Think not of me, but save yourself ! " cried Carver to Osbert. "I shall not quit this spot."

So suddenly had the daring deed we have described been executed, that surprise took away the power of opposition from the constables and halberdiers, but they now took heart, and encircled the horsemen, who had drawn their swords, and kept them off. At the same time, Captain Brand, who was issuing from the inn-yard with his men, vociferated,—

"Stay them, in the Queen's name !—let them not pass !—they are rebels and traitor !"

"Touch us not, good friends," cried Osbert. "We are true men, and would deliver you from Spanish bondage and Popish thraldom."

Upon this several of the crowd called out,—

"We are for you, masters. This way !—this way !"

And, seconding their words by deeds, they threw themselves upon the constables in front of them, and speedily opened a passage, through which Osbert and his companions got out of the ring, and dashed up the High-street.

A number of persons instantly started in pursuit, and as the West-gate was closed, it was thought that the fugitives must infallibly be captured; but those who entertained the notion were wrong, since instead of seeking an exit by that gate, Osbert and his companions turned off on the left, and dashing down another thoroughfare as steep and narrow as St. Mary's-lane, descended it in safety, and on reaching the bottom of the hill, found that the Water-gate was open, and rode through it ere the warder had time to shut it. Being now out of the town, and all admirably mounted, they set pursuit at defiance, and in less than an hour were safe on the other side of Kingston Hill.

CHAPTER VI.

THE MARTYRDOM OF DERRICK CARVER.

SO great was the confusion in the High Street after the flight of Osbert Clinton and his companions, and so threatening were the language and attitude of the populace, that it became a question with the sheriff whether it would not be prudent to postpone the execution to the following day. As a matter of precaution, Derrick Carver was taken into the entrance-hall of the hostel, the door of which was closed, and a guard placed before it.

Here he was kept for nearly an hour, when Captain Brand returned with the intelligence that he had failed in capturing the rebels. These were joyful tidings to Derrick Carver, and he exclaimed, "Now I shall die content!"

After a brief consultation between the sheriff and Brand, it was decided that the execution should be proceeded with, upon which Brand went forth with his men, and soon succeeded in clearing a space, as before, round the stake.

This done, Derrick Carver was again brought forth, and when he appeared on the threshold of the inn, a great cry arose from the people, and it became evident from the violence of their gestures and vociferations that another disturbance was at hand.

Alarmed by these menacing demonstrations, Sir Richard de Warren, who was of a somewhat timid nature, ordered the prisoner to be taken back, but Brand insisted that the sentence must be carried out.

"We must not yield to intimidation," he said. "The law must be carried out at all risks,"

Still the sheriff hesitated, when Derrick Carver interposed :—

"I pray you, Sirs, let me speak to them," he said. "They will listen to me."

"Speak to them if thou wilt," rejoined Brand. "But say nought to inflame them further, or it shall be worse for thee."

Having obtained this permission, Carver called out in a loud voice to the assemblage, that he desired to address them, upon which the tumult and clamour instantly ceased.

"Hear me, good friends," he cried, amidst the sudden silence. "I am come here to give testimony by my death to truth and pure religion against Antichrist and false doctrines, and I beseech you, if you hold with me in the faith, to let me die in peace. I would have my ending profitable to you, and not the cause of bloodshed and destruction even of my enemies."

This address produced the effect desired, and from that moment the crowd became tranquil, and offered no further interruption to the proceedings.

Seeing that order was restored, the sheriff committed the further conduct of the ceremonial to Brand, and withdrew to the upper window overlooking the street, whence he could contemplate the tragical spectacle as from a tribune.

Meantime, Derrick Carver, pushing aside Father Josfrid, marched up to the stake, and after embracing it tenderly, knelt down, and in tones of the utmost fervour prayed for strength and heavenly grace that he might by his death glorify the Saviour's holy name, ratify his Gospel, comfort the hearts of the weary, confirm his Church, and convert such as were to be converted. He further prayed for support during the grievous torments to which he was about to be subjected, offering himself up as a willing sacrifice and burnt-offering, and concluded by imploring that the blessing of the Word, of which the realm was at present unhappily deprived, might be once more vouchsafed to it. This prayer, uttered aloud and with great earnestness, produced a profound impression on all who heard it.

Seeing this, and anxious to efface the impression, Father Josfrid advanced towards him and said,—

"Wretched man, thy last hour is arrived; but there is

yet time to save thy soul if thou wilt recant thine heresies, and return to the Church thou hast abandoned, but which is willing to receive thee."

" Hence with thee, tempter ! " cried Carver, rising to his feet. " Wert thou to offer me all the riches of the earth, I would not become an idolater."

Thus rebuked, Father Josfrid withdrew, and his place was taken by two rough-looking men, one of whom rudely ordered the prisoner to make ready.

Upon this, Carver proceeded to divest himself of a portion of his apparel, and while he was thus employed, several persons among the crowd called out to him for a memorial, upon which he threw his garments amongst them, and they were instantly seized upon by a hundred eager hands, and rent in pieces, the fragments being carefully preserved by those who were fortunate enough to secure them.

As he was taking off his doublet, the sacred volume which had been the solace of his long imprisonment, and which he had kept about him to this moment, fell to the ground ; seeing which, Captain Brand, who was standing by, picked it up, and with a look of disdain, tossed it into the tar-barrel near the stake.

The two rough-looking men, who had remained near the prisoner, now took hold of him, and raising him in their arms, set him within the barrel. Thus disposed, Carver's first business was to take up the Bible, and after pressing his lips to it, he threw it amidst the crowd.

Greatly enraged by the act, Captain Brand called out in a furious voice to the person who had secured the prize to restore it instantly on pain of death, whereupon it was flung back, and was subsequently consigned to the flames.

A heavy chain was then passed around Carver's body and made fast to the stake. Left to himself for a moment, the martyr then called out in a loud voice, " Farewell, dear brethren, farewell ! Our Church is encompassed about by deadly enemies, who seek its destruction, and it is for the restoration of that Church that my blood is this day freely poured forth. It will not be shed in vain. Comfort ye amid your troubles, and remain stedfast in your faith ! Happier days shall soon dawn upon you. Farewell, O, farewell ! '

No sooner had he concluded this valediction, which was

responded to by loud lamentations from the majority of the assemblage, than the men began to heap fagots around him, filling the barrel with dry gorse and brushwood.

Before the pile, which was heaped up to his shoulders, could be lighted, the martyr exclaimed, " Blessed are they who die in the Lord. Thrice blessed are they who die in the Lord's cause. Fear not them that kill the body, for they cannot kill the soul. He that shall lose his life for my sake shall find it, saith our blessed Saviour, in the which hope I now die. Again, dear brethren, I bid you farewell!"

" A truce to thy blasphemy!" cried Brand, seizing a torch and applying it to the pile.

Fast and fierce burnt the fire, and quickly mounted the flame, but, to judge from the serene expression of his countenance, it might have been as innocuous to the martyr as was the blaze of the burning fiery furnace to the three Israelites. Not a groan escaped Derrick Carver, and his last words were, " I go to obtain my reward."

Captain Brand was as good as his word. A rare bonfire was seen that day at Lewes. Fagots and brushwood were heaped upon the pile till the flames rose up higher than the upper windows of the old hostel, and the heat was so great, that those nearest the blazing mass drew back half scorched.

When the fire had burnt out, all that remained was a heap of ashes, in the midst of which stood a charred stake with an iron chain attached to it.

Such was the martyrdom of Derrick Carver.

His memory is not forgotten in Lewes ; and on the fifth of November in each year, a great torchlight procession, composed of men in fantastic garbs and with blackened visages, and dragging blazing tar-barrels after them, parades the High Street, while an enormous bonfire is lighted opposite the Star Inn, on the exact spot where Derrick Carver perished, into which, when at its highest, various effigies are cast. A more extraordinary spectacle than is presented by this commemoration of the Marian persecutions in Lewes it has never been our lot to witness.

End of the Sixth Book.

BOOK VII.

THE TREASURE-CHESTS.

CHAPTER I.

THE LOVES OF OG AND LILIAS.

T will probably be recollected under what singular circumstances the acquaintance began between Og the gigantic and Lilias the fair. From the very moment when the damsel, seated behind the giant on the broad back of Arundel, passed her arm round his waist, a flame was kindled in his breast never afterwards to be extinguished.

A magnetic influence was exercised over him by Lilias, and he speedily became so much enthralled by her fascinations as was Sir Bevis of Southampton, whom he then represented, by the charms of the peerless Princess Josyan. When he and his gigantic brothers, with Sir Narcissus and Lady le Grand, proceeded to Winchester to take part in the pageants displayed there during the royal nuptials, Lilias accompanied them, and, before many days had elapsed, her conquest of Og was complete. She had him, as Gog confidentially remarked to Magog, "entirely under her thumb."

"Will he be fool enough to marry her, think you, brother?" observed Magog, shrugging his shoulders, and thinking of Dame Placida.

"Hum! I cannot say, but I shall do my best to dissuade him from the step," rejoined Gog.

So the brothers laid their huge heads together, and the result was that they devised a plan by which they hoped to get rid altogether of the fair syren, and cure Og of his ridiculous passion, as they deemed it. Their plan was to send back Lilias to Southampton, and persuade Og that she had left him of her own accord to return to her former admirer, and they managed the matter so adroitly, that Og was completely duped, and, after a tremendous burst of indignation against the fickleness of the sex, vowed he would never think of the false jillflirt again. His brothers commended his resolution, and told him he had had a narrow escape.

"If you are wise, you will take warning by me, and never marry," said Magog.

"If he must needs marry, let him choose a buxom widow, and not a tricksome girl like Lilias."

"I don't mean to marry at all," cried Og, resolutely.

But the fangs of disappointment gnawed his heart. He grew moody and dull, and avoided the society of his brothers.

After a month's absence from the Tower, the three gigantic warders returned there, and resumed their ordinary duties. But Og's melancholy increased, and his brothers at last began to feel uneasy about him, and to regret the part they had played.

"It would be a grievous thing were he to break his heart for this silly girl," remarked Gog. "He seems pining away for her."

"He may be pining away," observed Magog; "but he is in good case still, and his appetite is not amiss, judging by the havoc he made with the cold chine of beef and lumbar-pie at breakfast this morning, to say nothing of the stoup of ale which he managed to empty. Nevertheless, I agree with you, brother Gog, that he is not himself, and hath quite lost his old pleasant humour. He never jests, as was his wont, and I have not heard a hearty laugh from him since we sent Lilias away."

"I begin to think we did wrong in meddling in the matter," observed Gog. "I shall never cease to reproach myself if anything should happen to him."

"Well, we acted for the best," said Magog. "I only wish my marriage had been prevented," he added, with a groan. "Let us see how he goes on. Perchance, he may recover."

But Og did *not* recover, and, although he did not exhibit any of the usual symptoms of despairing love, as loss of appetite, or flesh, a lacklustre eye, and disordered manner, still he became more gloomy and sullen than ever, and rarely exchanged a word with his brothers.

Nearly eight months had now flown since he had beheld Lilias, and still her image was constantly before him, and the witchery she had practised upon him by her fascinations and allurements had not lost a jot of its power. He was still as much under her sway as if she had been with him all the time.

One evening, while he was taking a solitary walk upon the ramparts, and thinking of Lilias, he saw Xit hastening towards him, and would have avoided him, but the dwarf stopped him, saying,—

"Give thee good e'en, Og. I was looking for thee. I bring thee good news."

"Out of my way," rejoined the giant, gruffly. "I am in no humour for jesting."

"I know thou art become as surly as a bear with a sore head," replied Xit; "but thou hadst best not provoke a quarrel with me, or thou wilt rue it."

"Pass on," roared Og, "and exercise thy wit at the expense of those who are amused by it — my brothers for example. But meddle not with me. I am dangerous."

"Big words do not terrify me," rejoined Xit, with a mocking laugh. "Furious as thou art, I can tame thee with a word. I have but to pronounce the name of 'Lilias Ringwood,' and thou wilt straight become as gentle as a lamb. Ha ha! ha! Was I not right?"

"Hast thou aught to tell me concerning Lilias?" cried

Og, suddenly becoming as meek as the animal to which he had been likened. "If so, speak quickly !"

"Soh ! thou art in the mood for converse now, and my jests do not appear tiresome to thee," rejoined Xit; "but I will not gratify thee. Thou art dull company. I will go to thy brothers."

"Nay, but Xit, sweet Xit, if thou hast any love for me, tell me what thou knowest of Lilias."

"Thou dost not deserve that I should tell thee aught, uncourteous giant," said Xit. "Nevertheless, out of compassion for thy miserable state, I will speak. Know, then, most amorous Titan, that I have seen the lady of thy love ——"

"Thou hast seen Lilias !" interrupted Og. "Oh ! thou art my best friend. How doth she look ? Is she comely as ever ? Or is she changed and married to another ? Tell me the worst. It may break my heart—but spare me not."

"I will tell thee the best and the worst as quickly as may be," rejoined Xit. "The best is, that Lilias is still true to thee, and looking lovelier than ever—and the worst is, that she is coming to the Tower in a few days, and therefore thou wilt soon behold her again."

"Why, the worst is best of all !" cried Og, transported with delight.

"Nay, it is worst," rejoined Xit; "because, when she comes, thou wilt be compelled to marry her."

"But I say to thee again that it is best, for I desire nothing so much as marriage with her. But thou art not making merry with me all this while ? 'Twere a sorry jest to trifle with me thus."

"I am not trifling with thee, incredulous giant," replied Xit. "If the hand of the fair Lilias will make thee happy, thou shalt have it. That I promise thee. Now listen. Compassionating thy woful condition, I have been to Southampton, and seen the mistress of thy affections, and finding her still unfettered by matrimonial ties, still amiably disposed towards thee, I proposed marriage to her in thy name, and the offer was—accepted."

"Thou hast done me an incalculable service !" cried Og, taking him in his arms, and hugging him tightly.

"And so thou hast been to Southampton, and seen Lilias, and won her for me—eh? I have missed thee for the last week, but fancied thou wert with her Majesty at Whitehall."

"Set me down, and I will talk to thee," replied Xit. "Thou hast almost squeezed the breath out of my body;" and as Og placed him gently on the ground, he continued, "I will now let thee into a secret. But first promise not to be angry."

"I am far too happy to be angry with any one now," rejoined Og. "Speak out. What hast thou to reveal?"

"I must set thee right upon one point. When Lilias quitted thee so suddenly at Winchester, it was not, as thou wert led to suppose, from a desire to be reconciled to her first lover. Her disappearance was contrived by Gog and Magog, who did not wish thee to wed the damsel."

"Thunder and lightning! was it so?" roared Og, with sudden fury.

"Remember thy promise," said Xit.

"Well, proceed," cried Og, trying to calm himself.

"Perceiving the mischief they had occasioned, and despairing of remedying the matter, thy brothers applied to me, and out of my love for them and thee, I offered to go to Southampton to see what could be done with Lilias. Accordingly I went, and how I succeeded in my mission thou art already aware."

"I am for ever beholden to thee," said Og. "And so Lilias will certainly be here in a few days. Why didst thou not bring her with thee?"

"I would fain have done so," replied Xit; "but she had preparations to make before her departure. However, she will be escorted by a young gentleman whom you may remember, Captain Rodomont Bittern, of Cardinal Pole's household."

"Rodomont Bittern!" exclaimed Og, knitting his bushy brow. "Why should he escort her?"

"Because he chances to be coming up to London at the same time—nothing more, thou jealous and suspicious fool," rejoined Xit. "Captain Bittern's errand to Southampton was very different from mine. He did not go to propose a marriage, but to attend a funeral. You remember Constance Tyrrell?"

"Daughter of a wealthy Southampton merchant," replied Og. "Yes, I remember her. It was whispered that the King was enamoured of her, but that she preferred young Osbert Clinton. She is now at Lambeth Palace, under the guardianship of Cardinal Pole."

"I see you are well informed about her," replied Xit. "Well, old Tyrrell, her father, is just dead, and has made a very singular will. Since his daughter has become tainted with heresy, he has lost all affection for her, and has now disinherited her, and left the whole of his immense riches to —whom think'st thou?"

"Nay, I cannot guess," replied Og. "Not to Rodomont Bittern, I trust?"

"No, not to him," returned Xit. "He has made Cardinal Pole his heir, and the sum he has bequeathed is such as not even a Cardinal need despise. This was the reason why Rodomont Bittern and others of the Cardinal's household were sent down to Southampton to bury the old merchant and take possession of his property, and as I chanced to be there at the same time, I naturally came in contact with them, and on acquainting Captain Bittern with mine errand, he proffered his services, and accompanied me when I called on Lilias. It is but justice to him to add, that he pleaded thy cause with the damsel as warmly as I could do myself. When the affair was arranged, and Captain Bittern found that a longer stay at Southampton was inconvenient to me, he obligingly undertook to escort thy destined bride to London. Thus thou hast now the whole affair before thee. Methinks I have some little claim on thy gratitude. So if you will come with me to thy brothers, and assure them they are forgiven, I shall deem myself amply requited."

Og readily assented, and quitting the ramparts, they proceeded to the Byward Tower, where they found Gog and Magog at supper, an immense pasty, with a cold ham, a mountainous loaf, and a mighty mazer filled with ale, being set before them.

As Og and Xit entered, they both rose from the table at which they were seated, and seeing there were no traces of anger on their brother's countenance, they held out theii hands to him, which Og, so far from refusing, shook very cordially.

In a few moments all explanations were over, and the brothers amicably seated at the table, discussing the pasty, ever and anon applying to the mazer, and talking, when they were able to talk at all, of the approaching marriage.

CHAPTER II.

PRECISELY at the time that Lilias was expected, the King paid a visit to the Tower. He came from Whitehall by water, and was attended by Sir John Gage and Sir Henry Jerningham. On landing, he was received by the Lieutenant of the Tower, Sir Henry Bedingfeld, and a guard, among whom were the gigantic warders, and by his own desire was at once conducted to the Jewel House, where his chests of bullion were deposited.

This building was situated in a court belonging to the old palace, its precise position being on the south of the White Tower, between the Queen's lodgings and the Cold Harbour Tower. At the door of the Jewel Tower, the King was received by Master Thomas Lovel, the keeper, who seemed to expect his Majesty, and took him forthwith to the strong-room containing the treasure. After satisfying himself that the coffers were safe, Philip informed Lovel that he was about to place them in the Exchequer, and gave him some directions respecting their removal.

Before leaving the Jewel House, the King had some private converse with Lovel, who, it appeared, had an important communication to make to him. Having given further instructions in secret to the keeper, Philip proceeded to the White Tower, where he ascended to the great council-chamber, and after surveying it with much curiosity, repaired to the ancient Norman chapel dedicated to Saint John the Evangelist, and passed some time in devotion within it.

His examination of the White Tower ended, the King was proceeding with Sir Henry Bedingfeld towards the lieutenant's lodgings, and they had just reached the Tower Green, which was then, as now, shaded by noble trees, when lively strains greeted their ears, and other joyous sounds proclaimed that some festivities were going on.   Turning to Sir Henry Bedingfeld, Philip inquired the cause of this rejoicing, but the latter looked perplexed, and being unable to obtain any information from those about him, despatched a warder to ascertain the meaning of the gleeful sounds.   While the man was gone on his errand, Philip occupied himself in examining the exterior of the Beauchamp Tower, opposite which he had halted.   In another minute the warder returned, with a broad grin upon his face, and imparted something to Sir Henry Bedingfeld, which at once caused a corresponding smile to illumine the lieutenant's grave countenance.

"An please your Majesty," said Sir Henry, addressing Philip, "I have just ascertained that those sounds of rejoicing are occasioned by the arrival from Southampton of the destined bride of one of our gigantic warders, Og—there he stands to answer for himself, if your Majesty will deign to question him."

"From Southampton!" exclaimed Philip.   "I should not be surprised if it were the fair damsel I beheld there at the time of my arrival, who enacted the part of the Princess, when the giant himself personated the redoubted Sir Bevis."

"'Tis the very same, Sire," replied Og, advancing towards the King, and making a profound obeisance.   "'Tis Lilias Ringwood, whom your Majesty deigns to remember.   It would appear she has just arrived, though I myself have not had the gratification of beholding her."

"Thou shalt have the gratification anon," returned Philip; "but where are thy brothers?   They were with thee just now.   Are they with Lilias?"

"I conclude so, Sire," replied Og.   "While your Majesty was in the White Tower, they were summoned by Xit, with what intent I knew not then, though I can guess it now. They are giving Lilias a joyful welcome preparatory to our meeting.   Under these circumstances, may I crave your gracious permission to join my intended bride?"

"Control thine impatience for a moment, and answer me one question," said Philip. "How long is it since thou hast seen her?"

"Not since your Majesty was espoused to the Queen at Winchester," replied Og.

"And she has not changed her mind during that long interval? By my faith, she is a very model of constancy!" exclaimed Philip, laughing. "Sir Henry Bedingfeld," he added to the lieutenant, "I would fain witness the meeting between this loving pair. Let the damsel be brought hither."

Whereupon an order to that effect was instantly given by Bedingfeld.

Shortly afterwards the sound of a tabour and fife were heard, while the trampling of feet and other confused noises announced that a number of persons were coming up the road leading from the Bloody Tower to the Green, and in another moment a little procession came in view.

At the head of the train strutted Xit, in a jerkin and mantle of crimson velvet, embroidered with gold, and carrying in his hand a pole decorated with ribbons of various colours, and hung with bells. Behind the mannikin marched Gog and Magog, sustaining between them a chair, in which sat Lilias Ringwood, arrayed in a very becoming green kirtle, and her pretty countenance suffused with blushes. Some twenty or thirty persons in holiday attire followed the bride, amongst whom were Rodomont Bittern, and his friends Nick Simnel and Jack Holiday. Besides Lady le Grand and Magog's wife, Dame Placida, there was a troop of young damsels, several of whom had considerable pretensions to beauty

As soon as the procession reached the green it came to a halt, and Xit advancing alone towards the King, and making a very ceremonious obeisance to his Majesty, desired to know his pleasure.

"Let the damsel approach," said Philip.

Whereupon Xit signed to the two giants to advance with their fair burden, and as they drew near, the King bade Og go forward and help her to alight. It is needless to say that the command was promptly obeyed. With a few mighty strides Og cleared the space between him and his mistress, while his brothers elevated the chair on which she was seated, as if to place her out of his reach. Lilias, however, did not hesitate to spring from the giddy height into her gigantic lover's outstretched arms, and was instantly clasped to his mighty breast. After gazing on her rapturously for a moment, and uttering a few passionate words, he deposited her gently on the ground, amid the shouts and laughter of the beholders.

"Welcome !—thrice welcome !" he cried. "This moment amply repays me for all the misery I have endured."

"And have you really been unhappy without me?" inquired Lilias.

"Unhappy !" exclaimed Og ; "I have been so wretched that it is a marvel I didn't drown myself in the Tower moat. However, it's all right now."

"To be sure it is," interposed Xit. "You will have plenty of time for explanations hereafter. Your first business is to present your bride to his Majesty."

"Come, then," said the giant, taking her hand, and leading her towards the king.

Lilias displayed no bashfulness, but tripped gracefully by the side of her gigantic admirer, and made a profound reverence to his Majesty as she was presented to him.

"By my faith, good fellow, thou art to be envied," said Philip. "I would not advise thee to let this fair creature cut of thy sight in future."

"I do not intend to give him the opportunity, Sire," replied Lilias, demurely.

"Wisely resolved," rejoined Philip, laughing. "As I chanced to witness the commencement of your love affair, I am glad to see it brought to such a satisfactory conclusion. Make merry with your friends, and that you may do so without scruple, here is that shall help to pay for the wedding feast."

So saying, he took a well-filled purse from the velvet pouch depending from his girdle, and gave it to Sir Henry Bedingfeld, by whom it was handed to Og.

"We thank you most heartily for your bounty, Sire," said Og, bowing as he received the princely gift, "and shall not fail to drink long life to your Majesty."

"Ay, long life to his Majesty," cried Gog, in a stentorian

voice, "and may Heaven shower its choicest blessings on his head. Shout, friends, shout!" he added, turning to the others, who instantly responded by loud cries of "Long live the King!"

Bowing graciously in acknowledgment, Philip moved away with his attendants, and proceeding to the lower end of the Green, entered the lieutenant's lodgings, where he remained for some little time.

No sooner was the King gone, then Xit called out, in his shrillest tones,—

"A dance! a dance! Let us not separate without some mirthful pastime suited to the occasion. A dance, I say, and as the merriest and best, let us begin with a brawl."

The proposition meeting with general concurrence, the minstrels began to play a very lively air, while the entire assemblage, with three exceptions, took hands, and formed an immense ring. The three persons excepted were the giants, whose stature forbade them to join in the dance; but as the others wheeled round them, they found it impossible to keep their limbs quiet, and began to execute such grotesque movements that the dancers were scarcely able to proceed for laughter.

CHAPTER III.

HE next day was a joyous one for Og, since it saw him indissolubly bound to the object of his affections. The marriage took place in the little chapel on the Tower Green, and the edifice was crowded during the ceremonial.

At its close, the happy couple adjourned, with their kins-folk and friends, to the Stone Kitchen, where a copious and excellent repast had been prepared by Peter Trusbut, the pantler, who still exercised his vocation as purveyor to the warders of the Tower; and it need scarcely be said that full justice was done to the many good things provided by him on this auspicious occasion.

It was always agreeable to Peter Trusbut and his worthy dame to see their guests enjoy themselves, and the rapidity and gusto with which the dishes were now demolished per-fectly satisfied them. Gog and Magog ate more than usual in honour of their brother's marriage, and the bridegroom's prowess was hardly inferior to their own.

Of course Xit had been present at the wedding, and was likewise a principal guest at the breakfast that followed it. He was in high spirits, and diverted the company by his lively sallies. When the dishes had been removed, he leaped upon the table, goblet in hand, and, in appropriate terms, proposed the health of Og and his bride—a toast which was drunk with great cheers. While they were in the very midst of enjoyment, the door suddenly opened, and a man of exceedingly sinister aspect, and habited in a tight-fitting leathern doublet, appeared at it. At the sight of this ill-favoured personage, the countenances of the company fell, and their laughter ceased.

"Who is that strange man?" inquired Lilias of Og, in an under tone.

"It is Mauger, the executioner," replied her husband. "What brings thee here?" he added, half angrily, to the headsman.

"I am come to congratulate you on your marriage," replied Mauger. "Am I not welcome?"

"Sit down, and take a cup of wine," rejoined Og, filling a goblet.

"Here's health to the bonny bride!" cried Mauger, eyeing her curiously as he raised the flagon to his lips.

"I do not like his looks," said Lilias, clinging to her husband. "I wish he had not come."

"Harkye, Mauger," cried Xit, who was still standing upon the table, "thy presence is unsuited to this festive occasion, and we can, therefore, dispense with thy society."

"I shall not go at thy bidding, thou malapert knave," rejoined Mauger. "I came to see the bride, not thee."

And he was about to seat himself in the chair left empty by the dwarf, when the latter prevented him, exclaiming,—

"That chair is mine. Begone instantly, if thou wouldst not be unceremoniously thrust from the room."

Og seemed inclined to second the dwarf's threat, but his wife interposed, saying,—

"Let him not be turned out, or it may bring us ill luck."

"It *will* bring you ill luck if I be so dealt with, fair mistress," rejoined Mauger, with an uncouth attempt at gallantry.

And, pushing Xit aside, he sat down in the vacant chair.

"I have a present for you, fair mistress," pursued the headsman to Lilias. "Here it is," he added, producing a silver box from his doublet. "This pomander was given me by Queen Catherine Howard on the day of her execution, and I have kept it about me ever since, but I will now bestow it upon you, and I will tell you why. You have a neck as long, and as white, and as snowy as Queen Catherine's, and she had the whitest and slenderest throat my axe ever touched—therefore you well deserve the box. Take it, and if you ever need my services," he continued, with a grim smile, "you shall give it me back again. Smell to it—it is filled with delicate perfumes—ambergris, storax, benjoin, labdanum, civet and musk. You will find it a preservative against infection."

"It seems to me to smell of blood," said Lilias, tossing back the box. "I will not have it."

"As you please," said Mauger, returning it to his doublet. "Yet it is not a gift to be despised."

"Enough of this," said Og, somewhat sternly. "Do you not perceive that you interrupt our festivities? My wife thanks you for your intended present, but declines it."

"I have nothing else to offer her, unless it be an earring worn by Queen Anne Boleyn ——"

"I would not touch it for the world," cried Lilias, recoiling with horror.

"You know not what you refuse," said Mauger, testily; "but it is in vain that I try to render myself agreeable. Since I am an unwelcome guest, I will go. But I will tell you a word in parting. This day has begun blithely enough, but it will not end so merrily."

"What meanest thou?" cried Og, angrily. "Wouldst thou insinuate that something is about to happen to me and my bride?"

"Or to me—or to any other among us?" added Xit, with equal fierceness.

"No, I mean not that," replied Mauger. "But I tell you that the day will end differently from what you expect."

"Pshaw! thou art only saying this to frighten the women," said Og. "Sit down again and take another cup of wine."

"No, I have had enough," rejoined Mauger, in a surly tone. "I came here with presents to the bride—presents such as none other in the Tower could offer her—and they have been scornfully rejected. Be it so. A day may come for some of you when it may be necessary to bespeak my favour."

And casting a stern and vindictive look around, he limped out of the room.

"I am glad he is gone," observed Lilias. "And yet I wish he had not left us in anger."

"Pshaw! heed him not," rejoined Og. "His odious office causes him to be generally shunned, and hence he is sour-tempered. He is gentler than usual to-day."

"Then he must, indeed, be savage," said Lilias, forcing a laugh.

"He is strangely superstitious," pursued Og, "and pretends he has warnings beforehand of the persons he is to put to death. From what he let fall just now, I fancy he has had one of those warnings."

"Saints preserve us! I hope not!" cried Lilias, turning pale. "I declare I feel quite ill. Did you not remark that he compared my neck to that of Queen Catherine Howard."

"Nay, he meant that as a compliment," said her husband. "In good sooth, thou hast a dainty neck, sweetheart."

"Dainty or not, I like not the comparison," said Lilias. "When he looked at me, it seemed as if I felt the sharp edge of the axe—oh! take me into the air, or I shall faint."

Og instantly took her in his arms, saying, as he carried her forth, "If aught betide thee, sweet chuck, the day shall not end merrily for Mauger."

"Do nothing to him, I charge you," rejoined Lilias, faintly. "We have offended him enough already."

CHAPTER IV.

HOW THE TREASURE-CHESTS WERE CARRIED TO
TRAITORS' GATE.

THE bride's sudden indisposition naturally put an end to the breakfast, and ere many minutes all the guests had quitted the Stone Kitchen. On being brought into the open air, Lilias speedily revived, and the bloom which had temporarily deserted them returned to her cheeks. A stroll on the green completely restored her, though she was nearly made ill again by an injudicious remark of Xit, who pointed out to her the spot whereon the scaffold was usually erected.

In order to divert her from the gloomy thoughts which seemed to have been inspired by Mauger, Og took her to the palace and showed her over the royal apartments, with the size and splendour of which she was much astonished. They next visited the garden, with which she was also delighted, and were crossing the outer court towards the Cold Harbour Tower, when they encountered Lovel, the keeper of the Jewel Tower, who, courteously saluting the bride, volunteered to show her the treasures under his custody.

Lilias gratefully accepted the offer, and was taken with her husband and the whole party into the Jewel House, where the many precious articles contained in it were displayed to them. After they had feasted their eyes on this rich collection, Lovel said to the bride.—

"You shall now see the coffers containing the bullion deposited here by his Majesty. This is the only opportunity you will have of viewing them, for they are to be removed to the Exchequer to-night."

Upon this he unlocked the door of the strong-room, and showed them fifteen mighty chests piled within it. Each chest was wrapped in a cover emblazoned with the arms of Castile and Aragon. Removing the cover from one of them, Lovel disclosed a handsome coffer made of walnut, strengthened by bands of brass, and secured by two locks.

"Oh! how I should like to see what is inside it!" cried Lilias, after she had examined the exterior of the box.

And she looked so beseechingly at Lovel that he could not refuse to gratify her curiosity.

"It is against my orders to open the chests," he said. "Nevertheless, I will yield to your wishes."

And taking a bunch of keys from his girdle, he unlocked the coffer, and raising the lid, revealed the bars of gold to Lilias's admiring gaze.

"Oh! how beautiful they look!" she cried, clapping her hands. "Cannot you spare one of them?—it would never be missed."

"Were the gold mine, you should have one, and welcome, fair mistress," replied Lovel, gallantly. "But this is the King's treasure, and I am bound to guard it."

"But suppose it were carried off by force, what would you say then?" pursued Lilias, playfully.

"I cannot entertain any such supposition," he replied, shutting down the lid, and locking the coffer. "There! now I have removed temptation," he added, with a smile.

"That chest must be enormously heavy," observed Lilias to her husband. "Do you think you could lift it, Og?"

"I don't know," he replied; "but if Master Lovel will allow me, I will try."

"Make the attempt, and welcome," replied Lovel, with a laugh.

Seizing hold of the chest with a herculean grasp, Og threw it over his shoulder.

"There, now you have got possession of it, away with you," cried Lilias. "Master Lovel will not prevent you."

"Hold! hold!" exclaimed the keeper of the treasure. "This is carrying the jest rather too far."

"Did you really think I was making off with the chest, Master Lovel?" cried Og, setting it down with a great laugh.

"Well, it looked like it, I must own," returned the other. "But you couldn't go very far with such a burden as that."

"Couldn't I?" rejoined Og. "You don't know what I could do if I tried. Why, I would carry the chest from the Tower to Whitehall, if the King would only bestow it upon me for my pains."

And he burst into another tremendous laugh, in which his brothers heartily joined.

"That were a feat worthy of Samson," observed Lovel, dryly. "Suppose I put your strength to the test."

"Do so," rejoined Og. "What would you have me perform? You have just told us that the chests are to be removed to the Exchequer to-night. You don't want me to carry them to Westminster Hall?"

"No, no! I don't want that," said Lovel, laughing. "They are to be transported by water, and it will save time if they are taken at once to Traitor's Gate, where they will be embarked."

"Say no more—we'll do it, won't we?" cried Og, turning to his brothers, who readily assented.

Without more ado, he again took up the ponderous coffer, and called out, "Now, I'm ready."

"So are we," cried Gog and Magog, as they each shouldered a chest.

Upon this, the whole party went out of the chamber, the door of which was carefully locked by the keeper. It was a striking sight to see the three giants, laden in the manner we have described, cross the court of the palace, and descend with slow but firm footsteps the slope leading to the Bloody Tower, each having upon his broad shoulders a weight sufficient to call into activity the full forces of three ordinary men, and yet bearing it—if not easily—yet stoutly. It was true that the muscles of their bull throats and brawny legs were tremendously developed, and looked almost as large as cables, but these were the

CHAPTER V.

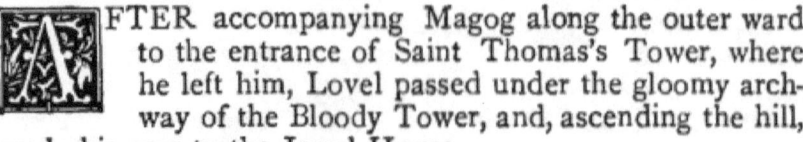FTER accompanying Magog along the outer ward to the entrance of Saint Thomas's Tower, where he left him, Lovel passed under the gloomy archway of the Bloody Tower, and, ascending the hill, made his way to the Jewel House.

Arrived there, he did not proceed to that part of the building which we last visited, but sought his private chamber, and having entered it, and bolted the door inside, he tapped at the door of a small inner room, and called out "You may come forth, Sir."

The summons was promptly obeyed by a young man, who stepping quickly towards him, said, "You have been long absent, Lovel. What news do you bring?"

"Excellent news, good Master Osbert Clinton," replied the other. "If all goes well, you will have the treasure tonight. It will delight you to hear that the coffers have been transported by the gigantic warders to Traitor's Gate, and are now lying there, ready for you and your friends to take them away. So far all has gone well—far better than could have been expected—and I hope the rest will turn out equally prosperously. Indeed, it can scarcely fail to do so, unless from ill management."

"What course do you advise us to pursue, Lovel?" demanded Osbert.

"First of all, there must be no delay in the execution of

the project," replied the other. "The business must be done to-night. A boat capable of containing the chests must be brought to Traitors' Gate. I shall be in Saint Thomas's Tower, and after going through the usual formalities, will cause the great wooden gate to be opened. If no untoward circumstance occurs, the coffers can thus be readily carried off and conveyed to a place of safety."

"Once out of Traitors' Gate, all the rest will be easy," said Osbert. "Your plan promises well, good Lovel, and I trust nothing will occur to mar it. Possessed of this gold, we shall be able to carry into immediate effect our grand enterprise. It may be wrong to seize this treasure, but neither I nor my associates have any scruples on the subject. We know that this gold is intended to be employed to bribe our nobles to enslave the country, and we consider it lawful plunder, of which we may rightfully possess ourselves by force or stratagem."

"I take precisely the same view of the matter as yourself, Sir," said Lovel; "and, as you, know, have engaged in this enterprise without fee or reward. I am anxious, as you and your friends are, to see the country delivered from Spanish thraldom, and the Protestant religion restored. While martyrs are giving up their lives in testimony of their faith, I do not hesitate to jeopardise mine to benefit the same cause. If this Spanish gold can be employed against our enemies, instead of being used by them to our disadvantage, I shall be content."

"In three day's time there will be a rising in Essex and S ffolk," said Osbert; "and in less than a week an army of insurgents, larger than that commanded by Wyat, will be marching to London, its battle-cry being, 'Down with the Spaniard and the Pope!' This gold will give us all we need. And so you positively refuse any reward for the great service you are rendering us, Lovel?"

"Were I to take a reward, I should consider that I had violated my trust," replied the other. "My object is to serve my country, and if it be freed from oppression I shall be amply rewarded. But now to proceed with the business. No time must be lost in communicating with Sir Henry Dudley, Sir Anthony Kingston, Master Udal, and the rest of your associates."

"That can be quickly done," replied Osbert. "They are close at hand—at the 'Rose and Crown,' on Tower Hill. There can be no difficulty as to a boat, since one has been already provided. At what hour ought the attempt to be made?"

"Let me see," said Lovel, reflecting. "The tide will serve at nine. The boat should be at Traitor's Gate at that hour."

"Good," returned Osbert. "Now then to communicate with my friends."

"Leave that to me," said Lovel; "you cannot quit the Tower with safety, as, if you should be seen and recognised, your instant arrest would follow. I will go to the 'Rose and Crown' at once, and give full instructions to your friends. Retire to the inner room, and do not stir forth from it till my return."

And as Osbert complied, the keeper of the treasure left the Jewel House, and set out on his errand.

CHAPTER VI.

HOW THE PLOT WAS DISCOVERED BY XIT, AND DISCLOSED BY HIM TO MAGOG.

EANTIME, Magog, with whom Lovel had parted at the entrance of Saint Thomas's Tower, had gone in, and made his way through the side-passage, previously described, to the interior of Traitors' Gate. He found the chests lying upon the platform, just as they had been laid there by himself and his brothers, and sitting down upon one of them, presently fell asleep, and made the vaulted roof resound with his deep breathing. How long he remained in this state he could not say, but he was roused by feeling something crawling, as he thought, over his face, and supposing it to be a gigantic water-rat — the place being infested with such vermin—he put out his hand, and catching hold of the noxious creature, as he deemed it, was about to throw it into the water, when a shrill cry admonished him that the fancied water-rat was no other than Xit.

"Wouldst drown me, Magog?" shrieked the dwarf, clinging to him.

"Drown thee—not I!" replied the giant, laughing. "But I took thee for a rat or an otter."

"None but a sleepy dolt like thyself would have made such a mistake," said Xit. "I could not waken thee without plucking thy beard. Call'st thou this keeping guard over the treasure? I call it gross negligence."

"Well, well, I am vigilant enough now," rejoined Magog. "What hast thou to say to me?"

"Something that will keep thee wakeful, I trust," said Xit. "Lend me thine ears, and I will disclose it to thee. I have discovered a plot."

"Poh! thou art always making some silly discovery that leads to nothing," rejoined Magog.

"But this will lead more than one man to the scaffold," pursued Xit, mysteriously. "'Tis an important discovery I have made."

"Indeed!" exclaimed Magog, with some curiosity. "What is it? Let me hear and judge."

"It relates to the chests on which thou art sitting," replied Xit. "There is a plot to carry them off. Master Lovel, the keeper of the treasure, is concerned in it, but the principal contrivers are Osbert Clinton, Sir Henry Dudley, Sir Anthony Kingston, Udal, and the others connected with the late outbreak."

"Ah, this is indeed important!" cried Magog. "And how didst thou make this discovery?"

"You shall hear," replied Xit. "Suspecting all was not right, I followed Lovel to his lodging, and by listening at the keyhole, managed to overhear a conversation between him and Osbert Clinton, who is at present concealed in the Jewel House. From this I learnt that the treasure is to be carried off by the traitors, in order to assist them in getting up another insurrection of a far more formidable character than the last. Their plan is to bring a boat to Traitors' Gate at nine o'clock to-night, when, feigning to be officers sent by the King to remove the treasure to the Exchequer, they will present a warrant, and Master Lovel, being their accomplice, the coffers will be delivered to them—so at least they calculate."

"A well-devised plan, I must own," observed Magog, "and like enough to have succeeded."

"It would infallibly have succeeded but for my shrewdness in detecting it," said Xit.

"Well, thou wilt, doubtless, receive due credit for thy penetration from Sir Henry Bedingfeld, to whom the matter must be forthwith communicated," observed Magog, getting up.

"What art thou about to do, thou foolish giant?" cried Xit. "We can manage this affair without Sir Henry Bedingfeld's assistance. Recollect that a heavy price is set upon the heads of all these offenders, and if we can effect their arrest—as we shall do if my counsels be followed—the reward will be ours. We must take them all, like fish in a net. Not one must be allowed to escape. Listen to me, and I will show thee how it can be done. The moment the barge is admitted into this place, Traitor's Gate must be closed by thee or by thy brothers, and we shall then have them like rats in a trap. Though they may offer some resistance at first, they will soon be forced to surrender. Osbert Clinton is sure to be on the spot with Lovel, and we can arrest them both at the same time. What think'st thou of my plan?"

"By my faith, it promises well," replied Magog.

"We shall need assistance," pursued Xit; "and besides Og and Gog, I propose to call in the aid of Captain Bittern and his friends. They are men of discretion, and can be relied on. Care must be taken not to awaken Lovel's suspicions, or our plan will be defeated. And now let us quit this damp place. I am half choked by the mist. I wonder thou couldst sleep in it. Come! There is no fear of the treasure being carried off just yet."

Upon this Magog arose, and they adjourned to the guard-chamber.

Xit's plan was carried out. About eight o'clock in the evening, Og tore himself from his bride, promising faithfully to return to supper, and, accompanied by Gog, Rodomont Bittern, Holiday, and Simnel, to all of whom the dwarf's important discovery had been communicated, repaired to Saint Thomas's Tower, and mounted to an upper chamber overlooking the river, where they held themselves in readiness for whatever might occur, beguiling the tedium of waiting with some flasks of wine which they had brought from the Stone Kitchen.

Xit, meanwhile, had kept watch over Lovel's movements. He saw the keeper of the treasure return from his errand to Tower Hill, and cautiously following him, and adopting the same plan of espionage which he had previously employed, he heard him inform ⌐ ⌐ ⌐ had seen

Sir Henry Dudley and the other conspirators, who were well pleased with the arrangement, and undertook to bring a barge to Traitor's Gate at the appointed hour that night.

"The coffers once secured," pursued Lovel, "your friends propose to take them up the river to Chelsea and land them there. No time must be lost in disposing of the treasure, for the moment it becomes known that it has been carried off, a general search will be made."

"Once in our possession, the treasure will never find its way to the royal Exchequer—of that you may be quite certain, Lovel," replied Osbert. "But what do you propose to do? Your connection in the affair will assuredly be suspected."

"I shall provide for my safety by flight," said Lovel. "This very night I shall quit the Tower secretly, and remain in concealment till your proposed insurrection will enable me to appear with safety."

"If we succeed, as I trust under Heaven we shall, your services shall not be forgotten, Lovel," observed Osbert. "You shall have a better post under Elizabeth than that which you now occupy under Philip and Mary."

"I have said that I do not seek reward," rejoined Lovel ; "but since, in abandoning this post, I shall sacrifice all, it is but just that I should have some compensation."

"You shall have compensation in full, doubt it not, Lovel," said Osbert. "And now let us finally arrange our plans for to-night. How many persons are there in Saint Thomas's Tower?"

"Only three," replied Lovel. "Croyland, the keeper of the gate, his man, and a sentinel. Stay! I had forgotten. One of the gigantic warders, Magog, is there at this moment, but I do not think he will remain there till night, and if he should, he will be no hindrance to us, since all will be conducted with so much formality that suspicion will be disarmed. We will go together to Saint Thomas's Tower, and if my instructions to Sir Henry Dudley are carefully carried out, no difficulty will be experienced."

What answer was made to this by Osbert, Xit could not tell. Fancying he heard a movement towards the door, he beat a hasty retreat, and left the Jewel House, perfectly content with the information he had obtained.

CHAPTER VII.

HOW THE CONSPIRATORS WENT IN AT TRAITORS' GATE BUT CAME NOT OUT AGAIN.

NIGHT, anxiously expected both by plotters and counter-plotters, arrived at last. Within the lower chamber of Saint Thomas's Tower were Magog and Xit, but the two other gigantic warders, with Rodomont Bittern and his comrades, kept out of sight, lest Lovel's suspicions should be awakened.

Croyland, the keeper of the Tower, had been made a party to the plan, and consented to act as Xit directed. The night was dark, and the mist hanging over the river, and almost shrouding Saint Thomas's Tower from view, was favourable to the project of the conspirators.

Some quarter of an hour before the time fixed for the arrival of the barge, Lovel, accompanied by Osbert, who was well armed, and wrapped in his cloak, quitted the Jewel House, and proceeded to Saint Thomas's Tower. The door was opened by Croyland, who had a lamp in his hand, which he raised for a moment to survey Osbert, and then, apparently satisfied with his scrutiny, ushered them into the guard-chamber, which done, he returned to fasten the door.

Within the guard-chamber were Xit and Magog. The giant appeared to be fast asleep, with his huge head resting on a table, and did not move on their entrance ; but Xit immediately arose, and after a word with Lovel, was informed by the latter that the gentleman with him was an

officer sent by his Majesty to take charge of the treasure. With this information the dwarf seemed perfectly content, and bowed ceremoniously to Osbert, who slightly returned the salutation. In another moment Croyland returned with a lamp, and taking it from him, Lovel beckoned to Osbert to follow him, and led the way to the platform on which the chests were laid.

No sooner were they gone than Magog raised his head, and said in a whisper to Xit, "Is it Osbert Clinton?"

The dwarf replied in the affirmative, but added, "Don't ask any more questions, or you will be overheard. Here they are coming back. Down with your head!"

On this, Magog resumed his previous posture. Next moment Lovel reappeared with the lamp, but Osbert remained in the passage, so as not to expose himself to observation.

"The coffers are all right, I perceive," remarked Lovel, as he set down the lamp upon the table. "I sha'n't be sorry when they are gone," he added, with a laugh. "They have been a great source of anxiety to me."

"I daresay they have," replied Xit. "Your office wouldn't suit me at all, Master Lovel."

"Wherefore not?" demanded the other.

"Because my honesty would never be proof against the temptation I should be exposed to. The sight of so much treasure would exercise a baneful influence over me, and I should long to appropriate it to my own use. Whereas, you, worthy Lovel, are of an incorruptible nature, and can see gold without coveting it. You would never dream of making free with the contents of those coffers."

"Certainly not," replied Lovel.

"Therein we differ," pursued Xit. "Had those coffers been confided to me, I should have fallen. The Arch Enemy could not find a more certain means of destroying me than they would afford him. Knowing my own frailty, I respect your honesty the more, worthy Lovel. You can touch gold without being defiled by it. Unluckily, such is not my case."

Ere Lovel could reply, Osbert called out from the passage:—

"The barge is at hand. I hear a noise outside in the river."

And, as he spoke, the bell hanging above the outer arch of Traitors' Gate was rung.

"Here they are!" cried Xit, shaking Magog. "Rouse thyself, thou great sluggard."

"Who are here?" cried the giant, pretending to waken from a sound sleep.

"Why, the officers sent by the King to take away the treasure," rejoined Xit.

"Oh, indeed!" ejaculated Magog, with a prodigious yawn.

Meanwhile, Lovel, followed by Croyland, had mounted a spiral stone staircase, which quickly brought them to the summit of the round projecting tower at the western angle of the fortification. On reaching the battlements, they could discern through the gloom a large barque lying in the river immediately beneath them. The barge was rowed by four stalwart oarsmen, and its head was brought close up to Traitors' Gate.

At the prow stood a tall man, apparently in command of the party, and who was no other than Sir Henry Dudley. The barge had already been challenged by the sentinel, and a short parley had taken place, but when Lovel and Croyland appeared, Dudley called out in a loud, authoritative voice :—

"Open the gate quickly. We are officers sent by the King to bring away the treasure."

"Have you a warrant for its removal?" inquired Lovel.

"Ay," returned Dudley, "a warrant you will not care to dispute."

"Enough," answered Lovel. "The gate shall be opened immediately."

With this he disappeared from the battlements, while Dudley, turning to his companion in the barge, said in a low, exulting tone, "The prize will soon be ours. We shall get in without difficulty."

"Heaven grant we may get out as easily!" rejoined Sir Anthony Kingston, who was standing near him. "More people go in at Traitors' Gate than come out from it."

As he spoke, the ponderous wooden valves, worked by some machinery in the upper part of the tower, began slowly to revolve upon their hinges, disclosing the interior

of the passage, which was now illumined by torches held by
Magog and Croyland, who, with Lovel and Xit, were
stationed near the head of the steps.   In the background,
partly concealed by the coffers, stood Osbert Clinton.

As soon as the valves had opened wide enough to admit
the barge, Dudley, who was all impatience to secure the
prize, called to the oarsmen to push in, and the order being
promptly obeyed, the barge entered the channel, and was
propelled to the foot of the steps.   Sir Henry Dudley then
leaped ashore, and was followed by Sir Anthony Kingston
and some four or five others.

"Here is the order for the delivery of the treasure, Sir,"
said Dudley, presenting a paper to Lovel, who advanced to
meet him.

Lovel glanced at it for a moment, and then, apparently
satisfied by the inspection, observed,—

"We have been expecting you, Sir.   The chests are all
ready, as you see."

"That is well," said Dudley, scarcely able to conceal his
satisfaction.   "Let them be embarked at once."

While this brief dialogue occurred, Traitor's Gate was
noiselessly returning to its place, and in another minute was
closed.   The conspirators, however, were too much occupied
with what they had in hand to notice this suspicious circumstance.   The oarsmen now got out of the barge, and were
preparing to place the uppermost chest on board, when
Osbert Clinton suddenly stepped forward, and said, in a
low voice, to Sir Henry Dudley,—

"We are betrayed.   See you not that the gate is
shut?"

"Ha! so it is!" cried Dudley.   "Why is this, Sir?" he
added, fiercely, to Lovel.   "How comes it that yon gate is
closed?"

"I did not know it was so," replied the other.   "There
must be some mistake.   But I will cause it to be reopened
instantly."

"There is no mistake," cried Xit, in his loudest and most
important voice; "it is by my orders that Traitors' Gate
has been shut, and it will not be opened again.   Traitors, ye
are caught in a trap.   Ye have come here, with wicked and
felonious intent, to carry off the King's treasure, but instead

of departing with your plunder to stir up rebellion, you will be lodged in the dungeons of the Tower, and ere long expiate your manifold and dire offences on the scaffold."

At this address the conspirators stared aghast, and laid their hands upon their swords.

Osbert Clinton, however, signed to them to keep quiet, and said to Lovel, "What means this, Sir? Is it some ill-timed jest?"

"I will tell you what it means, Master Osbert Clinton," interposed Xit. "It means, that you, and all those with you, are my prisoners. I arrest you all for high treason. You yourself, Master Osbert Clinton—you Sir Henry Dudley—you, Sir Anthony Kingston—you, Master Udal, and all the rest of you. Deliver up your swords."

"This is droll," cried Osbert Clinton, forcing a laugh; "but the jest may prove no laughing matter for thee. Get the gate opened," he added to Lovel. "We will have the treasure in spite of them."

"Traitors' Gate shall *not* be opened," screamed Xit. "I forbid it, and ye shall find whether or not I shall be obeyed. Stir a single foot, thou traitor Lovel, and thou art a dead man." And drawing his sword, he presented it at the breast of the keeper of the treasure, exclaiming, "I arrest thee, also, on a charge of conspiracy and treason."

"An end must be put to this folly," cried Osbert, fiercely. "By the time you have got the treasure on board I will have the gate opened," he added to Dudley. Then drawing his sword, he commanded Xit to stand out of the way.

"Help me, my faithful giants!" cried Xit, retreating. "Help me!"

And at the words, Og and Gog issued from the passage where they had remained concealed, and with their halberds opposed Osbert's advance.

"Back!" roared Magog, in a voice of thunder, "or you rush upon your death."

"You had better yield," cried Xit. "You cannot escape. You will more easily cut your way through the solid beams of Traitors' Gate than you will hew a passage through these living walls."

"I will cut a way through both sooner than surrender," rejoined Osbert. "Follow me, friends."

And he was about to fling himself upon the giants, who awaited his attack unmoved, when his desperate purpose was averted by the sudden ringing of the alarm-bell. This sound, which proclaimed that the fortress was alarmed, paralysed his energies, and caused him to drop the point of his sword, while the rest of the conspirators looked equally disheartened. Other sounds, calculated to increase their apprehensions, were now heard, and the trampling of feet, accompanied by the clatter of arms, showed that a number of men were collecting in the outer ward. It was plain that the conspirators were betrayed, and the glances they exchanged betokened that they felt so.

"You had better yield with a good grace," cried Xit, "and not compel us to take your swords from you by force."

"I will die rather than yield," cried Osbert Clinton.

"So will we all," responded the others.

"Resistance is in vain," cried Lovel, suddenly changing his manner. "It is time to throw off the mask. You are prisoners to the King."

"Ha! it is thou who hast brought us into this snare," cried Dudley. "Take the reward of thy treachery," he added, passing his rapier through his body.

"Ha! I am slain!" exclaimed Lovel, as he fell backwards into the water.

At this moment the massive portal communicating with the outer ward was opened, and an astounding spectacle revealed.

Beneath the gloomy archway of the Bloody Tower stood the King, the torchlight flashing upon his stately figure, and communicating to his countenance a stern and sinister expression.

With him was Sir Henry Bedingfeld. At the back of the archway rose a grove of pikes, while on the right and left was ranged a strong guard of halberdiers, several of whom held torches, which gleamed upon the steel caps, corslets, and partisans of their comrades.

At this unlooked-for spectacle the conspirators recoiled in confusion and dismay. Flight was impossible, and as Bedingfeld advanced towards them with an officer, and demanded their swords, telling them they were his prisoners, they had no alternative but submission.

By the King's commands, the conspirators were then brought before him, and he surveyed them for some moments with a smile of gratified vengeance.

"Soh, traitors!" he exclaimed, at length, "you thought you had devised a cunning scheme to carry off my treasure. But you have been outwitted. Your plans have been revealed to me, and I have allowed you to proceed thus far in order to ensnare you all. You have fallen like wolves into the trap set for you."

"The wretch who betrayed us has met his reward," cried Sir Henry Dudley. "He has perished by my sword."

"Is Lovel slain?" exclaimed Philip. "I am sorry for it."

"He richly deserved his fate," cried Osbert. "I see now how we have been duped."

At this moment Xit made his way towards the King, and said, "An please your Majesty, these rebels and traitors were captured by me. I claim the reward."

"Retire, thou presumptuous and intrusive varlet," cried Bedingfeld. "This matter is too serious for thy interference."

"But for my interference, Sir Henry," rejoined Xit, proudly and indignantly, "the plot would not have been discovered."

"There thou art wrong," rejoined Bedingfeld; "the plot has been all along known to his Majesty. It was revealed to him by Lovel, who, it seems, has gone to his account."

"Lovel is killed, sure enough," said Xit. "But I trust my services will not go unrewarded."

"Thy claims shall be considered hereafter," said Philip. And as Xit, satisfied with this assurance, bowed and retired, he addressed the conspirators : "For the heinous crimes and offences you have committed, you cannot doubt what your sentence will be."

"We are all prepared for our fate," said Dudley, resolutely. "In engaging in this enterprise we well knew the risk we incurred. Having failed, we are ready to pay the penalty."

"Do you deem your base attempt consistent with the principles you profess?" demanded Philip, contemptuously.

"Ay," rejoined Dudley. "Your gold has been one of the

chief weapons used against this unhappy land, and it was the part of true Englishmen—as we are—to deprive you of it."

"Ye are robbers and felons, and shall die the death of such vile miscreants," said Philip, coldly. "By this foul act you have forfeited your privileges as gentlemen."

"What!" exclaimed Osbert Clinton. "Are we to die like common felons?"

"Such will be your doom," rejoined Philip, sternly.

"Your Majesty is too magnanimous to stoop to such an unworthy revenge," said Osbert Clinton. "Let us die upon the scaffold. 'Tis the sole grace we ask of you."

"Ay, spare them this ignominious ending, I beseech you, Sire," said Mauger, advancing from the guard, among whom he was standing, "and let them fall by my hand."

"I owe thee a guerdon," rejoined Philip, "and will give thee their heads. As to you, Osbert Clinton," he added, "I could devise no worse torture for you than your own bitter reflections will furnish. Had you not engaged in this last design, you might have been pardoned your former offences, have been restored to my favour, and have wedded Constance Tyrrell. Reflect upon this when you are alone in your dungeon."

"This is only said to torture me!" cried Osbert.

"It is said that you may be aware of the happiness you have so recklessly thrown away," rejoined the King. "At the intercession of Cardinal Pole, I had consented to pardon you, and, moreover, had promised his Eminence not to oppose your marriage with Constance. But there will be no pardon for you now—no Constance."

Osbert made no reply, but covered his face with his hand.

After a brief pause, the King turned to Sir Henry Bedingfeld, and ordered him to remove the prisoners to their dungeons. "To morrow they will be privately interrogated," he said, "after which their arraignment, condemnation, and execution will speedily follow. You will not have to wait long for your fees," he added to Mauger.

"I humbly thank your Majesty," replied the headsman.

On this, the conspirators were led off by the guard, and placed in different state prisons in the inner ward, a cell in the Flint Tower being assigned to Osbert Clinton. Shortly afterwards, the King rode back to Whitehall, attended by a mounted escort.

As soon as tranquility was restored, Og returned to his bride, whom he had left in the care of Dame Trusbut, at the Stone Kitchen. A very substantial supper was in readiness for him, and to this he sat down with his brothers, Xit, Rodomont Bittern, Simnel, and Holiday, and, despite the previous occurrences, they made a right merry night of it.

Next day, the treasure-chests, which had been left on the platform in Traitors' Gate, were removed from the Tower, and safely deposited in the Exchequer.

End of the Seventh Book.

BOOK VIII.

CONSTANCE TYRRELL.

CHAPTER I.

BOUT a month must now be allowed to elapse.
During this time, the whole of the conspirators,
with the exception of Osbert Clinton, had
suffered death on Tower Hill. But though
Osbert's execution was thus delayed, no hope of pardon
was held out to him. On the contrary, he was told by Sir
Henry Bedingfeld, who visited him almost daily, that his
sentence would infallibly be carried out, and that he ought
to be prepared for a sudden summons to the scaffold. "I
will give you notice when I am sent for by his Majesty," he
said. "That will be an intimation to you that the hour is
at hand."

The Queen's accouchement being now daily expected,
great preparations were made for the important event;
religious processions thronged the streets, prayers were
offered for her Majesty's safe deliverance, and couriers kept
in constant readiness to bear the gladsome tidings to

foreign courts. While all were on the tenter-hooks of expectation, the Romanists were gratified, and the Protestants deeply chagrined, by the sudden and, as it turned out, unfounded intelligence that her Majesty had given birth to a son. The news spread with extraordinary rapidity, not only in London, but throughout the whole kingdom. Public rejoicings were made. Bonfires were lighted in the streets. *Te Deum* was sung in the churches, and one preacher—the priest of St. Anne's in Aldersgate—went so far as to describe the personal appearance of the new-born Prince, depicting him as a miracle of beauty and proportion. But next day all was changed. The Romanists were mortified by the authoritative contradiction of the report, whilst the Protestants exulted. Other rumours were then circulated, and it was said that the Queen had died in child-bed. But this statement was soon discovered to be false, and it eventually became known that the disease under which her Majesty was labouring, and which had deceived her physicians, was dropsy.

For some days Mary continued in a very precarious state, and serious apprehensions of a fatal result were entertained ; but these dangerous symptoms abated, and in less than a week she was pronounced out of danger. During her illness she had been sedulously attended by Constance Tyrrell, for whom she had sent when she supposed herself sinking, and it was to Constance's unwearying attentions that she mainly attributed her recovery.

Naturally, the Queen's state of health had been a source of the deepest anxiety to Cardinal Pole, and the news of her amendment was a proportionate relief to him. Having received permission to wait upon her, he immediately repaired to Whitehall, and on arriving at the palace he was met by Doctor Ford, the Queen's physician, who conducted him to her Majesty's presence.

Mary was in her cabinet, reclining in a large easy-chair, propped up by cushions, wrapped in a loose gown of purple velvet, lined with miniver, and with her feet supported by a tabouret. Her features were swollen, and her complexion turbid, and she had an air of extreme lassitude and debility. The only person by whom she was attended added, "I pray your Eminence not to retire. The matter is one that will interest you. Not to keep you in suspense, I will state at once, and in a word, the purport of the dispatch. The Emperor is about to abdicate, and resign his hereditary dominions to me."

"What do I hear?" exclaimed Mary, in extremity of surprise. "The Emperor about to abdicate!"

"'Tis exactly as I have stated, Madam," cried Philip. "I have it here under his own hand."

"His Imperial Majesty has for some months meditated this step, gracious Madam," interposed D'Egmont, bowing to the Queen, "but it is only recently that his final resolution has been taken. Of late a profound melancholy has seized upon him, which he finds it impossible to shake off. Tired of pomp and state, sated with glory and conquest, wearied with the cares of government, racked by a cruel disease, which allows him little respite from suffering, his august Majesty is about to put off the purple robe and crown, and, clothing himself in the lowly garb of a monk, to pass the remainder of his days in seclusion. I have been sent by the Emperor to announce his determination to his royal son, into whose hands he designs to relinquish his vast dominions."

"You hear, Madam—you hear what my father intends," cried Philip, with irrepressible delight.

"Yes, I hear it," rejoined Mary, mournfully.

"The solemn ceremony of abdication will take place at Brussels," pursued D'Egmont, "in the presence of all the nobles and deputies of Flanders, who, at the Emperor's request, will transfer their allegiance to his son. Subsequently, the sovereignty of Castile and Aragon will be ceded to King Philip."

"And what of the crown of Germany?" demanded Philip.

"That will deck the brows of your uncle Ferdinand, King of the Romans," said D'Egmont. "The Empire of Germany will be resigned in his favour."

"Is such my father's intent?" said Philip.

"I believe so, Sire—nay, I am sure," returned D'Egmont. "To prove the motives by which your august sire is actuated in his retirement, it will be enough to state, that out of his immense revenues he only intends to reserve himself a pension of a hundred thousand ducats."

"Only so much," cried Mary. "Why, 'tis less than a noble's revenue."

"It is more than the Emperor will need, Madam, in the solitary life he designs to lead," observed D'Egmont.

"I am filled with amazement," observed Pole. "That Charles V., the foremost monarch of Christendom, the greatest warrior of the age, who holds in his hands the destinies of Europe, should retire in the plenitude of his power, is indeed a wondrous circumstance, to which there is no parallel, save in the instance of Diocletian. May the Christian monarch be as happy in his retirement as was the heathen Emperor in his garden at Salona. Heavy, indeed, must be the weight of a crown, since its wearer desires to put it off thus."

"In his letter to me, the Emperor explains the motives of his intent to abdicate," said Philip. "Referring to the troubled and agitated life he has led, to his great fatigues and exposure, his frequent travels in Europe and Africa, the constant warfare in which he has been engaged, and his incessant labours for the public welfare and for religion, he observes : 'As long as my strength would allow me, I have fulfilled my duties, but now my infirmities counsel—nay, command—repose. Ambition, and the desire to rule, no longer sway my breast. The remainder of my days will be consecrated to holy thought and preparation for eternity. To you, my son, and to your care, I shall resign my vast possessions, conjuring you never to relax in your efforts for the welfare of the people committed to your charge. The time may come when, exhausted, loaded with infimities, and praying for release, you may desire to imitate your father's example.'"

"May that day be long distant!" cried D'Egmont. "A brilliant career is before your Majesty."

"Yet let the Emperor's words never be forgotten, Sire," remarked Pole, solemnly. "Lay them to heart, and be guided by them ; and so, when you arrive at that period which your august sire has reached, when earthly glories shall fade away and become as nothing in your sight, you will derive comfort from the happiness and prospenty you

26—2

was Constance Tyrrell, who likewise looked extremely pale and ill.

Having accompanied the Cardinal to the door of the cabinet, Doctor Ford retired.

"I am glad to see your Eminence," said Mary, as the Cardinal approached her. "Sit down beside me, I pray you. At one time I feared I should never behold you again ; but I am better, and I owe my preservation, under Heaven, to the ministry of this damsel. Without her I believe I should have died, and I never can forget the services she has rendered me—never sufficiently requite them."

"Your Majesty overrates my poor services," said Constance.

"She has poured balm into my wounded heart, as well as helped me to sustain my bodily sufferings," pursued Mary. "Oh, my good Lord Cardinal, how can I have so deeply offended Heaven that I should be thus severely afflicted !—that the boon I have so earnestly prayed for should be denied me. What have I done to merit this chastisement?—how have I sinned? I have searched my breast, but can discover no wickedness therein. I have swerved from no duty. It cannot be a crime to love the King my husband—though, perchance, I have made him an idol. But enjoin me any penance you please. I will perform it."

"I enjoin you only resignation to the decrees of Heaven, gracious Madam," returned Pole. "Your afflictions have been given you for some wise but inscrutable purpose, and must be patiently borne."

"I have borne them with patience," rejoined Mary ; "yet it is hard to be deprived of blessings which are vouchsafed to the meanest of my subjects. How many a poor cottager's wife can clasp her offspring to her breast !—while I, alas ! am childless."

"Your grief is shared by all your subjects, Madam," observed the Cardinal.

"Not by all," rejoined Mary, with asperity. "There are many who exult in my distress, who have prayed that I might have no issue, but that the sceptre might pass from my hands to those of my sister Elizabeth. And their prayers would seem to be heard, while mine are rejected. Oh, what happiness would have been mine had a son been granted me, for I feel all a mother's tenderness in my breast. A son would have compensated me for all my troubles—for the neglect I have experienced, and for the desertion which will ensue—but now I shall go to my grave broken-hearted."

"Be comforted, Madam, be comforted," said Pole. "All will yet be well. The King will *not* leave you."

"He *will* leave me, that is certain," rejoined Mary. "And then will come the severest part of my trial. When he is gone, all will be a blank to me. I would fain bury my woes in a cloister."

"No, Madam, you must rouse yourself," said Pole. "You must not give way to this excess of grief. It has pleased the Supreme Disposer of events to deprive you, and the country placed under your governance, of a great blessing ; but do not repine on that account. Rather rejoice that you have been afflicted. Devote all your energies to the welfare of your kingdom, and to the maintenance of religion. Peace will then be restored to your breast—peace, which nothing can disturb."

"I do not expect to find peace on this side of the grave," sighed Mary ; "but I will try to follow your Eminence's counsel."

"In time your wounds will be healed," rejoined Pole ; "and you will then understand why they have been inflicted."

"I humbly resign myself to Heaven's decrees," said Mary. "*Fiat voluntas tua.*"

At this juncture, without being announced, the King entered the cabinet, followed by Count D'Egmont. His Majesty's features did not wear their customary sombre expression, but were radiant with joy, and his deportment evinced considerable excitement.

Advancing quickly towards the Queen, and bowing reverently to the Cardinal, he said,—

"Count D'Egmont has just brought me a most important letter from the Emperor, and I lose not a moment in laying its contents before your Majesty."

Then, turning to Pole, who was about to withdraw, he

added, "I pray your Eminence not to retire. The matter is one that will interest you. Not to keep you in suspense, I will state at once, and in a word, the purport of the dispatch. The Emperor is about to abdicate, and resign his hereditary dominions to me."

"What do I hear?" exclaimed Mary, in extremity of surprise. "The Emperor about to abdicate!"

"'Tis exactly as I have stated, Madam," cried Philip. "I have it here under his own hand."

"His Imperial Majesty has for some months meditated this step, gracious Madam," interposed D'Egmont, bowing to the Queen, "but it is only recently that his final resolution has been taken. Of late a profound melancholy has seized upon him, which he finds it impossible to shake off. Tired of pomp and state, sated with glory and conquest, wearied with the cares of government, racked by a cruel disease, which allows him little respite from suffering, his august Majesty is about to put off the purple robe and crown, and, clothing himself in the lowly garb of a monk, to pass the remainder of his days in seclusion. I have been sent by the Emperor to announce his determination to his royal son, into whose hands he designs to relinquish his vast dominions."

"You hear, Madam—you hear what my father intends," cried Philip, with irrepressible delight.

"Yes, I hear it," rejoined Mary, mournfully.

"The solemn ceremony of abdication will take place at Brussels," pursued D'Egmont, "in the presence of all the nobles and deputies of Flanders, who, at the Emperor's request, will transfer their allegiance to his son. Subsequently, the sovereignty of Castile and Aragon will be ceded to King Philip."

"And what of the crown of Germany?" demanded Philip.

"That will deck the brows of your uncle Ferdinand, King of the Romans," said D'Egmont. "The Empire of Germany will be resigned in his favour."

"Is such my father's intent?" said Philip.

"I believe so, Sire—nay, I am sure," returned D'Egmont. "To prove the motives by which your august sire is actuated in his retirement, it will be enough to state, that out of his immense revenues he only intends to reserve himself a pension of a hundred thousand ducats."

"Only so much," cried Mary. "Why, 'tis less than a noble's revenue."

"It is more than the Emperor will need, Madam, in the solitary life he designs to lead," observed D'Egmont.

"I am filled with amazement," observed Pole. "That Charles V., the foremost monarch of Christendom, the greatest warrior of the age, who holds in his hands the destinies of Europe, should retire in the plenitude of his power, is indeed a wondrous circumstance, to which there is no parallel, save in the instance of Diocletian. May the Christian monarch be as happy in his retirement as was the heathen Emperor in his garden at Salona. Heavy, indeed, must be the weight of a crown, since its wearer desires to put it off thus."

"In his letter to me, the Emperor explains the motives of his intent to abdicate," said Philip. "Referring to the troubled and agitated life he has led, to his great fatigues and exposure, his frequent travels in Europe and Africa, the constant warfare in which he has been engaged, and his incessant labours for the public welfare and for religion, he observes: 'As long as my strength would allow me, I have fulfilled my duties, but now my infirmities counsel—nay, command—repose. Ambition, and the desire to rule, no longer sway my breast. The remainder of my days will be consecrated to holy thought and preparation for eternity. To you, my son, and to your care, I shall resign my vast possessions, conjuring you never to relax in your efforts for the welfare of the people committed to your charge. The time may come when, exhausted, loaded with infimities, and praying for release, you may desire to imitate your father's example.'"

"May that day be long distant!" cried D'Egmont. "A brilliant career is before your Majesty."

"Yet let the Emperor's words never be forgotten, Sire," remarked Pole, solemnly. "Lay them to heart, and be guided by them; and so, when you arrive at that period which your august sire has reached, when earthly glories shall fade away and become as nothing in your sight, you will derive comfort from the happiness and prosperity you have conferred upon your people. Rarely has a crown been similarly bestowed. Never could crown be more richly graced. Wear it, Sire, as it has hitherto been worn—wear it as your great father has worn it, and when you put it off, you will do so, like him, without a sigh."

"Once mine, I shall be in no haste to part with it," observed Philip. "But have I no congratulations from your Majesty?" he added to the Queen. "Do you not rejoice with me on my good luck?"

"Your good luck is my misfortune," rejoined Mary. "This unlooked-for act of the Emperor must cause our separation."

"Only for a season," returned Philip. "I must needs obey my father's summons to Brussels; but I shall speedily return."

"Impossible!" cried Mary. "As King of Spain, you will have much to do, and cannot quit your dominions, even if you should be so minded. No! I am not to be deceived. *I* cannot go to Spain, or to Flanders, and *you* will not come to England. Henceforward we must dwell apart."

"Nay, nay, you are wrong, Madam—by my faith, you are!" cried Philip. "I shall return before three months have elapsed. Meantime, I confide you to the care of his Eminence, who, I trust, will be rarely absent from you. It is my wish," he added, "that the Lord Cardinal be appointed chief of the Privy Council, and that nothing concerning the government of the realm be concluded without his sanction."

"All shall be done as you desire," rejoined Mary.

"Nay, Sire, I must decline a post for which I am unfitted," said Pole, "and which, as it would necessarily engage me in concerns of the world, is little suited to the spiritual character with which I am invested."

"But I will take no refusal," said Philip. "You must, at least, accept the post till her Majesty is perfectly restored to health."

"I shall have only your Eminence to look to when the King is gone," said Mary. "If need be, I must lay my positive commands upon you."

"In that case I have no alternative but submission," rejoined the Cardinal. "The sole condition I would annex to my consent is, that I may be allowed to exercise my religious functions as heretofore."

"Far be it from me to interfere with them," said Mary. "Apartments shall be assigned you in the palace, so that I may have an opportunity of seeing you more frequently, and profiting by your counsels."

CHAPTER II.

HOW SIR HENRY BEDINGFELD CAME FOR OSBERT'S DEATH-WARRANT; AND WHAT HE OBTAINED.

T this moment an usher entered, and informed the King that Sir Henry Bedingfeld was without, having come to Whitehall in obedience to his Majesty's commands.

"Admit him straight," replied Philip. And as the usher withdrew, Philip approached the Queen, and spoke a few words to her in a low tone. What he said was inaudible to the others, but its import could be gathered from Mary's troubled looks. She attempted some remonstrance, but the King appeared inflexible.

While this was passing, Constance stole softly towards the Cardinal, and said to him in a whisper, "Sir Henry Bedingfeld is come for Osbert's death-warrant. I am sure of it, from the look given me by her Maiesty. Oh! my Lord Cardinal, intercede for him with the King — intercede for him, I implore of you."

"I will do what I can," replied Pole, in the same tone.

Meantime, Philip continued urgent with the Queen, his manner becoming stern and peremptory.

"Must it be done at once?" inquired Mary.

"Ay, at once," rejoined the King. "I will have his head before my departure to-morrow. Then I shall be sure that my injunctions are obeyed. Here is the warrant," he added, placing a scroll of parchment before her. "Sign it."

Mary, however, manifested great reluctance, and was still appealing to the King, who continued inflexible, when Sir Henry Bedingfeld appeared, and making a profound obeisance to the royal pair, said, "I await your Majesty's commands."

"I shall be ready for you in an instant, good Sir Henry," rejoined the King. "Sign it, Madam—sign it," he added quickly to the Queen. "Why do you hesitate?"

"Because ——" And she glanced towards Constance, who had now turned aside, weeping. "I owe my life to her," she added. "Ought I to requite her thus?"

"I have said I will not depart without assurance of this traitor's death," rejoined Philip; "and your reluctance shows how my orders would be obeyed in my absence. Sir Henry Bedingfeld awaits the warrant."

Thus urged, Mary took up the pen, when Pole interposed.

"A moment, Madam," he cried. "Ere you sign that death-warrant, I crave permission to say a few words to his Majesty."

"I am entirely at your Eminence's disposal," rejoined Philip, advancing towards him.

"Sire," said Pole, "you will, I am assured, acknowledge that Heaven's bounties have been bestowed upon you with a lavish hand."

Philip assented, and Pole went on. "You have been summoned to the greatest throne in Europe, and while your heart is naturally elated by what you have gained, it should be opened to the kindliest and most generous emotions. Let your first act be one which shall show you are influenced by such feelings."

"What would you have me do?" replied Philip, somewhat coldly. "I am about to testify my gratitude to Heaven by public prayer and thanksgiving in Westminster Abbey, by largesses to my attendants, by liberal donations of alms to the poor, and in various other ways, as my confessor shall direct, and as I trust will meet with your Eminence's approval."

"All this is well," replied the Cardinal; "and yet your heart may not be touched as I would have it. Perform a noble deed. Osbert Clinton has deeply offended you. His life is in your hands. Pardon him."

"I cannot pardon him," replied Philip. "I have sworn that he shall die."

"I will absolve you of your oath," said the Cardinal. "The occasion is one that demands from you some self-sacrifice, and you must make it."

"I would do aught in my power to gratify your Eminence, to whom I am infinitely beholden, but I cannot forego an act of just vengeance," replied Philip. "I have purposely delayed this execution, not from any intention of sparing the traitor, but because I would prolong his punishment. To-morrow he dies. Press me no more, for I must perforce refuse your request. I will not be balked of my revenge."

"It is well, Sire," replied Pole. "But I warn you that you will repent your indulgence of this evil passion."

"You plead the cause of a rebel and traitor," cried Philip, impatiently. "Osbert Clinton has been justly condemned for his crimes."

"Search your heart, Sire," said the Cardinal, in a severe tone, "and you will find why Osbert became a rebel and a traitor. He was loyal and devoted till his wrongs—ay, wrongs, Sire—made him what he is."

"But he rose in rebellion against the Queen," cried Philip.

"I pardon him for his offences against me—fully and freely pardon him," interposed Mary; "and I pray your Majesty to pardon him likewise."

Philip made no reply, but his looks continued inexorable.

"Essay what you can do," said Pole, in a low voice to Constance.

"Alas, I despair of moving him," she rejoined. "Nevertheless, I will make the attempt." And casting herself at Philip's feet, she said, "Oh, Sire, if this sentence be carried out, and Osbert perish on the block, you will have my life to answer for as well as his, since I shall not long survive him. The blow which strikes him will reach me also. I am the cause of all Osbert's treasonable acts. But for his love for me, he would have been loyal and devoted to you and to her Majesty. Oh, that you had never seen me, Sire! Oh, that chance, on your arrival in this country, had not brought you near me! Since that fatal hour nothing but calamity has attended me. But now that you are departing, Sire, leave me not to wretchedness and despair. Pity Osbert, Sire—

overlook his offences, and pardon him. By so doing, you will save yourself from a remorse which no penitence will remove, but which will ever haunt you if you doom us both to death. But no, Sire, I see you relent—your nobler and better feelings triumph—you are yourself—the worthy son of Charles V. You forgive me — you pardon Osbert Clinton ? "

"Arise, Constance," said Philip, taking her hand and raising her; "you have conquered. That I have done you much wrong, and caused you great unhappiness, I freely confess. That I may have goaded Osbert Clinton into the commission of the offences of which he has been guilty, I will not attempt to deny. But I will make amends. He shall have a pardon."

"Nobly done, Sire!" ejaculated Pole. "Nobly done!"

"To make sure that Osbert is worthy of the grace bestowed upon him," said Philip, "he shall accompany me to Brussels, and thence to Spain, and when I have proved him, I will send him back to reap his reward."

"Oh, Sire, you overwhelm me with gratitude!" cried Constance. "Happiness, so long a stranger to me, begins to smile on me again."

"On his return, it will be for your Eminence to complete the work by bestowing upon him the hand of your ward," said Philip to the Cardinal.

"And at the same time I shall surrender the fortune which I hold in trust for her," said Pole.

"Sir Henry Bedingfeld," said Philip to the Lieutenant of the Tower, whose looks manifested the lively interest he took in what was passing, "you will return to the Tower, not with a death-warrant, but with an order for Osbert's immediate liberation."

"Here it is, Sir Henry," said Mary, tracing a few lines on a sheet of paper, and giving it to Bedingfeld. "Tell him that he has our full pardon."

"I shall not fail, gracious Madam," rejoined the Lieutenant of the Tower, with a profound obeisance.

And he moved towards the door. Before reaching it, however, he was stopped by an usher, who placed a packet in his hands, saying it was important, and had just been brought from the Tower. The packet contained a letter, enclosed within which was a small piece of paper. On glancing at the letter, Bedingfeld started, and his countenance fell.

"What is the matter, Sir Henry?" demanded the King, remarking his altered looks.

"The prisoner, Sire!—the prisoner!" faltered Bedingfeld.

"What of him?" shrieked Constance, in tones that chilled those who heard her. "What has happened?"

"Read, Sire," said Bedingfeld, handing the missive he had just received to the King.

"Ha! is it so?" cried Philip, his countenance changing as he read the dispatch. "Remove her, I pray you, my Lord Cardinal," he added to Pole.

"I will not go till I learn the truth," cried Constance, distractedly. "Speak, Sir, I conjure you," she added to Bedingfeld.

"Better let her know the truth, be it what it may," said Pole.

"Ay, speak, Sir Henry—keep her not in suspense," said the Queen. "The prisoner was well when you left the Tower—ha?"

"He was, Madam, but ——"

"But what?" demanded Mary.

"Since then he has died by poison," said Philip.

"By poison! how could it be procured?" asked the Queen.

"It appears to have been contained in a ring which he was unluckily allowed to wear," replied Philip.

"Is there no poison left for me, that I may join him?" cried Constance.

"Kind Heaven support her!" exclaimed Pole. "Her reason wanders."

"No, I am calm enough now," she rejoined.

"Then you may bear to hear that Osbert's last thoughts were given to you," said Philip. "This scrap of paper was found clutched in his dying grasp. On it are written the words, 'Farewell for ever, beloved Constance!'"

Taking the piece of crumpled paper from the King, she gazed at it for a few moments, and then pressed it convulsively to her lips.

"Farewell, Osbert—farewell for ever!" she cried.

" No, not for ever," rejoined Pole, solemnly. " You will be united in a better world."

Praying the Cardinal to stay with her and console her, the King withdrew with D'Egmont and Bedingfeld.

Left alone with Pole and the Queen, Constance was permitted by them to indulge her grief without restraint before any attempt at consolation was made ; but when these paroxysms were over, and she became calmer, the good Cardinal poured balm into her bruised spirit, and ceased not till his efforts were successful.

From that moment Constance became perfectly resigned —and though all youthful gaiety and lightness of heart deserted her, and her features wore an unvarying expression of melancholy and sadness, she never uttered a murmur. She would fain have spent the rest of her life in solitude and retirement, but the Queen refused to part with her, and retained her with her to the close of her days.

With remarkable consideration, Mary did not interfere with her religious observances, but allowed her what she denied all others, freedom of conscience. This concession, however, on the Queen's part, was made on the earnest recommendation of Cardinal Pole. Thus Constance continued unshaken in her faith. By her gentle assiduities she was enabled materially to alleviate the anguish of mind endured by the Queen during Philip's absence, and when at length Mary sank after protracted suffering, her last moments were soothed by Constance Tyrrell.

CHAPTER III.

TWO LIGHTS EXTINGUISHED.

UPWARDS of three years had flown since the occurrences last narrated—three terrible years, during which religious persecution never ceased. Bradford and Marsh had perished at the stake, so had Ridley and Latimer, with many others, and Cranmer had won a martyr's crown. Gardiner had long gone to his account, being stricken with a mortal disease, while reading a letter describing the torments of Ridley and Latimer. He lingered for a month, and then dying, was buried with great pomp in Winchester Cathedral. But though Gardiner was gone, Bonner yet lived, and the barbarous proceedings against the Protestants were unrelaxed.

On Cranmer's death, Pole was immediately created Archbishop of Canterbury, and began to put into execution the plan he had long designed for reforming the abuses of the Church. Notwithstanding the opposition of the clergy, aided as they were by Paul IV., the then ruling Pontiff, whose displeasure Pole had incurred, he succeeded in effecting many beneficial changes, and would doubtless have accomplished much more, had he been spared, but in the very midst of his exertions he was attacked by a quartan ague, engendered by the pestilent exhalations from Lambeth marshes. By its extreme violence, the fever threatened from the first a fatal termination.

Though not unconscious of his danger, and, indeed,

scarcely entertaining a hope of recovery, the Cardinal continued his labours during the intervals when he was free from fever. His chief cause of concern at this moment was, that the Queen also was lying upon a sick couch, from which it was scarcely probable she could rise. Foreseeing the disastrous consequences to the Church of Rome which must inevitably ensue from her death, he felt so troubled in spirit that his mental anxiety added force to the attacks of the ague.

Throughout the Cardinal's illness, Priuli watched over him with unremitting solicitude, and such entire reliance had Pole in the judgment and devotion of his friend, that he confided everything to him. One day, when the Cardinal was free from fever, and he and Priuli were alone together in the library of Lambeth Palace, he requested his friend to unlock a small coffer which he pointed out, and at the same time gave him a key. Priuli obeyed, and on opening the coffer perceived within it a parchment, so endorsed as to leave him no doubt as to its nature.

"That is my will," said Pole. "I desire you to read it."

On perusing the document, Priuli found that the Cardinal had appointed him his sole heir and executor, whereupon, looking Pole earnestly in the face, he said, "I am glad you have consulted me on this matter, dear friend, and allowed me the opportunity of expressing my opinion upon it. It would have grieved me to disobey your injunctions, and yet I cannot conscientiously fulfil them. Readily will I undertake the office to which you have appointed me, and will carefully attend to your directions as to the distribution of your property, but with regard to the rich inheritance you would bestow upon me, I must peremptorily decline it. I cannot—will not accept any part of it. I thank you for the intent, but I am rich enough without this augmentation of my worldly goods."

"Distribute my possessions among the poor, or build churches and hospitals with them," rejoined the Cardinal. "Whatever you do, will, I am sure, be for the best. But if you decline my bequest, at least accept some slight object, be it only a jewel or ring, to be kept as a memorial of our long friendship."

"I desire neither jewel nor ring, nor any other memorial

richer than the breviary you constantly use," replied Priuli. " Of all gifts, I should value that the most."

" It shall be yours, dear friend," rejoined Pole. " I shall keep it as long as my eyes are able to fix upon it—as long as my hands will hold it—then take it. May it afford you the comfort it has ever afforded me, and draw you towards Heaven, as it has never failed to draw me."

Pole was constant in his inquiries after the Queen, and on her part Mary was equally anxious for information as to the state of his health. Messengers were continually passing between Lambeth Palace and Whitehall, but from neither place were the tidings satisfactory. On the contrary, the reports of the condition of both illustrious sufferers grew worse, and it became a question as to which of the two would be the survivor. Pole prayed that he might be the first to depart—but it was not so ordained.

The grief felt by every member of the Cardinal's vast establishment for the deprivation which they felt they must soon undergo, was sincere and profound, but no one deplored his exalted master's precarious condition more deeply than Rodomont Bittern. The poor who thronged the gates of the palace, and received alms and food from Priuli, put up earnest prayers for their benefactor's recovery.

But the fever abated not, and though its attacks were somewhat mitigated in severity, still the Cardinal's debilitated frame was less able to withstand them. He daily grew weaker and weaker.

Notwithstanding his prostration, however, he was carried twice in each day to the chapel to hear mass. One evening after vespers, the large easy-chair in which he reclined was wheeled into the library, and Priuli, who now seldom left him, took his accustomed place by his side. Four days having elapsed since the Cardinal's last attack, it was certain that the night would not pass without a return of the fever. Notwithstanding this, Pole was conversing cheerfully with his friend, when Rodomont Bittern entered to say that Mistress Constance Tyrrell was without, and desired to see his Eminence.

" Admit her straight," replied Pole. " She is ever welcome."

And the next moment Constance came in. The

expression of her countenance, which was as pale as death, struck Priuli, but did not appear to attract Pole's attention. Moving noiselessly towards the Cardinal, Constance knelt before him, while he spread his thin white hands over her head, and in feeble tones gave her his benediction.

"How fares the Queen?" inquired Pole, as Constance arose. "She was somewhat easier this morning, as I understand."

"Her Majesty is easier now," replied Constance. "She is free from all pain."

"Is she gone?" inquired Pole, while a premonitory shiver shook his wasted frame.

"She is gone," rejoined Constance. "The heart that has so long suffered has ceased to beat."

"May the angels of Heaven receive her soul and present it before the Lord!" exclaimed Pole. "And may whatever sin she has committed in life through human frailty be forgiven her! Did her spirit pass away easily?"

"Most easily," replied Constance. "Her sole concern was for the welfare of her Church."

"The chief pillar of the Church is broken," cried Pole, in a voice of anguish; "and my hand, which might have helped to support the falling structure, is also powerless. *Domine, salva nos, perimus! Salvator Mundi, salva Ecclesiam tuam.*"

For some moments he remained in fervent prayer, after which he seemed calmer, and inquired if the Queen had said aught concerning the King her husband.

"She spoke not of him at the last," replied Constance, "but it would seem that the loss of Calais produced a deep impression on her, for she said, 'My physicians seek to know the cause of my malady. Let them open my breast, and they will find "Calais" graven on my heart.'"

"It was not the loss of Calais that broke her heart," said Pole. Heaven forgive him who has brought her prematurely to the tomb. England has lost a great sovereign, and our Church its chief defence. Elizabeth is now Queen, and with her the Protestant Church will be restored. Fortunately, I shall not live to see that day. Farewell, dear daughter. My blessing be ever upon you!"

Finding that the fever was coming on, he caused himself

to be transported to his chamber, and was laid upon the couch which he was never again to leave with life.

Towards morning his condition became alarming, and he received extreme unction, the last rites being performed by the Bishop of Asaph. This done, after some words to Priuli, he clasped to his breast the crucifix, which he had ever with him, and seemed to sink into a gentle slumber. And so he breathed his last.

Crucifix and breviary were kept as sacred relics by Priuli.

In the chapel of Saint Thomas à Becket, which he himself built in Canterbury Cathedral, rests the saintly Reginald Pole. This simple inscription is placed over his tomb :—

DEPOSITUM CARDINALIS POLI.

THE END.

PRINTED BY W. H. SMITH AND SON, 186 STRAND, LONDON, W.C.

18—12—76

www.ingramcontent.com/pod-product-compliance
Lightning Source LLC
Chambersburg PA
CBHW030813110726
47900CB00006B/1607